THE RIVER IS HOME

and

ANGEL CITY

A Patrick Smith Reader

Novels by PATRICK D. SMITH
THE RIVER IS HOME
THE BEGINNING
FOREVER ISLAND
ANGEL CITY
ALLAPATTAH
A LAND REMEMBERED

THE RIVER IS HOME

and

ANGEL CITY

A Patrick Smith Reader

PINEAPPLE PRESS, INC.
SARASOTA, FLORIDA

Inquiries should be addressed to:

Pineapple Press, Inc.
P.O. Box 3889
Sarasota, Florida 34230

www.pineapplepress.com

Library of Congress Cataloging-in-Publication Data

Smith, Patrick D., 1927–
     [River is home]
     The river is home; and, Angel city / by Patrick D. Smith.
       p.   cm.
     "A Patrick Smith reader."
     ISBN 978-0-910923-64-4
       1. Migrant labor—United States—Fiction. I. Smith, Patrick
D., 1927–   Angel city. 1989. II. Title. III. Title: River is home.
IV. Title: Angel city.
PS3569.M53785R58   1989
813'.54—dc19
                                          88-37479
                                          CIP

First Edition
20 19 18 17 16 15 14 13 12 11 10 9 8

CONTENTS

INTRODUCTION

THE EASYGOING NATURE and Mississippi drawl of author Patrick Smith will set you at ease the first time you meet him. In fact, it may be hard for most people to imagine him boating through the Ten Thousand Islands in search of crocodiles or working with the Seminole Indians or picking tomatoes as a migrant laborer. His story is that of a man who has led two lives or, more accurately, many lives, depending on the book he is researching and writing.

Readers of the present volume can glimpse several of those lives in the two novels included here, which are his first, *The River Is Home*, and one of his latest, *Angel City*. This collection follows the first Patrick Smith Reader that Pineapple Press published in 1987, a work that included *Forever Island* and *Allapattah*.

The two novels here offer quite a contrast for the reader: one is set in Mississippi, the other in Florida; one centers on a river, the other on a migrant labor camp; one was published in the early 1950s, the other in the late 1970s. What could they possibly have in common? The answer to that provides insight into why Patrick Smith has had a successful and consistent writing career over the past 35 years.

The two novels show one writer's development over a long career, and that will interest the student of stylistics and writing; but they also demonstrate two variations on the same theme, namely, that how one treats his fellow man can determine not only the future of the environment but also the future of mankind. The stories behind both novels reveal a great deal about a popular writer's personal growth.

In 1950, Patrick Smith was a 23-year-old who had grown up in a small Mississippi town during the Depression. Having been an avid reader from his early days and a writer whose local paper published his poems and sports columns, he finished writing a novel, but shelved it for two years, possibly apprehensive about its rejection and unsure of just how to get a book published. He finally showed it to one of his English professors at the University of Mississippi and received enough encouragement that—with some confidence—he sent it to Little, Brown and Company in Boston without an agent, without any fanfare. And they published it. Such is the printing history of Smith's popular but long-out-of-print novel, *The River Is Home.*

Set on the lower Pearl River in southern Mississippi at the turn of the century, when steamboats ran the river from New Orleans to Jackson, it is the story of a young boy growing up in a family poor in material goods but rich in spiritual values, a family that lived in harmony with their surroundings. Those surroundings consisted of swamps, woodlands, and the ever-present river that connected them to civilization, provided them with an abundant food supply, and challenged them with periodic floods. How each member of the boy's family did or did not adapt to the demands of the river is a study in contrasts.

If one recognizes in this story themes similar to those of Marjorie Kinnan Rawlings' *The Yearling* and *South Moon*

Under, it is no surprise since Smith did a critical analysis of Rawlings' work for his master's thesis, one of the first of its kind, in the late 1950s. Like the two Rawlings' books, Smith's novel is also about a boy growing up and learning to come to terms with his family and those who felt different than he did about the river and its creatures. Young Skeeter lived close to nature, so close in fact that he believed he could communicate with the animals:

'Shucks,' said Skeeter, 'you know I ain't skeered of them snakes. I was in the swamp one day by myself and I seed a big otter stalkin' one of them buggers. I sot real still in the skiff and watched what was goin' to happen. That dern otter snuck up to that snake backwards and waved his tail at him. When the ole snake struck at that bugger's tail, that otter turned so quick and sunk his teeth behin' that snake's head I hardly saw it happen. I asked the ole otter to tell me how he done it, and that sapsucker showed me all about it. I'll show you how hit's done fust time I gits a chance.'

Smith's dialect writing and ability to evoke a sense of place remind one of another river book, Mark Twain's *Life on the Mississippi*. Like Twain's book, Smith's also has several points that stretch our credulity, like the daughter in the family who is too beautiful to take to town and the insistence by young Skeeter on killing the huge alligator with a knife rather than a rifle, but on the whole it is a good story well told.

Much of the appeal of the story comes from its people. One might expect monochromatic stereotyping in a first novel: all the townspeople would be bad, and all the river people would be good. But not so here. While most of the townspeople are mean to Skeeter's folks, the old man that he befriends shares with Skeeter herbal secrets and the wisdom of his years. And while most of the river people are honest and decent, the Hooker family, especially the ten sons, present a particularly coarse side to living on the river. At least the despicable steamboat pilots enable the reader to focus an enmity on someone all of the time as they take every opportunity to cause as much trouble and grief for the river people as possible.

The setting of the swamp, full of mosquitoes and gators, would turn up again in Smith's Florida books, especially *Forever Island* and *Allapattah*, with the latter novels dealing not so much with white men as with Indians living in and near the swamp. Smith's emphasis on the importance of place in establishing one's identity would turn up in his future novels, whether of Seminole Indians trying to fit in with, or isolate themselves from, the white man or in the migrant workers' dream of having their own plot of land and a wayside stand.

If Smith had stayed in Mississippi, he might have followed the literary footsteps of fellow writers William Faulkner and Eudora Welty. Instead, he and his wife moved to Merritt Island, Florida, in 1966, where he became director of college relations for Brevard Community College in Cocoa. In the mid-1970s, after reading a newspaper article about the plight of migrant workers in south Florida, he found an issue that would absorb his spare time for several years. The newspaper told about a migrant crew chief who had enslaved his workers for more than two years, who wouldn't pay them or let them out of the camp, and who beat them regularly. The police finally arrested the crew chief and took him to court, but had to release him when none of the workers, all of whom were scared of him, would testify against him.

Alarmed that such migrant camps still existed in the 1970s, Smith went to Miami and read through old newspapers, where he found a number of stories about migrants being enslaved by the crew chiefs, often without the knowledge of the owners of the fields. Smith then began spending his weekends and vacations doing what he calls "physical research." He would don scruffy clothes, let his beard grow, and show up in Homestead to join migrants picking tomatoes or okra or cucumbers or squash, whatever was in season.

Earning a meager $35 a week, sleeping in buggy hovels, and trying to keep out of the frequent knife fights, he made mental notes of the sights and smells and noises. Apparently no one ever suspected that the quiet fellow with the Mississippi drawl was actually a writer. It was just as well since the crew chiefs in the migrant camps were very leery of investigative reporters, especially after Edward R. Murrow's 1960 documentary, "Harvest of Shame," had shown the world the tragic plight of Florida migrant workers. After spending more than a year doing "research" for the novel, which he entitled *Angel City*, Smith wrote it in just a few weeks, so filled was he of the sordid conditions of the camps and fields. When asked why he wanted to write such a novel, Smith replies, "The first step toward eliminating injustice is to expose it, and this was my primary goal in writing this novel."

And expose it he did, not only in the novel, but also in the movie based on the book. When he returned to the Homestead area several years later for the filming of *Angel City*, the film crew used an actual migrant camp, although obviously not one of the infamous "closed" ones, and hired migrant workers as extras in the film. For those workers who were between pickings, the $50 a day plus three meals a day must have seemed unreal. For readers unfamiliar with the movie, be forewarned: the endings are different. The film replaced the pessimistic ending of the novel with a hopeful scene, the father speeding away from the camp with his family. The moviemakers told Smith that people don't want to watch a movie anymore that doesn't end with hope, and so they brightened up the conclusion. Smith still contends that the pessimistic ending of the novel is more realistic.

Once the book revealed the terrible condition of the migrant camps, newspaper editorialists pressured the state and federal government to pass laws improving the plight of the workers so that today, according to Smith, those hell-holes that he witnessed probably don't exist. "Probably." One cannot be completely certain of this because of all the many hidden pockets where migrant camps might exist in the vast Everglades. It is a life completely alien to the glitter of Miami Beach to the east or the elegance of Naples to the west. Travelers speeding along the Tamiami Trail or Alligator Alley between the two coasts cannot imagine what inhumane conditions existed just off the highway along the dirt roads leading into the swamp.

Once the new regulations came out, not all the Florida newspapers supported them. One South Florida newspaper published a nasty article about Smith, claiming that he had completely fabricated the story and that the migrant laborers there belonged to the Chamber of Commerce and the Rotary Club and attended weekly meetings.

When Smith visited Russia in 1983 as a guest of the Soviet Writers' Union, he spoke at Russian universities about his novels, including *Angel City*. The Russian students asked him many questions about the book, not because it showed a bad part of American society, but because, according to the Russian students, it reflected the similarly harsh conditions that their Russian grandparents had suffered under the czars. The students told him that the migrant labor camps of mid-20th-century south Florida were similar to those of late 19th-century Russia.

Between *The River Is Home* and *Angel City* Smith published two other books: *The Beginning* (1967) about race relations in the South and *Forever Island* (1973) about the adaptation of the Seminole Indians to the encroaching white civilization, a theme also expanded in his later book, *Alla-pattah* (1979). After *Angel City* he published *A Land Remembered* (1984), a very popular historical novel covering three generations in Florida from the 1850s to 1960.

Smith is a quiet crusader, content to let his characters speak for him and reluctant to mount any soapbox. Edwin Granberry, another Florida writer and a winner of the O'Henry Prize for Fiction, once said, "I know of no other person who writes so eloquently about the poor, the unfortunate, and the underdogs in life as does Patrick Smith." Both of the novels in the collection do just that, although from different settings and with different characters. One can begin to see from the style of writing and intensity of feeling in these two books just why Patrick Smith has been nominated for both the Pulitzer Prize and the Nobel Prize in Literature. Readers will also be pleased to know that Smith recently retired from his eight-to-five job at the community college and, for the first time in his life, is writing fiction full-time; he has already begun a new novel.

—Dr. Kevin M. McCarthy
Department of English
University of Florida
Gainesville, 1988

THE RIVER IS HOME

ONE

A GENTLE BREEZE was blowing through the cypress trees, as Abner Corey sat on the stoop of his shack, mending fish traps. There had been a light rain that morning, and now the sun was sending long shafts of light into the swamp to draw the water up again. The drops of rain, clinging to the cypress boughs, glittered like thousands of diamonds in the air. The cries of wood ducks and cranes mingled with the chatter of squirrels and the incessant bellowing of frogs for more rain. Everything was full of activity but the Corey family. Abner's wife, Glesa, was stretched out on the back stoop basking in the sun. The two boys, Jeff and Skeeter, were throwing knives into the bare plank floor, while Theresa, the only daughter, was helping Abner mend the fish traps. The traps were the most valuable possessions of the Coreys because they represented their only means of getting cash money.

The Coreys had been living in the swamp for five years now. They had previously been sharecroppers, wandering to and from different parts of Mississippi and Louisiana year after year, getting what jobs they could and eating when they

could, but always being without much of either. And then
Abner had brought them to the Pearl River swamps of lower
Mississippi to begin a new and strange life. They arrived
with nothing and had to build their small shack with their
bare hands. Abner had chosen a little clearing on a bayou
several hundred yards from the muddy Pearl. The clearing
was bounded by tall, moss-covered, cypress trees, mingled
with magnolia and willow. From their clearing to the river
lay long stretches of flat marsh grass, and behind the clearing was the almost impenetrable swamp. The swamp was
joined by long, rolling hills covered with pine and scrub oak,
but the only way to cross from the clearing to the hills was
by boat through the murky swamp. Five miles down the river
was a little settlement called Mill Town, and twenty miles to
the north was Fort Henry. Once a week Abner and the boys
would row to Mill Town and trade fish for money and supplies, and once a year they would go to Fort Henry to sell
their winter trappings of hides. Fort Henry was a bustling
port town on the steamboat route to Jackson, far to the
north. Abner had promised the family if they ever got
enough money he would take them on the steamboat to
Jackson, but that time never seemed to come.

Most of the Coreys' time was spent on the river and in
the swamp—Abner and the boys fishing, hunting, and trap-
ping, while Glesa and the girl did the house chores and
tended the small garden on the edge of the clearing. They
grew a few onions, peas, and peppers, but their main diet
usually consisted of fish, game, and the wild poke salat that
grew along the clearing. They were planning this year to
have pork, because Abner had traded for three hogs in Mill
Town and had built a pen on the banks of the bayou.

The Corey shack was built of drift lumber and cypress
logs. The house had three rooms and no windows, and the
roof was made of hand-hewn cypress shingles stuffed with
moss. Two rooms of the house were used for sleeping, and

the other for cooking and eating. There were two beds in one room and one in the other. The beds were made of cypress slats, and the mattresses were made of croaker sacks sewn together and stuffed with moss. Ma and Pa Corey slept in one room and the boys and Theresa in the other. The kitchen contained a bare plank table, a washstand, and a clay hearth in one corner for cooking. All the water for cooking and drinking came from the bayou. The Coreys used the banks of the bayou for their privy and bath.

The oldest of the children was Jeff, who was nineteen. Theresa was fifteen and Skeeter thirteen. The Coreys had named their youngest boy Skeeter because he was born prematurely, and Pa Corey said that he was no bigger than a good-sized mosquito. Even now he was small and runty for his age, and did not have all that he should have had in the way of book-learning. Jeff was tall and skinny with short-cut, blond hair. Theresa was the most unusual of the Corey children. She was like a rose growing in a field of cabbage. She was an unusually beautiful girl with long, flaming-red hair, brown eyes, and a complexion as white as snow. It was strange that such a child could have the same blood as the haggard pair that had borne her. Ma Corey was a fat, sloppy-looking woman with straggly gray hair. Her teeth were stained brown from the long years of snuff dipping, and her skin was wrinkled and tanned from the long hours of working the fields before they came to the swamp to live. Pa Corey was built much the same as Jeff, tall and skinny, with short-cropped gray hair. Ma had always said that he could make more money hiring out as a scarecrow than he could any other way.

Pa Corey would not go into the swamp with Jeff and Skeeter to set and run their animal traps. He was more afraid of snakes and alligators than he was of the devil himself. In the spring and summer, Jeff and Skeeter would go into the swamp to kill snakes and catch young 'gators, so they could sell the snakeskins and young 'gators in Mill town. In the winter they would trap for mink and otter. Pa Corey was a fearless man on the river and bayou, but nothing could induce him into the swamp. The boys had built a flat-bottomed skiff to use in the swamp and a rowboat for the river.

As Pa Corey sat mending the traps, he often talked to himself, as he was doing now. "Dern gars," he said, "don't make nothin' but trouble fer me. Wish the slimy devils would stay out'n my nets and traps! Jest like hangin' a bull 'gator by the tail. I wish the good Lord would have a big fish fry in Heaven and use all the gars they is in the river. Pesky devils."

"Pa," said Theresa, "why is it that the gars won't stay in the traps like the catfish and the buffalo do?"

"Well, hit seems that the Lord equipped the muddy bastards with saws on their heads jest so'es they could saw their way out of anything. I've heard they can cut clear through a cypress log, jest as easy as nothin'. I caught one on a trotline once, and even the niggers wouldn't et him. They said he were a brother to the devil, and if'n you et him you would shore go below onced you was dead."

"Pa, Skeeter told me onced that he saw the devil up in the swamp one time. He said hit were jest afore dark and he come through a gap in the saw vines and there the devil set chewin' on a big ole water moccasin. He said when the devil seed him there, he swollered the snake whole and run off through the swamp belchin' smoke and bellowin' like a bull. Do you reckon hit were so, Pa?"

"Now don't you pay no mind to what Skeeter says, you hear? He's lible to come home one day sayin' he seed two bull 'gators doin' a dance in the top of a cypress tree."

"Jest the same, Pa," Theresa said, "hit shore would scare me if'n I was to see somethin' like that. That dern Skeeter jest ain't skerred of nothin', and I onced seen him ketch a live snake with his hands and pop its head clear off its body. Whut makes you so skeered of snakes, Pa?"

"Now you shet up and go tell them two boys to come here and help me git these traps in the boat. If'n we don't get 'em out soon, hit's goin' to be too dark. And I jest got a feelin' that them big ole catfish is goin' to be on a party tonight."

Theresa jumped up and ran to the room where Jeff and Skeeter were throwing the knives and said: "Pa said fer you two to git them traps in the boat so'es you can git 'em out afore it gits dark. You know Pa don't like to be on the river at night with them steamboat fellers runnin' over everything that gits in the way."

"Who's afraid of 'em?" Jeff said. "Skeeter, throw yore knife through her big ole toes."

Skeeter rose, drew back the blade, and before Theresa could run, the knife went slicing through the air and buried itself in the floor between her toes. "Oh my gosh, Pa," wailed Theresa, "Skeeter is in here tryin' to split my feet in half with his knife."

The boys jumped up and followed Theresa to the porch where Pa was sitting. Jeff said, "Dern fool! You ain't got no cause to go around the house bellowin' like that. I've seed Skeeter shave the whiskers off a tick's face at ten feet with that knife. You know dern well he don't never miss whut he aims at."

"Yeh, but they're always a fust time for everthing," said Theresa. "So jest you don't be doin' that no more."

"You dad-burned kids would make a hog's jaw bust carryin' on the way you do," said Pa. "Now git them traps on out there in the boat and let's git goin'. Theresa, you tell yore Ma to git up off that floor and hoe the garden like I tole her to. And you better help her, too."

*　　*　　*

Pa and the boys loaded the traps in the boat and shoved off down the bayou toward the river. They had about two miles to row before they got to the place where they were to set the traps. They did not put them in the river where it was deep but set them in little coves and branches running into the river. They set their trotline in the river and ran it along logs or sunk it deep into the water by putting heavy iron weights on the line. Pa was in the rear of the boat, and the boys sat in the middle and rowed.

They passed through the area of flat marsh grass and into the dense vegetation of the river bank. The entrance of the bayou into the river was so thick with cypress and magnolias that a person not familiar with it could pass right by, without knowing it. Pa said that was a good thing because it would keep the river folks and the sporting men from Fort Henry from messing around their place. The water, where the bayou met the river, looked like a pot of boiling mud. The Coreys could never remember the river when it wasn't muddy, but the bayou was always clear. Pa believed the big gar fighting on the river bottom kept the mud stirred up all the time.

When they reached the river, Jeff and Skeeter had to put all the strength they had into rowing the boat upstream. The river was always swift; even in the summer when there was not much rain and the water was low, it was full of trick currents and whirlpools. They had once seen a big log go down in the middle of the river and shoot high into the air a hundred yards from where it went under. Sometimes the channel would change overnight, and the steamboats would run aground and have to be pulled out of the mud.

About a mile above the Corey bayou, the river made a big turn and cut to the west for a few miles. This was known as West Cut. Along the turn there were several coves and creeks running into the river. When they reached the turn, they cut into an almost hidden cove along the west bank.

This cove was Pa Corey's favorite place for placing his fish traps. The big cats and buffalo would come into the cove at night to feed on the smaller fish and swim into his cone-shaped traps. He had caught as much as two hundred pounds of fish in one night here.

After they had carefully laid the traps and tied the trap lines to stobs, they cut back into the river to see about their trotline. When they came to the line, the boys headed the boat downstream so Pa could work it from the back of the boat. The hooks were baited with big chunks of squirrel and rabbit meat, and Pa had several piles of the cut meat in the boat to bait the hooks that were empty. About halfway down the line he jumped up and started shouting wildly: "Gol dern sons of bitches! Why can't the dirty devils let a feller make a livin' in peace?"

"Whut's the matter, Pa?" asked Jeff.

"Matter!" cried Pa. "Look at this! A dern catfish head without no body. That cat woulda weighed at least twenty pounds. Hit's the dad-nabbed turtles did it. If'n it ain't them thievin' devils, hit's the blame gar tearin' up the traps and nets. They ought to be some way to outdo these critters."

"I knows a old nigger down at Mill Town that could fix it so the gar and turtle wouldn't mess around with no fish lines," said Skeeter. "He done learned to mix up some potion you kin rub on the lines that makes them critters turn their tails and run. Let's see whut he kin do next week, Pa."

"We'll shore have to do somethin', Skeeter," said Pa, "or hit won't be wuth while to even fish in this muddy ole river."

"Pa," said Jeff, "hit's goin' to be dark pretty soon and it's jest about time fer that steamboat to come round the bend. You better hurry up or we all lible to be swimmin' home stead of ridin' in this here boat."

"You mighty right," said Skeeter. "You shore better git done with them lines, Pa, afore that steamboat feller gits here."

Pa Corey finished baiting the last hook, and they turned the bow of the boat downstream towards home. The last rays of light were fading through the tall cypress trees, when they reached the mouth of the bayou that led to their home. About halfway through the marsh flats, they heard a loud blast and saw fire and smoke belch above the treetops.

"Jest listen to that feller sound off," said Pa. "You would think the idiot owns the river the way he tries to blow the tops off all the trees."

The steamboat men did not like the people who lived along the banks of the river and in the swamps. They felt that the families, like the Coreys, who made their living along the river were always getting in their way and slowing down their speed. Sometimes the boatmen would purposely go close to the bank and run through trotlines just to get rid of them, and when they caught the swampmen on the river with their small boats, they would try to sink them with their wake. Once, below Mill Town, a swampman had shot a deck hand on a boat when they passed and tried to sink him, and the people in Mill Town had lynched the man without giving him a trial. The townspeople and the men on the river boats called the Coreys and their kind swamp rats, and said they were no better than the vultures living along the river banks. There was no law to protect the swamp rats, so they preferred to stay to themselves and avoid trouble as much as possible.

By the time the Coreys had put the few cats they had caught into the fish box and secured it in the bayou, Ma Corey was calling them to supper. Jeff took a bucket from the rear of the house, went to the bayou to bring in water for washing the dishes, and Pa and Skeeter went in search of wood, to keep the fire going through the night. The fire at night was their only protection against the mosquitoes, which were especially bad in the spring of the year. It was dark by the time all three got back to the house, and, as they climbed the steep steps to the kitchen, they could smell the aroma of frying fish and boiling coffee. Theresa was setting the table with their only setting of tin dishes, and Ma was bending over the mud hearth getting the pan ready to fry the corn pone. The Coreys in the last five years had eaten tons of fried fish and corn pone, which was their regular supper most every night.

"Gol dern it, Ma," Pa said, "I shore wish we hadn't had to build this blame shack so high off the ground. Hit nearly breaks my pore tired bones to climb the steps ever day."

"You jest better thank the good Lord that we did build the shack high off the ground stead of fussin' about it," said Ma. "You know dern well what will happen when the rains come and that muddy ole river comes messin' aroun' tryin' to git in the house with us."

"I reckon you right, Ma, but it shore do tire a pore ole fool like me climbin' them steps all the time."

Pa and the boys took the bar of yellow soap off the cabinet top and began washing the river slime from their hands before supper. Each took his turn at the one cloth towel that hung on a nail over the washstand. When they had finished, they sat at the table, and Theresa poured hot coffee into the tin cups before them.

"They ain't no more sugar for the coffee, Pa," said Theresa. "You better git some the next time you is in Mill Town."

"Yah," said Ma, "and if'n you don't git some more corn meal, they ain't gonna be no more pone on the table afore long. If'n you two boys would stay out'n that swamp long enough to clear me a little patch of land, I could grow us some corn to eat and to feed them pore old hogs. Them hogs air gittin' so thin hit's a wonder the snakes ain't done et 'em afore now."

"Now, they ain't no use to worry none," said Pa. "Me and the boys air goin' into town Satterday and we'll git some sugar and meal if'n them dern turtles and gar will jest leave us be long enough to haul in a mess of fish."

"You goin' to take me to town this time, Pa?" asked Theresa. "You been promisin' to take me for quite a spell now. Please take me this time, Pa."

"Now, you know why I ain't took you to town, Theresa," he said. "I done tole you a thousand times that if'n them dern town boys was to ever see you, they'd come sniffin' aroun' here and jest cause us a heap of trouble."

"Well, that ain't no reason why you can't ever take *me*," said Ma. "You know dern well ain't even no old hound dog gonna come sniffin' aroun' after me."

Ma Corey finished the frying of the bread, dumped it onto a plate and set it, with the fish, on the table. They all gathered at the table, and Skeeter slapped a fork into a big piece of the fried catfish.

"Now, jest a minute, Skeeter," said Pa. "I think I better turn up some thanks tonight afore we eat this meal." Pa turned his head towards the roof, and the others bent their heads.

"Good Lord," he said, "thank ye fer this meal. And please, Lord, keep them dern turtles and gar away from the lines afore Satterday so'es we can have some more pone on the table next week. Thank ye. Amen."

"Damn critters," he murmured to himself, as he carved a big piece from the pone before him.

"Pa," said Jeff, "me and Skeeter was thinkin' 'bout goin' into the swamp tonight after we eat and giggin' us some frogs. I heered one bellowin' last night what sounded like he was as big as a bear. Shore would be good to have some frog legs to eat in the mornin'."

"You boys had orter stay out'n that swamp in the night-time. You know the good Lord didn't make that place fer us human bein's to go into. One of these nights you goin' to go into that place and ain't gonna come out at all."

"They ain't nothin' in there that could hurt a feller if'n he jest keeps his eyes open and don't act a fool," said Jeff. "Anyhows, we ain't skeered of hit like you air."

When they finished the meal, Theresa put the dishes on the stand and began heating some water to clean the grease left on them by the fish. Ma put a big dip of snuff in her bottom lip and got the sage-straw broom to sweep the floor. Pa ambled out to the front porch to sit and think about ways to get more traps set, and Jeff and Skeeter got out their frog gigs to sharpen the points on the old whetrock that the family had had for as long as they could remember.

"Jeff," said Skeeter, "if'n we see a big moccasin in the swamp tonight, I'll show you how to ketch the varment. Maybe we kin swap him fer some likker sticks when we go to town Satterday."

"You better quit messin' with them snakes so much without any help," said Jeff. "One of them varments is goin' to knock a hole clear through you one of these days."

"Shucks," said Skeeter, "you know I ain't skeered of them snakes. I was in the swamp one day by myself and I seed a big otter stalkin' one of them buggers. I sot real still in the skiff and watched what was goin' to happen. That dern otter snuck up to that snake backwards and waved his tail at him. When the ole snake struck at that bugger's tail, that otter turned so quick and sunk his teeth behin' that snake's head I hardly saw it happen. I asked the ole otter to tell me how he done it, and that sapsucker showed me all about it. I'll show you how hit's done fust time I gits a chance."

"One of these days you goin' to turn into a gar fer tellin' them big tales like you do," said Jeff. "Sometimes you scare me when you start talkin' like what you do."

"I ain't tellin' no tale, honest, Jeff," said Skeeter. "You kin see sights sech as I do if'n you jest goes about hit in the right way."

"If'n I ever see some of the buggers you do while I'm in that swamp alone, they ain't even goin' to be no swamp left where I come tearin' my way out of there. Now, you better shet up sech talk and go git us a good lidard knot so'es we kin git goin'."

Skeeter took a burning stick from the hearth and went to the back of the clearing where they stacked the wood to get a fat pine knot to use as a torch. When he got back, he was slapping his neck and howling with pain. "We better git some of that oil I got and rub on us afore we leave," he said. "Them skeeters is shore out to kill a feller tonight. Dern if'n I couldn't feel the blood runnin' out'n me when that devil sucked."

"I don't know which would be the wust," said Jeff, "havin' them skeeters suck the hide off'n me or have that stinkin' crap you made smeared all over me. Hits like choosin' betwix a turtle and a gar. What you put in that stuff, anyway, Skeeter?"

"Hit's a potion a ole nigger give me at Mill Town onced. Hit's got jest about everthing in it."

"Well, I don't doubt that a bit. Now go get the stuff and let's git on in the swamp."

Skeeter went into the room where he and Jeff slept and pulled a long box from under the bed. The box contained many odds and ends and several bottles of potions that Skeeter had made for different purposes. He selected a bottle with a murky red fluid in it and went back to the kitchen where Jeff waited by the fire. When he opened the bottle, Ma dropped the broom and ran from the kitchen.

"Good gosh a mighty, Skeeter," Theresa shouted, "whut in the world is hit you got in that bottle? Hit smells like the devil's breath itself."

"Damn, Skeeter," said Jeff. "If'n hit's all the same to you, I'll jest stick by the skeeters and let you keep that stinkin' stuff to yoreself."

Ma Corey came running back to the kitchen, dragging Pa with her. "Jest git you a whif uv that stuff," she said, "and you won't worry bout eatin' no food no more. Now, you tell that dern youngin' to git that stuff out'n my kitchen and don't never bring nothin' like that in here no more. I'd jest as soon sleep with a bed uv skunks."

"Yore Ma's right, Skeeter," he said. "You'll have all the buzzards comin' from the swamp to see what's dead in the house."

"Derned if'n I'm goin' to have the skeeters eatin' on me, even if'n I do have to smell like a barrel of skunk juice," said Skeeter.

Jeff lit the pine knot, and they went into the yard. Skeeter stopped and rubbed the mosquito potion on his face and arms, and they loaded the gigs and poles into the light skiff and shoved off up the bayou.

"Who's goin' to pole, and who's goin' to gig tonight, Jeff?" asked Skeeter. "If'n I'm goin' to pole, you better git up here and hold this lidard knot afore we gits into that thick brush."

"You mout as well stay up there and do the giggin' whilst you're there," said Jeff, "cause you're a sight better shot with that thing than I am."

"Well, if'nt I'm goin' to stay up here, you be shore and go slow, so if'n I see me a snake I kin ketch him."

"I'll be derned if'n you do," said Jeff. "If'n you start draggin' live snakes in this here boat with me in here where I can't see good, I'm lible to pull down yore pants and spank yore rear plenty good."

A few hundred yards from the house the straight banks of the bayou melted into a seemingly unending lake of water and trees. This was the beginning of the great swamp. The water was shallower and darker, and the trees and vines looked almost impenetrable from a distance. It would be suicide for anyone not familiar with the swamp to venture into the place at night; even Jeff and Skeeter would not go in then, but they had made many trips around the edges in search of frogs. Danger dwelled in every tree and vine, and at any minute swift death could strike out of a dark shadow. The low-hanging branches and vines were covered with water moccasins, which had crawled there in search of safety from the alligators that lurked around the logs and shallow places. The alligators would conceal themselves during the day and come out at night for food. Deeper in the swamp there were even more dangerous enemies—panther and wild cat, and they had been known to attack a man by day or night. The water itself smelled of death and decay.

"Jeff," said Skeeter, "let's go over to that mudbank close to that old fallen magnolia tree. I seed sign there the other day where them big ole bull frogs had been sittin' on their haunches and rubbin' each other."

"O.K.," said Jeff, "but you hold that light good and high so'es I kin see some. Hit's so dark in here tonight that you could see a nigger's eye ten miles off. And I derned shore don't want to git this skiff stuck and have to pull it out."

"Pole her a little mite to the left, Jeff," said Skeeter. "They's two eyes over there as big as saucers starin' at me."

Jeff poled the skiff gently to the left, while Skeeter stood in the bow with the torch in his left hand and the gig in his right.

"Lordy me, Jeff," said Skeeter, "look at the size of that feller. I'd bet that bugger would weigh five pounds. I'd hate to see that sucker jump as high as he could. He'd probably land down at Mill Town."

"Well, quit runnin' yore mouth so loud and drop that gig betwix his eyes afore he leaps in the water and makes some big 'gator a good supper."

Jeff stopped the skiff and dug his pole deep into the muck to hold it steady. Skeeter raised the gig high above his head, took a steady aim, and sailed it towards the white eyes of the frog. The gig struck the bank with a thud and dropped into the water.

"Did you git him, Skeeter?" asked Jeff.

"I ain't sure. I didn't see him jump when the gig struck, but the gig didn't stick to the bank. Pole her up and let me git the gig out'n the water."

Jeff drew the pole out of the soft muck and shoved the skiff further towards the bank. "Hold her there," said Skeeter. "I think I kin reach hit from here."

Skeeter bent down in the skiff and reached into the black water for the long handle of the gig. When he raised it from the water, one end had sunk so he knew that his aim had been true.

"My gosh, Jeff," he said, as he pulled the gig back into the skiff. "Look at them legs. Bet they air at least two feet long."

"One more like that will be all we kin eat fer breakfast," said Jeff. "Let's find one more so'es we kin git the heck out'n here."

Jeff poled the skiff further along the edges of the swamp, while Skeeter held the torch high in search of more eyes. At times Skeeter had to lie flat in the skiff to pass under the low-hanging buck vines. They pushed farther and farther into the swamp.

"Hold her, Jeff," said Skeeter, "I think I seed some eyes a little over to the right uv you. Push her over there and let's see what hit is."

Jeff swung the skiff further to the right until the owner of the eyes came into the range of the light. "Hit shore air another big frog," said Skeeter. "He looks like he mout be as big as the other one. Pole her in and let me git a throw."

Jeff dug the pole into the muck, and Skeeter again took aim with his right hand, while holding the torch with his left. He raised the gig high, and it hit the bank with a dull thud. Only this time the gig pinned the frog to the bank.

"I shore got me a perfect hit that time," said Skeeter. "Pole her up and let me git the bugger in the skiff."

Jeff poled the skiff close to the bank, and Skeeter put the frog in the bottom of the skiff with the other one. "How's you and the skeeters gittin' along, Jeff?" he asked. "Bet them buggers has sucked you dry by now, ain't they?"

"Yeh, but I'd still ruther they kilt me than to die of that awful stuff you put on you. Now let's git back to the house afore that lidard knot has done burned out and we air left in a mess."

Skeeter laid the gigs flat in the bottom of the skiff and crouched in the bow to hold the torch so Jeff could see. They were slowly making their way back through the vines towards the bayou, when Skeeter saw the biggest pair of eyes he had ever seen in the swamp at night.

"Look over there, Jeff," he said. "Do you see them lights what I see? Them looks like the runnin' lights on the back end uv a steamboat. Let's go see if'n one of them blame boats has done run into the swamp."

Jeff poled the skiff closer so that Skeeter could get a better look at the enormous eyes which had caught the glare of the torch. As they got nearer, the eyes grew larger and larger. "Hit must be the reflection of the moon on the water, only they ain't no moon out tonight," said Skeeter. "And look, Jeff, they air turnin' as red as a tomato."

"Them shore ain't the eyes of no frog," said Jeff, "so'es you better be careful up there in the front of this thing."

After they had moved a few more feet forward, Skeeter signaled Jeff to stop. He stood up and held the torch higher so he could get a better look. "Pole her back a mite," he said. "They's a bull 'gator lyin' there that must be a grand-daddy to all the 'gators in the swamp. I'll bet his hide would be wuth more'n all the snakeskins in the swamp."

"Yeh, but don't go gittin' no funny idea 'bout me and you tryin' to git that hide. I'd jest as soon that critter keep his hide and me keep mine. I'm goin' to pole this skiff out'n here and leave well enough be."

"Jest a minute, Jeff, don't go fer a little yet. I got a idea where we mout be able to take this critter home with us to-night. If'n I could jest sink this gig deep enough betwix his eyes, we could let him flounce till he's dead and then drag him in. He's bound to be wuth enough to keep us in sugar and meal fer a month."

"I'd druther do without no corn pone and drink my coffee straight than wrestle with that big devil. So'es you jest forget them ideas and let's git out'n here."

Jeff pulled the pole from the muck and started to back the skiff out, and Skeeter realized what he was doing. Skeeter was not willing to leave the prize without even a try, so when Jeff started backing the skiff away, he lifted the gig and let it fly with all the strength his body could give forth, straight at the red eyes of the bull alligator. The shaft sailed true and struck the alligator between the eyes with a sickening thud. When the gig struck, the 'gator bellowed with such force that it nearly knocked Skeeter from the bow of the skiff.

"I got him, Jeff, I got him," cried Skeeter. "Pole up a little closer so'es I can see if'n he's dead."

Jeff poled up close to the burning eyes, and the 'gator did not move. The gig was planted solidly between its eyes. When he got a little closer, Skeeter signaled for him to stop and said, "He shore am dead, Jeff. I'll grab hold of the gig shaft and you back off till we git him to floatin'. Then we'll work him to the back, and you kin hold the shaft while I kin pole from up here. We kin drag him in home, and won't Ma be proud when she sees this?"

Skeeter grabbed the shaft, while Jeff poled the skiff back into deeper water. Suddenly the entire swamp seemed to turn over and cry to heaven. The skiff went round and round with Skeeter holding his grip on the gig shaft. Jeff was thrown to the bottom of the skiff.

"Turn loose that thing, Skeeter," cried Jeff, " 'fore that critter turns us over and kills the both of us!"

Before Skeeter could turn loose the shaft, he was slung through the air and thrown bodily into a group of cypress knees. The torch hit the water and went out in a sizzle of smoke. Skeeter was still holding to the shaft, and he felt himself being pulled through the murky slime at a fast rate of speed. Finally, from sheer exhaustion, he relaxed his grip from the shaft, and sank slowly into the muck.

Jeff was knocked dizzy for a moment, but raised slowly to his feet. "My God, Skeeter," he cried. "Where are you?" No sound came from the darkness except the echo of his own voice. In a few moments he thought he heard a faint moan to his right. It sounded as if it was about twenty yards from the skiff.

"Skeeter," he cried aloud, "kin you hear me?" Still no answer. Oh my Lord! he thought to himself, Skeeter's done bin kilt.

But then a second moan came, and now he heard it clearly. He took the pole and edged the skiff in the direction of the sounds. The moans became louder, and he cried out again. This time Skeeter answered him in a low voice: "Jeff! Air that you? Is the frogs still in the skiff?"

"Dern fool," said Jeff, "you askin' 'bout them frogs and me worried sick that 'gator done kilt you. Where is you? You better git in here afore them snakes finish you fer sure."

"Jest hold the skiff still and keep talkin', and I'll come to you," said Skeeter.

"Well, if'n you don't git here afore long, I'm shore goin' to be shoutin' so loud them folks in the hills will hear me."

Jeff felt a pull at the side of the skiff and knew that Skeeter had reached him. "Wait jest a minute and let me git

up there and help you in," he said. "We don't want to turn
this thing over."

Jeff crawled to the bow of the skiff and grabbed Skeeter
by the arms. He slowly pulled him forward until he felt his
body roll into the bottom of the skiff. Then he inched his
way back to the rear. They sat in silence for a minute, trying
to get their eyes accustomed to the darkness.

"Now ain't you done got us in a hell uv a mess!" said
Jeff. "How you think we is ever goin' to get home without
no light? And I done tole you to let that damned 'gator
alone."

"We kin git home," said Skeeter, "if'n we kin jest holler
loud enough to git Pa to hear us. Then he kin holler back
and we kin go to his voice."

"Yeah, and have them moccasins drappin' all over our
shoulders. I'll swear, Skeeter, I shore ought to whop the stuf-
fin' out'n you if'n we ever git out'n this."

Skeeter and Jeff stood up in the skiff and shouted as
loud and as long as they could, but they received no answer.

"Hit's only about nine o'clock," said Skeeter. "If'n we jest
sit still a few more minutes till the stars come out I kin
shore git us home. I know one star that lies right over the
house. I've laid awake plenty of nights and looked up and
seed it. And onced when I were in the swamp a 'gator tole
me that if'n I ever git lost at night jest to make fer that star,
and I would shore git home again."

"Well, I hope to the good Lord that this air one time
when yore tales makes some sense," said Jeff.

Jeff stuck his pole deep into the muck to keep the skiff
from drifting, and they sat waiting for the stars to come out
to show them the way home. Even after so much time had
passed, their eyes still could not penetrate the dark of the
swamp. They heard noises that they knew to be frogs and
'gators, and other noises that they had never heard before.
Once they heard an awful scream that Jeff said was a

panther, deep in the swamp. They could feel the flesh creeping along their bones as the swamp became more murky and mysterious. Finally the stars came out, and the moon broke through the seemingly impassable barrier of blackness.

"You see that big star at the end of the Big Dipper?" asked Skeeter. "Well, you jest count six stars to the left and four to the right in a straight line, and you'll come to a star that air a whole lot brighter than the ones around hit, and hit seems to turn to red and blue and green all the time. You see it now, Jeff?"

"Yeah, I sees hit. So you sit down in the middle and I'll start polin' towards it. And for God's sake, if'n I drap a snake off'n one of these vines on yore neck, don't turn the skiff over."

"You better be the one to worry about that," said Skeeter. "I wished you would drap one of them critters in here so'es I could show you how to ketch him. Then you wouldn't be afeered of him no more."

Jeff poled the skiff steadily in the direction of the star that Skeeter had pointed out to him, and before long they came out at the head of the bayou. "From now on," said Jeff, "I think I'd believe you if'n you tole me Ma was a wildcat. I shore am proud that you weren't tellin' no big tale this time."

They glided down the bayou to the landing at the clearing, and Skeeter slipped into the kitchen to get a lighted stick to clean the frog legs by, while Jeff secured the boat and put up the pole and the one gig they had left. After they had cleaned the frogs, they pulled off their overalls and slipped into bed.

Pa stirred in his bed and asked: "Air that you boys comin' in now?"

"Yeah, hits us, Pa," said Jeff.

"Well, you boys ought not be galavantin' around in the swamp havin' a good time til this time of night. Hit worries

yore ma and me to know you air frolicin' round in them
swamps."

"Yeah, Pa," said Jeff, and they pulled the covers over
their heads and went to sleep.

TWO

WHEN THE FIRST RAYS of the sun were beginning to penetrate the darkness, the Corey household showed some signs
of life. Theresa, who was always the first one up, was in the
kitchen stoking up the coals with fresh sticks to get the fire
started. By the time the sun had sprung to life, Ma Corey
was pouring fresh water into the old coffee grounds and getting out the pans to prepare breakfast. Pa was standing on
the front porch stretching his arms and yawning loudly. Jeff
and Skeeter were still in bed with the covers pulled over
their heads. Pa came into the room and shook them.

"You boys git on out of there so'es we kin go and run
them traps afore some nigger beats us to 'em. The way the
air smells this mornin' I'd near abouts bet a coon that them
traps is plum full of fish. I kin smell 'em clear to the house
here."

Jeff and Skeeter slowly arose from the bed, and made
their way to the back of the house and the washstand. They
took turns dousing cold water on their faces and rubbing the

sleep from their eyes with the towel. Skeeter was a little sore from last night's ordeal in the swamps.

"For the love of God," said Ma, "you boys git back in there and put on them overhalls. Hit jest ain't decent runnin' aroun' here naked as a couple of jaybirds."

They hurriedly left the room and returned shortly, fully dressed. "I guess we jest didn't realize that we wasn't dressed, Ma," said Skeeter.

"Well, you be shore and examine yoreself afore you come runnin' aroun' here like that no more," said Ma. "Now you take this here bucket and go git me some fresh water so'es I kin boil this corn mush."

Skeeter took the bucket and started to the bayou, while Jeff went to bring in a supply of wood to be used during the morning. The fire was never allowed to go out in the Corey house. Pa went to the back stoop and brought in the frog legs that the boys had hung there after their return the night before.

"Jest look at the size of these legs, Ma," he said. "Them shore air goin' to be some good eatin' soon as you git 'em fried."

"They'll be good if'n I kin jest keep 'em in the fryin' pan long enough to git 'em cooked. You'd think that when them things hit that hot grease they was goin' to git up and walk right back into the swamp."

"Skeeter tole me onced that he had seed a snake swoller one of them small frogs," said Theresa, "and after a while that frog jumped plum back out uv that snake's belly."

"Well, when I git him in my belly, he shore ain't goin' to jump back again," said Pa, "and I tole you afore not to pay no mind to what Skeeter has done tole you."

In a few minutes Skeeter returned with the water, and Ma put the corn meal mush on to boil. When Jeff came in, they all sat down at the table and began their breakfast of mush, frog legs, and coffee. Jeff and Skeeter did not say a word about their encounter with the big bull alligator on the previous night. After the meal was finished, Theresa and Ma started their morning chores as Pa and the boys left the house and went to the boat landing.

"Hit shore air goin' to be a purty day, ain't hit Pa?" said Skeeter. "When we gits back from the fishin' this mornin', I think I'll go into the swamp and see if I kin git me some snake hides to trade whiles we're in Mill Town tomorrow."

"Tain't goin' to be no use to go into town tomorrow if'n they ain't no fish in the traps and on the lines this mornin'. We hardly got enough in the box at home to eat ourselves. But I jest got a feelin' that we shore made a good ketch last night. You boys put yore arms to them oars and let's git on up the river."

Jeff and Skeeter glided the boat down the bayou and out into the river. The water of the river was red with the reflection of the rising sun. Gray wisps of fog floated from the water and into the trees along the bank. The river was always beautiful early in the morning. The air had a sweet, clean smell about it, and even the mud seemed not so thick. White cranes with long legs and bills were standing in the shallow water along the banks pecking at minnows and small frogs. The trees were alive with birds and squirrels, all blending their voices to make a gay musical sound drift across the river. High overhead, the cawing of the crows mingled with the call of the wood ducks coming in from their roost in the marshes. All the creatures of the air seemed to be glad to be alive on this beautiful spring day.

When they reached West Cut, Jeff took in his oar and crept to the rear of the boat to help pull up the fish traps. Skeeter steered the bow into the cove by himself, then dropped the anchor over the side. It was always exciting for Skeeter to watch them pull up the traps. Pa took one stake line while Jeff took the other, and they slowly raised the first trap from the water. With one quick motion they flipped the trap into the bottom of the boat.

"Jest look at the fish in there!" cried Jeff. "Boy, ain't they some pretty ones!"

Pa was too excited to talk. He was running his hand into the trap and pulling out fish. Skeeter stood up and looked on with glee.

"How many air hit, Pa?" asked Skeeter.

"They's eight cat and two buffalo in here," cried Pa.

When Pa had removed all the fish from the trap, they tied the stake lines and threw the trap back over the side. Skeeter drew in the anchor and rowed the boat further back in the cove where the other trap was set. He dropped the anchor again and they pulled the trap into the boat.

"We didn't do as good here," said Pa, "but they's about four good-sized cats here. Now let's hurry up and git to that trotline out in the river and see about hit afore them gars gits to work on hit."

Jeff climbed back to the middle of the boat, and he and Skeeter backed the boat out of the cove and into the river. They always liked going back better than they did coming. The swift river current caught the boat and sent it sailing downstream, like a feather floating on the water. They glided out of the swift water and pointed the bow toward the log where one end of the trotline was tied. Just before the bow touched the log, Jeff pulled hard with the oar on his side, and it swung round and pumped Pa right into the beginning of the line. When Pa had the line in his hand, the boat gently swung back around and pointed the bow downstream. Then he started pulling along the line.

The first few hooks he came to were empty of bait, but he could feel a hard pulling of the line a few feet on down and knew that he had a fish. He pulled the line up slowly. It was impossible to see below the surface of the muddy water so, in order to find what was on the hook, it was necessary

to pull the line all the way out of the water. Since Pa certainly did not want to jerk any gar into the boat, he was always very slow in seeing what was on the hook. When the
top of the line came out of the water, it was covered with a
white, silky slime, so he knew at once without raising it any
further.

"One of you boys mout as well hand me yore knife," said
Pa, "they's a fish eel on this 'un, and I could shore never git
him off."

Skeeter handed him his knife, and he wrapped the line
around his hand several times and cut it from the trotline.
Then he pulled the eel into the bottom of the boat. It was
about five feet long and bigger around than Pa Corey's arm.
"Hit's shore a nice 'un," said Pa, "and hit weighs 'bout six
pounds."

"That's the best eatin' they air in the river," said Skeeter.
"I'd heap ruther have hit than cat or buffalo."

"You mighty right," said Jeff. "I don't believe I ever could
git me a bellyful of that fish eel meat."

Pa pulled the boat slowly on along the line and took off
two more small catfish. At the far end he thought it had
hung on a snag, so he asked Jeff to help him pull it loose.
Jeff crept to the back of the boat, and they both took the
line and pulled. All at once it snapped from their hands and
disappeared beneath the water. "Well, I'm damned!" said Pa.
"We shore got us somethin' here. Hand me the gaff Skeeter."

He took the gaff from Skeeter, and he pushed the hook
deep under the water to catch and bring the line back up.
When he had it again, he and Jeff grabbed the line with both
hands and pulled with all the strength they could gather.
They would pull up a little and then the line would go back
down. They battled back and forth for a half hour and finally
succeeded in getting the fish's head to the surface of the
water. Pa grabbed the gaff and sliced the point through the
bottom jaw of the fish. They let the line go and both took

the handle of the gaff. With a mighty heave they pulled in the fish. It stretched half the length of the boat. The big cat would weigh at least eighty pounds.

"We shore got us one this time, ain't we Pa!" said Jeff.

"I knowed whut hit was goin' to be this mornin'," said Pa, "'cause I could smell hit in the air. A feller kin jest 'bout tell whut he's got afore he leaves the house if'n he'll jest smell the air."

"If'n we would of caught one more, this boat would have shore sunk," said Skeeter. "She's jest about under the water now. How much do you suppose all this fish will weigh, Pa?"

"Best I kin figger is that they'll weigh nigh on three hundred and fifty pounds with whut we got at the house. And they was bringing five cents a pound last week in Mill Town. We'll have enough left over after gittin' the supplies to buy us a few more shot and some powder fer the gun. We's jest about out."

On the way back downstream, Jeff and Skeeter didn't use the oars for fear of tipping the boat too much and swamping it. The sides were only a couple of inches out of the water, and a slight dip to one side would have sent it under. They let the current take the boat, and Jeff used his oar for a rudder. About a half mile from the mouth of the bayou they heard a loud blast around the bend.

"Oh my Lord, have mercy on me!" cried Pa. "Hit's one of them steamboat fellers, and with this load on here they will swamp us shore."

"Do you reckon we kin make hit to the bayou afore they gits to us, Pa?" asked Skeeter.

"We'd nary make it, Son," said Pa. "If'n you and Jeff was to use the oars fer speed you'd turn the boat over afore we got near 'bouts there."

The blast sounded again, and then they could see the steamboat come around the bend and head straight for them.

"Head her into that little creek comin' in there!" cried Pa.

Jeff turned the oar hard to the left, and the boat began to swing slowly into the right bank of the river. A little creek flowed into the river just below them, and Jeff pointed the bow of the boat into it. All three jumped out into the neck-deep water, and guided the boat behind a clump of bushes hanging over the water. Skeeter could hardly keep his nose above the water by standing on his toes. Just as they got behind the bush the steamboat passed, with its stern wheels churning madly. The waves from its wake rolled into the creek and knocked Skeeter from his feet. Jeff and Pa clung to the sides of the boat to keep the water from rushing over it and turning it over. Skeeter was knocked under the boat and then into the bank. When he came up, his eyes and mouth were filled with the foul-tasting, muddy water. He pulled himself onto the bank and began to belch the water from his stomach. Pa and Jeff still clung to the sides of the boat, with the waves rushing over their heads. When the water finally calmed again, they crawled onto the bank with Skeeter.

"You hurt, Skeeter?" asked Pa.

"Naw," he said, "jest got me a bellyful uv mud."

"How we goin' to git back in the boat without turnin' her over?" asked Jeff. "That sucker jest air goin' to stay out'n the water by itself now."

"I guess they ain't but one thing fer us to do," said Pa, "and that be to cling to the sides of the boat and float her in home. Me and you kin git on one side apiece and Skeeter kin hang on to the rear. We kin drift to the bayou and then kick her on up home."

Pa and Jeff got on opposite sides of the boat and Skeeter clung to the rear; they paddled with their hands and feet and pushed the boat into the swift current of the river. They fought the boat to the left side of the river and barely managed to turn it into the mouth of the bayou. Once out of the swift water, they all three clung to the rear and kicked up their feet, and slowly moved up the bayou to the landing. Ma and Theresa ran from the house to meet them.

"Whut in the world air you fellers hangin' on and kickin' like a bunch of hound dogs fer?" asked Ma. "You ain't got tetched in the head, has you?"

"That dern steamboat jest liked to have sunk the boat and drowned us all," said Pa, "and we couldn't git back in without swampin' her. You see whut a load we got in the boat, don't you? We shore got to git us a bigger boat somehow."

"Hit's a good thing you come home with some fish this mornin'," said Ma, "or hit would have been mighty pore eatin' aroun' here soon. Now you kin jest git me a fresh bottle of snuff fer some of that fish tomorrow."

"And if'n you kin, I'd like a hair comb, Pa," said Theresa.

"The both of you better be glad if'n I bring home plenty of meal and sugar," said Pa, "cause we come mighty nigh losin' the whole bunch of hit."

"Well, I'm goin' an' hoe in the garden some more," said Ma, "so'es hit won't be too long afore we has some peas and onions on the table. Theresa, you better go see if'n you kin get some of that poke salat to fix fer dinner. And while you is out there, git some fer them hogs. They been rootin' in that pen so much hit looks like where a bunch of bull 'gators been fightin'."

Pa and the boys pulled the boat up on the landing and took the fish out and put them in the fish box. When they had finished, they turned the boat up on one side and dumped the water out of it. "Jeff," said Pa, "I speck me and you better row over to the woods on the other side of the river and git some pine fer the fire. They ain't too much left, and we shore won't be able to go afore next week."

"Do you want me to go too, Pa?" asked Skeeter.

"I'm afeared they won't be enough room in the boat fer us and the wood too if'n you go," said Pa.

As soon as Jeff went to the house and brought back the ax, he and Pa shoved off down the bayou in the boat. Skeeter stood on the landing and watched them until they were out of sight. He was glad that they had not wanted him to go along with them. He liked to be alone, especially if he could go into the swamp by himself. He ran to the back of the house and got the pole for the skiff and started up the bayou toward the swamp. The sun felt good, so he pulled off his shirt and threw it in the bow. He felt good all over, knowing that he could do as he pleased the rest of the morning.

When he reached the edge of the swamp, he would give a hard push with the pole and then lie down in the bottom of the skiff and glide along, looking up into the trees and at the clouds in the sky. It gave him a dizzy feeling to lie in the skiff and watch the white clouds sail by over him. He would lie on his stomach and push the skiff along by pulling his hands through the cool water. He felt more at home in the swamp than any place he had ever been. He couldn't understand why anyone would be afraid of the swamp like Pa was.

A thought suddenly struck him that made him get to his feet and start poling the skiff swiftly through the water. He would go back to the place where they had fought the 'gator last night and see what had happened to him. He guided the skiff around trees and through vines, toward the place where they had been. Ahead of him he heard a splash in the water and knew that a snake had heard him coming and dropped from a limb or a vine. He could see turtles resting on logs and minnows shoot out in all directions. Sometimes he would pass a frog bed and see thousands of the small black eggs stretched out in long lines of white slime. As he went further into the swamp, the trees grew thicker, and the sun was almost shut out from him. He did not think that they had gone this far the night before.

Presently he came to the spot where they had first seen the burning red eyes. He found the mudbank where the 'gator had been lying and could see signs of the struggle. He poled in the direction the 'gator had pulled him, and could see broken vines for several hundred yards until he came to a limb of a tree hanging low over the water, where he found the shaft of the gig floating in the water. The 'gator must have gone under the limb and broken the shaft from the steel gig. He knew that the gig was still solidly planted in the 'gator's head. He said to himself: "Them dern 'gators must be awful hard critters to kill. Next time I go after me one of them buggers I'm shore goin' to take that shotgun with me." Without the gig shaft sticking up to break the vines, the trail was harder to follow and, when he came to a pool of deeper water, he lost it completely. He made several circles around the place, but could never pick up the trail again. Then he poled the skiff slowly in the direction of the bayou, stopping several times to watch a fight between a hawk and a catbird, or a snake stalking a small, unsuspecting frog, but he could never get close enough to one of the snakes to have a try at catching it. Sometimes it seemed that the snakes knew that he was after them and would glide away.

When he saw several small streaks of mud shoot through a shallow place by an old log, he knew that it was a crawfish bed, so he stopped the skiff and eased over the side into the water. He sunk down halfway to his knees in the soft black muck, and could feel it ooze up through his toes. He liked the feel of the cool muck on his feet. As he walked slowly through the shallow water to the log, he could see the crawfish backing around through the muck, so he stopped down and grabbed at them with his hands. When he would catch one he would put it in his pocket and then look for others. He ran his hands along the bottom of the log and caught several each time. After a while he had both of his pockets full and all he could carry in his hands, so he made his way back through the muck and dumped them into the skiff. Then he repeated this until he could find no more. He knew that his mother would be real proud, for now she could make them a big pot of crawfish gumbo. His mouth watered at the thought of this favorite dish. They could not catch crawfish in the bayou because the turtles would eat them as fast as they would come out of their beds.

It was about an hour before high noon when he reached the head of the bayou, so he lay down in the bottom of the skiff to enjoy the warm sun. A gentle breeze pushed the skiff slowly down the bayou. The breeze made the tall marsh grass look like a sea of swaying dancers. Skeeter thought that he would be content to drift forever with the sun and breeze and water about him. Why would anybody ever want to live anywhere besides along the swamp and river? When he raised up, he saw that he had already drifted past the landing, so he poled the skiff back to the landing and pulled it up on the bank.

He walked to the house and got a bucket and went back to the landing. He scooped several handfuls of the soft, cool, bayou muck into the bucket, and then put several layers of grass on top of it. When he had put in about a cupful of water and dumped the crawfish into the bucket, he walked back to the house and climbed the steps to the kitchen, where Ma and Theresa had already started preparing the noon meal.

"Guess whut I got in the bucket, Ma?" said Skeeter.

"Hit's probably a bucketful of them swamp snakes," said Theresa.

"Well if'n that's whut hit air you shore better git out'n here with hit in a hurry," said Ma. "You oughta know better than to bring a bunch of them varments in here."

"Hain't neither one of you got the right idea," said Skeeter, "I got a plum bucketful of crawfish here that I caught in the swamp."

"Well, now, ain't that nice?" said Ma. "I'll get yore Pa to git me a few things in town tomorrow, and we'll have the best pot of gumbo you ever tasted. I'm shore right proud of you, Skeeter."

"Whut's that you got cookin' fer dinner, Ma?" he asked.

"Hit's somethin' you like a lot," said Theresa.

"We got a pot of young poke salat with little onions and peppers chopped up in hit, and I'm makin' a corn pone with onions fried in hit. And best of all, I'm fryin' that fish eel. Now ain't that a right fancy dinner, Skeeter?"

The mention of the food and the smells coming from the hearth made Skeeter's mouth water with hunger. He put the bucket of crawfish in the corner of the kitchen, and slipped up to the hearth where the eel was cooking, to steal a piece. Ma saw what he was doing and grabbed him by the arm. "Now you git on out of here and wait fer yore Pa and Jeff to git back afore you start snitchin' food. All you'll do is ruin yore dinner."

Skeeter went out the kitchen door and down to the landing. He broke sticks into little pieces and threw them into the water and imagined they were boats on a big ocean and he was sailing them. He looked down the bayou and saw Pa and Jeff coming with the load of wood. When they were close enough, he waded into the water and grabbed the bow of the boat and pulled it to the bank, as Pa and Jeff started throwing the fat pine wood out of the boat.

"You should have been with us this time, Skeeter," said Jeff. "We saw a big buck over in the woods. We had sot down on a log to rest, and we were real quiet when we heard him comin' through the bresh. He run right up to us and jest stopped and looked at us fer a spell. If'n we'd had the gun, we coulda kilt him as easy as shootin' a squirrel."

Skeeter's eyes grew wide at the mention of the deer.

"I ain't never seed as many deer signs as they were over there this mornin'," said Pa. "I guess they ain't been none of them slickers from up at Fort Henry messin' aroun' over there and skeerin' 'em fer a long time now. We'll go over there next week and git us one of them buggers."

"Kin I go too, Pa?" asked Skeeter.

"Shore you kin go. Hit's jest that when we go after wood they ain't no room to take you, and other than that we jest don't have no call to go into the woods very often."

Skeeter had never been into the big woods on the other side of the river, and the thought of getting to go made him feel wild with excitement. He could picture all kinds of mysteries that he had never seen, but he didn't think that he would like it better than the swamp.

He helped Pa and Jeff store the wood beside the house, and then they all went in to wash up for dinner. Each took his turn at the washbasin and towel. Skeeter had become so excited at the thought of the deer hunt that he forgot to tell Pa and Jeff that he had caught the crawfish.

Ma put the dinner on the table, and they sat down to begin the meal. The young poke salat, hush puppies, and eel tasted so good that they all put large quantities of the food in their mouths and ate in silence. About halfway through the meal several of the crawfish escaped from the bucket in the corner and were crawling toward the table. Pa happened to glance at the floor and saw them coming toward him. He tried to jump from his chair, but his feet caught the bottom of the table and turned him over, rolling him backwards over the floor, right into the middle of the crawfish. The half-swallowed food stuck in his throat, and he fought madly to get back to his feet. Finally he dashed to the door and looked back and saw that his assailants were only harmless crawfish.

"Where in the tarnation of hell did them things come from?" he bellowed. "I thought all the devils in the swamp were comin' after me. That liked to have scared me to death."

"Skeeter caught 'em in the swamp whiles you were gittin' the wood," said Ma. "Now come on and finish yore dinner and stop actin' like an idiot."

Everyone had to hold their breath for a minute to keep from laughing at Pa.

"Well, if'n hit weren't for the fact that I could eat six barrels of that gumbo you make, Ma, I would whale the daylights out uv Skeeter right here and now. Ain't no use in scarin' the livin' out'n a feller like that."

Skeeter got up and caught the crawfish, put them back into the bucket, got a pan and covered the top of the bucket so that they could not escape again, and the meal was finished in peace.

When the last person got up from the table, there was not a crumb of the dinner left. Theresa stacked the dishes on the stand, and she and Ma went to the other room to lie down and rest a few minutes before washing them and cleaning the kitchen. Pa and Jeff lay down on the front porch, and Skeeter went down to the bayou to lie in the grass and look up at the clouds. The sun sent pleasant waves of simmering heat into the Corey clearing, and the breeze brought cool air from the bayou. In a few minutes the entire family was fast asleep.

It was midafternoon when the blast from the steamboat whistle awakened Pa Corey from his deep sleep. He grumbled something about where he wished the steamboats would go, and rose slowly to his feet. Ma and Theresa were cleaning up the kitchen. Jeff was still asleep on the porch. Pa walked into the kitchen, took the gourd dipper from the shelf, dipped it in the bucket, and took a long draught of the cool water. He walked back to the front porch and shook Jeff. "You better git up, Son," he said. "We got to string them fish afore hit gits dark."

Pa went into the kitchen and took the long fish string from a nail on the wall. On one end of the string was a slim copper spike, and on the other a copper circle. He went down the back steps and to the landing. Skeeter was not there, and the skiff was gone. Pa found a small round stick about a foot long, pulled a loop of the line through the copper circle and pushed the stick through the loop. Then he pulled tight on the string, and the stick was tied fast against the circle. In a few minutes Jeff came down to the landing, and they pulled the fish box out of the water. Pa took a fish out of the box, ran the spike through its gills and out its mouth, and then let it slide down against the stick. He handed the spike to Jeff, and as he would take the fish out of the box, Jeff would string them. When they had finished, they put the fish back into the box, closed the lid, tied the end of the string to a bush on the bank, and shoved the box back into the water. Jeff took his knife and started cleaning one of the large buffalo he had left out for their supper, and Pa went back into the house.

Jeff was washing the fish in the bayou, when he saw Skeeter coming toward him in the skiff. When he pushed in at the landing, Jeff saw three large water moccasins lying in the bottom. Their heads had been neatly popped from their bodies. Skeeter threw the snakes on the bank and got out of the skiff.

"I'll give you one of these skins to trade in town tomorrow if'n you'll help me clean 'em," he said.

"I'll shore do hit," said Jeff, "cause I need somethin' of my own fer to trade. Whut you reckon them folks do with these here skins, Skeeter?"

"I heard that they makes belts and purses out of 'em."

"Well, I shore wouldn't want no snakeskin hangin' aroun' my belly or in my pocket," said Jeff.

Jeff put the cleaned fish on the grass and grasped the tail of one of the snakes. Skeeter took the other end and ran the sharp blade of his knife down the underside of the snake. When they had split the snake in half, they trimmed the meat and bones from the skin. Then Skeeter washed it in the water. When they finished cleaning all three of the snakes, they hung the skins over a limb of a tree to dry, and went into the house. Ma was giving Pa instructions as to what to bring from town the next day. Jeff took the bar of yellow soap from the shelf and went up the bayou to take a bath, and Skeeter stood at the door looking after him.

"Why air hit that Jeff's been takin' a bath afore we go to town the last few times?" asked Skeeter. "I can't see no use in him gettin' all that fancy."

"I've heard that he's sparkin' some gal in town," said Pa.

"Yeh, and he better stop that sparkin' aroun' them town girls afore he gits us all in trouble," said Ma. "You know dern well whut them folks thinks of the likes of Jeff, and they ain't no use askin' fer yore head to be chopped off."

"Whut's sparkin' mean, Ma?" asked Theresa.

"Hit's jest as well you don't know and don't never find out. They ain't no end to a woman's troubles after a man comes sniffin' around her like she were a bitch dog in heat."

"Now, I wouldn't go so fer as to say that," said Pa. "You ain't did too bad fer yoreself."

"You call livin' in this swamp and bein' treated like a nigger by all the other white folks ain't so bad? Sometimes I think we would uv been better off if'n we would have stayed in the fields. Hit's been nigh on a year now since me and Theresa has seen airy other white folks, excusin' you and the boys."

Skeeter and Theresa couldn't understand what it was their folks were arguing about. They had seen these little spats before, and they always felt sorry for Pa, but they couldn't understand why Ma didn't love living on the river as they did. Skeeter couldn't stand the thought of not being around the swamp, and he liked not having other folks around them all the time.

"Jest the same," said Ma, "you better tell the boy to watch himself while he's messin' aroun' in that town."

"Leave the boy be," said Pa, as he walked to the front porch and sat down. Ma and Theresa started cooking the supper. After a while Jeff came in, and they all sat at the table and ate in silence. When they had finished, Pa and the boys sat on the front porch, while Ma and Theresa washed the dishes and cleaned the kitchen. When the work was finished, the family went to bed, for they all knew that they had to be up long before daybreak to start preparations for the trip to town.

A few hours after dark Pa was awakened by a loud splashing coming from the bayou. Jeff and Skeeter had heard the disturbance also and were pulling on their clothes. They went to the kitchen and lighted a torch and all three went down to the landing. They could hear the splashing continuing up the bayou. The fish box had been knocked from the water and was lying several feet up on the bank. They put it back into the water and stood for a few minutes in silence and could hear the noises continue past the end of the bayou and into the swamp.

"Whut in the world do you reckon that were?" asked Pa.

"Hit beats me," said Jeff. "I never heard of a critter pullin' a stunt like that there."

Skeeter didn't say a word because he thought he knew what had caused the disturbance and knocked the box out of the water.

THREE

SKEETER WAS AWAKENED by the smell of frying fish and corn pone coming from the kitchen. He jumped out of bed, pulled on his overalls and went into the kitchen. Pa and Jeff were already up and had gone down to the landing. Ma was cooking the fish and corn pone for their lunch on the trip to town, and Theresa was cooking grits and flapjacks for their breakfast. The smell of the coffee boiling made him hungry. He walked out onto the back stoop and breathed deeply of the fresh morning air. The sky was still pitch dark, and Pa and Jeff were loading the boat by torchlight. In a few minutes they had finished and they came back to the kitchen. Jeff was dressed in his best suit of brown khaki, and his hair was slicked back with water. Pa had on a pair of clean overalls, his best blue shirt, and his big black hat. Skeeter looked at them and grunted with displeasure. He was dressed in his same dirty overalls and was without shoes.

Ma finished cooking the lunch and wrapped it in a piece of soiled brown paper. They sat down and ate the breakfast of grits and flapjacks with thick brown molasses. When they

had finished, they took the lunch and went down to the boat
landing, and Ma and Theresa followed them. Pa sent Skeeter
back to the house to get the two croaker sacks that they
used to bring their supplies home in. Pa and Jeff turned the
bow of the boat down the bayou and tied the skiff on behind. Skeeter was to ride in the boat alone and guide it with
an oar, with Pa and Jeff in the skiff tied behind. This was
done to reduce the weight in the boat because Skeeter
weighed less. After everything was loaded, Skeeter got the
snakeskins and put them in his pocket. Ma was giving them
a few last-minute instructions about not forgetting the supplies, and when she finished, they shoved the boat down the
bayou. It was hard work for Skeeter to tow the heavy load
in the bayou, but when the boat was caught in the swift
water of the river, all he had to do was sit and guide with
the oar. It was nearly as much fun as being in the swamp.

They had just reached the river when the eastern sky was
filled with the gray streaks of dawn. The air was fresh and
sharp, and Skeeter trailed one foot in the cool water. Pa and
Jeff relaxed in the skiff for the pleasant ride. Life on the
river wasn't really so bad, thought Pa.

It was not yet midmorning when they reached the boat
docks of Mill Town, a small town of about four hundred
people. It had been named Mill Town because of the sawmill
on the bank of the river, and the only time the steamboats
stopped was when there was lumber on the docks for them
to pick up or a passenger to get on or off. There was one
street of business houses, two churches, a school, and the
rest were residential houses or shacks along the river. There
was a Baptist and a Catholic church, because many of the
people who worked at the mill were French Catholics, and
some of them could not speak English.

Along the business street there were several dry-goods
stores, a post office, a fish market, two saloons and a bar-
bershop. The south end of town along the river was the

Negro quarters. The best of the townspeople lived to the north and away from the river. None of the Coreys had ever been in that part of town.

Skeeter tied the anchor line to a piling, and Pa pulled the skiff alongside and tied it to the boat. Pa and Jeff got on the dock, and Skeeter handed them the fish line. Then he climbed up and helped. It was all they could do for the three of them to lift the string of fish to the dock. Pa put the lunch inside his shirt and Jeff took the croaker sacks, and they started carrying the fish to the market. Skeeter thought his arms would break before they finally arrived.

The man who ran the market was named Mr. Blanch, a short, fat man with jet black hair. He talked with a city accent and did not look like a native of that part of the country. They had heard tales that he was from somewhere up north and had moved down here for his health. He was the only man in Mill Town that treated Pa Corey with decency.

When they arrived at the back door of the market, he opened the door for them. "Well, come on in, Abner," he said. "You are certainly a welcome sight. This is the first fish I've had in two days. All the other men said that the gar have been so bad this week that they haven't managed to catch enough for their own families to eat."

"How much air you payin' this week?" asked Pa.

"With the supply so short, I'll pay you ten cents a pound if it's good fish."

It was all Pa and the boys could do to keep from shouting with glee. They hadn't felt so good in all their lives. Mr. Blanch started examining the fish and putting them on the large scales. He felt and smelled each one as he took it from the string. "You sure got a nice one here," he said, when he came to the large cat they had caught on the trotline.

"Yessah," said Pa, "and that bugger shore give us one heck uv a time afore we got him in the boat."

Mr. Blanch turned to Pa and said: "You've got exactly four hundred and ten pounds of first-class fish here, Mr. Corey. At ten cents a pound that will amount to forty-one dollars."

He walked over to the cash drawer and took out four tens and a one dollar bill and handed them to Pa.

"I shore thank you, Mr. Blanch," said Pa.

"And I thank you, too, Abner. If you have any more next week, bring them to me. Your fish are always fresh, and I like that."

Pa and the boys walked out the front door of the market and down the street, their heads held a little high.

"That's the most money I've seed in a long time," said Jeff.

"I guess the good Lord must have heard my prayer the other day and showered this goodness down on us," said Pa.

"Kin I have a nickel fer some likker sticks?" asked Skeeter.

"Let's go to the store and git the supplies fust and see how much we has left," said Pa, "then we kin tell how much each kin have to do whut he wants to with."

They walked to the big supply store on the first corner and went inside. A clerk at the counter looked at them with contempt, but when Pa took the bills out of his pocket, the clerk immediately grabbed a pencil and started writing down his order for supplies. When Pa finished, the clerk told him that it would take better than an hour to fill the order, so Pa paid him and they went back outside. Pa had several bills and coins left in his hand. He put the bills in his pocket and handed Jeff and Skeeter fifty cents apiece. He took the lunch from his shirt, and they sat on the porch of the store and started eating.

"If'n hit's goin' to be a good whiles afore that clerk gits our supplies ready, why don't we jest meet back here in front of the store, Pa?" said Skeeter. "I wants to go see Uncle Jobe a whiles afore we has to start back."

"Now who in tarnation is Uncle Jobe?" asked Pa.

"He's a ole nigger friend uv mine down in the quarters. Me and him always visits when I gits the chance. He's the one I'm goin' to git to give me the potion fer the gars."

"Well, I guess that be a right good idea at that," said Pa. "We'll jest all meet back here in about two hours. Now don't nary one of you be no later than that. You know how Ma feels 'bout us comin' in home too late."

They finished eating the cold fish and corn pone, and each walked off in a different direction. Skeeter headed south towards the Negro quarters, Jeff headed north towards the store that Clarise Smith worked in, and Pa headed across the street towards the River Side Saloon. All three looked forward to a pleasant two hours.

Skeeter walked down the dusty lane that led to the Negro section of town. Most of the shacks were built along the river so that outhouses were not needed. They were built of cull scraps from the mill and were in much worse condition than even the Corey house. Skeeter walked to a one-room shack where the old Negro known as Uncle Jobe lived alone. Most folks said that the Negro did not know his own age, but he must have been at least ninety years old. His hair was white as silver, and his face was wrinkled with old age. The only means he had of keeping body and soul together was selling the different potions he made to the other Negroes and some white people. He had a potion for almost every ill known to mankind, and some people swore by him and would seek the advice of no other. The old man was sitting on the front porch when Skeeter arrived. When he recognized the boy, he stood up and motioned him in.

"How be ye, Massah Skeeter?" he asked. "Welcome back agin."

"I'm shore mighty proud to see you," said Skeeter, "and I done brought you a little present that I caught in the swamp."

Skeeter took one of the snakeskins out of his pocket and handed it to the old Negro. He turned it over and examined it and stroked it with his hands. "How did you ever figger that I has always wanted one of these big snakeskins?" he asked. "This is jest about the best thing anybody done ever give old Uncle Jobe."

"I shore am glad you likes hit," said Skeeter. "I was afeered you wouldn't."

"Don't you be afeered that old Uncle Jobe won't like anything that you brings him. I jest wishes they were more white boys like you aroun' to visit with me."

"Uncle Jobe," said Skeeter, "I shore wants you to do somethin' fer me if'n you kin."

"Why you knows that I'd do most airy thing fer you that air in my limits, Massah Skeeter. Now whut is hit you wants?"

"We bin havin' a heap of trouble with them dern gar messin' with our traps and lines lately. I heard that they was a potion that would keep them critters from messin' around with any hooks."

"Why, you is sho' right," said Uncle Jobe. "I have jest what you wants right here in the house. I'll git hit fer you."

Uncle Jobe got up and walked into the dim interior of the shack with Skeeter close behind him. One complete wall of the shack was shelves filled with bottles of different colored fluids. The old Negro looked through several bottles and selected a small one with a dark yellow liquid inside. Then he walked back and sat on the porch.

"This air jest whut you wants," he said. "You jest put a drap of this stuff on each bait as you fixes yore lines, and you sho' won't be bothered with no gar no more."

"I shore don't know how to thank you well enough fer this," said Skeeter. "I know Pa is goin' to be real proud when he sees hit."

"Jest you don't forget that old Uncle Jobe will help you ary time hits in his power to do so, so'es you jest bring yore problems to me and we'll see whut' we kin do abouts fixin' 'em."

They sat in silence for a long time enjoying each other's company. They seemed to understand that being together and sharing their problems was enough to satisfy each other. Finally Skeeter realized that it would soon be time to go. He hated the thought of time going by so quickly, for he would like to sit with Uncle Jobe the rest of the afternoon.

"Uncle Jobe," he said, "they's one more thing I would like to ask you about afore I has to go."

"Well, you jest go right ahead, Massah Skeeter."

"Whut kin you do about a critter in the swamp that has gone plum crazy? Hit ain't really his fault, but somethin' done happen to him that has caused him to plum lose his mind."

"Whut makes you ask me a question like that? I've heard of folks doin' that, but I ain't never heard of a critter goin' crazy. Leastwise, I sho' wouldn't like to be aroun' when that happens."

"Oh, hit ain't nothin' really, I guess. I jest wanted to ask and see."

"Well, that's one thing that I can't give you no answer on."

"I speck I better be goin' now," said Skeeter, "cause Pa tole me not to be late in gettin' back."

"If'n that's whut yore Pa said, you better be on yore way. Don't forget to come and see me agin, Massah Skeeter."

"Good-by, Uncle Jobe."

Skeeter walked back down the lane towards town, and when he reached the store, neither Pa nor Jeff was waiting for him. He went into the store and walked to the counter. When the clerk came to him, he pulled the other snakeskin from his pocket. "How much in trade will you give me fer this?" he asked.

The clerk took the snakeskin and examined it. Then he walked to a room in back of the store and stayed gone for a few minutes. He returned without the skin. "What did you want to trade it for?"

"I wants to trade hit fer some likker sticks," said Skeeter.

"We'll give you five sticks for it," said the clerk.

"That sounds like a pretty fair trade. I guess I'll jest take you up on hit."

The clerk reached under the counter and laid five of the black licorice sticks in Skeeter's hand. Skeeter put one of them in his mouth and the rest in his pocket, and went back out and sat on the porch. Pa and Jeff still were not in sight.

Skeeter sat in the warm sun and watched the wagons rolling into town. The people were coming in from the swamps and hills to do their Saturday buying and to talk with neighbors they hadn't seen for a week. The mill had shut down at noon, and little groups of men were beginning to gather on the street. There was a lot of noise coming from the saloon across the street. Now and then Skeeter thought he could hear Pa's voice sound out in loud laughter. He remembered that he still had the fifty cents in his pocket, but decided to wait and spend it some other time. He looked across the street and saw Pa come out the saloon door. Pa had a bottle in one hand and weaved back and forth as he crossed the street. As he looked at Skeeter his eyes were a little hazy.

"Where's Jeff?" he asked. "Hain't he got back yit?"

"I ain't seed him, Pa," said Skeeter.

"Well hit's time we got started back towards the house."

Pa uncorked the bottle, took a deep drink, and started to sit down. A loud noise sounded up the street, and Jeff sailed out the door of a store and landed on the wood platform in front. Three men a little larger than he were on top of him immediately, kicking and hitting with their fists. Pa recognized them as the brothers of Clarise Smith. "So that's who he were sparkin'," said Pa. "Skeeter, you go on in the store and start gittin' them supplies down to the boat as soon as you kin."

Skeeter ran into the store and started carrying supplies to the boat. Pa put the bottle in his back pocket and weaved slowly up the street. The brothers had Jeff in the dust and were kicking him with their feet. Clarise was standing in front of the store yelling for them to stop.

"Ain't no yellow-bellied swamp rat goin' to spark around my sister!" said one of the brothers.

"Let's kill the low-down son of a bitch!" said another.

Jeff was fighting back as best he could, but he was no match for the three men. People were running down the street to watch the fight. There was already a big circle formed around the men. Blood was running from Jeff's mouth, and he wasn't fighting back as hard. Pa walked through the circle of people and grabbed one of the brothers by the arm.

"Now jest a minute," he said. "You boys air goin' to kill that boy if'n all of you don't stay off him at one time."

"Air you his Pa?" asked the man.

"I shore air," said Pa, "and I aim to see that you all don't beat on him like that. Hit ain't nearbouts a fair fight."

The man drew back his fist, and before Pa could say another word, he hit Pa full strength in the eye. Pa flipped backwards and rolled through the people in the crowd. Clarise ran through the crowd and stood in the middle of her brothers.

"Now ain't you a big bunch of bullies," she cried, "beatin' up a boy and a pore ole man. If you don't stop this right now I'll never speak to none of you no more."

"Well, we'll let him go fer now," said one of the brothers, "but if'n we ever ketch the son of a bitch hangin' around here again we'll shore bust his brains out."

The three brothers walked away down the street, and the crowd began to fade away. Pa rose slowly to his feet, picked up his hat and walked over to Jeff. He took Jeff by the arm and pulled him to his feet. His mouth was badly bruised and both eyes were nearly closed.

"Air ye hurt bad, Son?" asked Pa.

"Naw, I guess I'll live."

Clarise was still standing there looking at him. They looked at each other for a few moments without speaking.

"I'm sorry," she said.

"Hit's all right," said Jeff. "Don't you worry none. I'll be back."

He turned and followed Pa toward the boat docks. When they got there, Skeeter was standing by the boat, and half the supplies were in the boat and half were in the skiff.

"Did ye git 'em all?" asked Pa.

"I shore did," said Skeeter, "and hit took me four trips. You two air a sight fer sore eyes."

They all climbed down into the boat. Pa and Jeff leaned over the side and washed their faces in the river.

"Air ye able to row, Jeff?" asked Pa.

"I guess I kin make hit all right. If'n I can't, I'll let you know."

They put the oars in the locks, Pa untied the line from the piling, and the boat floated out into the river. Jeff and Skeeter bent their arms to the oars, and the boat started upstream. Pa sat in the bow and uncorked the bottle. About halfway home the whiskey was gone, and he was sound asleep. He was still asleep when they reached the landing. Skeeter shook him to wake him, and he jumped to his feet and shouted: "Leave me at the sons of bitches!" His feet slipped in the boat and he fell backwards into the bayou. He came up sputtering and spitting water, and fighting for the bank. His hat was still on his head.

"Now ain't you a pretty sight," said Ma. "If'n you spent the money and didn't git all them supplies, you jest better git in the boat and head back to town."

"If'n you'll jest wait and see whut all I done brought you won't be fussin' at me none," said Pa.

"Whut's done happened to you and Jeff?" asked Theresa.

"Some of them mill hands tried to steal the boat and we got in a big fight," said Pa. "But we shore got the best of them."

Skeeter looked at his Pa but didn't say anything. They all gathered up bundles and went into the house. Jeff went to bed, while the rest of the family gathered in the kitchen.

"Jest look whut all I got," said Pa, and he started pulling things out of the sacks. "They's a bag of corn meal, a bag of sugar, a can of coffee, a sack of grits, a jug of molasses, a side of salt pork, a sack of okra, tomatoes, and celery stalks. That's fer the gumbo. And I also got some seed corn, some okra, tomato, collard, and radish seeds, and a sack of hog feed. Here's two bottles of snuff fer you, Ma, and a big comb fer Theresa, and a bolt of red cloth big enouf to make you and Theresa a new dress. And I also got me some gunpowder and shot. And whut do you think of this?" he said, holding up a small paper bag. "Hit's a dozen hen eggs fer us to eat."

Ma and Theresa were almost wild with excitement. Theresa ran the comb through her hair time and time again. Ma felt the cloth and then the snuff bottles. She was so happy she was about to cry.

"Now tell me, Abner," she said, "how did you git all this?"

"We had four hundred and ten pounds of the fish, and they was payin' ten cents a pound. I still got a little money left fer a rainy day."

They put up the supplies, and Ma put away the cloth and started some supper. Jeff didn't come out to eat, and Pa said to just leave him alone. They were all tired, so they didn't sit around long after supper. Skeeter and Theresa went to bed, and Theresa took the comb with her. As soon as Ma finished the dishes, she grabbed Pa by the arm and pulled him towards the bed.

"You jest come on now, Abner Corey," she said. "Me and you is goin' to imagaine we is twenty years younger than we is."

Night settled on the Corey family, and all was well except in Jeff's heart.

FOUR

THE SUN WAS ABOVE the trees when the Corey household came to life the next morning. It was Sunday, and there were no traps to check and no trotline to run. Pa didn't believe in fishing on the Sabbath, so Sunday was always a day of rest, and each member of the family could do as he pleased.

Theresa was slicing the pork side into thin, even strips while Ma was mixing flapjack batter. When the aroma of frying bacon drifted through the house, the Corey men began to arise, and Pa and Skeeter were soon in the kitchen. After the bacon was fried, Ma dropped the eggs into the hot grease, and put on fresh coffee to boil. When the eggs were done, she dropped in the flapjacks. In a few minutes she set the breakfast of fried eggs, flapjacks, bacon, molasses, and coffee on the table. Jeff was still in bed.

"You better go in there and git that boy up and make him eat some breakfast," said Ma. "He didn't eat no supper last night, and if'n he don't git somethin' in his belly, he'll shore be sick."

Pa went into the room and shook Jeff's shoulder. Jeff stirred from the bed and put on his clothes. Both eyes were almost closed, and his lips were swollen badly out of shape. His side was so sore he could hardly walk to the kitchen. He sat down at the table with the rest of the family, but the sight of food made him run to the back stoop and retch in the yard. He went back and lay down on the bed.

"I'm shore sorry that he has to be sick, with us sech a breakfast as this on the table," said Pa. "We'll have to save these other eggs till he's able to eat again."

"I'll make him a poultice after breakfast and take that swellin' out'n his face," said Ma. "And if'n Skeeter kin git me some sassafras roots, I kin make him some tea that will fix up that sore belly of his afore he knows hit."

"Well, I shore hope he won't be laid up too long," said Pa, "cause the work will be mighty hard fer me and Skeeter here to do."

"I hain't worried 'bout hit, Pa," said Skeeter. "I believe we kin manage fer a few days."

"Well, as soon as we git through eatin', you go look fer them roots," said Ma, "and, Theresa, you go git me some fresh poke salat and a few dead magnolia leaves, and I'll need a little black mud from the bayou."

They finished breakfast, and Skeeter brought in a bucket of fresh water for Ma to do the dishes with.

When Skeeter returned, Ma took the sassafras roots and put them in some water to boil. She added a pinch of salt and a small pod of red pepper. The steam from the pot filled the room with a bitter smell.

Then she started making the poultice. She tore the poke salat leaves into small pieces and put them in a pot. She crumpled the dry, brown magnolia leaves on top of them. She put in a handful of the black bayou mud and three handfuls of ashes from the hearth, added a cup of water, stirred the mixture, and put it over the hearth to heat.

When the sassafras had boiled until the water turned red, she poured out a cup and took it to Jeff.

"Now you jest hold yore nose and drink this," she said, "cause hit'll cure jest about ary thing known to man."

Jeff raised up in the bed and drank the hot tea. He had to hold his hand over his mouth to keep from throwing it up on the floor. Ma went back to the kitchen and brought in the pot of hot poultice. Jeff lay back on the bed, and she put a thick layer of the substance over his face.

"That will draw the swellin' out afore you knows hit," she said. "You'll be jest as good as new in a day or so."

She went back to the kitchen and started cleaning the crawfish for the gumbo dinner. She peeled the husk and heads from them, saving only the tails. Pa was sitting on the back stoop whittling on a stick.

"Abner," said Ma, "they's a powerful lot of crawfish here fer jest the few of us, and they won't keep no longer. Why don't we take all the fixin's and row up to the Hookers' and go neighborin', and I could fix hit up there. They's plenty fer everbody, and me and Theresa would shore enjoy hit. Hit's been nigh on a year since we been neighborin' with them."

"Do ye think hit would be all right to leave Jeff here by hisself?" asked Pa.

"I think hit would do him good to be able to rest without no noise abouts. And I kin fix him some broth to eat if'n he gits hongry."

"Well, I guess hit's all right with me," said Pa, "but you better hurry up and let's git goin'. Hit's a fer piece up there."

Ma and Theresa finished the housework and started dressing. Ma put on her old black dress and her hat with the big red feather on top. Theresa wore her snug-fitting, white cotton dress, and combed her flaming red hair until it looked like silk hanging down her back. Pa dressed in his best overalls and shirt and wore his black hat.

When they were dressed, Ma went into the room with Jeff and made him drink another cup of hot tea.

"We're goin' neighborin' up to the Hookers'," she said, "so'es you jest stay in bed and rest. They's a pot of broth on the hearth fer you to eat if'n you gits hongry. You leave that poultice on till this afternoon and then take hit off and put on a new one. And if'n yore belly don't git better soon, git you some more of that tea in there and drink hit."

Jeff didn't say anything, but nodded his head to show that he understood. They put the fixin's for the dinner in the bow to keep dry; Pa and Skeeter sat in the middle to row, and Ma and Theresa sat in the rear. The boat sank a little deep on the side where Ma was sitting. They shoved off down the bayou.

The Hooker family lived five miles up the river from the Coreys. They were swamp rats, but they did not make their living in the same way as the Coreys. They made whiskey and took it to Mill Town and Fort Henry to sell. There was good money in the whiskey trade, so they were always fixed better than the Coreys.

Cline and Bertha Hooker had ten sons, with ages ranging from sixteen to thirty. They were unusually large people, and even the youngest of the Hooker boys was as large as Pa or Jeff. Old Man Hooker was more than six feet tall and weighed over two hundred pounds, and even though he was ten years older than Pa Corey, his hair was still jet black, as was that of all his sons. There were legends told about them all the way from Jackson to New Orleans, and it had been told that they had once cornered a giant black bear and killed it with their bare hands. Everyone had heard of the Hooker brothers, and all men feared them.

The first of the Hooker boys had been born twins, and they were named Sun Up and Sun Down. Then in succession came High Noon, Low Twelve, Quarter Moon, Half Moon,

Fourth Moon, Full Moon, and No Moon. The night their last son was born the sparks from the fire nearly burned the house down, so they named him Sparky. He was the best looking of the lot. All but Sparky wore black beards to match their hair, but he had not yet begun to shave.

The Coreys reached the mouth of the cove that led to the Hooker house and turned the boat toward the landing. The Hookers' house was not set as far back as the Coreys', and they could see the river from their front porch. When the boat touched the landing, several hounds raced to the bank and barked madly. Old Man Hooker walked down from the house.

"Well, I'll be a dad-burned 'gator's uncle," he said, "if'n hit ain't the Coreys. Git out and come in the house. Hit's been a coon's age since we've seed you folks."

"We're shore glad to see you too," said Pa. "We come up to neighbor a spell today."

They got out of the boat and walked to the house. Ma brought the fixin's with her. Skeeter was scared of the dogs, so he stayed close to Pa. They climbed the steep steps and went in.

"Jest look who's come, Bertha," said the old man.

"Well, dog, if'n hit ain't the Coreys," she said. "I was jest about to believe that you folks had died or moved off."

The only one of the Hooker boys who was in the house was the youngest, Sparky. When Theresa came in, he stared at her with his mouth open, and she flushed and stared back. She had never had a boy look at her like that. The old man brought in chairs, and they all sat down.

"Don't jest stand there like a tomcat, Sparky," he said. "Go out to the kitchen and git us a jug of that best whiskey so'es we kin offer our guests a little nip."

Skeeter stared wide-eyed at the Hookers' collection of guns in the room. One solid wall was covered with guns. Skeeter didn't think that there were that many guns in the whole world. The old man saw him staring so he said to Skeeter: "You kin go look at them closer if'n you want to, but jest be careful, cause all them things air loaded."

Skeeter got up and went over to have a closer look. Sparky came back with a gallon jug of the white whiskey and handed it to the old man as he pulled out the corncob stopper.

"Take ye a good snort, Abner," he said. "That's the best white lightnin' that's made on Pearl River."

Pa took a deep drink and handed the jug back to the old man. Then the old man handed the jug to Ma.

"I'll jest take a little nip," she said. "I'm always afeered to take much afore dinner."

She took a short drink and passed the jug on to Ma Hooker. The old woman turned it up and took a deeper drink than Pa Corey. Then the jug was passed on to the old man, and he repeated the performance.

"They ain't nothin' like a good snort of white lightnin' to warm a person's belly and make him feel neighborly," he said.

"I done brought all the fixin's to make up a big pot of my special crawfish gumbo," said Ma, "so'es we better go on in the kitchen and git it started. Hit takes a long whiles fer it to git jest right."

The two women got up and went to the kitchen, and Theresa followed. Sparky was still staring at her. When she looked at him, it gave her a funny feeling.

"Where's yore other boy, Abner?" asked the old man.

"He's laid up in the bed at home. He got in a big fight down at Mill Town yestiddy and got beat up somethin' awful. Them three Smith boys down there jumped him cause he were sparkin' aroun' their sister. I run to help him, and that's how I got this busted eye I'm totin' aroun' with me."

"That weren't much of a fair fight, were hit? I'll tell my boys about that next time they goes to Mill Town."

"I shore wish they could git back on them Smith boys," said Pa. "They called us sons of bitches jest cause we lives on the river."

"Well, if'n they ever calls one of my boys that we'll pull down their pants and whop their butts till they looks like the sun comin' over the river."

They passed the jug again, and both took long draughts of the whiskey.

"Derned if'n that little gal of yorn ain't turned out to be a pretty thing," said the old man. "They ain't nothin' on the river whut looks as good as she do, and from the way Sparky's mouth air hangin' open, I believe he done taken a liken fer her."

In the kitchen the two women were preparing the dinner. Ma chopped up the okra, tomatoes, and celery stalks into a big iron pot. She dropped in a few small pods of red pepper, and added garlic and wild sage. Then she put in the crawfish tails and filled the pot with water and set it on the stove to simmer.

"I shore would like to have a nice stove like this," said Ma.

"Hit takes one that big to cook the rations fer a big bunch of overgrown hogs like I got stayin' aroun' here," said the old woman.

"I don't see how come hit don't near 'bouts kill you keepin' house fer so many men," said Ma. "Hit's all I kin do with jest three and Theresa to help me."

"Hit do nearbouts git a pore ole soul like me down sometimes," she said, "but I guess I'm jest used to hit."

Pa Corey and the old man went through the kitchen and out the back door to go look at the whiskey still. Skeeter followed them, but Sparky stayed inside so he could watch Theresa.

"I want you to see these new boats we air buildin'," said the old man. "They's made out of planed cypress and is put together with screws, and we's almost done with them."

They walked up to where the two boats were sitting on props. They were more than twice as long as the Coreys' boat and much deeper. There were two seats in the middle and locks for four oars instead of two. Pa had never seen boats like these before.

"Them shore air fine," he said. "Them's abouts the best I've ever seed."

"Hit won't take us no time to run in a load of whiskey in them boats," said the old man. "I'd near 'bout bet that when four of them boys sets behind them oars they can near 'bout outrun a steamboat."

He took Pa on through the woods to show him the still. The whole still was set high off the ground on pilings to protect it during the floods. The floor was made of thick cypress planking, and the roof was better than the Coreys had over their house. They had built it on the bank of a creek, so it would be near fresh water.

The Hooker boys were sitting around the still, and when Pa Corey came up they all gave him a greeting. Pa and the old man looked around for a few minutes and then went on to see the garden. Skeeter stayed behind to watch the workings of the still.

After he had looked at everything, he walked up to Sun Up and said, "I've got a potion to home that will keep gars from messin' with baits and gittin' in traps."

"Did you hear that, boys," he laughed. "He says he got some kind of potion to home."

"Let's give him a big snort," said No Moon.

Three of them grabbed Skeeter and held him on the floor. No Moon came over and forced some whiskey down Skeeter's throat. It burned like someone had put fire in his belly.

"Jest look at him," said Sun Up. "The little bugger looks like he's drunk already. We better sober him up."

They jerked Skeeter's overalls off and carried him to the side of the platform and threw him into the creek. He came up spitting water and fighting for the bank. He climbed up the bank and came back on the platform to put on his clothes. Pa and the old man came back just as Skeeter was thrown into the creek. The old man ran up to the boys.

"Now, air that any way fer you boys to be treatin' a guest of ourn," he said. "You ought to be plum ashamed of yore-selves."

"We's just havin' a little fun with him," said Sun Up. "We didn't aim to hurt him none."

"They ain't hurt me none," said Skeeter. He was kind of proud that he had been thrown in the creek by the Hooker boys. That would be something good to tell Uncle Jobe.

"Well, jest the same," said the old man, "if'n I ketch you doin' hit agin, I'll take me a stick and stir up a lot of brains."

Pa and the old man walked back toward the house, while Skeeter put his clothes on. He wanted to stay around and be with the boys.

"Whut you totin' that big knife fer?" asked Sun Down.

"I uses hit in the swamp sometimes," said Skeeter.

"Bet you couldn't hit the side of a barn with hit," said Sun Down.

"Bet a dollar he kin," said No Moon.

"That's a bet," said Sun Down.

They reached into their pockets, and each pulled out a dollar bill, throwing it on the platform floor. Sun Down took a cigarette paper from his pocket, spit on it, and stuck it to one of the posts holding up the roof. "Let's see him hit that," he said.

"That ain't no fair trial," said No Moon. "He couldn't hit that with a rifle."

"You kin back out on yore bet if'n you want to," said Sun Down. He knew that No Moon wouldn't back down because no Hooker had ever been known to back out on a bet already made. He also thought that he had tricked No Moon out of a dollar.

They drew a line with a piece of burned stick about ten feet from the paper, and they told Skeeter to stand there and not cross the line.

"I think I'll jest back up a little bit if'n you don't mind," said Skeeter. He walked all the way to the far end of the platform and turned around. It was sixty feet from the paper.

"Now jest look at that," said No Moon. "You and Sun Down must have had this made up. You jest tryin' to beat me out'n a dollar."

Skeeter drew back the knife, hesitated a moment, and sent it flying through the air. The point of the blade pinned the paper to the post. They all looked at Skeeter with amazement. No Moon danced around wildly and picked up the money.

Sun Down reached in his pocket, took out another cigarette paper, and stuck it to the post. He pulled the knife out and handed it to Skeeter.

"Let's see you do that again," he said.

Skeeter drew back the knife and again sent the blade into the center of the paper.

"Well, I'm damned!" said Sun Down. "This little bugger air shore good with that thing. Didn't think he could do hit."

Skeeter knew that he was in with the Hooker boys now, and that they wouldn't bother him any more. A bell rang from the back of the house, and they went up for dinner.

They went into the front room and passed around a jug while the women were putting the food on the table. Besides the gumbo there were baked sweet potatoes, dried peas, turnip roots, stewed spare ribs, and corn pone.

When they sat down at the table, the Hooker boys started grabbing plates wildly. The old man stood up and banged on the table with his fist.

"Mind yore manners with company here!" he shouted, "and put them vittles back till I turn up some thanks. You'll have the Coreys thinkin' I done raised a bunch of hogs."

They put the food on their plates back into the dishes, and lowered their heads. The old man stood up and raised his hands above him.

"Thank Ye fer these vittles," he said, "and have mercy on our pore souls. Amen." Then mayhem broke loose. There was a loud clatter of food hitting plates and forks hitting food. Conversation was out of the question during the meal, and as soon as all the food was gone, the boys got up and went back to the still to lie down and sleep. Skeeter went with them, but Sparky went to the front porch and sat down.

"That was the best crawfish I ever et in my life," said the old man. "I could have et a barrel of hit."

"I'm mighty proud you like hit," said Ma.

The women cleaned the table and went to the kitchen to wash the dishes. Pa and the old man sat down to talk. After the work in the kitchen was finished, Ma and the old woman came in and sat down to join the talk, and Theresa went out on the front porch. When she saw Sparky there, she turned and started to go back.

"Don't go back in," he said. "I been wantin' to sit and talk to you."

Theresa came over to him and sat down but didn't say anything. She didn't know what to say, because she had never talked to a boy before, except those in her family, and this was different.

"Want to see the biggest cypress tree on the river?" he asked.

"I guess I do if'n Pa and Ma don't keer."

"They don't keer if'n you do. Let's go."

They got up and went into the yard. He took her along a path that led down the river. The path was so narrow and the brush on each side so thick that only one person could walk along it at one time, so she had to follow behind him. As they walked on, the path got a little wider, and then they came out in a little clearing on the bank of the river. On the edge of the clearing there stood the tallest tree Theresa had ever seen. Looking up from the base, it seemed that the clouds were drifting through its top. Its branches were covered with moss swaying with the wind. It was beautiful standing there in its majestic silence. Theresa was thrilled.

"Pa says hit's twenty feet right through the middle," said Sparky.

"Hit's the biggest thing I've ever seed," said Theresa.

They walked over and sat down under a magnolia tree and watched the river flow by. The muddy water boiled and bubbled and left brown foam along the bank.

"You got a boy friend?" asked Sparky.

"No," said Theresa. "You got a girl friend?"

"Naw," he said. "Ain't never seed one before that I liked."

They sat in silence for a few minutes; Sparky turned and looked at her.

"You like me?"

"Yes."

He put his arms around her and drew her close to him. He ran his fingers through her long silky hair. Then he turned her face up and put his lips to hers. The bubbles on the river seemed to pop and send music through the air. Theresa had never known such a feeling. Her heart pounded madly, and the blood rushed to her head. So this was what sparking was like. She put her arms around him, and they held each other close.

"I love you," he said.

"I love you, too," said Theresa, "and I'm scared."

"You don't need to never be scared of me. I'll never do nothin' to make you scared or to harm you. And I'll never stand fer nobody else to make you that way."

They sat arm in arm and watched the water flow by. Theresa had never felt so happy in her life. She didn't believe what Ma had said when Ma had the argument with Pa.

She could not be happier, and could never be happy with anyone but Sparky.

"We better go back to the house," she said.

They got up and Sparky put his arms around her, and they kissed again. The wind played melodies through the branches of the tall cypress tree.

"Let's you and me be promised," said Sparky.

"Hit's all right with me if'n Ma and Pa say we kin."

They turned up the trail towards the house. On the way back the brush seemed much greener and the sky much brighter.

They crossed the yard, hand in hand, and went into the house. The old people were still sitting and talking. No one else was in the house, because the rest were still asleep at the still. Sparky broke in on their conversation. He turned to Ma and Pa Corey. Theresa stood beside him.

"We've got something to say to you," he said. "We want to be promised if'n you'll say hit's all right with you."

Old Man Hooker jumped to the floor and danced around and around the room. "You see, whut did I tell you!" he said. "I knowed he had takin' a likin' to her. I could tell by the way he's been lookin' moon-eyed ever since she's been here."

Ma and Pa Corey looked at each other, and Pa said, "Hit suits me jest fine. What about you, Ma?"

"I guess it suits me, too," she said. "I reckon she would be jest as good off with Sparky there as with airy other man. But I do want you both to wait a spell and git a little more age on you afore you do anything about hit."

"Did you hear that, Bertha?" shouted the old man. "Hit's all right with them. Our Sparky is promised to the best lookin' gal in Mississippi. I was jest about to think I would never be a grandpappy, with them boys turnin' their heads ever time they sees a gal. I shore air proud of them both."

The old woman was just as proud as her husband at the thought of having a beautiful girl like Theresa in the family. Pa was proud, too, much prouder than he had shown. The old man grabbed a gun from the wall and ran to the back door. He pointed it through the trees and shot it toward the still. Black-bearded men poured from the woods like bees from a hive, and swarmed toward the house.

"What air hit?" shouted Sun Up.

"Each one of you bring a jug and come on up to the house," cried the old man. "I've got news fer you."

They went back to the still and each of them grabbed a jug and came to the house. Skeeter followed behind them. They came in the front room and stood around expectantly. The old man signaled for them to be silent.

"Sparky and Theresa here are promised," he said.

He could just as well have said that the revenuers were coming. The brothers went wild. They ran around the room slapping each other on the back and slapping Sparky and passing jugs. The old man grabbed a jug and handed it to Pa and Ma Corey. They both took heavy drinks. Then fiddles and guitars were brought out, and the room was filled with music. The old man grabbed Ma Corey, and Pa grabbed the old woman and started a dance. Skeeter didn't understand what was going on so he sat in a corner to watch. Sparky and Theresa slipped out to the front porch to be alone. The jugs were passed again and again, and the old people danced until they fell exhausted to their chairs.

"We better git started towards home," said Ma. "Hit's gittin' kinda late in the afternoon."

"I guess we better at that," said Pa.

"Run put a side of pork and some sweet pertators in their boat, Sun Up," said the old man, "and put in a couple of jugs of whiskey fer Abner. I been noticin' the way old Skeeter been starin' at them guns." He walked over to the wall where the guns were and took down a small rifle. "This here's fer you, Skeeter. We'd never miss hit with all the guns we got and here's two boxes of shot fer hit, too."

The old man handed the rifle and shot to Skeeter. Skeeter stroked the barrel and turned it over and over in his hands.

"I don't know how to thank ye enough, Mr. Hooker," he said.

"You jest learn how to shoot like them boys says you kin throw that knife, and hit'll be enough fer me."

"You shouldn't be givin' us so much stuff," said Pa.

"Whut's the difference," said the old man. "We's goin' to be intermixed, ain't we?"

The Coreys walked down to the landing with the entire Hooker family following. Ma and Pa were both a little drunk. Theresa said good-by to Sparky and got in the bow of the boat. Pa and Ma sat in the middle, with Skeeter in the rear to steer with his oar on the trip back down.

"You folks has got to call more often now," said the old man.

"We will," said Pa, "and you call, too."

Skeeter shoved the boat off with his oar and paddled towards the swift water of the river. The Hookers waved good-by and went back into the house. When they reached the river, they could hear the music start up in the house again and the stomping of many feet. Sparky was still standing on the porch waving to Theresa as Skeeter turned the boat down the river towards home.

Pa looked at the pork and the potatoes and the whiskey in the boat and said: "Our little Theresa has done right well by herself, ain't she?"

"She shore has," said Ma.

The rest of the trip was made in silence, with Theresa dreaming of Sparky, Ma and Pa thinking whiskey thoughts, and Skeeter stroking the rifle with one hand.

"We should have gone neighborin' more often," said Pa.

"I guess we should at that," was the reply.

FIVE

PA WAS UP EARLY the next morning shooting squirrels around the clearing to use for fresh bait for the trotline. He killed a few extra ones for Ma to fix for dinner. Jeff was not as sick as he had been the day before, but he was still not well enough to get around much. Most of the swelling was gone from his face, and he was not sick on the stomach, but he was sore and wanted to rest another day. When Pa came in, he skinned the squirrels, cut them into pieces and put them in a bag.

When breakfast was done, Pa and Skeeter shoved off down the bayou in the boat, Skeeter taking his gar potion with him. They turned up the river and rowed to the cove where the traps were set. When they pulled up the first trap, Pa cursed loudly and slammed his fist against the side of the boat. The top netting of the trap was cut to ribbons, and there was not a fish left in it. They pulled it into the boat and went to the other one. It was not cut, and there were several small cat and buffalo in it. Pa took the fish out and pulled the trap along the side of the boat and back to the place where the first one had been set. They always caught more fish there, and he wanted to leave the good trap in that spot.

"Let me put some of this gar potion on hit afore you lower hit back," said Skeeter.

"Well, I guess hit can't hurt none," said Pa.

Skeeter rubbed some of the fluid on the mouth of the trap, and they lowered it back into the water. After they had tied the lines to the stakes, they went back down the river to the trotline. Most of the baits were gone, and two lines were cut. Two of the hooks had only the heads of fish on them, and they got one cat off the entire line. Skeeter rubbed some of the fluid on each fresh bait before Pa put it on the hook. When they finished, they rowed back home. Pa put their small catch in the fish box and carried the trap to the house, then spent the rest of the morning mending it.

Skeeter showed Jeff his new rifle and told him all about their trip to the Hookers' the day before. He didn't understand all about Theresa and Sparky, but he explained well enough for Jeff to understand what had happened.

"I'd shore ruther have them boys fer me then agin me," said Jeff. "Maybe they'll come in handy fer me sometime. Let's see how yore rifle shoots, Skeeter."

Skeeter got the rifle, and they went out to the front porch. He brought a couple of shots with him, and there was already one in the breech. There were several white cranes along the edge of the water down the bayou, so Skeeter picked one of them as his target. He pointed the sight at the feet of the crane and then raised it until it looked as if the crane was sitting on top of the sight. He pulled the trigger and the crane dropped to the water. Pa was watching while mending the trap.

"Hit shore do shoot true," said Skeeter. "I could jest about hit anything with this gun."

"Let me try hit now," said Jeff.

"Now, you boys quit shootin' them cranes," said Pa. "If'n you got to try that thing on somethin', try hit on somethin' we kin eat. Tain't no use in killin' them critters."

Jeff looked around for another target. He saw several mallard ducks swimming around in the edge of the marsh grass. He took a steady aim and pulled the trigger, and one of the ducks slumped over in the water. The other ducks did not fly away.

"I got one more shot here," said Skeeter, "so let me try hit again."

He took the rifle, loaded it, and sighted it at a duck. His aim was true, and another one slumped in the water.

"Now you boys jest go git them ducks and clean 'em fer Ma to fix fer dinner," said Pa. "We kin keep them squirrels I cleaned fer bait tomorrow. I'd heap ruther eat them ducks."

Skeeter got in the skiff, poled down the bayou, and brought back the ducks. They were plump and fat from their winter feeding. The Coreys seldom ever shot the ducks because they could not spare the shot. Skeeter and Jeff picked and cleaned them and took them in to Ma to bake for dinner, then they went back to the porch and sat in the sun.

"We goin' deer huntin' over in the woods tomorrow, Pa?" asked Skeeter.

"I guess we better wait till Wednesday fer Jeff to git a little better fust," he said. "Me and you wouldn't be able to tote one of them big critters out of the woods by ourselves."

"Why is hit that they's woods on that side of the river and swamp on this un, Pa?" asked Skeeter.

"I guess that's the way the good Lord wanted hit to be," said Pa. "He made all kind of critters on this river and they all has to have a home. The deer and bear and turkey and critter sech as that can't live in no swamp, so He made the woods fer them to roam in. And He made the woods high so the river couldn't come in during the floods and drown 'em. And then the frogs and the snakes and 'gators couldn't live in the woods so He made the swamp fer them. He's made a place for all folks and critters, and will look out fer them if'n they'll jest stay in their place and be sotisfied."

"If'n the floods don't go into the woods like hit do here, how come you to build the house here 'stead uv in the woods?" Skeeter asked.

"I'd heap ruther have the floods come at me than have them bear messin' aroun' the house and them deer eatin' the plantins as soon as they come out of the ground," said Pa. "The Lord made them woods fer the critters, and so fer as I'm concerned, they kin have whut was made fer them all to theirselves. I'd jest as soon stay here in the swamp."

"I'd heap ruther be here, too," said Skeeter.

"You better go out behin' the house and git that old ax and sharpen hit real good," said Pa. "Me and you have got to clear a little piece of ground this afternoon fer yore Ma and Theresa to set out them new seeds I got. Hit'll be full moon in a couple of days, and if'n they ain't set out then, they won't be no use to set 'em out at all."

Skeeter brought the ax to the porch and started sharpening it on the old whet rock. He rubbed it along the blade until the ax was as sharp as a razor. Ma came to the porch and called them to dinner.

After dinner, Pa and Skeeter started clearing a place for the new garden. Pa would chop away the brush and small trees and Skeeter would put them in a pile. When all the brush was cut away, Pa dug up the roots with a hoe, while Skeeter pulled the weeds from the ground with his hands. The hot sun bore down on them, and sweat rolled from their bodies. Their overalls were soaked, and their bodies were covered with the black grime of the soil. When the ground was cleared, Pa took the hoe and broke the soil into long even rows. Skeeter chopped up the brush and trees and carried them to the house to use as firewood. It was late in the afternoon when they finished. They went into the house and got clean overalls and went down to the bayou, washed their clothes and themselves, then returned to the house. They were very tired and after supper went to bed.

Pa and Skeeter set out up the river early the next morning with the trap Pa had repaired, and when they reached the cove, they pulled far in to set the trap before they looked at the one already out. After they finished, they went back and pulled up the first one. There was not a fish in it, and it had not been cut by a gar.

"Well, I'll be derned," said Pa. "That's the fust time I ever seed that happen. I ain't never knowed a trap not to have a single fish in hit 'ceptin' when hit was cut."

They lowered the trap back into the water and moved on to look at the trotline. They went the entire length of the line and not a bait had been touched.

"Well, I'm derned agin," said Pa. "I ain't never seed sech a sight. Hit's that potion of yores that done this, Skeeter. Whut did that nigger say was in that stuff?"

"He didn't say, Pa," said Skeeter, "but hit shore kept them gars away, didn't hit?"

"Yeah, and everthing else, too." Pa smiled. "I guess hit's worth hit jest to fool them gars out'n a meal this one time," said Pa. "Hit's a good thing I brought this new bait with us. Now let's go back along the line and put fresh bait on all the hooks." Pa threw the old ones into the river.

"I guess the water will wash that stuff off the trap afore tonight," said Pa. "If'n hit don't, them gars shore air in fer another surprise."

When they reached home there was nothing to do, so they sat around the front porch waiting for dinner. Ma was cooking some of the pork and sweet potatoes the Hookers had given them, and the smell made Skeeter's nose twitch with delight. Pa slipped into his room and took a deep drink from one of the jugs of whiskey.

After the meal, Skeeter poled off toward the swamp in the skiff. It was late in the afternoon when he returned.

"Whut you been doin' in that swamp so long?" asked Ma.

"I been lookin' fer a critter, but I didn't find him," he said.

"Whut kind of a critter?" asked Ma.

"Jest a critter," said Skeeter, and walked out of the room.

Skeeter was so excited that it was far into the night before he could stop thinking about the approaching hunt and go to sleep. Once during the night he thought he heard something flouncing under the house but decided that he was mistaken. Thet critter wouldn't come clear to the house looking fer me, he thought, and went back to sleep.

SIX

PA CAME INTO THE ROOM and awakened Skeeter and Jeff. It was pitch dark outside, but breakfast was already on the table when they walked into the kitchen. They sat down and ate while Ma and Theresa fixed them a lunch to take along. When they finished, Skeeter went back into his room and put on his old brogans. He strapped his knife around his waist, put a box of shells in his pocket, and picked up the rifle. Pa had the shotgun and a tin of powder and shot. Jeff picked up the bag of food, and they went outside.

"You better go back inside and git us a torch, Jeff," said Pa. "Hit's so dark out here I couldn't see a nigger two feet in front uv me."

Jeff went back into the house and came out with a lighted pine knot in his hand. The light cast varied shadows along the ground in front of him. Jeff climbed into the bow of the boat to hold the torch, and Pa and Skeeter rowed them down the bayou. The air was cold, and Skeeter shivered and pulled the collar of his shirt tight around his neck.

They reached the place where the muddy water merged with the clear, and pointed the boat downstream.

The river looked strange and forbidden with the torch as their only light. They pulled close along the bank, and the shadows of light made the tall cypress trees look like gray ghosts in the night. It started Skeeter thinking of the night he and Jeff had been in the swamp with no light, and then he remembered the giant 'gator with the frog gig in its head, and he didn't want to think about it any more.

They drifted slowly along the bank for about a mile, and then Pa and Skeeter turned the boat into a clump of bushes hanging over the water. Jeff pulled the bow of the boat up on the bank and tied the rope to a tree. They broke limbs from trees and piled in the boat to make it impossible for anyone passing on the river to see it. Then Pa took the torch and led them away from the water.

The brush was so thick that they had to walk single file, and the last person in the line could not get the benefit of the light. Skeeter had to feel his way along in the dark and keep in the direction of the light ahead. After they had traveled a short distance away from the river, they sat down to wait for the dawn, for Pa could not find the place he wanted to go with only a torch for light. They sat on a dead log, and Pa and Skeeter loaded their guns.

In a little while the sun sent long rays of light through the tops of the tall trees. The woods seemed to take on a different appearance as the light crept in and the darkness went away. The squirrels came out of their nests and began looking for breakfast and playing in the trees. There were big black ones, red fox squirrels, gray cat squirrels, all playing together—paying no mind to the humans sitting on the ground. The woodpeckers started the rhythmical beating of their bills against the trunks of dead trees. Birds of all colors and sounds flew through the air. A covey of quail flushed from their bed for the night and went out in search of grass seeds for their food. A mother coon walked along a path leading to a water hole with her litter of little ones following. Skeeter was fascinated by the sights that he saw. He almost had a feeling of regret when Pa told him it was time to move on, but then he remembered the hunt and got up eagerly to move to the deer grounds.

The woods were very thick for a long distance away from the river, and progress through them was slow. Skeeter thought that he had never seen so many different kinds of trees. The buck vines were laced from tree to tree, and it was impossible to see more than a few feet ahead. There were cypress trees, scrub oak and big water oaks, hickory trees, holly, beech, dogwood, magnolias, pines, and dozens of other different trees, all with vines running between them. Sometimes they had to crawl on the ground to move at all.

As they got further away from the river, the woods began to thin out, and the going was not so difficult. Finally, they came into a great open stretch of pine and hickory trees. Pa showed them scars on the trees where the big bucks had rubbed their antlers. Some of the scars were fresh, and they knew that the deer had been there the night before. They found a trail that the deer were using to go to water, and Pa told Skeeter to sit on a log and watch the trail.

"If'n you see a deer comin' slow, jest wait till he's on you and aim at his fore shoulder," said Pa, "but if'n he's runnin' fast, wait till he's right at you and let out a loud whistle. He'll stop and look at you ever time, and then let him have it. If'n we hears you shoot we'll come to you, and if'n you hears us shoot you come to us. We's goin' down the trail jest a piece and wait. Now be kerful and make yore shot count."

Pa and Jeff walked down the trail and left Skeeter by the log. He leaned the gun against a tree and raked the leaves and pine straw away from the log with his hands, so that he could stand up and turn around without making any noise. He sat down and began his wait. The squirrels were in the trees above him, and he watched them at their play. They would jump from limb to limb, and hang by their feet, and chase each other up and down the trunk. When a bird would light in the trees, they would chase it away and chatter loudly while doing so. He almost went to sleep watching them.

Skeeter could sit on the log and see for a hundred yards both ways down the trail. The brush and trees were thick along the sides of it so that it would not be visible in any direction except straight down. He had almost given up hope of seeing a deer, when he heard a clanking coming down the trail. He looked and saw a big buck coming straight toward him. The buck's antlers were hitting the trees close along the trail and making the noise. It had not seen Skeeter, and it kept coming straight toward him. He cocked the hammer of his rifle and waited. Cold sweat was pouring from his face, and his heart was pounding inside him. His hands shook so that he was afraid he could not aim the gun. He thought that the deer would never reach him, but when it was directly in front of him, he aimed at the fore shoulder and pulled the trigger.

The deer leaped forward and fell to its knees. Blood was pouring from its shoulder, as it looked around and saw Skeeter for the first time. The wind had been with it, and it had not smelled him. Skeeter could see surprise in its eyes, and he hurriedly breached the gun and put in another shell. As the deer rose to its feet and started to run, Skeeter's second shot grazed its eye, and it fell again. Slowly rising to its feet, it ran off through the woods before Skeeter could load the gun again. There were two pools of blood on the ground where the deer had fallen, and a steady stream of blood followed the wounded animal through the brush. Skeeter didn't know what to do, so he sat down on the log to wait for Pa and Jeff, and in a few minutes they came running up to him.

"Did you git him?" asked Pa.

"I knocked him down twice, but he still run off through the bresh," said Skeeter. "I don't see how that critter walked with lead in him like that."

"They're powerful hard to kill sometimes," said Pa.

Pa walked over and looked at the two pools of blood and the trail of blood leading through the brush.

"That critter's hurt bad," he said. "Let's trail him. He won't git far afore he falls."

They followed the trail of blood through the brush and vines and through open places in the woods. Every few feet they came to a pool of blood on the ground where the deer had stopped to rest, and blood was smeared on the sides of trees and on vines.

"That critter's blind as a bat," said Pa. "He's runnin' into trees and vines and anything that gits in his way."

"Where you reckon he's goin', Pa?" asked Skeeter.

"He's headin' fer the nearest water hole," said Pa. "When them critters gits a hole in them they jest has a natural cravin' to lay in a pool of water. And sometimes when they ain't hurt too bad, they gits well that way. I killed a big ole buck one time with gunshot all in him, but this un will never git there. He's 'bout done now."

The stream of blood became thinner and the pools nearer together. They came through some thick buck vines and found the deer lying on the ground and bleating. When he saw them, he raised his head and tried to get up. His legs were too weak, and he fell back to the ground. Pa ran up to him and grabbed his antlers, and the deer tried to struggle away from him, but it was too weak to do so. Pa pulled out his knife and cut the buck's throat. It quivered a few minutes and then lay still.

"You shore got you a nice one fer the first time you been deer huntin'," said Pa. "He's got ten points on his antlers, and I'd say he'll weigh mighty nigh four hundred pounds. We better go ahead and git this sucker bled."

They tied one end of a rope they had brought with them to the deer's hind feet and threw the other end of the rope over a limb of a tree. Then they pulled it into the air and tied the rope to the trunk of the tree so it would stay there. Pa took his knife and split the deer down the stomach and removed all its insides. Then he let it hang for the blood to drain out. While they were waiting they took out the lunch and ate.

"We goin' to skin him here?" asked Skeeter.

"We better take him home first," said Pa, "or else the meat will git mighty dirty when we have to take him back through all them buck vines."

When they finished eating, they cut a small sweet gum tree and trimmed the limbs from it. Then they lowered the deer to the ground and tied its feet over the pole. They picked up the pole and started walking with it, but the deer's antlers dragged the ground, so they stopped and tied its antlers to the pole.

Their progress was not too hard while they were in the big woods, but as they got closer to the river and the woods grew thicker, it became more difficult. They moved very slowly and had to stop often and rest. Sometimes they had to drag the deer along the ground. Sweat poured from them, and their muscles began to ache with tiredness.

They stopped once and laid the deer down so they could rest. Just as they sat down on the ground a young buck jumped out of the buck vines in front of them. Pa could not resist the shot, so he jumped to his feet, sighted the old gun, and pulled the trigger. The blast knocked him back several feet as the shots left the barrel. The deer fell dead in its tracks, and they walked over to where it was lying. It had two antlers, about five inches long, sticking straight out of its head.

"Hit's a nice young spike buck," said Pa. "That's the best eatin' there is. Hit's a lot better than a big ole buck. We ain't fur from the river, so let's tote the big un on down to the boat and come back and git this un. We kin take this un home fer us to eat and then come back and skin the big un on the river. We kin stop the steamboat and sell hit to them, cause I've heard that they'll pay a purty good price fer venison."

Before they left, they took a piece of the rope and tied the small buck to a limb. Pa split him and left him to bleed. Then they took the big one to the river and left him, and came back and got the small one. They tied the big buck to a limb, put the small one in the boat and rowed home. When they reached home, they hung the deer from a post and left it for Ma and Theresa to skin, and went back to the place where they had left the big one. It was not long before dusk when they finished skinning the buck and heard the steamboat coming up the river. They loaded the deer and the hide into the boat and rowed out into the river. When Pa saw the steamboat coming, he stood up and waved with his hands. The boat came alongside of them and stopped. The captain came to the side where they were.

"What you damned swamp rats mean by stoppin' the boat?" shouted the captain.

"We want to know if'n you wants to buy a nice deer," said Pa.

"Throw up your line and we'll have a look," said the captain.

Pa threw the line up to a man, and he made it fast to the rail. They lowered two lines into the boat, and when Pa and Jeff had tied the lines to the deer's legs they pulled it up to the deck. The captain examined the deer.

"I'll give you twenty dollars for it," shouted the captain. "Send the small boy up your rope and I'll pay him."

Skeeter climbed the rope to the deck of the boat and went up to the captain to get the money. The captain had untied the boat rope behind Skeeter and held it in his hand. He motioned for two deck hands to come over to him.

"Throw this little bastard over the side," he said.

The two men grabbed Skeeter and heaved him over the side of the boat. The captain shouted down to Pa, "That'll teach you damned swamp rats not to stop the boat. Thanks for the deer." He laughed and signaled the wheelhouse for full speed ahead.

The churning water from the stern wheel of the boat sent Skeeter all the way to the bottom of the river. He felt his body hit the soft mud of the river bed. He thought he would never come up. His lungs were hurting, and he had taken in a lot of water. When he came up, he was thirty yards down the river. He fought madly to get upstream toward the boat. When Pa and Jeff saw him, they rowed to him and pulled him into the boat. He coughed water from his throat and lungs.

"You all right?" asked Pa.

"Yeah," said Skeeter.

"The Lord ain't goin' to stand fer sech as that much longer," said Pa. "One of these days he's goin' to take them boatmen slam off the river. I wish they was all in hell, myself."

They rowed on home and told Ma about what had happened. She almost cried when she learned that they had lost the deer for nothing.

"The Lord will take keer of them in His way," she said.

She had some of the fresh deer steaks cooking in the skillet, and the aroma soon took the thoughts of the boatmen from their minds. The men washed up while Ma finished the cooking. She put a heaping platter of steaks and a big bowl of gravy on the table. There was also a big pot of grits. The meat was so tender it fell to pieces as it was taken from the platter. Skeeter thought he had never eaten so much in his life. They all ate until every piece of the meat was gone.

They had to sit at the table for a while before they could get up.

"Well, I'll be derned," said Ma. "I got so mad when you told me about them boatmen that I clear forgot to tell you that we lost a hog after you all went back after that other deer."

"How you mean we done lost a hog?" asked Pa.

"Well, after me and Theresa had skinned that deer I walked down to the bayou to throw away hits feet when I seed the biggest 'gator I ever seed lyin' along the edge of the hog pen. He were jest lyin' there and waitin' fer one of them hogs to come close to the water. I grabbed a stick and throwed at him, but it didn't seem to bother him none. Then one of the hogs walked to the edge of the water, and he hit it with that big tail of hisen and knocked it in the water. Then he tore it all to pieces with them big jaws and didn't even eat it. He jest let it float off down the bayou. It near 'bout give me the creeps jest watchin' hit. That 'gator had the wildest look I ever seed in a critter's eyes, and the strange part about hit were that hit had whut looked like a big piece of metal stickin' out betwix its eyes."

"I bet it were the same critter whut knocked the fish box out'n the water that night," said Pa. "That critter must be either loco or downright mean, cause I never heerd of a 'gator pullin' tricks like that."

Skeeter felt his stomach almost turn sick. He knew that it was his fault that the hog had been killed, and it would be his fault for everything else the 'gator destroyed. He knew he should have listened to Jeff that night.

"I know whut it is, Pa," said Skeeter. "I seed that big 'gator in the swamp the night me and Jeff was frog giggin', and I planted a frog gig right betwix his eyes. He got away and broke the shaft, but he's still got the gig planted in his head. That 'gator's plumb lost his mind, Pa."

"If'n he's done gone crazy he mout kill ary thing that gits in his way, jest fer the love of killin'," said Pa.

"Don't you worry none about hit, Pa," said Skeeter. "Now that I got this rifle I'll git him fer shore afore the week is out."

"I guess we better call that old 'gator Steel Head till we gits him killed," said Pa. "That's shore a good name fer him with all the metal he's totin' aroun' in his brain."

"That air a good name at that, Pa," said Skeeter.

"Call him whut you wants," said Ma, "but you better git him afore he has all them hogs and us kilt, too. I'll be scared to go into the yard at night knowin' 'bout that critter bein' loose."

After everyone had gone to sleep, Skeeter lay awake thinking of ways he could track down and put an end to the life of Steel Head.

SEVEN

THE NEXT MORNING Jeff went with them to run the traps and lines. The traps were not cut, but the catch was small. Both traps did not yield over ten pounds of fish apiece, and the catch was also poor on the line. They had four cats, but they were all small ones. Pa rebaited the hooks, and they went home.

When they reached home, Jeff and Skeeter tacked the two deer hides to the side of the house to dry and cut the antlers from the head of the big buck. Then they threw the two heads into the bayou.

"Kin I have yore deer hide to sell, Skeeter?" asked Jeff. "I got to git up a little extra money fer somethin'. Pa's done said I could have hisen."

"You kin have mine if'n you'll go with me into the swamp tonight to see if'n I kin find that dern loco 'gator," said Skeeter.

"I shore ain't hankerin' to be in that swamp at night with that critter runnin' aroun' loose," he said, "but I'll do hit fer that hide."

"I'm goin' to take the rifle this time," said Skeeter, "so they ain't no use to be skeered."

"Jest the same I don't like hit," said Jeff.

"I think I'll go kill us a rabbit fer dinner," said Skeeter. "I been havin' a cravin' lately fer some good rabbit stew. Want to go with me, Jeff?"

"I'm still too sore from the fight and all that walkin' yesteddy to go huntin' anymore," said Jeff. "I'd ruther stay here and sit on the porch."

Skeeter picked up his gun and walked to the woods at the back of the clearing. He walked along kicking the bushes and trying to scare up a rabbit. A big cottontail jumped from a bush, and he shot it on the run.

"I believe I'll try the next un with the knife," he said out loud. He pulled the knife from his belt and changed the rifle to his left hand. When he kicked up the next rabbit, he sailed the knife straight into its side. "Guess I'm ready to tangle with old Steel Head now," he said. He walked back to the house, cleaned the rabbits, and took them in to Ma. She put them into a pot to parboil before making the stew.

After dinner, Pa, Jeff, and Skeeter were sitting on the front porch when they heard loud shouting and guns shooting on the river. They jumped to their feet startled.

"What in tarnation do you reckon that air?" said Pa. "Hit sounds like somebody's done took up a feud on the river."

Two boats whipped into the mouth of the bayou and started toward the house. They saw that it was the Hookers in their new boats. The old man was standing in the bow of the boat in the lead, and he looked like an old Indian chief leading his warriors. The Corey men ran down to the landing.

"Howdy, Abner," said the old man. "We's jest out tryin' our new boats. Don't you and yore boys want to go with us fer the ride?"

"I'd be powerful pleased to ride in them things," said Pa.

Theresa came to the back door and looked down at the landing. Sparky saw her and climbed out of the boat.

"If'n hit's jest the same to you, Pa," he said, "I'd like to stay here till you gits back from down the river."

"Now, you jest go on up there and git you some good sparkin' done," said the old man. "I knows jest how you feels. Evertime I see that girl, hit makes me wish I were forty years younger."

As Sparky walked to the house, Pa got into the boat with the old man, and Jeff and Skeeter got into the other one. When the boats reached the mouth of the bayou, the old man signaled them to stop.

"Pass the jugs around fust, and then we's going to have a race to Mill Town," he said. "Git both boats in the middle of the river, and when I fire my gun, take off."

The jugs were passed around, and everyone except Skeeter took a deep drink. Then they rowed the boats to the middle of the river and lined them up side by side. The old man stood in the bow and raised his gun in the air. When he pulled the trigger, they let out a loud yelp, and the boats were off with a jerk.

Skeeter had never been on anything moving so fast in his life. The boats were almost skimming the water. Each of the four oars touched the water at the same time, and each came out of the water at the same time. The old man stood in the bow of his boat and shouted wildly for more speed. He reloaded his gun and shot it into the air. It didn't seem to Skeeter that they had been on the river but a few minutes when Mill Town came in sight.

The boats were still running neck and neck when they passed the dock at the mill. The old man signaled them to boat their oars, and they let the boats coast until they lost some of their speed. Then they rowed back up the river and tied the boats to the docks.

"We mout as well git some sugar and some meal while we's down here," said the old man. "And when we gits through, we kin go by the saloon and watch that nigger play the joos harp a little. You boys bring a couple of jugs along. We mout want to wet our whistles afore we gits back to the boat."

They all got out of the boats and walked up the lane to the business street. Each one had his gun in his hand, and two of the boys carried a jug of whiskey. The old man went into a store and bought a hundred pounds of sugar and a hundred pounds of meal. Two of the boys put the sacks on their backs, and they crossed the street to the saloon. As they entered the door, the bartender came around and stopped them.

"You can't come in here and bring your own whiskey," he said. "That's agin the house rules."

"Hit 'pears to me we is already in," said the old man, "but if'n you wants to put us out, that's another thing."

He turned around and faced the boys. "Boys, this here varment says we can't come in here with our own whiskey. Don't you think hits might stuffy in here. They ought to be a little more air comin' in."

The bartender heard the click of nine gun hammers being cocked at one time. They raised their guns towards the roof and fired, and when the smoke cleared there could be seen nine holes blown in the roof.

"Do you think we could sit a spell now?" asked the old man.

"Anything you wants is on the house," said the bartender.

"Well, you owes us a dollar fer puttin' ventilation in this here place," said the old man.

The bartender pulled out a dollar bill and handed it to him.

"Now git that little nigger out here to dance and play that joos harp afore my trigger finger gits itchy and my aim gits bad."

The Negro came out, but he was nearly scared to death. His eyes were as big as buckets, and his hands shook so that he could hardly hold the harp.

"That little bugger shore air nervous," said the old man. "Git a water glass and let's give him a drink to kinda settle him down."

The bartender handed them a water glass, and Sun Up filled it to the brim with the white lightning whiskey. The old man motioned to the Negro to come over.

"Let's see how fast you kin kill this whiskey," he said.

"Boss man, I can't git that much of that stuff down," said the Negro.

Pa clicked the hammer of his gun, and the Negro took the glass and started drinking the whiskey. Water poured from his eyes, but he drank it to the last drop. He put the glass down and staggered around the room.

"Jest look at him," said the old man, "he's as drunk as a jaybird in a chinaberry tree. Now, give us a little music, boy."

The Negro's nervousness was now all gone, and he played his jew's harp and danced as he had never done before.

The jugs were passed many times, and they sat and watched for more than two hours. Finally the old man told them it was time to go, but before they left, he called the Negro over to him and gave him a dollar bill. The Negro thanked him profusely, and they left the saloon. The bartender sighed with relief.

Pa had not noticed that Jeff was not with them until they got back to the boats. Jeff came down the street and joined them on the dock. When they got into the boats and started up the river, they made better time than the Coreys could make coming down. It was not long before they reached the landing at the Corey house.

"Won't you all git out and come in?" asked Pa.

"We better git on up the river," said the old man. "We got a batch to run off at the still afore hit gits dark."

Sparky came out of the house and down to the boat landing. As Theresa stood on the stoop and watched him, he got into one of the boats.

"Hit's goin' to be full moon Satterday night," said the old man, "and we air plannin' on goin' in the woods and runnin' the foxes some. We goin' to go in jest a little below yore house, and we kin pick you up if'n you wants to go."

"I'd be much obliged to you if'n you did," said Pa.

The Hookers rowed down the bayou, and when they reached the river, the Coreys heard a shot and much yelling. They knew that another race was on.

Pa had had a little too much whiskey during the afternoon, so he went to bed as soon as supper was done. Ma and Theresa stayed in the kitchen to work on their new dresses. Jeff and Skeeter were in their room getting ready for the trip to the swamp. Both had knives on their belts, and Skeeter was putting shells for the rifle in his pocket.

"We goin' to carry a frog gig with us?" asked Jeff.

"Naw," said Skeeter. "Tain't no use to fool with them frogs if'n we's goin' to try to git that 'gator. He'll give us all the huntin' we has time to do."

They selected the biggest pine torch they could find and lit it on the hearth. When they got outside, Skeeter rubbed some of the stinking mosquito potion on his face. Jeff refused when he passed the bottle to him, and they walked down to the landing. Jeff got in the back of the skiff to pole, and Skeeter stood in the bow. He laid the rifle down and held the torch as they started toward the swamp.

They made several circles around the edge of the swamp but didn't see any signs of the alligator. Each time they made a circle they would go a little deeper into the swamp. They saw several small alligators and many big frogs, but still no sign of Steel Head.

"Let's go in a pretty fer piece and work our way back," said Skeeter. "I know that 'gator ain't gone to the hills. He's bound to be here somewheres."

"Well, you be kerful up there and keep them snakes out'n the skiff," said Jeff. "First one of them snakes you lets git in here I'm goin' to quit and go home."

Jeff poled the skiff straight towards the heart of the swamp. They went around trees and through vines and sometimes had to back up and turn around when they came to a dead end. The further in they got the thicker was the foliage.

"I jest ain't goin' no further, 'gator or no 'gator," said Jeff. "I don't believe a person could go all the way through this swamp unless he got down and crawled on his belly."

When Jeff turned the skiff around and started back, they could see only the distance ahead of them that the light covered. It was like being in a lighted ball with the outside painted black. They did not head straight back toward the bayou, but made long sweeping runs back and forth so they could cover much of the swamp. They saw many strange sights, but no signs of the big 'gator. As they were getting close to the edge of the swamp, Jeff stopped the skiff.

"Whut's that?" he asked.

They sat in silence for a few moments and then heard loud bellowing noises and water splashing somewhere in the darkness. Jeff poled in the direction of the sound. Skeeter picked up the rifle and cocked it.

"Now, go slow," said Skeeter, "cause if'n that's him, I shore don't want to come up on him all at once."

As they eased through the vines and trees, the sounds became louder. All at once the noise stopped, and they could hear a splashing going away from them. Jeff speeded up a little and Skeeter signaled for him to stop.

"Jest look at that," said Skeeter. "Have you ever seed sech a sight before?"

"Hit beats arything I ever seed," said Jeff.

There was a big bull 'gator about twelve feet long lying on a mudbank. He was torn and slashed, and his tail was nearly ripped from his body. The water was stained crimson with blood. They had never seen anything torn up so badly.

"That's shore the work of old Steel Head," said Skeeter. "Wouldn't no critter in his right mind tear up one of his brother critters like that fer no reason at all. Let's see if'n we kin hear him."

They listened and heard a splashing not too far ahead of them. Jeff poled slowly in the direction of the sound, and then the sound stopped.

"He's stopped," said Skeeter. "He's lying up somewhere ahead of us, so go slow and keep yore eyes open."

As they poled slowly through the darkness, sweat was beginning to run down their faces. Skeeter's grip tightened on the rifle, and Jeff's hands shook a little as he pushed the pole. When they came into a group of big cypress knees, Jeff suddenly pushed the skiff sideways and started shouting wildly.

"There he is!" he shouted. "Right there in them cypress knees!" The 'gator was lying between two big knees and they had not been able to see him until they were right on him.

Skeeter wheeled around and aimed the rifle. The 'gator shot out of the knees like a bolt of lightning and went under the skiff. When his body hit the bottom of the skiff it knocked the skiff sideways. Skeeter fell off balance, and the gun fired into the water.

"Don't drop the torch!" shouted Jeff. "For gosh sake's don't drop the torch!" He was almost wild with fear.

Skeeter scrambled to his feet and held the torch above him as he hurriedly reloaded the rifle. The 'gator was lying right along the side of the skiff, popping his jaws madly. Skeeter took aim with the rifle. The 'gator hit the side of the skiff with his tail and knocked it several feet through the water. Jeff fell to the bottom of the skiff, and Skeeter had to grab the sides to keep from going into the water. He almost dropped the torch in the water, and the gun went off in the air. The 'gator came alongside of them and hit the skiff with his tail again, knocking it into the cypress knees. He bellowed loudly and went off through the darkness.

Skeeter and Jeff were lying in the bottom of the skiff, but they had not lost their light. Skeeter still had the torch in his hand. It was several minutes before either of them said anything. Jeff got up and pushed the skiff off the cypress knees.

"I wouldn't come in here again after that 'gator fer a thousand deer hides," he said. "A critter that could rip up a tough 'gator hide like that thing done wouldn't even need no teeth to tear me or you up."

Jeff poled the skiff out of the swamp as fast as he could. Skeeter didn't say anything for a long time.

"I'll git him afore I'm done," he finally said.

"Hit'll be more likely he gits you," said Jeff.

EIGHT

"DID YOU BOYS see that 'gator last night?" Pa asked.

"We seed him, Pa," said Skeeter, "but we didn't git him. He were too fast fer us last night."

"And that ain't the wust of hit," said Jeff. "I ain't goin' to see him no more if'n I kin help hit. That dern 'gator could snap a log in two with one whop. No, sir, I ain't goin' near that swamp at night agin fer nobody."

"I'll get him," said Skeeter. "You jest wait and see."

Ma was cooking the remaining eggs that Pa had bought, now that Jeff was fully recovered and could enjoy them. She fried some strips of salt pork and made a pot of grits. The food was steaming hot when they sat down to eat, and Pa took big helpings of everything because he was always especially hungry on a morning after he had been drinking white lightning.

The men got ready to go up the river. Pa was waiting for Jeff and Skeeter in the kitchen.

"If'n the ketch air as pore as hit were yesteddy we better stay up there and run them traps all day," said Pa, "so you better throw us somethin' in a sack to eat if'n we don't come back. Won't be no use goin' to town tomorrow if'n we don't git some fish today. Hit wouldn't be wuth the trip down fer what we got now."

Ma fried a few slices of pork and made a small corn pone and put it in a sack. Pa took the food and they left the landing. After they had run the traps and line, Pa decided they had better stay on the river all day, because the catch had been poor again. They had taken only about fifty pounds of fish. If they ran the traps all day, they could get the fish out before the gar could get in and tear the netting, and they could get the cats off the trotline before a turtle had a chance to eat their bodies. They went from the traps to the line continuously, except for the time they took to eat their small dinner. Pa believed that their labor had been worth it, though, because they made a good catch during the day. They caught a hundred pounds of fish, and with what they had caught all week, he believed they would have a good load.

After supper, Jeff took down the deer hides and rolled them into a bundle to take to town and sell the next day. Skeeter was going to take the antlers to Uncle Jobe as a gift, for he always had to take the old Negro some kind of a present. Pa sat on the front porch for a while before going to bed. When the moon came over the cypress trees, it was as red as a big ball of fire. Pa went back into the kitchen where Ma and Theresa were working on their dresses.

"The moon air full tonight," he said, "so'es you better plant them seeds tomorrow while we air in town. They always does better if'n they's planted on the first day of full moon, 'specially the corn. And mix up some of that hog feed and give them pore hogs in the morning. The way they looked today, I don't believe they's goin' to last till killin' time."

"They'd do all right if'n you'd feed 'em once in a while," said Ma. "The pore things done grubbed all the roots out'n the ground."

"I jest plum forgit about feedin' 'em," said Pa. "I'll git ole Skeeter to give 'em somethin' ever day from now on."

Pa and the boys reached the boat docks at Mill Town by midmorning. They pulled the string of fish onto the dock. It was not nearly as heavy as it had been the week before, so Pa and Skeeter could handle it by themselves. They started to market with the fish, while Jeff went to sell his deer hides. Skeeter had the deer antlers with him. After Pa had been paid for the fish, they came out on the street.

"Kin I go see Uncle Jobe while you air gittin' the supplies?" asked Skeeter.

"I guess you kin," said Pa, "but don't be gone too long, and meet me back in front of the store."

Skeeter skipped happily down the lane to the Negro quarters. He found Uncle Jobe, as he always did, sitting on the porch of his house.

"Howdy, Uncle Jobe," said Skeeter.

"Well, dog if'n hit ain't Massah Skitter agin," he said. "Come on in and sot a spell."

Skeeter crossed the yard and sat on the front porch.

"I went deer huntin' the other day, and I done brought you some antlers. I killed him right by myself, too."

"Did you now, child?" asked Uncle Jobe. "I'm right proud uv you. And I sho' likes the gift you done brought me."

"Has you ever seed ary deer, Uncle Jobe?" asked Skeeter.

"Lawsy me, Massah Skitter, when I was a boy yore age there was so many deer thet they would come up and run with the cattle and hosses. At the plantation where I was brought up, I seed as many as fifty crossin' a field at one time, and we used to find one near 'bouts every day with his antlers caught in a fence. Sometimes when one of them big bucks would git caught, he'd fight so hard thet hit would break his neck."

"They ain't near 'bouts that many now, air they?" asked Skeeter.

"No, they ain't. They's been too many kilt jest fer the pleasure uv killin' 'em. They's still more then 'nough aroun', if'n everybody would jest git whut they need."

"We killed two," said Skeeter. "We took one home to eat and tried to sell the other one to the steamboat men. They throwed us a line and pulled the deer up on the deck, and when I went up the rope to git the pay, they throwed me in the river and made off with the deer."

"I knowed they was things like thet goin' on," said Uncle Jobe. "I kin feel hit in the air. They's trouble brewin' on this river with all the sin and them people treatin' you swamp folks like you was lower than the dogs. The Lord didn't make this river fer hit to be this way, and one of these days He's goin' to fix hit so'es them boats can't even go up the river. And they ain't gonna be no more deer or no other critters left fer folks to eat, and all the folks am goin' to have to go away."

"I shore hope nothin' like that don't ever happen," said Skeeter.

"These folks is sho' goin' to have to change their ways," said Uncle Jobe, "or somethin' air goin' to happen to 'em."

"I better be gittin' on back now," said Skeeter. "See you agin, Uncle Jobe."

When Skeeter reached the store, Pa was waiting for him, and they carried the supplies down to the boat and waited for Jeff to return. In a few minutes Jeff came back, and they started up the river for home. This Saturday had been a lot different from the last, and they were all secretly glad of it, especially Jeff.

When they reached home, they took the supplies into the kitchen and went to the front porch to sit. It was a good while before supper, and they had nothing to do.

"You boys goin' on the fox run tonight?" asked Pa.

"I don't keer nothin' 'bout goin'," said Jeff. "I had enough fer one week myself."

"You goin', Skeeter?" he asked.

"Shore," said Skeeter. "It'd take a broken leg to keep me from goin' with 'em."

They sat around and talked the rest of the afternoon, and Skeeter told them what Uncle Jobe had said about the river people and what was going to happen. Finally the sun went down, and they went in and ate supper. It was not long after they had finished when they heard the Hookers coming up the bayou. Pa and Skeeter went down to the landing and were waiting when the boats came in. The Hookers had four hounds tied in one boat.

"Git out and come in a spell afore we go," said Pa.

"I don't speck we got the time," said the old man. "The moon will be up by the time we gits down the river, and these old hounds air about to go crazy to git in them woods. They near 'bout jumped out'n the boat comin' down. You all ready to go, Abner?"

"Jest me and Skeeter here goin'," said Pa. "Jeff says he don't want to go this time. I think he's done gone to bed."

"Sparky here ain't goin' either," said the old man. "That boy's got the sickness mouty bad. Says he ruther stay here with Theresa than go on a good fox hunt. Never thought I'd see the day, but I guess I's jest too old to remember when I were a young buck."

Sparky got out of the boat, and Pa and Skeeter got in, and they started from the house. Theresa met Sparky on the back stoop, and they went out and sat on the front porch. Jeff was already asleep.

*   *   *

By the time the Hookers tied the boat up down the river, the moon was out, and it was nearly as bright as day. Sun Up took the dog chains and pulled the hounds up the bank. Two of the boys brought jugs of whiskey, and one brought a whole, dressed pig. They made their way, single file, through the thick brush and vines and kept going until they reached a pine thicket in the big woods. They raked a big circle clean of pine straw and started piling up wood for a fire. When they had brought enough wood to burn all night and had a big blaze going, they cleaned another circle and started a smaller fire to one side. The old man cut two forked sticks, which he put in the ground on each side of the fire. Then he cut a straight one, sharpened it, and ran it through the whole length of the pig. He cut a small stick and tied to the end of the long one going through the pig so it would be easy to turn while the pig was roasting. Then he put the pig over the small fire and assigned Skeeter the task of keeping it turned.

"Well, you kin turn 'em loose now, Sun Up," said the old man.

Sun Up released the chains from the collars, and the hounds bounded off through the woods. They let out a low, wailing yelp as they ran, and the men gathered around the fire, waiting for the dogs to strike.

"Open up a jug and let's all have a little snort," said the old man. "They ain't nothin' like a good drink uv whiskey out in the woods at night." The jug was passed around, and everyone took a good drink. Pa and the old man took a second drink before they put the stopper back.

"When you goin' to teach that boy there to take a good drink, Abner?" asked the old man.

"He says hit burns his belly too bad, and he don't keer fer hit," said Pa.

"Well, I guess we'd be better of if'n we were like that, but I shore do enjoy a good drink uv whiskey."

When they heard the hounds let out a shrill yelp far in the distance, they knew that they had struck the trail of a fox.

"Jest listen to that music," said the old man. "They ain't nothin' like bein' in the woods at night and listenin' to the hounds run, and havin' plenty of good whiskey to drink, and a pig roastin' over a fire, and good friends about you."

"I likes hit mighty fine, too," said Pa. "I'm right pleased you axed me to come."

Skeeter was sitting on the ground turning the pig over the blaze. "Ain't we goin' to follow them dogs since they has struck that fox?" he asked.

"Tain't no use to do that, Son," said the old man. "They'll bring him right back around to here if'n they don't ketch him fust."

They could hear the yelping of the dogs as they made a wide circle around them. The jug was passed again, and everyone was beginning to feel in a good mood. The boys sang songs while Pa and the old man talked. After a while the sound of the hounds became louder, and the men could tell that they were coming straight back to where they had started.

"They ain't goin' to ketch that one," said the old man. "Go git him."

Two of the boys picked up their guns and walked off toward the sound of the hounds. In a few minutes a gun was fired, and they walked back to the fire carrying a red fox, which they hung by the tail in a tree. The dogs came in, sniffed the fox for a few minutes, and were gone again. The jug was passed to toast the first kill. In a few minutes, the dogs struck again, but this time they caught the fox and brought him back. He was hung up beside the other one, and the dogs were off again.

By midnight three jugs were gone, and everybody was getting pretty drunk. They didn't pay as much attention to the dogs. Conversation was flowing freely, and the boys were beginning to play a little rough.

"Let's have a bear rassel," shouted Full Moon. "Me and Sun Down, High Noon and Low Twelve will take on the rest of you."

They all stripped off their clothes and formed in two straight lines facing each other. When Pa shouted "go," they immediately became a mass of tangled flesh and bones. They threw each other on the ground and piled on, and rolled all over the thicket. Skeeter thought they were going to kill each other. The fight went on for a half hour, and finally the old man shouted for them to stop. He told them that it was a draw, so they took a big drink from the jug and put on their clothes.

By this time the pig was roasted to a golden brown, so the old man removed it from the fire and placed it beside a huge sack of corn pone and baked potatoes that his wife had prepared for the hunt. Each man came by and cut himself a big chunk of the meat, and then came back for seconds. They ate until there was not a piece of flesh left on the bones. As they washed it down with another drink of whiskey, the old man signaled for the boys to be quiet.

"Listen at that," he said. "That ain't no fox them dogs has got. They got a wildcat treed out there."

The dogs were yelping wildly and in a much higher pitch than they had been doing.

"Let's go git him," said the old man.

They picked up their guns and went off toward the dogs. When they reached them, the dogs were in a circle around a small sweetgum tree. They could see a big wildcat in its top, so several of the boys raised their guns to shoot.

"Don't shoot!" cried the old man. "Let's make a good fight out'n hit. A couple of you boys go over there and shake him out fer the dogs, but be shore and git out'n the way in a hurry, cause that critter kin tear the fool out'n you."

Two of the boys went over and shook the tree until the cat fell to the ground, and then ran as fast as they could. The dogs were on the cat immediately, and then the cat was on the dogs. The air was filled with the screeching and yelping of the fight. The dogs were trying to get their teeth on the cat's throat, and the cat was slashing long gashes in their flesh with its claws. For a few minutes it looked like the cat was going to win, but one of the dogs got it behind the neck with its teeth and the fight was soon ended. The dogs tore the cat to pieces, and then they ate its flesh.

"You better put the chains on them hounds now," said the old man. "Since they's tasted that wildcat meat we'd never git 'em out of the woods."

Sun Up chained the dogs, and they went back to the fire. When they finished the last jug of whiskey, they put out the fire. The dawn was just breaking when they reached the boat and started up the river. They were still so drunk when they reached the Corey house that they forgot about Sparky and went on and left him. Pa staggered into the house and fell onto the bed. Sparky was in the bed with Jeff, so Skeeter went out on the porch and went to sleep. He decided that he had had enough fox hunting to last him a long time.

NINE

IT WAS LATE that afternoon when the Hookers came back after Sparky, and only four of them came. Sparky said good-by to Theresa and left. Pa was still asleep, but Skeeter had just got up and gone to the back of the house to wash the sleep from his eyes. He went into the back yard to see if the foxes were still where he had left them. The Hookers had given them to him, and he had brought them home to give the hides to Jeff. He called Jeff to the back yard.

"We better skin these foxes afore they spoil," he said. "I thought they mout be worth somethin', so you kin take 'em to town the next time you go, and see."

They skinned the foxes, and Jeff tacked the hides to the side of the house, and they played mumble peg until darkness fell.

The next week did not bring as much excitement as the previous one had. They spent most of their time running the traps and the line. Three days they had to stay on the river all day to make a good catch, and one day they found the trap torn again. Skeeter spent all the spare time he could get killing snakes, so Jeff could have the skins to get the extra money he had secretly said he needed.

Jeff never mentioned what he wanted the money for, and Skeeter never asked, for they never pried into each other's private affairs.

By the end of the week they had made a good enough catch to make the trip to Mill Town. After they had tied up to the dock, Pa and Skeeter took the fish to the market, while Jeff went to sell the fox hides and the snakeskins. Skeeter went to see Uncle Jobe, while Pa bought the supplies, and then they met in front of the store and took the supplies down to the boat. Jeff was not there so they sat down to wait. They waited a long time, and Jeff still did not return. A small Negro boy came on the dock and walked up to Pa and Skeeter.

"Yore name Corey?" he asked.

"Hit shore air," said Pa. "Whut you got on yore mind?"

"This air fer you," said the Negro. He handed Pa a piece of paper and turned around and ran from the dock.

Pa turned it over and over and looked at it from all angles. Neither he nor Skeeter could read.

"Wonder whut this air," said Pa. "Hit's got writin' on hit. Don't know who'd be sendin' me some writin'."

"Why don't you keep hit till Jeff gits back?" said Skeeter. "He kin read a little bit."

"We'll jest do that," said Pa, "and if'n he can't read hit, we'll take hit home fer Theresa to read."

They waited a long time, and still Jeff didn't return. They heard the steamboat coming up the river, and they walked to the end of the dock to watch it pass. When it reached the big dock down the river at the mill, there was a white flag hoisted on a post of the dock, so the boat pulled in and tied up.

"Wonder whut the boat's stoppin' fer," said Pa. "They don't load no lumber on Satterday afternoon."

"Hit beats me, Pa," said Skeeter.

They could see two people walk up the plank and board the boat. Then the plank was pulled in, the lines cast off, and the boat came on up the river and passed out of view.

"Jest a couple of people gittin' on," said Pa. "Wonder who they was? Too fer off to see who they was."

They waited until late afternoon and still Jeff had not come back. Pa was beginning to get worried about him.

"Can't understand hit," said Pa, "I ain't never knowed that boy to stay off this long withouts him telling me somethin'."

"Maybe that note's from him, Pa," said Skeeter. "Why don't we go and git Mr. Blanch to read hit to us."

"That sounds like a right good idea, Skeeter. Don't know why I hadn't thought of that afore now."

They walked up the lane to the fish market and went in the back entrance. Mr. Blanch did not have any customers in the market, so he came back to meet them.

"Don't tell me you've caught some more fish already, Abner," he laughed.

"Tain't that this time, Mr. Blanch. I was jest wonderin' if'n you would do me a favor."

"Why sure, if I can I'll be glad to."

"I got a note here a nigger brought me down to the docks, and I left my specks at home, so I can't read hit. Skeeter here ain't never had a chance to git no schoolin', so we was wonderin' if'n you would read hit fer us."

Pa handed the note to Mr. Blanch, and he turned it over and looked at it for a long time. It was written in a very poor hand, so it took him a long time to make out the words. Finally he turned to Pa and started reading:

DEAR PA,

I don't know how you air goin to feel when you reads this but I hope you don't feels too bad to me. Me and Clarise

is leavin on the boat to git married and live up the river at
Monticello. I has been savin up fer this since I got beat up
and she has a little money too. The swamp woudn't be no
place fer her to live with her used to the town and if'n we
stayed aroun here hit would jest mean trouble fer all of us.
As soon as we gits settle and has time we will write you at
the post office at Mill Town and let you know how we are
and everythin. Tell Skeeter I thank him fer helpin me git the
money and tell Ma and Theresa goodby. You all take ker of
yoreself and we'll be thinkin abouts you.

Yore son,
JEFF

Mr. Blanch handed the note back to Pa, and nobody said
anything for a long time. Pa wiped a little mist from his eyes
with his dirty hands. Skeeter just stood with his hands behind him.

"I never thought the boy would go so fer as that," said
Pa, "but I guess he's got his own life to look out to."

They turned around and started out the back door.
"Thank ye fer yore trouble, Mr. Blanch," said Pa. Mr. Blanch
nodded his head.

They went back to the boat and rowed up the river in silence. It was dark when they reached the house. Ma and
Theresa met them at the landing.

"Whut's done kept you so long?" asked Ma. "And where's
Jeff?"

Pa didn't say a word but walked in the house with them
following. He handed the note to Theresa and she read it to
Ma. Ma sat at the table and buried her face in her hands for
a long time. Finally she got up to get the supper.

"I knowed hit was goin' to come to that," she said, "and
Jeff were right. The swamp wouldn't be no place fer them."

They ate their supper in silence, and the food did not
taste good to any of them. Pa knew that the work would be
harder now that Jeff was gone, and soon he would be losing
Theresa. Skeeter was thinking of having to do his and Jeff's

part of the work and how he wouldn't have as much time from now on to wander by himself in the swamp. Ma was just sick at losing her first-born son.

They went to bed, and the bed didn't feel the same to Skeeter without Jeff in it with him. He lay awake late into the night and could hear his mother crying in the next room. He didn't understand this part of life.

TEN

PA AND SKEETER went about the work and the fishing as best they could by themselves. It was a little harder running the traps and the line, without Jeff to help Skeeter row so Pa would be free to do the work, and it took them longer than it had before. The sun continued hotter, the rains were further apart, and it was as hot at night as it was in the day. The river dropped a little each day, and the further it dropped, the worse became the gar and turtle. Some weeks they had to stay on the river all day every day, and some weeks they didn't go to Mill Town because they did not have enough fish. They had to carry water in buckets from the bayou to the garden to water it, because the plants were almost fully grown.

It took the steamboats twice the length of time to make the trip up the river in the summer as it did at any other time of year. When the river was low, they had to creep along and take soundings every few feet, to keep from running on bars. The boats did not come by as often, because they could not pass each other on the river when it was low.

Some months during the summer only two boats ran the river. One would have to make the trip all the way up and wait for the other one to get there, before it could start back down.

One day Pa and Skeeter were working their traps at West Cut when they heard a steamboat coming up the river. West Cut was one of the most dangerous curves on the river during low water, and the boat was creeping along. They stopped their work to watch it make the turn. All the passengers were standing around the rails watching. When the boat passed the curve, it gathered speed to run over a bar; it hit the bar, and the jar turned the bow to the left, and the boat left the channel. It ran into a mudbank and tilted to one side. The engineer gave it full speed astern, and the paddle wheels sent tons of muddy water rising under the boat and onto the bank, but the boat did not move. It was stuck too tight to pull itself off. Pa and Skeeter rowed up to the side of the boat, and the captain came to the rail.

"I'll give you a dollar to help us get off this mudbank," he yelled.

"Give us the dollar fust," said Pa.

The captain cursed and threw a wadded dollar bill down to Pa. He unfolded it, looked at it, and put it in his pocket.

"Now, what you want us to do?" asked Pa.

"Row around to the stern and we'll lower an anchor down into your boat. You row back down the river until the line gets tight and then drop the anchor and get out of the way. We'll do the rest."

Pa and Skeeter rowed their boat to the stern and the anchor was lowered to them. They drifted back down the river until the line attached to the anchor became tight and then dropped it over the side. The men on the steamboat wrapped the line around the drum of a steam winch and took up the slack. Pa and Skeeter rowed over to the bank to watch. As the slack was taken out of the line, the anchor dug deeper into the mud at the bottom of the river. They intended to take up the line and pull the boat back to the anchor, and off the mudbank. As the line became tighter the boat moved a few feet and stopped. The engineer gave it full astern, and the men on the stern tightened with the winch. The line broke in the middle and sent a fine spray of manila hemp all over the river. The captain cursed and motioned for Pa and Skeeter to come back, so they rowed back to the boat.

"We can't get it off," said the captain, "and it'll be almost a week before they can send another boat up here to pull us off. I've got a lot of passengers on here and we couldn't bring much meat because of the heat, so I'll pay you to kill me a deer."

"Will you pay us afore you gits the deer on the boat?" asked Pa.

"Yes, damn you!" shouted the captain. "I'll pay you before we get the deer on the boat! And we'll buy some fish right now if you have any!"

The captain bought all the fish Pa and Skeeter had with them, and they rowed back down the river towards home. The next morning they were in the woods before sunup, and in an hour had killed a big buck. They bled him and skinned him on the bank of the river and loaded him in the boat. Skeeter cut off the antlers and threw the head in the river. They rowed back to West Cut, and the captain gave them twenty-five dollars for the buck, before they pulled it up to the deck. They sold them more deer before the other boat came, but what little fish they caught they had to take home to eat themselves. By the end of the week they did not have a single fish to take to Mill Town to sell, but they had the money to buy their supplies with.

Pa spent every bit of the money for food supplies, and Skeeter traded the deer hides for shot for his rifle. Pa knew that the fishing would become worse, and he wanted to have as much food as possible in store to tide them over.

As the days got hotter and the river dropped, the fishing became worse, and finally it was all Pa and Skeeter could do to stay on the river all day every day just to catch enough for the family to eat. The food supplies were getting shorter, and Ma would have to boil the same coffee for a week at a time. The traps would be torn nearly every day, and the turtles would eat the cat almost as soon as they would get on the line. The gars ate the bait so fast that it took more and more shot to kill squirrels and rabbits to keep the bait supply up. One day they came back home with both traps in the boat. Pa walked in the kitchen where Ma was and sat down.

"Tain't no use foolin' ourselves no longer," he said. "We can't make hit here with the fishin' like hit air now. They ain't even goin' to be meal to cook fish with soon, and I done et so much fish that my belly feels like a fish box."

"Whut you plannin' on doin'?" asked Ma.

"I was thinkin' 'bout goin' down to Mill Town and workin' at the mill till things gits better," he said. "We kin set the traps and the line at the mouth of the bayou here, and hit'll be easy fer Skeeter to run them. And they ought to be enough in the garden fer you to make out on. Skeeter kin come to town once every week, and I kin take my earnings and send the supplies back up by him."

"Now, you know Skeeter can't row that boat up the river by hisself."

"No, but I kin make him a paddle and he kin come in the skiff. The river ain't swift now, and he could make hit in that light skiff. I was goin' to take the boat with me."

Skeeter was sitting outside listening to the talk. He liked the idea of Pa being away for a while, for then he could have more time to himself, and could hunt old Steel Head again. He had not looked for the big 'gator since the night he and Jeff went into the swamp.

"But won't hit cost you as much as you make jest to stay in Mill Town?" asked Ma.

"I kin stay with that nigger friend of Skeeter's fer nothin'," said Pa, "and I kin eat light and save enough fer supplies. They was payin' fifteen cents an hour last week."

"Well, I guess hit beats stayin' here and starvin'. I hates to be left in this swamp with nobody but Skeeter and Theresa around, but I guess you better go. When you plannin' on leavin'?"

"Jest as soon as I kin git my few clothes together and git in the boat."

Pa went into his room and tied his belongings into a little bundle and came back to the kitchen. Skeeter was sitting on the floor.

"You go back up the river and take up that trotline and set hit down at the mouth of the bayou," he said. "And set them traps in the bayou. When the wood gits low, go over to the woods and git some more, but you be shore and be careful. Them critter over there gits mean this time of year. You do what yore Ma tells you, and look out fer them. If'n they's trouble, come down in the skiff and tell me."

Pa picked up the bundle and walked down to the landing with the rest of the family following him. He told them all good-by, got into the boat and shoved off down the bayou. When he reached the river, he stood up and waved back to them. Then he was gone from sight.

"He done went right off and forgot to make you that paddle," said Ma.

"Don't matter," said Skeeter, "I'll make hit myself."

Skeeter spent the rest of the morning making himself a paddle. When dinner was done, Ma called him to the house. Dinner didn't taste the same with only the three of them to eat, and he didn't feel quite as happy as he first had with the thought of being alone.

After dinner, he went up the river and moved the line to the mouth of the bayou and then came home to mend the traps. He took them to the front porch, and Theresa came out to help him. They sat in the hot sun, and Skeeter wanted to go to sleep. The heat felt good to him and seemed to draw all the energy from his body. In a few minutes his eyes closed, and Theresa went on with the mending.

He was awakened by loud shouting on the bayou. He looked up and saw the boats of the Hookers coming towards the house. Ma and Theresa were already down at the landing. He jumped up and ran down to meet them, but the boats had touched the bank when he got there.

"Howdy, Glesa," said the old man. "Where's Abner?"

"He went down to Mill Town this mornin' to git a job at the mill," she said. "The fishin' were gittin' so bad that our rations was gettin' mouty short. He's jest goin' to stay till the fishin' gits better."

"Well, I hates to hear that," said the old man. "Hits mighty bad when a family gits broke up cause of rations. If'n we had of knowed hit, we could have helped you out."

"I shore appreciate you sayin' that, but I know he'd ruther have hit this way. Abner never was much to ask fer help."

"I guess hits best fer a man to feel that way. Ever man feels like he'd best look after his family by hisself."

Theresa and Sparky were looking at each other and had not heard a word of the conversation. When they were together, they were not aware of anyone in the world but themselves.

"We were jest on our way to Mill Town and thought we would stop by and speak," said the old man. "You may as well git on out, Sparky, afore you has to ask me kin you stay."

Sparky got out of the boat, and the Hookers continued their trip to Mill Town. Ma went into the house to work on her dress, and Skeeter returned to the porch to finish mending the trap. Sparky and Theresa walked to the woods at the back of the clearing and sat down under a magnolia tree.

The tree was in full bloom, so Sparky climbed a limb and got Theresa one of the giant flowers. He put it in the side of her long red hair, and it was beautiful against its silky background.

"I wish we had a big cypress tree down here like you have," she said. "None of ours are near 'bouts that tall, and I think that tree is the purtiest thing on the river."

"I think you are the purtiest thing on the river," said Sparky.

Theresa blushed, and he took her in his arms and kissed her. He held her for a long time without speaking.

"When you think yore folks air goin' to let us git married?" he asked.

"I don't know," she said, "I ain't asked them. With things bein' so hard on us as they has been lately, I been ashamed to mention hit. I better stay around and help till things gits better."

"I guess that air the right thing to do," he said, "but I wish the time would hurry and come. I hates fer us to be apart so much."

"I hates hit, too, but maybe it won't be too long."

They sat for a long time talking and then got up and went back to the house. Theresa showed him the new dress she was making, and he told her that she would have to wear it when they went to the Christmas frolic at Mill Town together. Theresa thrilled at the thought of the frolic, for she had heard of it but never had been. She had never gone to any kind of a frolic in her life, for she had never known anything but work on a farm and the life in the swamp.

"You really goin' to take me to the frolic?" she asked.

"Shore, I am. And after we's married I'll take you ever year, and you'll have a new dress ever time to show them folks you air the best-lookin' woman on the river."

Theresa had never been called a woman before, and the word excited her. The thought of going to the frolic every year made her feel good, and she was so happy she thought she would cry. It made her sad when she heard the Hookers' boats come back to the landing. They walked down to meet them.

"Jest look at that," cried the old man. "Dog if'n that flower in that red hair don't make that gal look like some kind of a princess. I gets butterflies in my belly ever time I looks at her."

Theresa blushed and thanked him for the compliment.

"I seed Abner while we was there, Glesa," he said, "and he said to tell you he got the job all right, and air stayin' with Uncle Jobe, whoever that air. I didn't know you all had kinfolks down there."

"Hit ain't really kinfolks," said Ma, "hits jest a friend of Skeeter's." Ma didn't tell him it was an old Negro.

"He also said to tell Skeeter hit wouldn't be no use to come to town this week, to wait and come next Satterday. And he sent you this bag uv meal."

He handed the bag of meal to Ma, and even though she knew that Pa had not sent it, she took it. She knew that the old man had bought it himself, because Pa didn't have any money when he left.

"How about us comin' down and gittin' you folks early Sunday mornin' and you spendin' the day with us?" asked the old man. "We'd be mouty pleased to have you, and Bertha is cuttin' a fit to see that gal again."

"We'd be mighty pleased to," said Ma.

They waved good-by as the Hookers left and then went back to the house. Skeeter loaded the traps into the skiff and left to set them in the mouth of the bayou. When he finished, he came back and ate supper. Ma and Theresa worked on their dresses, and Skeeter cleaned his rifle. They all stayed up later than usual before going to bed. It was the first time Skeeter had ever spent a night without Pa, and it felt strange to him.

*   *   *

When Skeeter ran the line the next morning, there wasn't a fish on it, but he made a good catch in the traps. He knew that it was just that the fish were not used to the traps being there, and that the catch would not be as good the next time. It seemed that during low water the fish knew where the traps were, and would avoid them. But he was proud that he had made one good catch. It would make him feel big when he went to town next week and had fish to sell. He went back to the landing and put the fish into the fish box. The next morning when he went to the traps they were both torn up beyond repair, and new netting would have to be bought for both of them before they could be used again. He took them home and put them under the house.

It was early Sunday morning when the Hookers came for the Coreys. The old man had not come himself, but had sent four of the boys for them. He was waiting at the landing when they reached the Hooker place. He greeted them and they all went to the house together. The old woman met them at the door.

"Come on in, Glesa," she said, "I shore am proud to see you again. And there's that purty gal with you."

The old woman put her arm around Theresa and kissed her on the cheek. Sparky had not been in the boat that brought them, and Theresa looked around for him. In a few minutes he came in, and they went out to sit on the porch. Skeeter went down to the still, and the old folks sat in the front room to talk.

"I shore hated to hear 'bout Abner havin' to go off and work at the mill," said the old woman. "Hit's a shame when a thing like that happens to a woman. A woman jest naturally needs a man aroun' the house."

"I don't like hit a bit," said Ma, "but hit 'pears sometimes that the Lord jest don't want things to go too smooth fer a body. Seems like He wants to mix in a little of the bad with the good, so a person will appreciate the good more when he has hit."

"Well, I never thought about hit like that afore," said the old woman, "but I believe you is dead right. When things is too good, folks gits to takin' it fer granted, and then they don't 'speck nothin' no less. And when things gits bad, they don't know whut to do, and runs around like a bunch of lost hounds. I see now whut the Lord means when He gives folks a sort of a bad time."

"I believe if'n the Lord took some of them town folks and drapped them down on this riverbank like He did us, they'd starve to death afore they got their bearin's," said Ma.

"I 'spect you air right," said the old woman. "I 'spect you air right."

The two women went to the kitchen to prepare the dinner, and when it was done they called the boys in from the still. It was a big dinner, and after it was finished, the boys all went back to the still to sleep. When the dishes were done, the two women and the old man went to the front porch to sit and talk. Sparky and Theresa were walking towards the trail that led to the big cypress tree.

"Now jest look at that," said the old man. "Them two kids air goin' down to that big tree. Some days Sparky goes down there and jest sits fer hours by hisself. They must have some kind uv secret down there."

"Theresa talks about hit a lot, too," said Ma.

"I think when they gits married I'll build them a house down there so'es they kin spend all their time there," said the old man.

The old folks sat on the porch and talked for many hours, and it was late in the afternoon when Ma said they had better go. The old man gave them a side of salt pork and several jars of beans before they left. He told Ma that the boys would call for them next Sunday, and they would have another good visit. It was dark when the Coreys reached home and said good-by to the Hooker boys.

Sparky had made the trip back down with them, and Theresa hated to see him leave. They took the things the Hookers had given them into the kitchen, and Ma fixed some supper.

"Them Hookers air mouty good neighbors to have," she said. "We's lucky to have them aroun'."

"We shore air," said Theresa, but she meant it in a different way.

ELEVEN

THE WORK WAS EASY for Skeeter the next week without the traps to run. He had not told Ma about the good catch he had made the first night the traps were set in the bayou because he wanted to have fish to take to town Saturday. If they ate the fish, there would be no money to buy new netting for the traps. He saved what few fish he caught on the trotline to go with the others and kept Ma pleased by providing meat for the table by killing game. Now that the garden was grown, there was no danger of starving, but they had to have meat.

Ma had made Skeeter a pair of shorts from an old pair of overalls that he had outgrown, and they were the only clothes he wore. His skin was as brown and as tough as a piece of leather, and his hair was bleached yellow by the hot summer sun. He would spend long hours lying in the bottom of the skiff, drifting on the bayou, and when his skin became hot, he would slip off the shorts and dive into the cool water. He liked to swim naked in the cool black water of the bayou and lie among the marsh grass and water lilies. Sometimes he would chase a snake from a log or try to slip up on an unsuspecting crane.

He also spent many hours of the afternoons in the swamp, always on the watch for Steel Head. He found bodies of several small 'gators torn to shreds and knew that Steel Head was still in the swamp, but he could not find the big 'gator. He knew that his best chance to find him was at night, but he could not hunt him without Jeff to pole for him while he held the torch. But he never gave up the idea of killing the 'gator. He seemed to know that they would meet again in combat, and the next time was his turn to win.

Now each day he had a new task—watering the garden. He carried many buckets of water from the bayou and poured on the thirsty plants. The marsh grass and the trees and bushes were parched red from the lack of rain, and without the water the garden would dry in a few days. When he finished, he went back to the house and into the kitchen where Ma and Theresa were sweating from the heat.

"Let's go nigger fishin' today, Ma," he said. "The bream air bedded up now, and I know where they's a bunch of good beds. I'll dig the worms if'n you and Theresa wants to go with me."

"That's a right good idea, Skeeter," said Ma. "Hit would do us good to git out'n this hot house fer a change. And I'd like to have a good mess of them bream fried good and crisp."

Skeeter went to the back of the clearing to dig the worms, while Ma and Theresa finished their housework. When he returned, he took three slender cane poles from under the house and rigged them for bream fishing. He put on long lines and small hooks and quills he had made from the stems of marsh grass. Ma made a small lunch to take with them, and she and Theresa put on their sunbonnets and came down to the landing. Skeeter already had the poles and worms in the skiff.

"I got some of them long red worms," he said, "and a few grasshoppers. Them red worms is the best bait they air. We ought to ketch a barrelful. I brought a fish string with me."

"Well, I jest hope we ketch 'nough to make the skillet smell," said Ma.

"You better sit in the middle, Ma, so'es the skiff won't sink," said Skeeter.

"Why, you little varment," she said, laughing.

They got into the skiff, and Skeeter poled up the bayou in the direction of the swamp. When they reached the point where the bayou merged with the swamp, Skeeter turned the skiff to go along the south side. The edges of the swamp were not thick with vegetation as it was further in, so Ma and Theresa were not afraid to go there. Tall, towering cypress trees and cypress knees rose out of the water, and little islands of marsh grass were scattered about. The water was very still and clear, but the dead leaves and trash on the bottom made it look black. Tall white cranes and gray cranes and water turkeys stood around the islands of marsh grass pecking at the crawfish and minnows. Ducks floated lazily on the water, and turtles were sunning themselves on logs.

Skeeter stopped the skiff several yards out from a clump of cypress knees. There was a spot on the bottom, close to the knees, that was white instead of black, and that was where the bream had made their bed. He unrolled the lines, set the quills, and strung a worm on each of the hooks. Then he handed one to Ma and Theresa.

"You jest as well wait a minute afore you throw in," he said. "Them bream scare easy and hit'll be a little bit afore they comes back to the bed. And don't make no noise if'n you kin help hit."

They sat very still and quiet for a few minutes and then threw the lines over the bed. As soon as the baits sank to the bottom they shot off towards the knees and the thin cane poles bent double. They were catching the bream as fast as their baits hit the water. Some of the fish would weigh three pounds, and none were smaller than both Skeeter's hands put together. Bream that size were not found anywhere but in the swamp, as the ones in the creeks and bayou were much smaller.

A minnow swam lazily by the side of the skiff, and Skeeter scooped it up with his hands. He cut the small hook from his line and put on a larger one, and pulled the quill down until it was only a foot from the hook. Then he hooked the minnow through the tail and threw it away from the bream bed. The minnow pulled the quill around the top of the water for a few seconds and then went under with a splash of water. The end of the cane pole popped the water madly, and Skeeter thought it would break. He made no attempt to pull the fish in, but just let it fight with the line and the pole. Ma and Theresa stopped fishing to watch. The fish would take Skeeter's line in wide circles around the skiff and would come towards the skiff and then go the other way. Skeeter held the line tight but allowed the pole to play as much as it would. The fish tried to take the line into the cypress knees, but Skeeter would hold it back. The fight went on for a half hour, and finally the fish began to give up. Skeeter pulled it to the side of the skiff, grabbed the line and yanked it into the skiff. It was a bass that would weigh at least ten pounds.

His arms were tired from the fight, so he did not fish any more. He sat and watched Ma and Theresa catch the big bream until the bait was gone, and then they started home.

He poled the skiff close to the grass islands so he could watch the big cranes fly away, and he steered close to logs and knocked turtles into the water with his pole. He took them around big trees and through groups of cypress knees so he could show Ma and Theresa more beds that the bream had made and places where the 'gators made their dens.

They watched a snake stalk a small frog, then swallow it whole, and Theresa almost cried when she saw it. She wanted Skeeter to kill the snake and get the frog from its stomach, but he just laughed and went on.

Coming out of the swamp they passed a large mudbank, and Skeeter saw a moccasin curled in the muck. He poled the back of the skiff to the bank and stepped out. "I'm goin' to show you how to ketch that varment," he said.

"You better git back in here and leave that thing alone," said Ma. "You jest askin' fer trouble. Whut you think we'd do if'n that thing bit you, and us up here in this swamp?"

"He ain't goin' to," he said.

He broke a reed from a piece of grass, and holding it in his left hand, eased over to the snake. When he was close enough, he waved the reed in front of the snake. It raised up from the coil and held its head high for a few seconds, its tongue darting back and forth from its mouth, then it struck at the reed. Skeeter's right hand shot out as quick as a flash and grabbed the snake just behind the head. Ma and Theresa were terrified as they watched. He threw the reed down and transferred the snake to his left hand. It wrapped its body around his arm, and he started back to the skiff.

"Don't you dare bring that thing in this skiff!" shouted Ma.

"I were jest goin' to let you look at him," said Skeeter.

"I don't want to look at him!" said Ma. "If'n that's whut you been doin' whiles you is always up here in this swamp, I don't see how you has lived to be as old as you are."

"You want to see his brains pop out?" asked Skeeter.

"I don't keer whut you do with him, jest so long as you don't bring him in this skiff," said Ma.

He unwrapped the snake's body from his arm, took the end of it with his right hand, swung both arms back to the left, let go the head, slung it out with his right hand and jerked it back. The snake popped like a whip, and its brains hit the water ten feet away. Skeeter brought the limp body back to the skiff with him.

"I'll trade this fer some likker sticks Satterday," he said.

"Well, you shore better not ever do that again with me around," said Ma. "That dern near scared me to death, and jest look at Theresa shakin'. We don't want to see you git yoreself kilt." He threw the limp body into the skiff and poled back to the landing.

They all helped clean the fish, and Ma and Theresa carried them to the house. They had much more than they could eat, so Skeeter saved the smaller bream to put on his trotline. He knew that the big cat liked bream better than anything he could put on the hooks, but the turtle and gar liked them too, so he would have to run the line that night if he expected to catch a big cat. He put them in a bucket of water to keep. When he finished, he pulled off his clothes and swam in the water of the bayou. He baited the hooks just before dark and returned to the house.

Ma was frying the fish they had caught, and it smelled a lot better to him than the smell of catfish. He had eaten so much catfish that he didn't get any joy out of it any longer, but he liked the sweet crisp taste of the bream and bass. They were not full of muddy water as the cats were. Ma fried them to a crisp, golden brown and put them on the table, and Skeeter thought of Pa and Jeff as he ate, because he knew that they both liked the bream as well as he did.

Skeeter lay awake until about midnight, then got up and went down to the landing to go run the trotline. He got the gaff from under the house and paddled down the bayou. The water where the line was set was too deep to use the pole. The moon was out, and it cast a pale silver glow over the flats of marsh grass. The night air was making a thin fog rise from the ground, and the moon made it look like gray ghosts floating through the air. The place was enchanting, with the moon shining through the moss of the tall cypress trees and painting a silver streak down the bayou and the river, with the gray mist twirling in the air. Skeeter felt that he was in another world from that of the day. He felt like standing up and floating through the air and becoming a part of the beautiful miracle he was seeing. It was a simple miracle, one that he had seen many times before and never noticed, the miracle of day changed into night, creating an entirely different world. He felt that he could look at the scene forever.

The reality of the trotline broke the spell for him, and he almost resented the line being in the river. He thought it was not right that something man had made should be in the midst of what he was seeing, something much greater and more beautiful than man could make. His resentment was soon erased as he felt a pulling when he touched the line. He had a fish, and now his mind was occupied with only the thought of getting the fish off the line. He was brought back from the night down to man's world again.

He pulled the skiff down the line until he reached the hook that held the fish. He raised it to the top of the water and pulled it into the boat. He went on down the line and removed two more fish. Then he went back to the house and put them into the box. He stood for a long time in the yard, looking towards the bayou, and wishing he could recapture the feeling that had picked him up, when he first went out into the night. But now it was gone, and he went into the house and went to bed.

The remainder of the days before Saturday were spent in the same way as the ones before had been — running the line early in the morning, watering the garden, bringing wood and water to the house, and drifting on the bayou and in the swamp. Finally Saturday came, and it was time to make the trip to town. Skeeter strung the fish the night before and was ready to leave at daybreak the next morning. Ma had his breakfast on the table when he got up and his lunch already fixed and in one of the croaker sacks.

"You be shore and git a pail of lard today," she said. "They ain't no more in the crock, and I done strained this we air usin' till hits plumb wore out. Hit jest won't last till hog killin' time."

"Air they anything else besides the meal, sugar, and coffee?" he asked. He hoped he could remember everything, for this was the first time he had ever had to remember what to get. Pa had always done that.

"You better git some salt, too," she said. "I shore hope yore Pa has 'nough money to git everthing. If'n they ain't enough, leave off the sugar."

He put the fish in the skiff and paddled down the bayou. The sun was turning the treetops red when he turned down the river. This was his first trip to town by himself, and it made him feel big and powerful. He knew that Pa would be proud that he had caught some fish, and he hoped they would bring enough money to buy the new netting.

He noticed a lot of things, as he drifted down the river alone, that he had never noticed before. He saw how the willows dipped into the water as if drinking, and how the leaves fell from the magnolia trees and were caught up by little whirlpools and spun round and round, like small boats, and then went skimming along with the current. He saw the gray squirrels bundle themselves into the moss of the cypress trees when they heard him make a sound, and become invisible to him. A mother coon brought her young to the edge of the river to drink the water, and then led them silently back into the woods. Ducks picked up and flew ahead of him, and the birds sat in the trees and chattered at him as he passed. Only the turtles sunning themselves on logs seemed unaware of his presence. They were conscious of nothing but the sun and the water. He paddled close to logs just to disturb their sleep and laughed when they rolled over into the water. It was like watching a parade of all the creatures of the river.

When he reached the docks, he tied the skiff and took the fish to the market. He had a hundred and fifty pounds, and was paid fifteen dollars. It was enough to buy the new netting, and it made him feel good thinking about it. He thanked Mr. Blanch and started down the lane to Uncle Jobe's shack. When he reached there, Uncle Jobe was sitting on the front porch.

"Good mornin', Massah Skeeter," he said. "Yore Pa won't be in from the mill till noon, so come in and sot a spell."

Skeeter greeted him and sat down on the porch. He felt in his pocket to be sure that the money was still there, for he didn't want to lose it before Pa came.

"I didn't bring you nothin' this time," said Skeeter.

"Thet's all right, child, I's powerful glad to see you without you bringin' me nothin'. I'm right pleased you sent yore pa to stay with me. I's fixed him up a good place to sleep, and we gits along jest fine. Hit does a old soul like me good to have company around, and yore Pa air sho' a fine man."

They sat and talked until noon, and shortly afterwards Pa came to the shack. He was glad to see Skeeter and slapped him on the back. Skeeter took out the lunch Ma had fixed for him, divided it three ways, and they ate dinner. Skeeter told him all about the fish he had sold, the traps being torn up, what his Ma had said to bring home, and everything that had happened during the past week. After they finished eating, Pa and Skeeter walked back to town.

"We better git them supplies and let you start back as soon as you kin," said Pa. "Hit'll take you a good whiles to git back by yoreself."

"I still got that fifty cents you give me one time when we had that good catch," said Skeeter, "and I wonder if'n I kin spend hit fer anything I wants now."

"Why shore you kin," said Pa. "Hits yore money and you kin do with hit as you please."

They went to the store and bought all the supplies Ma had wanted and the new netting for the traps. Skeeter bought himself a piece of lead pipe, three feet long and three inches wide. Pa didn't ask why he bought it, though he wondered what it was for. It was Skeeter's money, and if he wanted to spend it on lead pipe, that was his business. They took the supplies down to the docks and loaded them into the skiff. Pa told Skeeter good-by, and he started up the river. He didn't have as much time going back to watch things as he had coming down, for it was hard work for him to paddle the skiff up the river by himself. When he reached home, he was tired and his arms hurt, but he was proud that he had remembered and brought home everything Ma had told him.

TWELVE

SKEETER AND THERESA spent most of their time the next few days putting the new netting on the traps. It was slow work weaving the nets around the framing without leaving any holes or weak spots, and it took them many long hours before the work was done. When they finished, Skeeter decided not to put the traps back out, because the few fish he would catch would not be worth the chance of having the traps destroyed again. The cost was too high to repair them. He fished for bream along the edges of the swamp and used them for bait on the line and ran the line every night. This way he managed to keep a few fish in the fish box and have a little to take to town and sell.

He fastened the pipe he had bought into the bow of the skiff to use as a means of having light at night. He would cut the end of the pine torches down until they would fit into the pipe, and this way he would not need anyone to pole the skiff for him. Now he could go into the swamp by himself at night. He decided to bait the line with squirrel meat so that he wouldn't have to run it at night.

Skeeter had stopped taking his rifle when he went squirrel or rabbit hunting and would use only the knife. It was very seldom that he missed a running rabbit or squirrel, and he had practiced so much that he was accurate at over a hundred feet. One day he hit a bird in midair, but he didn't try throws like that very often. He seldom killed anything for which he did not have a use.

One morning when he came in from running the line, Ma told him that the wood supply was out and there was no more pine under the house. He took the ax and went down the river to cut some pine in the big woods. He hid the skiff under some willow limbs and started through the thick buck vines. This was the first time he had been in the woods by himself, and he had a feeling of high adventure. He wanted to bring his rifle with him, but he knew that it would only be in the way bringing the wood back to the skiff. He would have to make several trips into the woods before he had enough.

He made his way through the thick growth and into the part of the woods where the big pines were. He cut a chip out of every tree on the way to be sure he would not lose his way coming back and miss the place where he left the skiff. He knew that he could find his way back to the river, but he didn't want to do any extra walking carrying the load of wood. He chopped the fat pine on the ground into sticks and made several loads back to the skiff. Coming back with his last load, he was working his way through some thick vines when he heard strange noises in a clearing ahead of him. When he remembered what Pa had said about the critters being mean during low water, he felt a little afraid. He sat for a few minutes in silence thinking they would go away, but the sounds became louder. He felt he had to see what it was.

He lay flat on the ground and crawled on his stomach through the vines, not daring to make a sound. It was slow progress, and it was several minutes before he reached a place where he could see into the clearing. He lay in silence and watched the strange spectacle taking place before him. Two big bucks were on each side of the clearing facing each other. They turned and walked in opposite directions around the clearing, then stopped and faced each other again. They lowered their heads and charged straight at each other. Their antlers hit with a clash and knocked them both from their feet. They scrambled up and walked back to each side of the clearing, walking around again in opposite directions, looking like two boxers feeling each other out in the first round of a championship fight. When they walked half the circle around the clearing, they stopped, faced the center, charged in, and clashed antlers again, only this time they reared up and kicked with their front feet instead of falling to the ground. The third time they made the charge their antlers became entangled, and they fought around and around until they came loose. Then they went back to the edge of the clearing. The fourth time they made the charge they did not go back to the edge of the clearing but stayed in the middle of the circle and kicked and bit and slashed out at each other with their antlers. Skeeter knew that he was witnessing a death battle between two great bucks of the forest.

The bucks fought and struggled and rolled over and over on the ground and tore great gashes in each other's sides. Blood dripped to the ground, and they were both rapidly becoming spotted with blood. Skeeter's heart pounded wildly inside him, and his hands shook with fright. He wished that he had his rifle or that Pa was with him or that he was in the skiff in the bayou. He had never witnessed such a fight, not even the night in the woods when the Hooker boys had the bear wrestle. He wondered what they would do if they were here. He could not stand to watch the big, beautiful bucks slaughter each other, and yet he could not make himself leave. The fight was getting more vicious as it went along, and finally one of the bucks knocked the other to the ground and backed off to charge it with his antlers, to end its life, and the fight. Skeeter could stand it no longer, and he didn't know what he was doing he was so excited. He jumped to his feet and shouted wildly. He jumped up and down and shouted as loud as he could. The buck stopped his charge, and the one on the ground jumped to its feet. They both looked at Skeeter with surprise and bounded off through the vines in opposite directions.

Skeeter sat on the ground and wiped the sweat from his face with his hands. His face was red, and his heart was still pounding so hard that it hurt him. He couldn't understand what had made him do what he had done, because if one of the bucks had charged him it would have meant the end of his life. He had never been scared by Steel Head as he was by this fight, yet he knew that Steel Head was a much greater danger to him. It was just that he could not bear to see the beautiful, proud bucks end their lives in such a way. He would not mind hunting them and killing them for food, but he didn't want them to kill each other. He sat for a long time and rested and then returned to the skiff with the load of wood. He paddled slowly up the river to home.

When he had unloaded the wood and put it under the house, he carried some into the kitchen. His face was white as a sheet, and his hands shook.

"Whut in the world air wrong with you?" asked Ma. "You look like you seed a ghost over in them woods."

"Tain't nothin'," he said, and walked back into the yard.

He couldn't eat much dinner, and as soon as he finished he went to the woods next to the clearing to kill squirrels. When he returned, he dressed four for their supper and cut the others up for bait. He got into the skiff and went up the bayou and lay in the sun. He pulled off his clothes and swam in the water and then lay in the skiff and watched the clouds fly by overhead. He poled the skiff into the marsh grass so it could not drift and went to sleep.

He was awaked by the gentle patter of rain on his body. He did not know how long he had been asleep, but it was still light. Excitedly he poled the skiff down the bayou to the landing. Ma and Theresa were standing in the back yard in the rain; their clothes were soaked, but they were happy. The black clouds were rolling in from the south, and soon the whole sky would be covered. It was a weird sight, with the sun shining and rain falling at the same time. A giant rainbow was forming in the east. Skeeter got his meat and left to bait the hooks. The warm rain felt good to him, and he wished he could stay out in it all night. All memory of the fight he had witnessed that morning was gone now. When he got back to the landing, the sky was completely covered by the black clouds, and it was almost dark. Ma and Theresa were still standing in the rain. They went into the house and changed to dry clothes and started frying the squirrels for supper.

"Thank the Lord hit's come at last," said Ma. "That pore old parched ground would have blowed away afore long if'n hit hadn't got no water."

Skeeter was hungry now, and the supper tasted good to him. He ate until he could hold no more and then lay on his bed and listened to the rain beating against the roof. It had prevented his going into the swamp that night, but he didn't mind. The fish would bite good during the rainy night, and he liked to listen to the rain against the roof. Sleep came easy, and it was a sound sleep. When he awoke the next morning, the sun was out, and the black clouds were gone from the sky.

That was the last rain they had for many weeks. The days got hotter, and the ground was parched red. The fishing became so bad that Skeeter took the line from the river and stopped wasting the squirrels and the bream for bait. He kept meat on the table by killing game and catching the bream in the swamp, but if Pa had not been at the mill, they would have had nothing with which to cook them. Skeeter made many trips into the swamp at night, killing frogs, but he never got another chance at Steel Head. The big 'gator seemed to come out and do his killing and disappear into thin air.

The days changed into weeks, and finally the nights began to be cool, and the rains came more often. Early in the mornings there would be a chill in the air, and the swamp was filled with fog. The marsh grass turned brown, and the leaves on the trees became tinted with red. The days were shorter and the nights longer, and the river began to rise. There were not as many snakes about, and the baby squirrels were playing in the trees. The robins were starting their migration south, and bobwhite could be heard late in the afternoon calling the young into covey. The stalks of corn in the garden were turning yellow, and the blooms of the magnolia trees were dying and turning into seed. All the animals seemed to sense that fall was in the air, and the squirrels carried nuts and acorns into their dens all day. The big bullfrogs could be heard less often in the swamp at night, and the opossums were eating the last of the wild persimmon. The big bass were beginning to strike in the river, and the minnows stayed close to the bank. One night they heard the honking of wild geese flying overhead and knew that the warm days would soon be gone. Pa returned from the mill.

Pa and Skeeter set the traps and the line up the river, and the fishing was better. The gar and turtle were not as bad, and they managed to catch enough fish to buy all the supplies the family needed. By the first of November the river was back to normal, and the leaves were falling from the trees. Every day they could see hundreds of ducks flying into the edges of the swamp and the bayou and along the river. It would not be long until the deer meat was at its best, and the young quail were large enough for Skeeter to trap. The entire river and swamp looked like a new world every time the seasons changed.

A week before Thanksgiving the family was sitting at the table eating a supper of baked ducks that Skeeter had killed on the bayou.

"Let's bait up some turkeys and have the Hookers down fer a big dinner Thanksgivin'," said Pa. "They ain't never et down here, and we been up there so many times. I knows a good spot fer me and Skeeter to bait 'em up."

"I think that'd be a mouty fine thing to do," said Ma, "bein' as we took ever Sunday dinner up theer whiles you was at the mill, and they give us a lot uv eatin', too."

"Well, you start thinkin' 'bout the fixin's, Ma," he said, "and leave the turkey and the meats up to me and Skeeter. We'll start on that in the mornin'."

The next day when they left to run the traps, Pa carried an ear of corn and the hoe with them. Skeeter had never been on a baiting before, and he didn't understand it. When they got down the river, they tied the boat up and went into the big woods. Pa dug a shallow trench in the ground about six feet long and four inches wide, sprinkled kernels of the corn the length of the trench, and then they built a blind of pine boughs in the vines away from the trench. That afternoon they went back and the corn had not been touched, but when they went by the next morning it was gone, and there were turkey droppings on the ground. They baited the trench with corn for the next three days, and each morning when they went back the corn was gone. Then they stopped putting out the corn.

Pa and Skeeter rowed up the river and asked the Hookers about coming for the meal. The old man said they would be glad to and would bring plenty of whiskey. He wanted to know if there was anything else they needed, but Pa assured him that they had all the provisions.

Two days before the big day Pa and Skeeter went into the big woods and killed a young buck and brought him home. They dressed him and hung him in the kitchen to be barbecued. Ma had made several quarts of crab-apple jelly that week and had all her things ready to start cooking the dinner the next day. Early the next morning Pa and Skeeter went back to the trench in the woods and put corn in it again and hid behind the blind and waited.

"Now be shore and don't make no noise when they come," said Pa, "and don't miss no shot. You make the first throw with that knife, 'cause hit won't make no noise. Then when it hits one, if'n it does, be ready to shoot on the fly when the rest of them takes off."

They sat behind the blind for about an hour and nothing happened. Then they heard the slapping of big wings coming down through the trees, and nine turkeys lit on the ground and started eating the corn. Pa motioned for Skeeter to go ahead and throw, but Skeeter was a little slow in doing so. He had never wanted so much for his throw to count, for he wanted to show Pa that he could do it. He raised his arm and sent the knife straight into the breast of a turkey. When it hit, the turkey screamed, and the others took to the air. He threw up his rifle and shot almost at the same time as did Pa. They stepped from behind the blind and found three turkeys dead on the ground.

"Didn't think you could do hit," said ·Pa. "You must have learned a lot whiles I was gone last summer."

Skeeter didn't say anything, but he felt proud inside. They took the turkeys back to the house and dressed them and hung them beside the deer. Skeeter went out late that afternoon and killed a dozen ducks with the rifle and brought them home. Ma said if they didn't stop, the kitchen would be so full they couldn't get inside and it would take her a year to cook it all.

The family was up before dawn the next morning, preparing for the dinner. Ma had only one broiler big enough to hold a turkey, so she would have to bake them one at a time, and then there were all the ducks to bake. Pa and Skeeter did not run the traps that morning, for they were digging the pit in the back yard to barbecue the deer. When the pit reached the depth of three feet, they cut small sweet gum trees to lay over the top. Then they built a fire in the pit with hickory limbs and put the deer on the sweet gum poles. It would have to be watched all day to keep the fire just right and keep the meat turned.

Ma baked the turkeys and the ducks in their own fat, and then used the broth to make the dressing. She used corn pone for the base of the dressing and mixed in sage and onions. She mixed three big pots of dressing and set them aside to be cooked the next morning, so it would be hot for the meal. It was late in the night when they stopped and went to bed.

They were up again at dawn the next morning to finish the preparations before the Hookers came. There was the dressing to cook, the corn pone to make, and Ma was going to make some big, sweet-potato pies. They did not have enough plates for so many people, so Pa sent Skeeter up the bayou to get giant lily pads to use instead. They wouldn't need plates for anything but the dressing and the pie, so the pads would do fine. It was a clear, warm day, so they moved the table into the back yard to have the meal in the open.

It was midmorning when the Hookers arrived, and the men had several jugs of whiskey and their guitars and fiddles with them. They stayed in the yard and passed the jugs, and the women went into the kitchen to finish the cooking. The men talked and drank until the meal was ready and then helped put all the food on the table. The deer was left on the pit so that everyone could go around and cut his choice piece, and they put the turkeys, the baked ducks, the dressing, corn pone, crab-apple jelly, and potato pies on the table. After Pa returned thanks, the meal was begun, and it lasted for over three hours. Then the boys went to sleep, and the old people went to the front porch to sit and talk. Sparky and Theresa walked into the woods to be alone.

"That's about the biggest feast that's ever been put on along Pearl River," said the old man. "I'm afeered that my britches air goin' to bust."

"It were about the best I ever seed," said the old woman.

"Well, I'm shore glad that you all enjoyed hit," said Pa. "We been owin' you a feed like this. I shore appreciate yore keepin' company with my family while I was gone this summer. Hit makes a body feel better to know his family air aroun' friends."

"Well, don't forget we're goin' to come by and take you all to the Christmas frolic in Mill Town with us," said the old man. "We been countin' on hit fer a long time."

"We'll be much obliged to go," said Pa.

They talked for a while and then all dozed off to sleep. They woke up late in the afternoon and the men went to the back yard. The two women stayed on the porch to talk. The jug was passed several more times, and then it was time to eat again. No one ate as much the second time as they had the first. When the second meal was finished, the boys started some music, and a dance was begun. They took turns dancing with the three women, and the jugs were passed so everyone was feeling good and happy. It was late at night when the Hookers bade their farewell.

THIRTEEN

THE DAYS were getting colder, and some mornings Pa and Skeeter had to wear their wool jackets while on the river. It was time for Skeeter to set his animal traps and almost time to kill the hogs. They were already making preparations for the hog killing. Pa and Skeeter were building a temporary smokehouse out of sweet gum poles and pine boughs and were getting a good supply of hickory logs together. They would kill the hogs the first morning there was a frost on the ground.

"I wish the frost would hurry and come," said Ma. "I got a hankerin' fer a bait of chitlins and cracklin' bread."

"Hit do sound good," said Pa. "The way the air felt this mornin' I believe the ground will be white in three or four days."

Skeeter went to the swamp that day and picked the places to set his traps. He had six of them, and he placed them on mudbanks and small islands of high ground around the edges of the swamp. If they didn't do good, he would move them around during the winter and try new places. He came back to the house and helped Pa sharpen the knives for the hog killing.

The nights were cold now, and the quilts felt good to Skeeter. He liked to sleep rolled up in a ball like a squirrel, and he hated to get out of bed in the morning. Late that night he heard a noise come from the hog pen, and the hogs squealed loudly. He jumped from the warm bed and slipped on his clothes. Pa had heard it too, and he dressed and came into the room with his gun. They lit a torch on the hearth and slipped into the yard and down to the pen. They found one of the hogs dead and badly torn and heard a splashing up the bayou.

"Hit's that kill-crazy 'gator agin," said Pa. "I wished I could git a bead on that varment with this gun. I'd blow them loco brains of his'n all over them marsh flats."

"Let's go git him now," said Skeeter. "He couldn't be too fer off time we gits started."

"Tain't no use runnin' that varment in the dark," said Pa. "He knows the swamp a heap better'n we do."

They climbed into the pen and examined the dead hog. The big 'gator had mangled it badly.

"They's still some good left," said Pa. "We kin cook out the lard and git the chitlins, and maybe a little meat. You run to the house and git the knives and we'll gut him now so'es he won't spoil till mornin'."

Skeeter ran to the kitchen to get the knives, while Pa brought the hog to the back stoop. Ma and Theresa were in the kitchen.

"Whut were hit?" asked Ma.

"Old Steel Head done got another one of the hogs," said Skeeter. "But Pa says they's still some good left on him. We's goin' to gut him now."

"I knowed that varment would come back," said Ma. "Hit ain't safe fer a body to be outside at night with that devil around."

"Tain't that bad," said Skeeter. "That's the fust time he's been around here in a long time."

"But hit shore won't be the last," said Ma. "He'll git us all afore he's done with it."

"I'm goin' to see if'n I kin git him tomorrow," said Skeeter.

He took the knives to the stoop, and they hung the hog up and dressed it as best as they could. It was hard to clean being torn up so badly. When they finished, they washed the blood from their hands and went back to bed.

Skeeter and Pa were up earlier than usual the next morning to run the traps and line, and when they returned home, Ma and Theresa had already started on the hog. They scalded it with hot water, scraped it, and then removed the skin and fat to fry down as lard. The rest of the meat they would grind up as sausage. Skeeter got his knife and his rifle, filled one of his pockets with shells, found half of a corn pone in the kitchen and put it in his pocket, and went down to the landing and got into the skiff.

"You be kerful in that swamp," shouted Pa, "and be shore and git out of there afore hit gits dark." Pa was not afraid for Skeeter, because he knew that he could take care of himself during the day.

Skeeter poked the skiff up the bayou and tried to think of every place that the 'gator might be in the daytime. He figured that it would be asleep and he could slip up on it. He made long sweeps along the edges and then worked his way further into the swamp. He raked his pole along logs and in grassy spots and looked around all the mudbanks and cypress knees.

The swamp had taken on a desolate look with the coming of winter. The trees no longer had leaves, and the vines were bare. Only the moss on the cypress broke the monotony of limbs against sky. The sky was cloudy that day, and the grayness gave an eerie atmosphere to the already dismal surroundings.

Skeeter worked his way back and forth along the swamp with no sign of the 'gator, and when he thought it was noon, he stopped and ate his corn pone. He drank some of the swamp water, and it didn't taste good, so he swallowed a little and spit the rest out. A fine mist was beginning to fall, so he pulled the collar of his jacket tight around his neck and continued his relentless search for the alligator.

He pushed deeper and deeper into the swamp, and he was already farther in than he had ever been before. The trees were much thicker and the vines more entangling, and the water was getting shallow. Sometimes he had to lie in the bottom of the skiff to pass under the vines, and he could hear an occasional snake, that was late in hiding away for the approaching cold winter, dropping into the water ahead of him. Even the water was changing color. It was turning from black to green, and the green slime covered the top so that he could not see past the surface. An irresistible force pushed him farther and farther into the swamp. Many times he found himself trapped by vines, and he would have to back the skiff out and go another way. The sickening stench of the slime was so bad that he could hardly bear it, but he pushed on and on. The vines and the trees and dead limbs were so thick that he could not see the sky, and he did not know what time it was. The mist was beginning to soak down through the trees, and he was wet and cold, so he decided to give up the hunt for the day. He started back and then realized that he was lost, and the sun was gone from the sky. The thick trees and the clouds had fooled him, and he had not realized that it was so late. In a few minutes the last gleam of light would be gone and there would be no moon or stars to guide him out. He didn't know what to do. He was scared, and he was wet and hungry, and his mouth ached for a drink, but he dared not drink the slimy water.

He realized for the first time that this was what men feared most—being lost in the swamp at night.

The mist was turning into rain, and he poled the skiff under some thick vines to escape as much of the rain as possible. When the last light was gone, he became engulfed in a great sea of darkness, a darkness that would even bring terror to a man's heart. He wished he were in his warm bed or that he would wake up and find that this was only a bad dream. He wished that he could jump up and fly from the swamp, but he knew that his condition was hopeless, and no amount of wishing could get him out. He lay down and tried to sleep, but sleep would not come. He saw a pair of green eyes coming at him through the trees, and when they were above him they stopped, and something screamed. It was a panther, and the scream made the flesh crawl on his bones. He picked up his rifle and aimed what he thought was the sight, at the eyes. He would shoot if it came at him, but it did not. It continued its journey through the night and was soon gone. Skeeter lay on his back and soon fell asleep from sheer exhaustion.

His eyes had been closed only a few minutes when he felt something drop across his neck. It was round and cold, and he knew that it was a snake, but he dared not move for fear it would strike. He could feel its smooth body slowly inching across his face. Cold sweat broke from his face, and his blood turned to ice. The snake was making a coil on his neck because it liked the feel of his warm body. Skeeter knew what was happening, and he wanted to jump up and scream, but he also knew that one strike from the snake would mean sure death. His hands shook, and he tried to stop them for fear it would shake the skiff. He looked into the blackness above him, trying not to think. Sweat was pouring from his face, and he thought he would go crazy at any moment. Finally, he felt the snake's body move again, and it moved slowly across his neck. He heard a splash in the water, and it was gone.

Now sleep was out of the question. He sat in the skiff and shook, and his heart pounded madly, until at last the streaks of light broke through the haze, and it was dawn. He had never seen a dawn that was so beautiful to him. His stomach ached from hunger, and his throat was dry, but it was light, and he was not afraid any more. He could not stand the thirst any longer, so he raked the green slime from the surface and drank some of the water. The stench would not stay on his stomach, and he retched it back up. It made him feel sick, and his head hurt. He eyes were red from lack of sleep and his clothes were soaked with water. He looked at the moss on the trees to tell directions, and then started his slow journey back through the swamp. He did not think of Steel Head on the way back; his only thought was of getting out. He had to turn around many times and backtrack, and it was almost dark when he reached familiar ground and knew that he was out. He poled the skiff to the bayou and down to the landing. He was weak and sick, but he knew that he had been where no man had ever been before, and possibly would never be again. He picked up his gun and went into the house. Pa grabbed him, and Ma and Theresa were crying.

"You done give us the biggest skeer we ever had," said Pa. "If'n I weren't so glad to see you I'd whale the daylights out'n you. Where you been all this time in that swamp?"

"Lookin' fer Steel Head, but I didn't git him," was all that he said.

He took a big drink of the clean fresh water in the bucket and then put on dry clothes. Ma fixed him a bowl of hot gruel and a corn pone, and he ate it slowly to keep from retching it up. The warm food settled his stomach, and he felt better. He got in the bed and rolled up in the warm covers, and the bed never felt so good to him before in his life. He immediately fell into a deep sleep.

"I shore thought we had lost our last son," said Pa. "Hit would be mouty hard without him."

"He's got to quit doin' things like that," said Ma.

FOURTEEN

A FEW DAYS LATER, the frost was on the ground, and it was time to kill the last hog. Ma and Theresa heated the water, while Pa and Skeeter killed it. They scalded and scraped it and hung it up to bleed; and before the day was through they had cut up the fat and skin for lard, separated the hams, shoulders, backbone, ribs, and all the scraps they would use for sausage. The next day they would pack the meat in salt to prepare it for smoking with hickory limbs. Then they would use part of the intestines for sausage casings and save the rest to fry as chitterlings. When the sausage was ground and stuffed, they would hang the casings beside the hams to be smoked, cook backbone and ribs and store them in the fat, and make cheese from the head. It would be soaked in vinegar and called souse. That night Ma mixed up the crisp pieces of skin with the corn pone and cooked the chitterlings, and they ate till there was none left. They would save most of the meat for the flood season when they could not get outside.

Pa and Skeeter ran the traps and line every morning, and when they returned, Skeeter would run his animal traps. When he caught a mink, he would tack its pelt to the house to dry. The days passed on, and soon it was Christmas time. Pa cut a small cedar tree and put it in the house, and they decorated it with bits of bright paper and cloth left over from the dresses. There was no money for presents, but Ma had planned to have a good dinner, and the trip to Mill Town would be enough. The two red dresses were finished and hanging on the wall to be worn to the frolic. The Christmas frolic was the only time during the year that the townspeople would let the swamp rats join in their festivities, and they looked forward to it through the year. It was held in the one-room school, where there was dancing and food, and the men would have jugs of whiskey to pass around. Theresa could hardly wait until Christmas Eve.

Each family was supposed to bring food, so Pa and Skeeter baited the turkey trench again, and the day before Christmas Eve they killed two turkeys. Ma baked one to take to the frolic and saved one for their Christmas dinner. There was not much sleep that night, for everyone was too excited.

They were up at dawn the next morning, hurrying to get the housework done, the traps run, and the final preparations for the trip made. After dinner, Ma and Theresa put on their new dresses, and Pa put on his best pants and shirt. They made Skeeter put on a clean pair of overalls. Theresa combed her long hair and tied a white ribbon in the back— she was beautiful. She hoped Sparky would be proud of her. About midafternoon the Hookers came, and they all loaded into the boats and started the trip down. Pa thought he had never seen as many jugs of whiskey as there were in the boats. There was hardly enough room for the passengers. The men emptied one jug on the way down.

When they arrived at the docks, there were many boats tied to the pilings, and there were a lot of people on the streets. Wagons were rolling into town, and there were many horses and mules tied to the hitching posts. The people from all the surrounding territory were coming in for the frolic. Everyone seemed in a joyous mood, and much talk and laughter were heard on the street. The women took the food and went on to the schoolhouse, while the men stayed on the street to talk with friends they had not seen for a long time. The Hooker men passed the jugs to a number of people on the street, and a good deal of conversation went around. When it started getting dark, all the men went to the schoolhouse.

The food was laid out on long tables on the school grounds, and there were oil lamps around for light. There was every kind of food a person could imagine: turkeys, venison, chickens, fish, ducks, big pots of dressing, potato salad and baked sweet potatoes, many different kinds of pies and cake, and big tubs of coffee for the women and children. Tin plates and forks were stacked high; everyone could pass by and get what food he wanted, then get off in little groups of his own. The eating went on for several hours, then the preachers said a few words of welcome and about Christmas, and all the folks went inside for the frolic. Most of the young boys stayed on the outside to play and fight and tear the good clothes that their mothers had fixed for them.

The inside of the school was decorated with holly and pine, and mistletoe hung over the door. Some of the boys would stand by the door and try to kiss the young girls as they came inside. The girls would giggle and try to stop them.

Chairs were placed around the outside of the large room so the old folks could sit and watch, and for the people who didn't want to dance. Lanterns were swung from the roof, and the old, pot-bellied, iron stove in the corner was red with the glowing coals of a warm fire.

One end of the room contained a platform for the string band, and the fiddlers were already taking their places. There were several fiddles and guitars, and one bass fiddle. The fiddlers were tuning up their instruments, and the drone of the waiting crowd drowned out all sound. People were laughing and talking, and the dancers were lining up their partners for the first dance. Theresa had many offers for the first dance, but she would have no one but Sparky.

The caller climbed to the platform and raised his arms for silence. Everyone faced the front and listened.

"Now git yore pardner, and let's git ready for the lead out," he shouted.

Everyone got his partner, and they lined up facing each other. Those who were not going to be in the dance backed off the floor and took the chairs around the room. Each member of the band stood up, and after they played the first few notes of a tune, they stopped. The caller sang out:

> Git yore pardner,
> Swing her around,
> Come on now
> And go to town.
> Right foot up,
> Left foot down,
> Come on now
> And swing her around.

Then the dance was started. The two lines of men and women came to the center and bowed and skipped back. They came back and locked arms and swung to the left, then skipped back, then returned and swung to the right, and then did do se do and started swinging down the line. When the dance was finished, new sets took the floor. The men went outside to drink from the jugs, and the spirit of the frolic grew as each new set of dancers took the floor.

As Skeeter entered, the three Smith brothers stopped him.

"Ain't you a Corey?" one of them asked.

"Yeah!" said Skeeter.

"I thought you was a brother to the bastard whut run off with our sister," he said. "Let's rough him up a little, boys."

One of them shook Skeeter, and another slapped him. Sparky and Theresa were dancing on that end of the floor, so they saw what was happening. They dropped out of the dance, and Sparky went over and said something to the rest of the Hooker boys. They all crossed the room toward the door.

The three men were still shaking and slapping Skeeter, so without saying a word, the Hooker boys made a circle around them. Sun Up and Sun Down grabbed one of the boys and threw him through the glass window before he knew what had happened. Glass and window framing shattered all over the end of the room. The music stopped and a few women screamed. Then the caller jumped to the platform, the music started again, and the dance went on. A fight was nothing new at the frolic.

The Hooker boys dragged the other two brothers out the door and picked the third up from the ground. Pa and Old Man Hooker and a lot of other men followed them outside. A crowd had already formed around them. Sun Up explained to Pa and the old man what had happened.

"Well, them yellow varments," said the old man, "pickin' on a little feller like Skeeter." He turned and faced the crowd. "If'n they's ary of these fellers' friends here that wants to git in this, you mout as well step up now."

All of the Smith brothers' friends looked at the Hooker boys, and nobody moved.

"Well, git their pants down, boys," said the old man.

The Hooker boys held the brothers and dropped their pants to the ground. They bent them over, and the old man came around with his belt. He took them one at a time and strapped them twenty licks each. They let the brothers pull their pants back up, but they kept the circle around them. Laughter could be heard in the crowd.

"I 'spect their ends air a little hot," said the old man. "We better carry 'em down to the river and cool 'em off a bit."

They dragged the brothers—by their feet—down to the boat docks. The crowd and Pa and Skeeter followed. When they got to the end of the dock, all the Hookers stopped and passed the jug.

"We'll git even with you damned swamp rats," said one of the brothers.

"We ain't worried 'bout the likes of you none," said the old man. "But jest fer sayin' that, I think the boys had better have a little contest. The oldest of you boys divide into teams of fours and see who kin throw one each of these yellow bastards the furtherest in the river, and then the team that wins kin throw the last one in. And afore the contest starts, I want to say a word." He turned to the three brothers. "If'n we ever hear of you sons of bitches botherin' a Corey agin, they'll be iron weights tied to yore backs next time we throws you in the river. Now start the contest."

Four of the boys took the first brother by the hands and feet, swang him back and forth a few times, and sent him tumbling, end over end, into the cold, muddy water. They could hear him come up snorting and fighting for the bank. This was repeated until all three had been deposited in the river. Then all the people went back and joined the dance.

It was well after the hour of midnight when the dancing stopped and the people started their journeys home. Ma and Theresa were very happy because they had made nearly every one of the dances. They were tired, and yet the trip was beautiful. The moon was high above the trees, and it made the muddy water of the river change to silver and gold. Sparky and Theresa sat in the back of one of the boats and made a wish on the Christmas moon, which was supposed to come true.

*   *   *

The Coreys got up late the next morning, ate a light breakfast, and Ma put the turkey and dressing on the hearth to bake for their big meal that night. Skeeter ran his animal traps, but they let the fish traps and the line go since this was to be a day of rest and pleasure.

In the middle of the afternoon they were sitting on the front porch when they saw a boat turn up the bayou from the river. A man was rowing, and a woman was sitting in the back. When it got closer, they saw that it was Jeff and Clarise. Pa and Skeeter jumped to their feet and ran into the house.

"Hit's Jeff and Clarise comin' up the bayou in a boat!" cried Pa.

Ma and Theresa stopped their cooking, and they all ran to the landing to wait for the boat. When it touched the bank, Jeff and Clarise jumped out, and there was much hugging and kissing and warm greetings. They went into the house and sat in the kitchen.

"We jest come to spend Christmas Day," said Jeff. "We got to catch the boat back in the mornin'."

"Tell us all about yoreself," said Pa. "We ain't heerd a word from you since the two of you been gone."

"We're livin' up at Monticello," said Jeff, "and I'm workin' in the mill. The pay's a heap better then hit air down at Mill Town. Clarise air workin' in a store, and we live in one of the mill houses. We likes hit jest fine."

"We's mouty glad to hear that, son," said Pa.

"We had to slip off the boat down at Mill Town and borrow this boat so'es we wouldn't have no trouble with them brothers of Clarise's," said Jeff.

"You don't need never to worry about that again," said Pa. "Last night down at the frolic they tried to ruff up Skeeter, and them Hooker boys got 'um and pulled their pants down and whopped their butts with a belt, and then they throwed 'em in the river. Old Man Hooker told 'em that if'n they ever messed with any of us again, they would throw 'em in the river with iron weights on their backs."

"Serves them right," said Clarise.

"I shore wish you could have been there, Jeff," said Pa.

Ma and Theresa finished the cooking, and then they had the big supper. When it was finished, they sat around and talked and sang Christmas songs until late in the night. Pa moved in and slept with Skeeter, and Ma moved in with Theresa, so Jeff and Clarise could have the big room to themselves. Pa said that this was the best Christmas he had ever spent, and they all agreed.

FIFTEEN

THE DAYS OF THE SUN were now gone, and as the weeks wore on, the days were darker and drearier. There was fog on the river every morning, and the sky was filled with clouds. The wind blew from the north, and it was cold, so it made Pa and Skeeter shiver as they went about their daily work of running traps and lines. Sometimes there was ice along the edges of the river and bayou; there was frost on the ground nearly every morning. The piles of wood did not last as long, and they had to make more and more trips into the big woods. The singing birds were gone, and they did not often see the squirrels. The nights were long, and the days were short. The snakes had disappeared completely from the swamp, and many times the trees were covered with ice. The dead limbs would break from the weight of the ice, fall into the water, and it was always a danger to Skeeter when he went under the trees. Great swarms of blackbirds flew around the clearing and the woods, and ducks were plentiful on the bayou.

The trips to town were no longer a pleasure to Pa and Skeeter for it was cold, and the wind went through their clothes, chilling their bones until they ached. The vegetables had long been gone from the garden, and since the wild poke salat was also gone, there were no greens of any kind on the table to eat. But the deer were plentiful, and this was the best time of the year to kill them. The meat was sweet and thickly coated with fat. There were plenty of ducks, and they could still now and then kill the rabbits and the squirrels, and sometimes Skeeter killed the blackbirds and Ma made pies of them. They were good, stewed tender with plenty of dumplings. Winter was not too bad in the swamps, except for the wind and the cold.

Skeeter was running his animal traps in the morning and the afternoon for fear of losing a catch, because it would not be long before he had to take the traps up. The rains would come in March, and they would have to go to Fort Henry and sell the pelts before then. They depended on the money to buy supplies to last them during the flood. The Hookers did not come by as often, because many days the weather was too bad to be on the river, and they could not take their whiskey to Mill Town.

One afternoon Pa went with Skeeter to run the animal traps. It was bitterly cold, and the swamp was filled with mist and fog rising from the water. The sky was cloudy, and it looked as if it would sleet, so they hurried from one trap to another. The first traps had nothing, but in the last they had caught a mink. Skeeter removed the animal and reset the trap. This trap was the farthest one in the swamp, and it was a long way from home; so Skeeter poled the skiff as fast as he could through the vines and cypress knees. It looked as if the clouds were flying through the tops of the trees. Pa pulled his jacket tight and wished that he had stayed at home. Skeeter brought the skiff through a group of knees and made a sharp turn along the mudbank and had almost passed it when he dug the pole into the muck and stopped. Pa looked up and saw that Skeeter's hands were shaking, and Skeeter motioned for him to look at the mudbank. Pa saw the top of a giant 'gator head with a piece of steel sticking from it. Steel Head was asleep on the mudbank, and had not heard them coming. Skeeter picked up the rifle and aimed, but then he put it back down.

"Whut's the matter with you?" asked Pa. "Go ahead and shoot whiles you got the chance."

"I started hit with a piece of steel," said Skeeter, "and I'm goin' to finish hit that way. You take the rifle, and if'n I don't kill him, then shoot."

Skeeter took his long hunting knife from his belt. He drew back the blade and threw it with all the force of his body. He had never thrown the knife so hard before, and he almost fell from the skiff. The blade buried to the hilt in the 'gator's head, just below the frog gig. Steel Head flopped over twice on the mudbank and lay dead.

Skeeter didn't trust the big 'gator even in death. He took the rifle and shot it between the eyes, then reloaded and shot it again. He would have shot again, if Pa had not told him he was wasting shells and to stop. He sat in the skiff for a few minutes and didn't say anything. He thought of the dead hogs, of the many nights and days he had hunted the 'gator, of the night he spent in the swamp and nearly lost his own life, and now the end had come so easily. He had always thought of it as being a death struggle with the 'gator, but Steel Head had not known what had hit him. It was too easy, and he almost wished he had not seen the 'gator, so that he could have tracked it down and engaged it in combat. Pa seemed to understand what was going on in his mind, for he sat in the cold wind and mist and didn't say anything. Finally Skeeter poled the skiff back to the landing.

Taking a coil of rope, they went back to the swamp in the rowboat. They tied the rope around Steel Head and pulled him from the bank, then dragged him back to the landing. He was so heavy they had to pull him up the bank an inch at a time. Ma and Theresa came out and looked and went back into the house.

When they finally got him to the back yard, they measured him; he was twenty-two feet long. Then they rolled him on his back and split him open with an ax; Skeeter pulled out his knife and worked on him. They removed all the meat and bones and threw it in the bayou, then scraped until they had all the flesh from the hide. It was dark and had started sleeting, so they went into the house and left the 'gator until morning, when they could finish with him. Ma, Pa, and Theresa were in a mood of celebration, but for some reason Skeeter did not feel as they did. He had wanted to fight the 'gator as the big bucks had fought, to slash out at each other, to tear each other until the water was red with blood, and one of them had died and sunk into the muck of the swamp. But when he remembered that it was he who had caused Steel Head to go crazy, and everything that the 'gator had killed was his fault, he was glad that it was dead—even if the end had come in the way that it had. He went in and joined in the supper, and the worries left his mind.

The next morning when they finished cleaning the hide, Skeeter pulled the gig from the alligator's head. They cut out all the meat from the neck and head, leaving the head attached to the hide. Pa said it would be best to take it to Fort Henry for it would be worth more there, so they stored it under the house.

The work was the same day after day, and the weather stayed misty and cold. Skeeter longed for the hot summer days when he could drift in the skiff and swim naked in the bayou. He would be glad when the flood came, for he wouldn't have to go out of the house. He could sit by the hearth in the kitchen, eat, and then sleep and be warm.

One day when they were up the river, Pa took up the trotline, pulled the traps into the boat, and brought them home. He told Skeeter it was time to take up the animal traps, for they would have to make the trip to Fort Henry in plenty of time, before the flood came. When Skeeter made his rounds that day, he brought the traps home with him and put them back under his bed.

"Hit's goin' to be too hard fer you and me to make that long a trip up the river by ourselves," said Pa. "Let's go up to the Hookers tomorrow and see when they air goin' next, and maybe we kin go with them."

"I think that's the right thing to do," said Ma. "You and Skeeter could never row that boat all the way to Fort Henry by yoreself."

The next morning they rowed up the river to the Hookers and asked about the trip. The old man insisted that they stay for dinner.

"We's goin' to run up a load in three days," he said, "and we'll be more then glad to have you go with us."

"Will hit be all right if'n we tow our boat behind with our pelts and supplies?" asked Pa.

"Shore hit will," he said. "Them boys could tow a barge if'n they had a mind to. And you kin bring Glesa and Theresa up here, and they kin stay till we gits back. Hit wouldn't be good to leave them down to yore place with all this bad weather we is havin'. I'm leavin' Sparky and No Moon to look after things."

"Now that's a right good idea," said Pa, "and I shore do appreciate yore invite."

"Be shore to bring some kever to take on the trip," he said, "fer hit'll take us two nights sleepin' out on the trip up, with the river gittin' swift like hit air. Hit gits mighty cold on the river at night."

Pa and Skeeter stayed for dinner and then returned home. They spent all the next day bringing pine from the big woods, so the work would not be so hard when they returned, and the following day they made ready for the trip. They rolled the pelts into little bundles and put them in croaker sack. Ma made them a bundle of sausage, corn meal, and strips of dried fish. There would be no need to take any cooking utensils, for the Hookers would have plenty.

The next morning they rolled their quilts into bundles and were on their way up the river before daylight.

The 'gator hide was so large it couldn't be put in the boat, so they tied it in the skiff and pulled it behind. The river was swift, and the boat was overloaded; it was hard work for Pa and Skeeter to row against the current. There was ice along the river, and the cold wind burned their faces. Ma and Theresa shivered in their thin cotton dresses. But despite the cold, Pa and Skeeter were sweating when they reached the Hooker landing.

They went into the house, were greeted by the old man and woman, and sat by the fire to warm. The boys were preparing for the trip, so Pa and Skeeter went back to the landing and moved the 'gator hide into the boat so they would be ready to leave when the others had finished. The fire was warm and felt good to them, and they hated to leave when the Hooker boys came in and told them it was time to go.

Pa got into the boat with the old man, Skeeter got into the other one, and they tied Pa's boat behind and started up the river. Both boats were heavily loaded, but the Hooker boys didn't seem to mind. Their backs and arms were hard from the many trips they had made up the river, and they fought the current with steady determination.

"Where in tarnation did you git sech a 'gator hide?" asked the old man.

"That's the loco 'gator what's been givin' us sech a bad time," said Pa. "Killed two of the hogs afore we got him. Skeeter killed him the other day with his knife."

"You mean that youngin' killed that big 'gator with a knife?"

"He shore did," said Pa. "Buried hit up to the hilt in its head. That boy beats ary thing I ever seed throwin' that thing."

"Well, I'm shore glad he's yore boy and a friend," said the old man. "I'd ruther be shot betwix the eyes with a gun then stuck with a knife. I'm jest downright skeered of them things."

"I don't think Skeeter would ever hurt ary man," said Pa.

At noon they pulled the boats to the bank to eat a cold dinner that the old man had brought. They rested a few minutes and moved on. The day was getting colder, and Skeeter sat in the boat and shivered, thinking of warm fires and his comfortable bed at home. Their progress was very slow, for they were fighting directly into a strong north wind. Skeeter didn't see how the Hooker boys could keep such a steady pace, but their oars never faltered for a moment. They bent forward and backward, their oars touching the water, pulling, and then coming out, shoving the boat forward a little at a time. Occasionally they would stop and take a deep drink of whiskey to warm their bodies and their spirits as well.

When the light began to fade away, they stopped at the foot of a bluff to make camp for the night. The top of the bluff was covered with tall magnolia trees, so they made camp under them to keep off some of the mist. A big fire was built, and they cooked a supper of salt pork, grits, and corn pone. The men drank some of the whiskey, then piled enough logs on the fire to keep it burning all night. They laid out their bedding in a circle around the fire. The Hookers did not stay up all night and play as they did on the fox hunt, for they were tired, and soon everyone went to bed. Skeeter rolled up in his quilt on the cold ground, tried to get warm, then moved closer to the fire and was soon asleep.

They were up by daybreak the next morning cooking breakfast and breaking up the camp. Skeeter was stiff from sleeping on the ground, but the Hookers didn't seem to be bothered by it. They cooked the sausage Pa had brought and made a corn pone. They boiled coffee in a big bucket, and the smell mixed well with the cold morning air. When breakfast was done, they put out the fire and moved on again.

The banks of the river changed appearance as they moved further north. There was not much swamp along the banks; sometimes they passed fields and meadows running right down to the water. There were hills, then long flats, and then great stretches of the swamp again. The pines grew closer to the river; sometimes they passed fields and meadows running right down to the water; sometimes they saw cottonfields lying idle or cows grazing along the river. But they never went too far at a time without seeing stretches of swamp, and the water was just as muddy and brown as it was at Mill Town. There were many ducks on the river, and Skeeter shot them as they moved along that afternoon. When it was time for them to stop to make camp, he had twelve in the boat.

They picked a thick pine grove along the river to make their camp that night. They built the fire, then cut small pine saplings to make lean-tos to sleep in. They covered the lean-tos with pine boughs and piled pine straw inside them. The pine trees were green all year, and their branches made a good roof when in the woods at night. After this was finished, they cleaned the ducks and roasted them with sticks over the fire. When they finished eating, they went to bed. The lean-tos were warm and kept out the cold wind, so the sleep was much better that night.

By noon the next day they reached the outskirts of Fort Henry. At the south end of town there was the mill that most river towns had, the mill houses, and then the Negro shacks. The boat docks were a half mile up the river from the mill, and there were many more docks than there were at Mill Town. There were several big docks for the steamboats, and wharves along the bank on which to stack the cotton and other goods that were shipped out on the river. They tied their boats to a dock and started unloading.

"Let's go uptown and git us rooms at the hotel afore we sells ary a thing," said the old man. "I looks forward to this trip ever time so'es I kin sit on one of them water fountains and git under one of them spigots of hot water and soap myself."

"Hit suits me jest fine," said Pa, "but we better sell this 'gator hide fust, cause hit's too big to tote around."

"Well, we'll leave the boys here to watch the stuff, and me and you and Skeeter'll go and sell hit."

They took the hide and carried it up the street to one of the trading posts, and the boys stayed on the docks. The street was much wider and had many more stores than the one at Mill Town. There were all kinds of shops and many saloons and show houses. The street was crowded with wagons and horses, and many people were on the sidewalks. A lot of people stopped and looked at the big 'gator hide as they passed, for they had never seen one so large before. Pa, Skeeter, and the old man carried it through the door of one of the big trading posts, and the owner came over to them.

"You let me handle this, Abner," whispered the old man. "I knows how to handle these fellows."

"That shore is a big one," said the man. "Is it for sale?"

"Hit's fer sale if'n you wants hit bad enough," said the old man.

"I'll give you twenty-five dollars," he said.

"You must want to buy jest the tail," said the old man. "They ain't many 'gators like this whut allows theyselves to git kilt."

"Well, I'll make it thirty," said the man.

"Now, ain't that jest dandy," said the old man. "Let's take hit somewhere else, boys."

He reached down as if to pick up the hide, and the man stopped him.

"Forty," he said.

"Now that sounds better," said the old man. "Make hit fifty and you got yoreself a hide. Otherwise, we's jest wastin' our time."

"Well, all right, I'll make it fifty," said the man. "You swamp rats give me a pain in the head sometimes."

He pulled out his wallet and counted out five ten-dollar bills and handed them to the old man. They went out to the street, and he handed the money to Pa.

"You see," he said, "you jest got to know how to handle them fellers."

"Well, I shore am proud," said Pa, "and I thanks you a lot."

When they were gone, the owner motioned for two clerks to help him carry the hide to the back of the store.

"I would have given a hundred dollars for a hide like this," he said. "It'll bring two hundred in Jackson."

They walked back to the docks to gather up all their supplies and goods and then went back up the street to get a room at the hotel. When they went in, the old man went up to the counter.

"Give us four rooms with big beds," he said, "and make 'em close to the water fountains and hot-water spigots."

"You mean toilets and showers," said the clerk. "Just sign here, please, and pay in advance."

The old man marked an X on the book and paid for the rooms. Pa tried to pay for his and Skeeter's, but the old man wouldn't let him. The clerk handed him the keys, and a Negro went with them to show them where the rooms were. They went inside and put all their bedding and supplies on the floor. The old man came back down to Pa's room.

"We's goin' to sell our whiskey now," he said, "but we'll save out enough to tide us over till we gits back. We's got a regular customer here that buys all we brings, so we won't have to shop around. You and Skeeter go on and sell yore pelts and meet us back here in a hour. You kin take them pelts back to the place where we sold the 'gator hide, and don't let him gyp you."

The Hookers went out with their jugs of whiskey, and Pa and Skeeter took the sack of pelts back to the trading post. They had twenty-five mink and otter pelts, and the man offered Pa a hundred dollars. Pa thought that was a good price so he took it. He thanked the man and they went back to the hotel. They waited a few minutes, and the Hookers returned.

"Let's all take one of them hot soapings and then go out and et and do the town," said the old man. "I got a hankerin' fer a bellyful of good beef steak."

Pa agreed, and they all went into the shower room at one time. They turned on only the hot water, and then took off their clothes and got under it. There were several big bars of soap in a bucket, so they passed them around and soaped each other until the floor was covered with soap suds.

"This water air hot enough to scald a hog," said the old man, "but I shore do likes it."

"I like it too," said Pa. "This air the fust time I ever stood under one of these hot-water spigots."

When they finished, the room was so full of soap suds and steam that it was almost dangerous for a person to go inside. They dressed and went outside the hotel. It was dark, and the lamps were lighted in the shop windows and along the street. They walked down the sidewalk and into a restaurant and sat at a long table. A waiter came over to them.

"Give us all one of the biggest beef steaks you got in the house," said the old man, "and bring plenty of them fried tators. Sun Up, you go back to the hotel and git a jug of whiskey. I wants to wet my whistle afore I eats."

Sun Up left and was back presently with a jug of whiskey. They passed it around the table. The waiter came over and placed knives, forks, and spoons at each place.

"What'll you folks have to drink?" he asked.

"We brought our own whiskey," said the old man. "Thank ye jest the same."

The waiter stared at the old man and then returned to the kitchen. In a few minutes he returned with the steaks and a big plate of fried potatoes.

"Don't know why he brought these knives," said the old man. "I don't never use 'em eatin' steak. I always said that if'n you had to use a knife to cut a piece of steak, hit weren't fitten to eat."

He picked up the steak with his hands and started eating. All the rest did the same. They grabbed handfuls of the potatoes and crammed in their mouths and ate a slice of bread with one bite. When they finished, they smacked their lips and all took a big drink of whiskey.

"I know where they's a good stage show," said the old man. "Do everbody want to see it?"

"I'd like to," said Skeeter. "I ain't never seed one."

"I'd like hit too," said Pa.

All the boys said they would go, so they went up the street to one of the show houses. The seats were nearly filled, so they had to sit in the back. There was a long aisle between the rows of seats, and the stage was at the rear of the building. Lamps were along both walls, and the front of the stage was filled with them. In a few minutes the curtain went up, and the show started.

In the first few acts were dancing girls, and then there was a singer and a magician. Then the girls danced some more, and there was a comedian. The old man and the boys would shout wildly when the girls danced. The last act on the program, they announced, would be Vetro, the world's greatest knife thrower. They brought out a target board, and the man made several throws at it. Then a woman stood against it, and he threw knives and made an outline against her body. Then they placed the ace of a deck of cards against the target, and he said he would perform the greatest feat of all time: he would split the center of the card at forty feet. He backed off and threw, and missed the first time. Then he threw, and the knife split the center of the card. The crowd shouted and clapped, and the women stared in wonder.

When the noise stopped, the old man jumped to his feet and shouted: "Who all wants to bet that this boy here can't do that from the door here?"

It was well over a hundred feet to the door. Several men jumped up and shouted for him to sit down, and then he pulled out a roll of bills and waved them, and several men came over to cover the bet. The old man bet every cent he had on the feat.

"How much money you got, Abner?" he asked.

"I got a hundred and fifty dollars."

"Hand it here and I'll bet hit fer you," said the old man.

Pa thought long and hard about handing over their supply money, but he finally gave it to the old man. Skeeter just sat and didn't say anything.

"We got some more here," shouted the old man, and several more men came over and got in on the betting. They let the house owner hold the money. The old man had bet three hundred dollars, plus Pa's money. When the betting was all done, everyone sat down. They turned the target towards the door, and Skeeter got up and pulled out his knife.

"If'n you'll hit that shot I'll buy you enough likker sticks to last a year," said the old man.

Skeeter thought of what would happen if he did not make the throw hit the card, of what Ma would say when they came back without supplies, and how they wouldn't have any money to buy food to last during the flood. He wished the old man had kept his seat, but now there was nothing to do but go ahead.

Skeeter walked back to the door and stood for a moment. A hush swept over the crowd, and the drop of a pin could have been heard. He raised his hand, hesitated for a moment, and sent the knife flying through the air. It sailed over the end of the stage and split the card dead in the center.

The old man and Hooker boys jumped up and down and shouted as loud as they could. The crowd went wild, and Pa felt a big relief. Skeeter just went down the aisle and got his knife, came back, and sat down. The old man got the money and counted out Pa three hundred dollars, then put the rest in his pocket. When they were out of the show house, the old man bought Skeeter a big bag of likker sticks. They went to see every other show in town, and the old man paid the admissions. It was after midnight when they returned to the hotel and went to bed.

The next morning they got up and went out of the hotel to get breakfast. It was sleeting, and the wind blew against their faces. Skeeter thought of the trip home and shuddered. They went into the same restaurant they had been in the night before, and each ate a half dozen eggs and all the hot biscuits the waiter could bring out. It was a real treat for Pa and Skeeter, for they could not afford the flour to make biscuits at home, and they very seldom ate eggs. When they finished, they went back to the hotel.

"They ain't no use in us goin' back in them boats and freezin' to death while I got all this money," said the old man. "I always did have a hankerin' to ride on them steamboats, so let's take hit back down. We'll be home a little after dark tonight."

"Whut about the boats?" asked Pa.

"We kin tie 'em to the side of the steamboat and pull 'em back down. Then we kin git off at the house and save comin' back from Mill Town."

Skeeter was thrilled at the idea of riding the steamboat. He had always wanted to ride one.

"We'll go with you and Skeeter to buy yore supplies, and then go on down to the docks. That boat'll leave in about a hour."

They took their belongings, left the hotel, and went to one of the stores for Pa to buy the supplies. Pa bought all the food they would need, and several sides of pork, and he bought both Ma and Theresa a new pair of shoes and a dress, and he got himself and Skeeter each a new pair of shoes and a new jacket. He bought Ma several bottles of snuff, Theresa a big bag of licorice sticks, plenty of shot for his gun, and several boxes of shells for Skeeter. They carried the supplies down to the docks and loaded them in the boats. The steamboat was at the dock, so the old man bought the tickets and they went aboard.

Sun Up and Sun Down rowed the boats around to the side of the steamboat and threw the lines up to the old man and Pa. They tied them to the rail and the boys climbed up. The lines were cast off from the dock, and the boat started down the river.

They stood around the rail and watched while the boat got under way, but the sleet was getting worse so they went inside. The stateroom was warm, and it felt good to them, so they started passing the jug. Before long they were all fairly drunk and were in need of excitement.

"Let's go blow the whistle," said the old man. "I always did want to blow one of them steamboat whistles."

They got up and went outside and climbed the ladder going to the wheelhouse. All of them carried their guns. The captain met them at the door of the wheelhouse and stopped them.

"You can't come up here," he said. "We don't allow passengers up here."

"We is here," said the old man, "and besides, we don't want to do nothin' but blow the whistle."

"We just can't allow that," said the captain.

"Well, if'n you don't mind," said the old man, "we jest goin' to do hit anyway. Now step aside if'n you don't want that little house blowed full of holes."

They shoved the captain aside and walked in the wheelhouse. The old man grabbed the whistle cord and pulled it. The whistle blew, and he shouted and pulled it again. Then he stepped aside, and the others came up one at a time and pulled the cord. One of the other passengers came up and wanted to know if the boat was in trouble, but when he saw the bearded men and the guns, he slipped back down the ladder.

When it was noon, they all went down to eat in the mess and then returned to the wheelhouse and started blowing the whistle again. The didn't stop until it was dark, and the old man knew they would soon be at the house.

"We wants to git off in a little piece," he said.

"I can't stop the boat till we get to Mill Town," said the captain. "It's against the rules."

"Well, you better jest break the rules and throw this thing in reverse," said the old man, "or I'll do hit fer you."

"I guess it'll be worth it to get rid of you," said the captain. "Both of my ears are busted now."

The captain stopped the boat, and they started down the ladder to get off. The old man turned and looked at the captain.

"Thanks fer lettin' us blow the whistle," he said, and went on down the ladder. They climbed down the lines into the boats, a deck hand cast them off, and they rowed over to the landing. The women were waiting for them at the landing.

"Whut in the world were that boat whistle cuttin' up so fer?" asked the old woman. "And whut air you all doin' gittin' off that boat?"

"Let's git out of the cold and we'll tell you all about it," said the old man. "Abner and the women air goin' to stay here tonight and go on home in the mornin'."

They walked into the house and warmed by the fire. The old man told them about the trip and about Skeeter throwing the knife and winning all the money. Pa told Ma what all he had brought and of the money he still had left. It made her very happy, and she could hardly wait to get home and try on the dress and shoes.

The women cooked supper, and the men brought out some more jugs. After supper the boys got out the fiddles and guitars and played lively music. They danced and drank and had a frolic almost as good as the one at Christmas.

SIXTEEN

THE COREY FAMILY was happy now, knowing they would not be hungry during the flood. The kitchen shelf was well stocked with meal, coffee, sugar, lard, salt, smoked sausage, and hams, and the salt pork hung from the rafters. There were ears of corn to be parched over the hearth, potatoes to be baked, and they had the crocks of fresh pork packed down in lard. Ma and Theresa tried on their new dresses and shoes many times.

There was much work to be done before the flood came. They had to bring in pine from the woods and stack it in the house, the roof had to be packed with moss, and everything they owned that floated had to be put in the house or stored on the roof. The nets and the line were brought in, and the skiff was tied to the side of the house. After they finished with the roof, they spent most of their time bringing pine from the woods. When there was no more room in the kitchen, they stacked it on the back stoop, because the pine would have to last several weeks.

One day they took their guns with them to the woods and killed a young buck. They built another smoke house in which to smoke it, and when they were finished, it was hung from the kitchen rafters with the other meats. The venison would taste good and would be a change from the pork.

When the work was finished, there wasn't much for Pa and Skeeter to do during the day, so they reset the trotline in the river. They could eat the fish until the rains came and save the other meats. When they finished running the line every morning, they spent the rest of the day hunting ducks on the bayou and along the swamp, and they went into the woods to hunt turkey. They did not bait the turkeys now but stalked them in the trees and on the ground, for one turkey was all that they could eat at a time, and they were hunting mostly to take up their time. They could have killed many bucks but did not do so. Once they killed a large buck and took it to the Hookers, for they knew that the Hookers did not have much time to hunt and would like the fresh venison. Other than that they watched the deer at their play and let them go. One night before supper Skeeter was sitting in the kitchen rigging a giant sethook and line. Ma stopped her cooking and watched him for a few minutes.

"Where in the world did you git sech a big outfit like that?" she asked.

"I got hit down at Mill Town one day," he said.

"Whut you plannin' on doin' with it?" asked Ma. "They ain't no fish big enough to swaller that thing."

"I'm goin' to ketch me a gar," said Skeeter.

"You goin' to fool around with them gar and git yoreself in another mess like you did with that big 'gator," said Ma. "You better worry 'bout ketchin' catfish and leave them big devils alone."

"How'd you like to have a good mess of gar meat fer supper tomorrow night?" asked Skeeter.

"Now you shet up sech talk as that or git out'n the kitchen," said Ma. "I ain't goin' to have you in here talkin' 'bout gar meat whiles we's fixin' supper."

"If'n you got hongry enough I bet you'd eat it," said Skeeter, "and then yore nose would grow long and turn to a sword, and yore arms would turn to fins, and you'd git scales all over you and then jump in the river, then fust things you knows you'd be eatin' raw squirrel meat and gittin' in traps."

"You shet up right this minute! You gives me the creeps talkin' like thet. Now git on out of here till I calls you." Skeeter got up and went to his room to finish rigging the line.

The next morning he went up the river and took the big hook and line with him. He selected a good, strong, willow limb that hung over the water and tied the line to it so, if he hung a gar, the limb would give and there would not be much tension on the line. If he tied it to a log or a stake or anything that would not give, the gar could easily break it. He put a whole squirrel on the giant hook and lowered it into the water and returned home.

The next morning when he went back, the willow limb was not moving, so he thought he had not made a catch. He grabbed the line to see if the bait was still on the hook, and it jerked back out of his hands. The whole willow limb shot under the water. He knew that he had something big, and it would be no use to try to pull it out of the water, so he left it and went on home. The fish would eventually wear itself out, and then he could pull it up. He didn't say anything about it when he reached home, but that afternoon he went to see if he could pull it up, and he still could not move it. The next morning it was the same way, and he left the line again. For three days he tried to pull the line up, and though he could get it up a little more each day, he could not get the fish to the top of the water.

The fourth morning he took the gaff and his rifle with him. He pulled with all his strength, and the line moved slowly upward. The point of a bill came out of the water, and before the head reached the surface, the bill was much higher than the sides of the boat. The gar shot downward and almost jerked Skeeter from the boat, but he held the line tight. When it was still for a minute, he moved the line to his left hand and grabbed the gaff and jerked it through the gar's mouth. Again he had to hold on with all his strength to keep from being pulled from the boat. When it settled down again, he held the gaff with his left hand and picked up the rifle, cocked it, and shot the gar through the head. It jumped so hard he had to let the gaff go. A thin streak of blood came to the surface, and the line was still. When he raised it this time, there was no resistance, but pulling in the dead weight was hard work. The gaff was still in its mouth so he pulled it up. When the gar finally floated up, it was almost as long as the boat and weighed at least three-hundred pounds. Skeeter thought it was the ugliest thing he had ever seen. It scared him just looking at it, so he tied the line to the rear seat and pulled the gar down the river.

When he reached the landing, he called the family out to look at it. They came down to the landing and stared at the gar floating in the water.

"How did you ever git that thing out?" asked Pa.

"Hit's been on the hook five days," said Skeeter, "and I was jest now able to git hit to the top."

"Hit scares me," said Theresa. "If'n I knowed that sech as that were runnin' aroun' in the river, I'd never even poke my hand under the water."

"Whut you goin' to do with hit?" asked Ma.

"I thought me and Pa would float hit down the river and show hit to Mr. Blanch," said Skeeter.

"Well, I'll be glad when you gits hit away from here," said Ma.

The next morning Pa and Skeeter pulled the gar down the river to Mill Town and got Mr. Blanch to come from the market and look at it. He said it was the biggest fish he had ever seen, and he didn't see how a small boy like Skeeter had landed it. It made Skeeter feel proud when he heard that, and it made Pa feel good too, for he knew that if Skeeter could land a gar that size he could do anything a man could do on the river. Mr. Blanch said he would like to have it to send away and have a trophy made of it, so they got two men to help and took it to the market. Mr. Blanch gave Skeeter a dollar and he was very happy for he did not think the gar would be worth anything. They rowed back up the river.

Each day Pa would watch the sky to see if he thought the rains were coming. Some days they had sun, but most of them were cloudy and dark. Even when the sun was out, the wind was still cold and burned their faces.

One night the wind became harder as it blew against the house, and they knew the rains would come the next day. When Pa and Skeeter went out the following morning, they had to fight against the wind to get to the boat. The marsh grass was bent flat against the ground, and moss was blowing from the cypress trees. The black clouds were flying by overhead, and there was hardly any light. The clouds were so low Skeeter thought he could reach up and touch them. When they reached the river, the rain started, and it felt like hail, as the wind blew it against their faces. It was hard to row the boat up the river. Leaves and moss and dead limbs were blowing into the water, and the wind made churning waves of water sweep down the river. When they reached the line, the rain was so heavy they could not see more than twenty feet ahead of them. They threw the fish from the line as they pulled it in, and started back down the river.

The rain was cold, and they thought they would never reach the landing. When they finally got there, they pulled the boat up the bank and tied it to the house. They brought the oars and the line inside with them. It was near noon, but it was dark as night. Limbs blew against the house, and the clouds dropped lower and lower until it looked as if they would come into the house. Great sheets of rain beat against the ground and the bayou so that even the water in the bayou was muddy.

The wind continued for another day and then stopped. The rain got harder until finally they could not see as far as the bayou. It beat against the roof and tried to come in, but Pa and Skeeter had done a good job, and the roof turned it away.

It was warm and pleasant inside. They liked the noise of the rain beating against the house, and the sleep at night was sound. Skeeter liked to lie in his bed and listen to its patter on the cypress shingles. Each did what he pleased during the day; the meals were bountiful; and at night the family sat around the hearth and parched corn and told each other tales that had been kept secret to tell during the rains. Skeeter told of the day he had seen the two bucks fight, but he never told about the night in the swamp. They sang and played games, and sometimes Pa and Ma drank too much whiskey the Hookers had given them and showed Skeeter and Theresa how they danced during their courting days.

The rain lasted for six days, and the water rose a little each day. When the water from far up the river started down, it rose much faster. When the rain had stopped, it was still cloudy and was bitterly cold outside. The water crept up the bank of the bayou and into the yard, and finally they could look out and see only a sea of muddy water. The top of the marsh grass could not be seen, and the water rose to within five feet of the floor of the house. The Coreys had many more days yet to stay in the house.

Finally the sun came out, and the water stopped rising. They could stand on the porch and see water in all directions. Logs and trash swept against the side of the house and stuck against the pilings, then went under and floated away. The water was very swift and left brown foam floating everywhere.

Then the water began to fall, dropping lower and lower each day, until finally the marsh grass could be seen, and the water was back in the banks of the bayou. They had been in the house three weeks without touching the ground.

The first day Pa and Skeeter went out they bogged up to their knees in mud, so they did not try it again for several days. In a few days the ground was dry enough to walk on. They pulled the boat and the skiff back to the landing and put the fish box back in the bayou.

There was almost as much work to be done cleaning up after the flood as there was preparing for it. Big drifts of trash and logs were all over the clearing and under the house, and it took days to clean them up. Sometimes the boat or the skiff was hit by a drifting log and had to be repaired. The pine was nearly gone, and they had to bring more from the woods. After several days the work was done, and they were ready to start fishing again.

"I shore am glad to see the bayou clear again," said Pa. "I done got me a bait of drinkin' that muddy water. Hit'll take a month to wash the mud from my belly."

"Where we goin' to set the traps, Pa?" asked Skeeter.

"Let's set 'em at the head of the bayou," he said. "They's lots of them big catfish been washed up into the swamp, and we kin ketch 'em as they start back to the river."

"We goin' to put out the line, too?" asked Skeeter.

"Tain't no use to put the line back in the river fer a while yet," said Pa. "They's still too much trash and logs washin' down it. That line would git tore up afore we got hit in the river good."

"After we gits the traps sot, let's go in the swamp giggin'," said Skeeter. "Last year after the flood I seed lots of them big catfish swimmin' aroun' in the shallow water."

"We'll give hit a try," said Pa, "but fust let's git these traps on out. You go in the house and git the stakes whiles I loads 'em in the boat."

When Skeeter came back, they got into the boat and went up the bayou. They placed the traps at the head of the bayou, facing the swamp, so they would catch all the fish that tried to get back to the river. When they returned to the house, dinner was ready, so they washed up and sat down at the table.

"You and Skeeter don't plan nothin' fer tomorrow," said Ma. "Everthing we got in this house has to be washed, and hit's jest too big a job fer me and Theresa. We better git it done whiles this weather air good, so'es you all kin jest stay here and help."

"I wasn't cut out to be no washwoman," said Pa, "but we'll stay and help jest to keep peace."

After dinner, Skeeter got out the gig, and he and Pa poled up the bayou in the skiff. Skeeter stood in the bow, and Pa handled the pole.

"Hit shore feels a lots better to be polin' aroun' the edges of the swamp knowin' that ole Steel Head ain't behind some log waitin' fer us," said Pa. "I jest couldn't feel safe knowin' that varment were runnin' aroun' loose."

"Hit do feel a mite better," said Skeeter. "Pole her aroun' that hollow log, Pa."

Pa poled the skiff alongside a hollow log that was half submerged in the water, and Skeeter lay down in the skiff and ran his hand into the log. He moved it around and around the inside of the log, and then drew it out. He had a catfish gripped by the mouth, and he held it up for Pa to see.

"Now, where in the world did you learn to do a thing like that?" asked Pa.

"Old Uncle Jobe told me that's the way they used to ketch fish all the time," said Skeeter. "He said they did hit along the rocks in the river when hit was down and caught lots of fish that way."

"You goin' to stick yore hand in the wrong thing's mouth, too. Whut if'n you reached in there and pulled out a snake?"

"They ain't no snakes out yit, and if'n they wus, he'd probably run out the other end of the log. I ain't skeered of hit, Pa."

"Well, you be careful and don't let none of them fish bite a plug out'n you. And if'n you pull out a bull 'gator and ain't got no hand left, don't come pore-mouthin' aroun' me."

"I think I seed a big 'un swimmin' aroun' over there. Pole over a little closer and let's have a look at hit."

Pa poled the skiff slowly forward, and Skeeter kept the gig raised in the air above his head. He looked around carefully and then sent the gig flying into the water. He grabbed the handle and pulled a large catfish into the skiff.

"Got him right betwix the eyes. I bet you we fill up the skiff afore we gits done."

"Well, if'n we do, we'll jest have to go to Mill Town and then fight that river back up. Them fish you hits with the gig ain't goin' to live long enough fer us to wait fer the river to slow down."

Pa poled the skiff all around the edges of the swamp, and Skeeter reached in logs and threw the gig until the skiff was loaded to capacity with fish. When it would hold no more, they started back to the bayou.

"We should uv been doin' this after the flood ever year," said Pa. "This air more fish then we kin ketch in the traps."

"Hit does do right good, don't it, Pa? I ought to take Uncle Jobe one of these fish fer givin' me that idea. He tole me when I come back again he were goin' to tell me another way we could ketch fish in the river jest after the flood."

"If'n we kin keep gittin' 'em like this, we may kin get enough money to buy us stuff to make a new boat. That old one shore ain't much longer in this world."

"I believe we kin do hit, Pa."

When they reached the landing, they strung all the fish and put them in the box in the bayou. They washed their hands in the bayou and went in the house for supper. It was not ready, so they sat at the table and waited.

"I think we better put off that wash till day after tomorrow," said Pa. "Me and Skeeter done caught a plum boatload of fish in the swamp this afternoon, and we better take 'em to town tomorrow."

"Why can't you put that off instead?" asked Ma.

"Most of 'ems got holes in their heads and won't live. Mr. Blanch don't like hit when the fish ain't fresh, and he's always give us more than the others cause we don't never bring him no bad fish."

"Well, me and Theresa will jest do hit ourselves. You and Skeeter git that washpot from under the house and build a fire under hit afore you leaves in the mornin'. And I don't see how you figger you'll ever git back up the river with hit runnin' like a hound dog chasin' a fox."

"We'll stick close to the bank and make it somehow. I shore ain't goin' to let that fish stay here and sperl. We goin' to try to git enough spare money to build us a new boat."

"Well, jest the same you better be mouty kerful on that river tomorrow. I ain't aimin' to be no widder woman and be left in this swamp by myself."

"Why, purty as you air you'd have another man in no time at all," laughed Pa.

"Now, quit makin' fun of me, afore I throw the supper out in the back yard, and then you would come sniffin' aroun' and talkin' to me." She had a smile on her face so Pa knew that he had not made her mad with his teasing.

"I were jest tryin' to tell you how purty you are, and don't worry about bein' no widder woman, 'cause I ain't got no hankerin' to be gar bait on the bottom of that muddy river."

After breakfast was done the next morning, Pa and Skeeter brought the big iron washpot from under the house and filled it with water. They built a fire under it for the water to boil, then tied a rope from the back stoop to a tree to use for a line to hang the clothes on when the washing was done. They put the mattresses out to sun and brought all the quilts and clothes out to the washpot. When this was done, they loaded the boat to leave.

They did not mind getting a late start, for Pa was afraid of being on the river before daylight. The river was most dangerous just after the flood. The current was swift and treacherous, and big logs raced down the middle. Whirlpools would suck logs under, and then send them shooting back into the air. If one hit a boat, it would smash it to pieces. They stopped the boat at the mouth of the bayou and watched the boiling muddy water race by in front of them.

"I almost hates to go out in hit," said Pa. "Hold on to yore backbone when we hits that current, and if'n you see a log go under, head fer the bank as quick as you kin, and fer gosh sakes don't let the boat git sideways, or we'll be gone fer shore."

"I think I kin handle my side if'n you kin handle yores," said Skeeter.

They slowly rowed the boat into the river, and when the current caught it, the boat shot downstream like a bullet. The water boiled and splashed around it, and Pa and Skeeter fought to keep the bow pointed downstream.

"Even the Hookers ain't never gone this fast," shouted Pa. "I believe she's goin' to take to the air and fly."

The trees seemed to fly by as the boat sped along with the current. The water was filled with trash, logs, and the dead bodies of small animals, all engrossed in a mad race down the river. When Pa and Skeeter came to curves in the river, they had to fight with the oars to keep the boat from being smashed into the bank. Big whirlpools were around the edges, and the water boiled and bubbled around them. Bits of trash would go around and around in them and then disappear beneath the surface. Pa kept glancing back to keep a watch for logs. He saw a big one hit a whirlpool, spin around, and then disappear.

"Let's fight her into the bank quick!" he shouted. "They's a log comin'!"

They pulled with the oars and maneuvered the boat close to the bank. Limbs were hanging just over the water, and they had to lie down sometimes to keep from being knocked from the boat. They looked down the river and saw the log shoot out of the muddy water and sail high into the air. It came down with a splash and raced on in front of them.

"What will happen if'n one of them logs were to come up under a steamboat like that?" asked Skeeter.

"I guess hit would go right up through the smokestack," said Pa. "I shore wouldn't want to ride one of them boats with the river like this."

They pulled the boat back into the middle of the river, and the docks at Mill Town came into sight.

"Whut we goin' to do now?" asked Skeeter. "If'n we head her into them docks goin' like this we'll take docks and all on down the river with us."

"I don't know jest exactly whut to do," said Pa, "but we shore got to do somethin' quick or we'll be past Mill Town afore we sees hit good."

"Why don't we turn around in the boat and row back the other way, Pa? Maybe that'll slow her down a mite."

"I guess that's 'bout the only thing we kin do."

They turned around and started pulling the oars as hard as they could. It slowed the boat down a little but not enough. They steered it out of the current, and it headed straight for the docks. They pulled the oars with all their might, but they couldn't stop the movement of the boat. It was nearing the end of the docks.

"You stand up and grab one of the pilings and hold on," shouted Pa, "and I'll try to throw the rope over hit."

When the boat reached the end of the docks, Skeeter grabbed one of the pilings and hooked his feet to the side of the boat. He thought his body would break in two. The boat swung around, but before Pa could throw the line over the piling, Skeeter's feet slipped and he was left dangling on the piling. The boat swung around and hit the bank, and stuck against a tree in the water. Pa jumped out, tied the line to another tree, and raced back up the bank to the dock. He pulled Skeeter up from the piling, and they both went down and pulled the boat along the bank to the dock. Then they tied it up.

"That's the dernest landin' I ever seed made," said Pa. "I shore don't want to do that again."

"I ain't got no hankerin' to try hit again neither."

They got the fish out of the boat and started to the market, and Skeeter kept one to give Uncle Jobe.

"You run on down there and take him that fish whiles these air bein' weighed, and then hurry on back," said Pa. "We got to start back jest as soon as I gets paid, 'cause hit's goin' to be somethin' tryin' to git back up that river."

"Ain't you goin' to buy any supplies?" asked Skeeter.

"We still got enough at home without buyin' none today," said Pa. "And hit'll be all we kin do to pull ourselves back without tryin' to take any supplies."

They took the fish to the market and Skeeter ran down the lane to Uncle Jobe's. They greeted each other, and Skeeter handed him the fish.

"I brought you a catfish to et," said Skeeter. "I done like you tole me about them logs and got a bunch of 'em."

"I knowed you would," said Uncle Jobe. "I'm goin' to give you somethin' else to git 'em with, too."

He got up and went into the shack and returned with a paper bag in his hand. He handed it to Skeeter and then sat back down.

"Now you do jest like I tells you and you'll git plenty," he said. "Git you a gallon jug and pour this stuff in hit. Don't put no top on hit, neither. Then tie a short piece of rope to the top of the jug, and git you a weight and tie to it. Find you a place in the river where they's a cove and the water ain't runnin' swift, and throw this in. Jest git back a ways and hit will do the rest."

"I shore thanks you," said Skeeter. "Me and Pa air tryin' to git enough extra fish to git up the money to build a new boat."

"Well, you air sho' welcome, and jest bring me another cat next time you comes. I sho' like them cats when they air fried good and brown."

Skeeter skipped back up the lane with the bag. Pa was waiting for him in front of the market.

"Whut's that you got in that bag?" asked Pa.

"Hit's somethin' Uncle Jobe give me to catch us some more extra fish. I'll show you how hit works when we gits the chance."

They went back to the dock and got into the boat. Skeeter untied the line, and they started the trip home. Several times they didn't think they would make it. They had to stay close to the bank and row hard to move the boat forward. Many times they grabbed limbs and held the boat so they could stop and rest. The current shoved them back every time their oars came out of the water, and the boat moved forward only a little more than it moved back each time. It took them the rest of the morning and all afternoon to reach the mouth of the bayou, and when they finally reached the landing, they had to sit and rest before they could get out of the boat. Their arms and backs ached worse than they had ever done before. They went into the house and went to bed without eating any supper.

"Never thought I'd see the day when you two would go to bed without eatin' no supper," Ma said, the next morning. "That river must have really been somethin' to git you that way."

"Hit were like tryin' to tow one of them steamboats up stream with a paddle," said Pa. "I ain't got no hankerin' to try that again afore the river slows up a mite."

Pa and Skeeter didn't gig any more fish, but they caught so many in the traps that the fish box wouldn't hold any more. The river didn't go down any, and the current stayed just as swift, so they finally had to make another trip to town and fight the river as they had before.

"Hit looks like we mout as well git used to fightin' the river and go on abouts our business," said Pa, "cause hit don't look like it's goin' to slow down fer a while yet. They must have been a powerful lot of water som-ers fer hit to keep comin' like this."

"Why don't we go up to West Cut and try this stuff Uncle Jobe give me?" asked Skeeter. "Today would be a good day fer hit."

"I guess hit suits me," said Pa. "If'n we keeps gettin' the fish likes we is now we'll shore have that new boat afore long."

"We'll need one of them empty whiskey jugs, a piece of rope and a weight," said Skeeter. "You git the jug, and I'll git the rest."

This was the first time they had been to West Cut since the flood, and the cove had been washed out and was much bigger than it was before. The water in the cove was not swift, and now it hardly moved at all. When they had pulled the boat to the bank, Skeeter started doing what Uncle Jobe had told him to do.

"Let me look at that stuff," said Pa. Skeeter handed him the bag and he examined it and handed it back to Skeeter. "Hit looks like some kind of lime."

Skeeter poured it into the jug and tied the rope to the weight and mouth of the jug.

"He said to jest throw it in the water and git out'n the way," said Skeeter.

"I don't see whut hit kin do to ketch fish," said Pa. "Maybe the fish air supposed to eat the stuff as it comes out'n the jug and git sick. But I'd shore hate to have to sit here and wait that long."

"Well, I mout as well throw hit in and see whut happens. Push her out in the middle."

Pa pushed the boat out in the cove and Skeeter threw the jug into the water. The weight pulled it down, and it sank from sight. Pa rowed the boat back out of the way.

"I ain't seed nothin' happen," said Pa.

"Maybe hit ain't had time yit," said Skeeter. "They's bubbles comin' up now."

They sat for a few seconds watching the water, and then a muffled explosion went off deep below them. A geyser of water shot into the air and poured down on them. The boat rocked and nearly threw them into the river.

"Whut in the hell air that nigger tryin' to do!" shouted Pa. "He done dern near got us kilt, and I ain't seed no fish yit!"

"Look at that!" shouted Skeeter, and pointed to the middle of the cove.

Dozens of fish were rising to the surface and floating around in the water. There were big ones, little ones, and they kept coming up until the water was filled with fish.

"Well, I'll be derned," said Pa. "I wouldn't believe it if'n I weren't seeing hit with my own eyes. Let's git busy."

They rowed the boat around and scooped the fish out of the water with their hands. When they were through, the boat was loaded with fish.

"Whut you think of hit now?" asked Skeeter. "Old Uncle Jobe shore do know a lot of things, don't he?"

"I's powerful glad to git all these fish," said Pa, "but I'll be dogged if'n we air ever goin' to do that again. We could have got blowed slam out'n the boat foolin' with that stuff, whutever hit were. You jest thank Uncle Jobe, but don't take none uv that stuff no more."

They made one more trip down the raging river, and then the current began to slow down. The water dropped a little each day, and finally it was back down to normal. The trips to town were not so hard now, and they went every Saturday and brought back supplies. Each time they had a little money left and put it with their other savings. They put the line back into the river, and the fishing stayed good. The Coreys were beginning to prosper a little.

"If'n this keeps up we'll have enough money to git the boat and maybe enough to tide us through the low water this summer," said Pa. "Hit shore would please me if'n I didn't have to work at the mill this summer. Maybe me and Skeeter would have enough time to clear enough land to have a big corn crop, and we could stop havin' to buy so much meal."

"Hit would shore be nice," said Ma, "and maybe the Lord will be good to us, and hit will be that way."

"I shore hope He is," said Pa. "I shore hope He is."

SEVENTEEN

IT WAS NOT LONG before all traces of the flood were gone. The wind blew the drifts of trash and leaves from along the river banks, and the sun dried out the low places of ground. Buzzards flew along the bank in search of the dead animals, and when found, devoured them. The winds still blew, and sometimes it was cold, but the days were more sunny than cloudy. When they had rain, it was gentle, and the sun was setting later in the west.

One day Skeeter found a group of small, blue violets growing in the clearing, and a few days later he saw a robin, and he knew spring had come again. It could be felt in the air, on the river, and even the trees seemed to sense it and sway in anticipation of the new coat of leaves they would get. The marsh grass was turning green again, and the ducks were flying away to the north. The trees were covered with small buds. The sky was filled with great white clouds, mixed with patches of deep blue, and the sun was beginning to feel warm and pleasant. The thick wool jacket was not comfortable during the day, the shoes would soon come off, and the water of the bayou would soon be warm enough to swim in.

Each day the tiny buds on the trees grew; the snakes and turtles came out to sun themselves on logs; and the grass turned greener. The squirrels came out early in the morning, played in the trees all day, and the baby frogs began to bellow in the swamp at night. The katydids chirped at sundown, and the fireflies filled the night with thousands of small diamonds sparkling in the darkness. The tiny buds of the trees grew until they burst, and everything was splashed with green. Spring had arrived with all her glory, and the river was beautiful again.

Gone were the bare limbs that raised themselves in solemn submission to the black clouds of the sky, and gone were the cold winds and rains that burned the face and chilled the spirits. The minnows swam in the bayou, the birds sang to the air, the animals rejoiced that the dark days were behind, and the sky was filled with light.

The clean, black ground of the garden was broken into rows, and the seeds were covered with the cool soil. The sun would warm them, the gentle rains would quench their thirst, the rich black soil would nourish them, and they would burst from the ground in appreciation of spring. It was a wonderful time for the birds of the air, the animals of the woods, the reptiles of the swamp, the plants of the ground, the humans of the clearing. All were glad to be alive, and they drank of the sun and air until they were drunk with the intoxication of spring.

The trips to town were pleasant again. The trees and vines were beautiful, and Pa and Skeeter could see the small animals at play. Birds sang to them, crows shouted at them, squirrels talked to them, and the turtles paid no heed to them. Everything looked different, except the water of the river; it kept its muddy color even though all else had changed. There could be sun, or rain, or it could be winter or spring, but the brown water of the river stayed the same. If it was low, or if it was raging across the marsh flats and into the clearing, it made no difference. It paid no heed to what was going on around it; it was unchangeable in its ways. It seemed that God made it to be muddy, and muddy it would be, regardless of what came or went, of what traveled up and down its far reaches.

The days rolled on, and the fishing stayed good, and sometimes Pa and Skeeter had to make two trips to town a week to sell the fish. This turn of good fortune made the family happy, and there were no flashes of temper or ill feelings among them. The days seemed more sunny than ever, and the sky seemed bluer than they had ever known it. Finally Pa decided that the savings were enough for the new boat and to keep him at the clearing all summer, so one morning they rowed up to the Hookers to see about the supplies to do the building. The old man saw them coming and met them at the landing. They exchanged greetings and went to the house.

"You ain't goin' to Fort Henry ary time soon, air you?" asked Pa.

"Why shore," said the old man. "We's goin' the fust of the week. Hit's the fust time we been up this spring, and we got a big load to run up. Air they somethin' we could git fer you?"

"Yes," said Pa, "if'n you don't mind. The fishin' has been good, so me and Skeeter has saved up enough to git the stuff to build us a new boat. That old one air jest about shot, and we wants one that air bigger and kin haul more stuff. I knowed you was mighty good on buyin', and you knows more about buildin' boats than ary man abouts here, so I'd shore appreciate hit if'n you would git the stuff fer me."

"I'll shore be glad to do hit, Abner," he said. "I'll git the best stuff I kin find, so'es you will have as good a boat as ary man on the river. When we gits back, me and the boys will build hit up to the house and bring hit down to you. We kin git it done in a day."

"That'd be mighty nice," said Pa, "but we shore willin' to help with the buildin'. We ain't askin' fer you to do it all."

"I know you ain't," said the old man, "but we'd right well enjoy hit, and then it would be a good surprise fer you when you first sees hit."

"Well, they's one more thing," said Pa. "Skeeter here wants the boat painted, so git enough paint to do hit and one of them breshes to put it on with."

"Whut color you want?" asked the old man.

"Red," said Skeeter.

"Then red it will be," said the old man. "That'll shore make a purty-lookin' boat."

Pa gave the old man the money, and they went back down the river. They were both excited the rest of the week and could hardly wait until the Hookers got the material and finished the boat. They did not even enjoy their Saturday trip to Mill Town for thinking about the boat. It was the only thing on their minds, and they could have no peace until they saw the finished boat. Ma and Theresa were excited, too, but not as much as Pa and Skeeter.

One morning, the first of the week, Pa was at the landing and saw a boat with three men in it coming up the bayou, and he watched as it came toward the landing. The men were dressed in fancy hunting clothes and carried guns, so Pa knew they were not swamp folks. When they got closer, he recognized them as the three Smith brothers and could see that they were drunk and had several empty jugs in their boat. They pulled the boat to the landing and walked up the bank, one of them bringing his gun.

"Howdy," said Pa. "Glad to see you fellers done got friendly and come a callin'. Come on in and sit a spell."

"Shet yore goddam mouth," said one of the brothers. "We ain't come callin' on no low son of a bitch like you. You got whiskey to sell?"

"I shore ain't," said Pa. "I don't make no whiskey; I jest fish."

"He's lyin'!" said one of the men. "All these damned swamp rats lie like that."

"I ain't tellin' no lie," said Pa, "and I ain't wantin' no trouble from you fellers. I jest ain't got no whiskey, but if'n I did, you'd be welcome to hit. You kin git some 'bout five mile up the river, if you wants to go there."

"We want it now," said the brother. "He's lyin'. Hold the gun on him, and I'll go look in his house."

The brother with the gun pointed the barrel at Pa, while one of the others staggered to the house. He climbed the back steps and went in.

"Don't make a move," said the one with the gun. "I been wantin' to kill me a swamp rat, and I'd jest as soon blow yore brains all over this bayou."

Pa did not move, and then he heard Theresa scream. He turned and saw the man shove Ma down the back steps and drag Theresa by her arm across the yard. He shoved Ma ahead of them.

"I didn't find no whiskey, but look what I did find," he said. "I didn't know they was anything that looked like this hid out in these swamps."

"She sure is a beauty," said the one with the gun. "What you got in mind?"

"Well, if we can't have any whiskey, we can sure have some fun," he said. "You hold the gun on these two, and I'll take her first. Then I'll come back and you all can have her."

He started dragging Theresa towards some bushes up the bayou, but she fought back, and he was having a hard time.

"She sure is a little wildcat, ain't she?" he said.

"You jest don't know how to handle these swamp rats," said the one with the gun. "Hold her arms and I'll show you how to quiet her down."

The brother pinned both of Theresa's arms behind her, while the one with the gun walked over to them. He drew back the gun and hit her hard behind the head with the butt. She slumped to the ground and blood trickled down her neck. Then he came back and held the gun on Ma and Pa. "She won't give you no trouble now," he said.

None of them had seen the figure of the small boy crawling across the clearing towards them. Skeeter had seen the man hit Theresa with the gun, and he was creeping silently into range. When he saw the man start dragging Theresa's limp body into the bushes, he pulled his knife from his belt and drew it back. The blade spun through the air and struck the man with the gun. He slumped to his knees, screamed and fell to the ground. The gun went off, and Pa staggered backward. When Skeeter saw what had happened, he sat down and started retching violently. The other two brothers ran to the boat for their guns. Ma ran to where Theresa was lying.

In the excitement none of them had seen the two boatloads of men silently towing a new red boat up the bayou and pulling into the landing. As the brothers stumbled down the bank, the Hooker boys trained their guns on them.

"Now jest git on back up there," said the old man, "till we finds out what this air all abouts."

The two men retreated up the bank with the Hookers behind them. Pa had risen to his feet and came towards them. Skeeter was still sitting on the ground retching.

"Whut air all this?" asked the old man. "Whut's these low bred sons of bitches doin' here?"

"They were tryin' to ruin Theresa," said Pa, "but Skeeter planted his knife in that one there. When he fell, he shot me in the shoulder. They knocked Theresa in the head with the gun, and she's over there in the bushes."

When he heard this, Sparky ran to the bushes and picked Theresa up in his arms. Her red hair was stained even redder with blood, and she was unconscious.

"Git her on in the house so'es her ma kin see 'bout her," said the old man. "A couple of you boys git some rope and tie these bastards up. Sun Up, you git a fire started and boil some water so'es we kin treat Abner's wound. How bad air hit, Abner?"

"Hit ain't too bad," said Pa. "Jest knicked me a little mite in the shoulder."

Two of the boys returned with the rope and bound the two men's hands and feet.

"We'll git the law on you sons of bitches," said one of the brothers.

"You fellers better be makin' yore peace with the Lord, 'stead of studyin' 'bout the law," said the old man.

Sparky took Theresa into the house, put her on a bed, and Ma came in and bathed her face with a wet cloth. She opened her eyes and looked up at Sparky. "Oh, Sparky," she said, "I'm so sorry this had to happen."

"Hit's all right," said Sparky, "hit ain't none of yore fault."

"Don't leave me, Sparky," she said. "Please don't leave me."

He bent down and kissed her on the lips and laid his head on her shoulder. Ma came back into the room with a bucket of water and a clean cloth. "Hold her hands while I bathe that wound," she said.

Sparky kissed her again and held her hands in his. He could feel her grip tighten as Ma touched the wet cloth to the deep cut.

The old man walked over and lifted Skeeter from the ground. Skeeter was still retching and crying bitterly. "I done kilt a man," he sobbed. "I ain't never thought I would kill a man."

"Don't you fret none," said the old man, "cause you done the right thing, Skeeter. You done right in the sight of the Lord, so don't worry 'bout hit. We all right proud of you."

He led Skeeter to the bayou and bathed his face in the cool water, then led him to the back of the house. They had taken Pa's shirt off, and the old man examined the wound. "Tain't too bad," he said, "we'll have it fixed up in a little. It jest might be sore fer a day or so."

When he had finished with Pa, the old man started into the house to see how Theresa was doing. As he entered the kitchen, Sparky was walking from the room.

"How air she?" he asked.

"She got a pretty bad cut," said Sparky, "but she's goin' to be O.K."

"Well, you go back in the room and stay with her and help her ma," said the old man.

Sparky started towards the back door. "I'm goin' out in the back where them two . . . "

"Goddammit!" shouted the old man. "You do like I tole you! I'm goin' to handle them two out there, so'es you git back in that room."

The old man walked out the back door and over to where the two brothers were lying. "Everybody come on over here," he shouted. Pa and all the Hooker boys came over to him.

"Whut we goin' to do?" asked Pa. "We goin' to turn 'em over to the law in Fort Henry?"

"Tain't no use in that," said the old man. "They'd jest git some of them slick lawyers and come down here and hang Skeeter from a cypress tree. We'll have the trial right here. I'll be the jedge, and you all be the jury."

"The law will git you if you mess with us," said one of the brothers.

"Tain't no law on this part of the river but the law of right and wrong," said the old man, "and you two bastards oughta know which is which."

The old man turned to the others and spoke: "Men, you know whut the charges is again these two. They has tried to ruin a innocent young girl and could have ruint the happiness of two young children and broke the hearts of two families. They also would have committed murder if'n we hadn't come up. Do ary one of you say they ain't guilty?" No one spoke or raised a hand. "Then I commits them to the muddy water of the river, and may the Lord have mercy on their damned souls."

The two brothers didn't say anything for they didn't believe what was happening. They thought the men were only trying to scare them.

"We better not do that," said Pa. "Whut we goin' to do if'n the law comes around here lookin' fer 'em?"

"Damn the law!" shouted the old man. "The law wouldn't do a damn thing but turn these bastards loose and hang Skeeter. We'll put guns in their boat and turn the boat loose in the river. With all them empty whiskey jugs in there folks will think they jest got drunk and fell in the river. Besides, the law can't see to the bottom of that muddy river, if the law even comes." The old man turned and faced his sons. "Sun Up," he said, "git them sons of bitches on out of my sight, and when you gits done, turn the boat loose on the river." He turned and walked into the house, and Pa followed him.

Sun Up looked under the house and found three heavy trotline weights and tied them to the men. They loaded them in the boat and rowed to the river. Sun Up lifted one of them from the boat and lowered him until only his head was above water. "Got any last words to say?" he asked.

When the man started to speak, Sun Up released his grip, and only bubbles came to the surface of the muddy water.

When the other brother saw this he fainted, and they threw his body and the dead one into the water. Bubbles rose to the surface for a few minutes, then the water flowed as usual. They returned to the house, towed the brothers' boat to the river and turned it loose, then went back to the landing. Pa and the old man came out of the house as they returned, and Skeeter walked to the landing with them. He had stopped crying and didn't look as scared as he had.

"In all this excitement you ain't even seed yore new boat, Abner," said the old man. Pa looked down the landing at the sleek new red boat.

"Hit shore air a beauty," said Pa. "Hit gives my pore old soul a thrill jest to stand and look at it. I never thought I'd be goin' to town in somethin' that looked as purty as that."

"Hit may leak a little at first," said the old man, "but jest as soon as hit's been in the water long enough hit's goin' to start swellin', and them cracks will seal up so tight you can't even git a gnat's eyeball through 'em."

"I can hardly wait to try it out," said Pa.

"I know jest how you feels," said the old man. "We was jest like that when we built our new ones. I brought a little mite of white paint in case you wants to name hit. A purty boat like that ought to have a name."

"I guess hit do at that," said Pa. "Whut you wants to call it, Skeeter?"

"Let's name it Steel Head," said Skeeter. "If'n hits as tough as that critter were, it'll shore be a good one."

"'I think that suits hit real well," said Pa. "Kin ary one of you fellows write?"

"Can't none of us do it," said the old man.

"Me and Skeeter can't do it either," said Pa, "but Theresa kin, so soon as she gits over that lick on the head we'll git her to do hit fer us."

"We better git on back up the river, boys," said the old man. "One of you run to the house and git Sparky." One of the boys ran to the house, and Sparky returned with him. They all got into their boats, and the old man turned to Pa. "Abner," he said, "we shore sorry this had to happen, but I guess hit would have come sooner or later. Them bastards was rotten through and through. The best thing is that we all forgets it ever happened. Let's don't none of us ever say another word about hit."

"I guess that suits me fine," said Pa.

"Well, you and yore folks come up to the house Sunday and we'll have dinner and celebrate yore new boat," said the old man.

"We'll shore be proud to be there," said Pa.

The Hookers pushed away from the landing and rowed down the bayou. Pa and Skeeter watched them until they turned into the river and disappeared from sight.

EIGHTEEN

THE COREYS left early Sunday morning for the Hookers' with everyone dressed in his best. Pa's shoulder was sore but not too sore to row, and Theresa felt good though she wore a large bandage on her head. Ma and Theresa had on the new dresses Pa had brought them from Fort Henry before the flood. Ma had made herself a jar of sassafras tea to take along, for she didn't feel very good that morning. The trip up was very pleasant, and the rowing was a joy instead of a hardship to Pa and Skeeter, for the new boat skimmed the surface of the water with the grace of a swan. It was a beautiful day, and the air was filled with the clean, sweet smell of late spring. Flowers of all colors were growing along the banks, and the wistaria vines in the trees had burst into bloom, dotting the green of the trees with their purple. Dogwood trees were white with their blooms, and the honeysuckle blended in with its pink and red. The buds of the magnolia had opened, and the women thrilled to the beauty of the great white flowers. Pa and Skeeter were not so aware of this beauty as were Ma and Theresa.

After they arrived at the Hookers' landing and exchanged greetings, they sat on the front porch to talk, with no mention being made of what had happened to the Smith brothers. The old woman admired the new dresses that Ma and Theresa wore, and the men talked of nothing but the new boat and what a pleasure it was to use it. All the men went down to the landing and took turns rowing it on the river. They were so interested in the boat that they forgot to pass the jugs around before the noon meal, and when they got back to the house, the food was already on the table. When the meal was finished, the men went to the porch to make up for the time they had lost on the jugs, and the women cleaned the table. When the work was finished, Ma lay down on a bed to rest for she still wasn't feeling any better. After she rested, she went to the porch to join in the talk. The boys and Skeeter had gone to the still, and Sparky and Theresa were down at the giant tree, so it was quiet and peaceful, and Ma felt a little better.

"I shore am glad you folks has been blessed with goodness lately," said the old man. "Hit's about time you got some of good 'stead of the bad."

"Hit pleases us well, too," said Pa, "and we're mighty thankful fer it. I always said that sooner or later times would git a mite better fer us, cause we's always minded our own business and let the other feller be. I believe that if'n a man tries to do right, and don't give trouble to other folks, the Lord will look out fer him and show him some of the goodness."

"You air shore right," said the old man. "They would never be no trouble on this river if'n folks would jest learn to stop messin' with other people and treat each other as the Lord intended for them to do. They ain't no cause fer them town people and them boatmen to come through here actin' high and mighty like they was the only ones on the river fit to live."

"That don't matter too much to me," said Pa. "Hit don't make me no mind what they think of me and my family jest so long as they let us be and the Lord keeps on givin' us a little goodness."

"Well, hit matters to me," said the old man. "If'n them fellers come aroun' here puttin' out trouble, they'll git more than they bargained fer."

Skeeter came around the side of the house, climbed the steps, and sat on the floor by the old man. "Has you ever seed the big river?" he asked.

"You mean the Mississippi?" said the old man.

"Yeah, that's hit," said Skeeter.

"I seed hit when I were a young buck 'bout like Jeff air."

"I heard niggers talkin' 'bout hit down to Mill Town one day, and I been wantin' to git somebody to tell me 'bout hit whut had been there."

"You git on out of here and play with them boys and quit worryin' Mr. Hooker with all them questions," said Ma.

"Let him stay," said the old man. "I don't mind tellin' him 'bout hit."

Skeeter was glad that the old man had said he could stay, and he settled back against a porch post to listen. The old man looked at him and started talking.

"When I were a young buck, I come from a family as big as this'n I got now, and hit were all boys, too. We lived over in Hancock County on the Wolf River and made whiskey jest like we do here now. Ever once in a while my pa would git the hankerin' fer killin', and he'd git all his boys together and head fer the woods. He always said that when he got that way, he'd 'truther go to the woods and kill the animals then stay around and shoot up some white folks or niggers. We'd take to the woods and stay fer three or four days, sometimes a week, and kill ary thing that walked on four feet, and then go on back home when he were satisfied. Sometimes we'd go clear over to the Pascagoula River and come back along Red Creek."

"Did you see ary bears?" asked Skeeter.

"We seed plenty," said the old man, "and killed plenty, too.

"Then one year my ma died, and pa took the killin' spells soon after that. He made us board up the house, put everthing away, and told us that we mout be gone a long time. He said we was goin' slam to the big river and back. That suited us boys jest fine, cause we wanted to see hit, too. We struck out afoot north till we hit the Black River and then followed hit to where hit started from. We made camps all along the way and et the game we killed. We kept headin' north, and soon came to the Strong River and camped there fer a couple of days. That were one of the purtiest little rivers we seed. Hit were full of rocks and falls, and they were plenty of game along it. We moved on till we hit this muddy Pearl and made a camp on the top of Le Fleur's bluff. The next day we walked right down the streets of Jackson, whiskey jugs, hound dogs, and all. Them people shore thought we was a sight.

"All that country up in there were mighty purty. They were long rollin' hills, and big pines, and they wasn't much swamp. We cut straight across from Jackson, and crossed the Big Black, and then come out on the Mississippi down from Vicksburg. We throwed up a camp and killed deer and stayed there till Pa was tired of lookin' at that big river."

"Were they ary steamboat on hit like they air here?" asked Skeeter.

"We seed steamboats on hit what would make the ones here look like rowboats," said the old man. "Hit nigh on scared Pa to death furst time we seed one of them big buggers churnin' up the river.

"After we camped there fer a spell, we headed south and left the river. We cut back in and camped along Bayou

Pierre fer a while. They were the biggest bluffs and hills through that country that I ever seed, and we most near broke our necks fallin' over 'em. When we left there, we went on down and camped along the Homochitto River, and then went on down into Louisiana. We hit the Amite River and followed it until hit met the Blind, and then went slam on down to Lake Maurepas. The country were gittin' full of marsh and swamp, and the skeeters were powerful bad, so we cut north and went aroun' the lake. We run into the top of Lake Pontchartrain, and I'll never fergit the look on Pa's face when he took a drink and found out that that water were salt. That salt water give Pa a bellyful, so we cut back towards home. We crossed the Tangiapahoa, the Tchefuncta and Bayou Chitto and then run back into the Pearl. We headed down through the marsh country and come out at Saint Louis Bay, and follered it around to where the Wolf ran into it. Then we went back up the Wolf to home. Hit took us nigh on three months to make that trip, and when we got back, somebody had done stole our whiskey still. Pa went on a rampage and got hisself shot by one of the Cajuns, and I come here to live."

"You've jest about seed everthing, ain't you?" asked Skeeter. "But how did you all know all them rivers when you come to them?"

"Hit weren't like it air here," he said. "They was a lot of people livin' all along up there, and lots of towns, and the people would tell us where we was. We didn't have to ask nobody when we hit the Mississippi though. We knowed whut hit were when we first seed it. Hit were the widest piece of river I ever seed."

"I shore wish I could see it and go aroun' like you did," said Skeeter.

"I been thinkin' 'bout gittin' the boys and makin' a trip like that sometimes, and if'n we goes, you kin shore go along with us."

"Well, right now we better make us a trip down the Pearl to home," said Ma. "I ain't feelin' a mite too good, and I better git home and lie on the bed."

Pa sent Skeeter to get Theresa, and he and Ma went down to the boat with the old man and woman following.

"I shore hope you ain't gittin' sick," said the old woman. "Hit would be mouty bad to have to lie in the house all the time with this purty weather we air havin'."

"I think I'll be all right after a good rest tonight," said Ma. "Hit ain't really nothin' mouch to worry 'bout."

In a few minutes Skeeter came down, and Theresa returned. They said good-by to the old man and woman and started down the river. The sun had sunk low in the west, and the shadows of the tall trees made dark avenues across the water. As Pa and Skeeter sent the boat skimming along, small circles of brown foam trailed behind them. It was not long before they were at the landing.

Ma drank some more hot tea and went to bed. Theresa fixed the supper for Pa and Skeeter, and they helped her clean up when they were finished. They sat on the porch until the moon came up behind the cypress trees casting its silver up the bayou, and then they went to bed.

Ma was not up the next morning when Pa and Skeeter left to run the traps and line. Theresa fixed their breakfast, and they let Ma sleep. When they returned, she was still in the bed. Her face was red, and she had quilts piled on top of her. Pa went into the room and felt of her face.

"Don't you feel any better yit?" he asked. "If'n you don't I'll fix you some more tea."

"I think that might help a little," she said. "I guess I'll be all right in a while."

Pa fixed her the tea and she drank it, but at noon she couldn't eat any food. They let her sleep most of the day, but when she awoke she was much worse. Her head burned like fire, and she could not lift herself from the bed. They sat up with her most of the night, and she finally fell asleep.

Pa and Skeeter were on the way to Mill Town at dawn the next morning to bring the doctor back to look at Ma. They were afraid and didn't know what to do, for they had never seen her sick like this before. When they reached the docks, they went straight to the doctor's house and persuaded him to go back with them. It was the middle of the morning when they got back to the house, and Ma was much worse. The doctor went into the room with her and told them to stay outside.

It seemed to Pa that the doctor had been in the room for hours. Finally he came back to the kitchen.

"What air hit, doctor?" asked Pa. "Air she very sick?"

"She's a very sick woman," said the doctor. "She's got a bad case of the fever, and if she doesn't get the proper care, she'll probably die. I think I can get a nurse to come up here and stay if you have the money, but if you haven't, you may as well start diggin' the grave."

"I got the money," said Pa.

"Well, let's get on back down the river as soon as possible so I can send the nurse up here with the proper medicine before the woman dies."

The doctor sat in the rear of the boat, and they started back down the river. They paid no heed to anything but the speed they could get out of the boat. Skeeter looked hard at the doctor seated before him. He was not such an old man, but his face was wrinkled as with age. He wore a beard on his chin, and an old black hat covered his thin, gray hair. His small, black eyes had a far-away and vague look in them, as if he had seen much of the world and was weary of it all. Skeeter hated him, and the hatred stood out in the way he tightened his mouth as he looked at the doctor. He blamed this man, this stranger, for what had happened. The man had no right to come in their house and say that his mother might die. Things had always been all right before this man came, and he should have stayed away. It was the first real hate Skeeter had ever known, and when the doctor saw the look in Skeeter's eyes, he would not look at him again. Skeeter had not hated even Steel Head like this.

When they reached the docks, they went back to the doctor's house. He told them he would go see the woman and that it would probably be a while before she could get her things to leave. He asked Pa for money to get medicine, and Pa gave him half the savings that he had. They waited at the house, while the doctor went for the woman. It seemed to them that he would never return and that Ma would surely die before they could get back, but finally the doctor did return. The woman had a small, black bag with her, so Pa took the bag and they went back to the boat.

Skeeter studied this woman on the trip back just as he had studied the doctor, and he hated her just as much. She had no right to be going to their house, but if it would help Ma, he would not complain. The woman was fat like Ma, and middle aged, and her face was wrinkled like the doctor's. Her hair was gray and unkempt, and her eyes had a hard and unsympathetic look in them.

When they reached home, the woman took the bag and went straight to the bed. She wouldn't let anyone come into the room, so they sat around the back stoop. She stayed in the room the rest of the day and came out only a few minutes to eat supper. When darkness came, she took a candle from the bag, so she could have light in the room. She lit it over the hearth and returned.

Pa got a quilt so he and Skeeter could sleep on the kitchen floor and let the woman stay in Skeeter's bed, but the woman did not go to sleep or come out of the room. Pa, Skeeter, and Theresa sat in the kitchen and stared into space. They did not talk, and they did not seem to see each other, but they were all thinking the same thing. They sat up that night until they fell asleep on the floor, and when they awoke at daylight, the woman was still in the room, and the bed had not been touched. About the middle of the morning she came out and asked for coffee.

"How air she now?" asked Pa.

"She's passed over the worse," said the woman. "She's not goin' to die, but she's still bad sick. It'll be a long time before she's well again."

"Well, thank God she's goin' to live," said Pa.

"She's asleep now," said the woman, "so don't any of you go in the room. I'm goin' to sleep some myself, so please wake me just after noon."

Pa sat at the table and buried his face in his hands. Theresa sat beside him, but Skeeter got up and went into the yard. He felt better now that he knew Ma would live. He did not hate the woman so much as he had, nor the doctor either. The bitterness went out of his face, and the sun was bright again. He got into the skiff and poled up the bayou and around the edges of the swamp. He tried to forget that the doctor had said Ma might die, and when he thought of the words, his face drew tight, and the hatred came back. He wished there was no such thing as sickness, so people like the doctor and the woman would never come to the swamp and to their house. When his mind was eased, he poled the skiff back to the house.

Theresa fixed dinner, but none of them ate very much. When they finished, Pa went in and woke the woman, and she went back to the room with Ma. Skeeter started in to see Ma, and the woman stopped him. She told him he couldn't come in and for none of them to ever come in the room until she said they could. The hatred returned to his face. Why should this woman tell him he could not go in the room to see his own mother? Why should she take away a privilege that he had known all his life? She was an outsider; she was not one of the family, so she had no right to do such a thing. He returned to the swamp and didn't come back until dark.

Pa and Skeeter ran the traps and line the next morning, and life returned to its usual path except for the woman's presence among them every day. She still would not allow them to enter the room, and the dark cloud of gloom hovered over the family. The food did not taste good, the river was not beautiful, and the joy of being alive had gone out of them. Things would be better if this woman would leave.

She stayed with them for two weeks, and then Pa took her back to town. She gave him several bottles of medicine to take back with instructions as to how to use them, and when Pa paid her for her services and the medicine, there was not a cent of the savings left. His chances for staying home during the summer were gone, but he didn't mind as long as Ma was going to live. When he returned home they all went in to see her for the first time. She was no longer fat, and her face was very pale. Her eyes were weak and drawn, but she gave them a faint smile. Skeeter left the room as soon as he could, for he didn't like to see his mother looking like this.

Theresa did the cooking and looked after Ma, while Pa and Skeeter carried on their work as usual. In a few days Ma could walk around a little with help, and she was gradually getting her strength back. The spring days vanished, and the hot summer came. The river was dropping, but the fishing was still good, even though they all knew that it wouldn't remain that way for long.

NINETEEN

FOR SOME STRANGE REASON the river didn't drop very fast that summer, and they still caught enough fish to keep them in supplies and save a small amount each week. By the middle of summer Ma was up and around again, though she would sometimes get weak and have to rest. She weighed much less than she had, and her face was still slightly drawn, but it would not be long until she was as well as she had ever been. The joy of living had returned to the family, and they were happy during the long hot days.

Skeeter was the happiest one of the family, for this was the time of year he loved most. He could go into the swamp at night to gig frogs, he could swim naked in the bayou, and he could drift in the skiff and let the hot sun tan his body as he watched the clouds roll by. Nothing was so wonderful as summer on the river, with the hot sun during the day and the big moon at night, and all the things he loved around him. He wished it would be summer the whole year.

The Hookers had been down to see Ma while the nurse was in the house, and they had not been able to see her. Pa and Skeeter were sitting on the porch one afternoon when they saw one of the Hooker boats coming up the bayou. The old man and woman and four of the boys were in it. Sparky was one of them. Pa and Skeeter went down to the landing to meet them.

"Howdy, Abner," said the old man. "Has that old woman left so'es we kin see Glesa yit?"

"She's been gone a good whiles now," said Pa. "Ma's been up and aroun' the house a lot lately. You folks git out and come on in the house."

They got out of the boat and went to the house as Theresa came to join Sparky. Skeeter stayed at the landing to be with the other three boys. The old people went to the front porch and sat down.

"We shore air glad to see you up and aroun' agin," said the old woman. "You give us a scare here fer a while."

"Hit give me a scare too," said Ma. "I could see them pearly gates openin' up fer a while. I shore thought I was gone, but I guess hit jest warn't my time yit."

"Well, I'm shore glad hit warn't yore time," said the old man. "We would have shore missed you if'n you had left."

"I think hit done her a little good," laughed Pa. "She's done lost all that weight, and now she looks to be a good twenty years younger."

"Well, derned if'n she don't at that," said the old man.

"You all jest teasin' me to make me feel good," said Ma. "You know I looks like a old scarecrow now."

"Well, if'n I thought hit would make me look twenty years younger, I'd git me a good case of the fever," said the old woman. "But you knows we jest teasin' you. You's lucky to be here now, cause don't many people git over the fever at all."

"I guess you air right," said Ma. "I'm jest plain lucky hit didn't git me."

"They's somethin' else we wanted to ask you folks abouts whiles we air neighborin'," said the old man. "Has you two ever decided ary thing yit about them two kids gittin' married? That boy of ourn air goin' to droop hisself to death if'n he don't find out somethin' soon. He droops aroun' like a sick cow ever' day, and spends most of his time messin' aroun' down by that big cypress tree."

"I think Theresa air jest about the same way," said Ma. "I don't think I ever seed two kids what had hit no worse."

"I been studyin' on that some myself," said Pa. "I thinks we ought to go on and sot a date so'es they kin know somethin'. Hit ain't fair to them if'n we don't. Whut do you all think would be a good time?"

"I don't rightly know," said the old man. "Some folks goes by the moon, and some folks the seasons, but I think one time air jest as good as another. I don't hold by them old ways no more. I think gittin' married air jest as good any time you wants hit."

"I likes Christmas mighty well," said the old woman.

"I think that's a powerful good idea too," said Ma. "We could git 'em married on Christmas Eve and then go down to the frolic at Mill Town that night to celebrate."

"I think that's the best," said the old man. "We'll jest call hit settled right here and now. They's goin' to git hitched Christmas Eve."

"I got to git the cloth purty soon to start makin' her a weddin' dress," said Pa. "Ain't no gal of ourn goin' to git married in nothin' less than the best."

"That shore air right," said Ma. "Hit'll take a long time to make that dress. You better git the cloth Satterday."

"I done got enough money put back to build them a house of their own right at the foot of that big cypress tree," said the old man. "And if'n they don't git busy right away and get me some little 'uns to play with, I'm goin' to move down there myself."

"Now you shet up talkin' like that," said the old woman. "You'll have the Coreys thinkin' you ain't got a brain left in you."

They all laughed and were in a good mood now that the plans had been completed for the wedding date.

"Who we goin' to git to do the marryin'?" asked Ma.

"We kin bring one of the preachers up from Mill Town that morning and take him back with us when we go down for the frolic that night," said Pa. "He kin be here fer the feast at dinner and git his bellyful fer a change."

"And I kin give him a snort of the best whiskey on Pearl River," said the old man. "That is, if'n he wants hit."

"Well, I don't speck he will," said the old woman.

"Why don't we call them kids in here and tell them the news and watch whut happens to their faces," said the old man.

"That would be a good idea," said Pa. "I'll go call 'em, and don't nobody let on likes they know whut hit is when they first gits here, and then we'll jest ups and tell 'em."

Pa went to the back stoop and called Sparky and Theresa and then hurried back to the front porch and sat down. In a few minutes they walked onto the porch and stood in front of the old people.

"Hit's a mouty purty day, ain't it?" said the old man.

"Hit shore air," said Theresa.

Sparky put his hands behind him and played with his fingers. They just stood there for a few minutes feeling awkward.

"We done decided to git you two married Christmas Eve," said the old man.

Sparky and Theresa turned and looked at each other for a few seconds without saying anything. Then he took her in his arms and kissed her for a long time. The old man jumped up and let out the loudest yell that had ever been heard on the Corey bayou. He jumped up and down and stomped his feet on the floor. Sparky and Theresa turned and ran from the porch.

"Sit down afore you stomps the house down!" shouted the old woman. "You gonna have the Coreys thinkin' you ain't got a speck of brains in you."

"I knowed that boy had it in him!" shouted the old man. "He's the only one that really takes after his Pa. I could do that back in my young days jest like he done it. I shore am proud of him."

"You jest carryin' on like a old fool," said the old woman. "Now sit down here afore you bust a blood vessel and falls out on the floor."

"Seein' somethin' like that makes me feel like a young buck again," said the old man. "I could go out right now and whup the biggest bear in them woods."

The kiss Sparky had given Theresa had affected all of them just as much as it had the old man, even though they didn't show it. The sight of such young love had thrilled them and warmed their old hearts.

"We better git on back to the house," said the old woman. "Hit's goin' to be dark afore long."

"I guess we had," said the old man. "I don't recall when I ever enjoyed a afternoon better, and I hates to leave."

When they got up and went down to the landing, Pa and Ma went with them. As Sparky left Theresa, he kissed her again, and the old man stood up in the boat and fired his gun into the air. He was still waving when the boat reached the mouth of the bayou and turned up the river. Theresa walked back to the house as if in a dream.

"Whut was all that about?" asked Skeeter.

"Sparky and Theresa air goin' to git married Christmas," said Pa.

"Aw, I thought hit were somethin'," said Skeeter.

*   *   *

When they were in town that Saturday, Pa went to buy the cloth for the dress while Skeeter went to see Uncle Jobe. Skeeter walked into the house and sat down.

"Howdy, Uncle Jobe," said Skeeter. "How you gittin' along now?"

"Old Uncle Jobe ain't fittin' fer nothin'," he said. "I ain't long fer this world, Massah Skeeter."

"You sick or somethin'?" asked Skeeter.

"I done been pegged, Massah Skeeter," he said. "They were a mean nigger come down here from the hills to work in the mill, and he were all time gittin' drunk and beatin' up folks, so nobody didn't like him, and he couldn't find no place to stay. He come here and asked me could he stay here, but I were afraid of him, so I told him no. He got mad and told me he were goin' to peg me. Ever time I done my job after that I kevered hit up so'es he couldn't find hit, but one day I done plumb forgot and didn't do hit. When I thought about hit, I went back to hide it, and afore I got there he had hit in a sack and were runnin' away, and now he done got me pegged."

"Whut you mean he done got you pegged?" asked Skeeter.

"When you pegs a feller, you bore a hole in a tree and then makes a peg to fit the hole. Then you take some uv his droppin's and puts in the hole, and everyday you knocks the peg in a little bit more. Ever time he hits that peg my body tightens up a little more, and the day that peg air knocked all the way in, my bowels air goin' to lock, and I's goin' to die a horrible death. Wouldn't nobody do sech a thing 'less he were in with the devil."

"Ain't they nothin' you kin do?" asked Skeeter. "Why don't you jest find the tree and pull the peg out?"

"Lawsy me, Massah Skeeter, I done looked at ever tree around here and ain't seed no sign uv hit."

"Can't you see the doctor and git some medicine fer it?"

"Hit ain't no use. They ain't nothin' you kin do once you air pegged but make yore peace with the Lord, and I's done that."

"I'll make Pa come early next Satterday and stay all day, and me and him'll shore find that peg fer you."

"I'd shore be mouty proud if'n you did."

"Well, don't you worry none. We'll git hit fer you fer shore."

Skeeter got up to leave, and the old Negro stopped him.

"Jest a minute afore you leaves, Massah Skeeter. Let this ole nigger give you a piece uv advice. I's done been here a long time, and these old eyes has seed a lot. I kin see things most folks can't, and I knows whut's goin' on along dis river. Dey's too much bad, and things ain't goin' right. De Lord ain't goin' to stand fer sech stuff much longer, people hatin' people and treatin' you river folks like skum. Tell yore pa to always stay as good a man as he is, and you do the same thing, Massah Skeeter. If things don't change, someday one of dem floods air goin' to fix dis river fer sho', and dem boats ain't goin' to be able to go up it, and you folks air goin' to have hit all to yoreself. Then you gwin know happiness."

"I'll tell him whut you said," said Skeeter, "and you take care of yoreself till we gits back next Satterday and helps you."

As Skeeter walked back up the lane to town, he had a funny feeling in his head. He didn't know what to think of the things Uncle Jobe had said for he had never heard talk like that before. He met Pa, and they made the trip back home in silence. Pa thought Skeeter looked strange, but he did not question him.

That night after supper the family was sitting on the porch, and Skeeter told them all about what Uncle Jobe had told him. He also gave Pa the message Uncle Jobe had sent to him.

"Them niggers with their hoodoo!" said Pa. "Hit beats ary thing I ever heard of. Tain't no use to worry 'bout him; he'll be all right."

"Whut if'n he ain't all right?" asked Skeeter.

"We'll go to town early next Satterday and make him take a good dose of medicine," said Pa, "and then we'll go out and find him a peg jest to make him feel good about hit. They ain't nothin' to that hoodoo, and hit couldn't possibly kill him."

"Whut about all that stuff he said 'bout the Lord goin' to do somethin' to the river?" asked Skeeter.

"That ain't nothin' to worry about, neither," said Pa. "Whut the Lord's goin' to do to a feller He's goin' to do anyway, so they ain't no use to try to run away from hit."

Skeeter thought about Uncle Jobe all the next week and kept wondering if the "hoodoo" was really true or not. He didn't believe it, but he couldn't forget the look of fear in the old Negro's eyes. It seemed to him that when Uncle Jobe talked of what the Lord was going to do he was looking right through him and into another world that he couldn't see. He would be glad when Saturday came and they could go back and see about him, but the days dragged by, and he thought the week would never end.

When the day did come, Skeeter could hardly wait until they reached the docks. He rowed the boat with all his strength, and several times Pa had to make him slow down. When the boat was tied, they took the fish to the market, and Skeeter started to leave.

"I'll be down there jest as soon as the fish air weighed and I gits the money," said Pa. "If'n he ain't all right, I'll come back up here and git the medicine."

Skeeter raced down the lane to the shack, and when he arrived Uncle Jobe was not sitting on the porch. He walked across the yard and sat down to wait. He thought Uncle Jobe should not have left, for he had told him they would be here early in the morning. A little Negro boy walked down the lane and stopped in front of the shack.

"You waitin' fer Uncle Jobe?" he asked.

"I shore am," said Skeeter. "You know where he's at?"

"Yassah," he said, "I knows where he's at."

"Then why don't you tell me," said Skeeter, "so'es I kin go meet him."

"He's daid. He died two days ago."

The thought didn't reach Skeeter at once, and he just sat and stared for a few minutes. Then he turned to the little Negro again.

"Where'd you say he was?"

"He's daid," repeated the little Negro.

This time the thought went through to Skeeter, and he fell to the floor and started crying bitterly. The little Negro moved away when he saw this. He lay on the floor and cried until he could not see. He was not aware that Pa was standing over him, and it startled him when Pa touched his shoulder. Pa did not have to ask what was wrong; he knew when he saw Skeeter lying there. He lifted Skeeter up, put his arms around his shoulders, and they started back to town. He did not try to stop Skeeter from crying, for he thought it would be best to let him stop when he wanted to.

He took Skeeter down to the boat and went back to town to buy the supplies. When he returned, Skeeter was still crying so he didn't bother him. He rowed the boat by himself and said nothing. When they were halfway home, Skeeter stopped crying and looked up at Pa.

"Why?" he asked.

"Hit's somethin' I can't explain to you, Son," said Pa. "When the Lord gits ready fer a person, he jest takes him back up where he come from, and they ain't nothin' we kin do about hit. Ole Uncle Jobe were mighty old, and he had seed his life, so hit were time fer him to go. He'll be a heap better off where he air now, and I know he wouldn't want to see you carry on so. You ought to be proud fer him, cause he's at a good place, and he's where he's been wantin' to be. They ain't nothin' but happiness there, and hit's all spring and summer. The rations is always good, and ole Uncle Jobe will like hit mighty fine."

Skeeter stopped crying and lay down in the bottom of the boat. Presently he leaned over the side and washed his face in the muddy water and then took his oar from Pa. When they got home, Skeeter went straight to his room and went to bed without eating supper. Ma started to call him, but Pa told her to leave him alone. He told her about Uncle Jobe being dead, and she understood.

The next morning Skeeter ate a light breakfast and left in the skiff. He wanted to go to the swamp for there was something about it that took the sadness and hatred from him. It gave him a feeling that nothing else could give him. He stayed there all day, and it was dark when he got back to the landing. The sadness was gone from him, and he was glad that Uncle Jobe would be happy. He walked into the kitchen and the family was all waiting there.

"I'm powerful hungry," he said, "and as soon as the supper air done I'm goin' in the swamp and gig us some frogs. Them legs shore would be good fer breakfast in the mornin'."

ANGEL CITY

ONE

THERE WAS an unusual chill in the mountain air for late
September, but winter comes early in West Virginia, especially on Teeter Ridge. The late afternoon sun was filtered by a
swirl of low-hanging clouds, causing the tops of ridges to
glow with a somber yellow. The unpainted clapboard house
clinging to the side of a hill looked forlorn and foreboding, as
if dreading that its aged timbers would once again be
drenched with chilling rain.

Jared Teeter stood on the front porch, gazing at the unplowed fields in the valley below, paying no notice to the
excited voices inside the house. He left the porch and walked
out to the barn with its empty chicken coops and silent stalls
– stalls also now empty but still smelling of fresh manure and
hot milk. A rat scurrying through a pile of hay in the loft
caught his attention momentarily, and he listened intensely,
as if expecting the sagging structure to come alive with
sounds; then he turned and walked back to the porch. Far in
the distance he could see a pickup truck winding its way
slowly up the mountain road. He called through the screen

door, "Cloma, I think they're beginnin' to come."

An answer came back, "You best feed the hogs now. There won't be time after everyone gets here."

He smiled, saying to himself, "She's as confused as I am. She knows darn well that the hawg pen's been empty now fer more than two weeks."

But just to be sure that it really was empty, he left the porch again and walked toward the fenced plot of barren ground.

Jared Teeter had been born in 1932 in this wooden frame house surrounded by a hundred and sixty acres of West Virginia soil which had been known for almost a century as Teeter Ridge. He was the only one of three Teeter sons to stay behind and live on the land. Both of the other brothers had left home before they reached age twenty, one supposedly going to Baltimore and the other to Chicago. Neither ever returned. Following the death of his father in 1950 and his mother one year later, Jared had lived in the house alone until he married Cloma when he was twenty-three and she sixteen. Their two children, Kristy, the oldest at sixteen, and Bennie, two years younger, were also born in this house. Cloma was now pregnant with a third child.

For several years after it became apparent that he would someday have to leave, Jared clung stubbornly to the land; but each year the tax bills and the cost of clothing and food and gasoline and farm supplies pushed him deeper and deeper into debt. When he finally sold the sturdy old house and the land and paid all the back taxes and the mortgage and the bills, he had only six hundred dollars in cash to show for his lifetime of trying and struggling and finally being forced to admit the stinging reality of defeat. With this money he would have to seek out and build a new life for himself and his family, and he had chosen to do this in Florida.

When the final realization came to Jared, and he had signed the deed to the land, he did not tell Cloma or the children for more than two weeks. They suspected something unusual was happening when Jared sold the milk cow and the hogs and chickens and then his old Cub tractor. Then one day he left in the pickup truck and returned with a 1960 Dodge van, a useless vehicle for a farm. At this moment Cloma knew, but she too remained silent in front of the children.

Jared told them one night at the supper table, and the news was more than they could at once comprehend. Neither Kristy nor Bennie had ever been further away from the farm than an occasional trip into Charleston, and to them this land and the school and church in nearby Dink was all of the world that existed. At first there was a lot of crying. Deep gloom enveloped them, but eventually they accepted the inevitable. And then both of them were pervaded with the excitement of soon seeing a part of the world that had, until then, been only make-believe.

This was the last day for the Teeter family to remain on Teeter Ridge, and that night all the friends from neighboring farms would come to pay their respects.

Jared walked back into the house and to the bedroom, where Cloma was packing the last of their clothes. She looked up at him and said hopefully, "Jay, the bed . . . can't we at least take the bed?"

He had anticipated she would ask this, and had dreaded the moment. He knew what the old brass bed meant to her. It had been his wedding present to her, and in this bed both Kristy and Bennie had been conceived and born; and now another child was within her as a reminder of what this bed meant to their lives together. She had expected that this new child would also be born here. Finally he turned his eyes from her and said softly, "No, Cloma. I'm sorry. There won't be room in the van. I'll get you another brass bed as soon as we're settled."

"It won't be the same," she said. "You know it won't be the same."

"I'm sorry," he said again. Then he turned and walked back to the front porch.

Again Jared watched as the pickup truck groaned up the last few feet of road and turned into the yard. Cloma's mother and father got out and walked to the house. The man was tall and lanky like Jared, but his hair was silver-white and the skin beneath his eyes was deeply marked with chicken tracks caused by too many years of squinting into the sun while following a plow. The woman also had a wrinkled face, but her body was rotund, and she wobbled as she walked.

Jared extended his hand and said, "Howdy. Come on in the house."

The woman greeted him warmly and then went into the house. The man shook hands and remained outside with Jared. He said, "We come a mite early so's I could bring you this. It's fer the trip."

Jared looked at the bills as the old man took them from his coat pocket. He said quickly, "No. I thank you greatly, but I don't need money. We have enough. But I do rightly thank you."

"Take it," the old man insisted. "It's only fifty dollars. We want you to have it as a gift — for the new baby when it comes."

"No," Jared said firmly. "You need it more'n we do."

Cloma's father knew it was useless. He put the bills back into his pocket, suspecting that Jared really needed the money but also knowing what was meant by mountain pride. He said, "Well, if you have need of us in the future, you just write and let us know. We ain't got much, but what we got we'll share."

"I appreciate that," Jared replied, wanting to drop the subject and say nothing more about the money. "Can you smell a storm comin'?" he asked.

"Yes. I smelled it all the way up the mountain. It's goin' to be a humdinger, too. You can bet on that."

Just then two more pickups and an old Chevrolet coupe pulled into the yard. These were followed almost immediately by two more trucks. As each vehicle arrived, the occupants came onto the porch and were greeted by Jared. The women then went inside to present gifts to Cloma of handmade aprons and pot-holders and baby clothes.

The men segregated themselves on the porch while the younger people and children chased each other around the house and through the yard. Conversation on the porch was lively: "We shore hates to see you go, Jay. Maybe you could stay yet and make it o.k."

"Ain't no way," Jared replied. "Use to be a man could make it on a farm just by growin' enough to feed his family and havin' enough left over to get stuff such as flour and salt and shoes. 'Tain't true no more. Now the taxes and the machines and the gasoline and the stuff at the store takes ten times what a fellow can make. The eggs ain't worth the price of chicken feed, and the milk ain't worth the cow feed. Just ain't no way anymore fer a poor man to make it here."

"That's the God's truth!" one man agreed. "Hit's got sometimes where I think I'm goin' to have to et the slop rather than feed it to the hawgs. Them hawgs can always run in the woods and dig out snakes and acorns, but a man ain't a mind to do that."

"Don't know what none of us is goin' to do if'n things don't change soon," another said.

"How fer down in Floridy you plan to go, Jay?" one man asked.

"A fer piece," Jared replied.

"You remember last year, ole Jim Bigley had to sell out

too and leave? He went down to Jacksonville. We got a letter from him sayin' he found work there in a shipyard. Maybe you could stop in Jacksonville and get work with ole Jim."

"Nope," Jared said. "I'll not stop in Jacksonville. So long as we're goin' to Floridy, I want to be where everything is covered with palm trees and oranges. Jacksonville would be 'bout the same as Georgie. I'll go as fer south as a man can go, slam down past Miami, to Homestead. I done looked it up on a map."

"That's a mighty fer piece, all right. But maybe we can all come down and spend Christmas with you. I hear they's a heap to see on one of them Floridy beaches in the winter."

One man laughed and said, "That's probably why ole Jay wants to go so fer down there, so's he can sit around all day and stare at them half-nekked women on the beaches. I've seen pictures of them beaches afore."

Jared said, "Well, you're all welcome to come and stay with us at Christmas time if you've a mind to. We'll be settled by then, and you'll be most welcome. And maybe we can leave the womenfolk at home fer awhile and sneak off to the beach."

· "You better shet that up for now," another man said. "Here comes Preacher Will and his missus into the yard. You know he ain't goin' to want to talk about no nekked women runnin' around on a beach."

"He might surprise you," another said, laughing. " 'Specially if they's vittles on that beach."

Kristy and Jeff Billings left the others in the front yard and walked to the fence by the abandoned hog pen. Jeff was one year older than Kristy, and they had been "promised" for the past year since Jeff had carved JEFF + KRISTY on the "promising tree" adjacent to the school in Dink. The old hickory was scarred with dozens and dozens of such inscriptions. Many of the inscribers later became lifemates while others eventually went their separate ways.

Jeff and Kristy's courtship had progressed according to normal mountain customs: passing notes in class, carrying books after school, sitting next to each other in church, long walks on Sunday afternoons, and slipping out of the Saturday night barn dance in order to hold hands and to dare one kiss that would send both of them into violent spells of dizziness.

Kristy was sad that she was going to leave Jeff, but she was too young and too filled with the excitement of life to constantly grieve over it. Jeff wanted to grieve, but instead he pretended that he didn't have that much interest one way or another. On this last night, both of them felt like throwing away their masks and pouring out their inner feelings, but the mountain urge to be above such emotion was prevailing.

Jeff finally broke the silence and said, "I don't care nothin' at all about movin' to Floridy. The mountains is good enough for me."

Kristy thought for a moment, and then she said, "Have you ever seen an orange tree?"

"No. And I don't want to either." Jeff pouted as he said it.

Both said nothing more for a moment, and then Kristy said, "Jeff, I really don't want to move away either. I cried about it for a long time, but I'll not cry any more. I don't really care about orange trees either. What I want someday is an old house just like this one here in the mountains, and a garden to grow things, and a stove to cook meals on, and a brass bed just like Mamma's, and babies . . . lots of babies . . . your babies, Jeff . . . that's what I want most of all. . . ."

Her face flushed as she said it, and Jeff could smell the sweetness of her reddened flesh as she brushed lightly against him. She took his hand in hers and said, "I'll miss you and the mountains, Jeff, but mostly I'll miss you."

Her words rushed through his mind like a mountain wind. He wanted to reach out and hold her close to him forever, but he restrained his emotions and said, "Will you write to me when you get to Floridy? I'll write you back, and then maybe I can come visit you when school ends and the spring plowin' is done."

"I'll write as soon as I can," Kristy promised. "And you better write back right away, you hear?"

Jeff then said, "I brung you a present. I'll go fetch it from the truck, and I'll bring a flashlight so you can see it."

It had now become so dark that Kristy couldn't see Jeff as he turned the side of the house and ran toward the pickup. She was excited by the thought of an unexpected gift, and she wondered what it would be. In a moment Jeff returned and said, "Bet you'll never guess what it is."

Kristy said impatiently, "Jeff, show me! We don't have much time left. They'll be callin' us to supper soon."

Jeff held his hand out and then turned the flashlight on a brightly colored rag doll. He said, "I know you don't play with dolls no more, but my Ma makes the best rag dolls in the mountains, and I had her make this one for you. I remember when you were about six, and we were playin' down by Panther Crick. You got mad and throwed your rag doll into the water, and then you cried somethin' awful as it shot away down the crick and disappeared around a bend. I wanted you to have another one now and take it with you as a reminder of the mountains."

Kristy took the doll and held it against her breasts. "I didn't think you could remember something that happened so long ago," she said. "And I do love this one. I'll keep it always."

"It ain't much," Jeff said proudly, glad that she liked it, "but my Ma made it, and I wanted you to have it. She wanted you to have it too."

"Could you turn off that light now?" Kristy asked.

"Yes. I just wanted you to see the doll."

As soon as the light clicked off, Jeff felt Kristy press against him. He also felt the coming of a violent dizziness.

Preacher Will was the only man present who sported a huge stomach and a fat face. His black wool suit also contrasted with the other men's faded overalls, dungaree pants, khaki pants, and denim windbreakers. For several minutes he stared intensely at the table laden with fried chicken, sliced ham, fried squirrels, venison roast, sweet potato pies, and corn pone. He seemed to be having a hard time restraining himself, and then he said loudly, "May I have yore attention, please?"

All the men came in from the porch, and the women became silent. The preacher said, "For the time bein', leave all them youngens out in the yard. It's time for grownups to have vittles, but afore we eat all this good food the ladies has brought, I best turn up thanks. And I can tell that some of you sinners needs blessin' too afore you gets into them jugs of corn likker I know you got in the trucks. So bow yore heads, please, and cut out that snickerin' afore the Lord sends down a thunderbolt amongst you."

As soon as all became silent again, the preacher said, "Lord, bless this food on this special day, but more 'specially bless the family of Jay Teeter as they depart from amongst us and seek a new life in strange places. Be with them as they search the way, Lord, and see to it they find the kind of home that all God's chillun deserve. They's good folks, Lord, and we'll all miss 'em mightedly, and we ask that You keep 'em in Yore hands and help 'em find the happiness they now seek. Bless us all, oh Lord, and watch over these mountains and all God's chillun. Amen, and let's eat."

Jared said quickly, "Thanks, Brother Will. We appreciate those words. But before everyone starts eatin' I got a few words to say too. When we leave in the mornin' we're not takin' anything in the house with us. They just ain't no room in the van. So I want all of you to come back here in the mornin' and take out what you want. Everything stays behind."

One man said, "That ain't right, Jay. We could sell all this stuff fer you and then send you the money. I'd buy some myself."

"Won't sell a piece of it," Jared said firmly. "All of you know that my Papa built this house afore the turn of the century, and most of this stuff has been in the house since then. Some of it he made hisself. I couldn't sell one piece of it, and I won't rest easy unless I know it's all in the hands of friends."

Cloma spoke up and said, "Don't nobody take the brass bed, though, if you get here afore Papa. Papa has said he'll take it to his place and store it for me, and then we can send for it when we get settled. Everything goes but the brass bed."

Jared was relieved to hear this and was glad that the bed would be safe with Cloma's father. He said, "I'll leave the house open in the mornin', and you can all come back and clean it out. Whatever you don't take will just be wasted with the real estate man, so take it all. Let's eat now, and then we'll have a little fiddle music and some stompin' before everyone goes."

No one needed a second invitation to fill their plates, but no one was as fast as the preacher in reaching the table.

Jared stood on the porch and watched as the last truck headlight disappeared around a bend in the road far below. He sensed that he might have seen the last of his friends for a long time to come, perhaps even forever. He turned and went into the house and said to Bennie, "You best go outside and fetch Skip in, and see to it he stays inside. We'll be leavin' afore dawn, and we won't have time to be chasin' a dog all over the woods."

"Yes, Papa," Bennie said, scrambling for the door.

Jared then took a kerosene lantern from the kitchen shelf, lit it, and turned to Cloma. "I'll be gone fer a bit, but it won't be too long."

She understood what he must do. She said, "You want that I go with you?"

"No. 'Tain't no use fer you to be out in the dark and the night air. I'll go alone."

A dome of orange light sprang outward as he went down the back steps and across the yard. He walked rapidly as he followed a narrow trail that turned north from the barn and ran along the edge of the ridge. Soon he entered a thick growth of hickory trees. The flickering light revealed two granite tombstones in a little clearing which was surrounded by a rusted cast-iron fence. He opened the gate and went inside.

He set the lantern on the ground and dropped to his knees in front of the graves. A glass vase holding faded plastic flowers sat between the two stones. Jared remained silent, thinking of those two times in the past when he had taken a shovel in his hands and physically dug the holes where the two bodies now lay. He had always assumed that he too would someday lie in this plot of ground, but now it seemed that this would never be, and he was afraid.

He also thought of his lifetime on this land, of how deeply his roots were sunk into the West Virginia mountain soil, and the thought of tearing them up so late in life was like ripping out his very heart. For weeks he had been consumed with doubts and anxiety, with a fear of leaving all that he knew and facing the unknown; but he had kept it all hidden within himself as best he could. He did not want Cloma and the children to see his true feelings, for he knew that he must show strength for all of them.

Finally he broke his thoughts and said, "I'm sorry, Papa ... and Mamma ... I done the best I could, but it weren't enough. I just couldn't make it no more ... I tried, but it just couldn't be done. I purely hate to go off and leave you here alone, and I never thought I would. But they ain't nothin' more I can do. I've made sure nobody will ever put plow or axe to this grove and disturb you. It's in the deed, writ right in there, so you can rest easy on that score. Maybe some day we can buy back the land and be with you again. I promise you I'll do my best, I'll try; but now we gotta go. The Lord be with you ... Papa and Mamma ... the Lord be with you. And rest well."

He then got to his feet quickly and walked back along the trail, not looking back again at the grove of darkened hickory trees.

When he approached the house, all was in darkness except for a dim glow coming from behind a drawn window shade in his and Cloma's bedroom. Sharp rumbles of thunder were rushing in from the west, signalling the coming of a storm. Brilliant fingers of lightning shot downward and disappeared into the black outlines of distant ridges. For a moment Jared watched as the lightning moved eastward, and then he opened the back door as quietly as possible and walked softly down the hall to the bedroom.

Cloma was in the bed asleep, so Jared tried to make no sound as he removed his clothes. He looked at Cloma's tousled blonde hair and marveled at how much Kristy looked like her. Both had the same blonde hair, delicate nose and cheekbones, and thin mouth. Bennie was just the opposite, with Jared's black hair, full face, and the tall lanky body of a mountain man. Although tall, Bennie still had the look of a boy, but Kristy — like most mountain girls her age — already had the fully developed body of a woman, a mountain child-woman. Jared had always said that both he and Cloma had been allowed to stamp one child each from their own individual molds. When Cloma had become pregnant again, Jared teased her that now they would have a sandy-haired boy who would have the features of both of them.

Suddenly Cloma said sleepily, "Is that you, Jay?" Then she pushed herself up and said, "The youngens was dog-tired from all the excitement of the day. They went on to bed right after Bennie caught Skip and brung him inside. I hope you didn't have much for them to do tonight."

"No, there wasn't nothin' more to do. It's best they went on to bed. We got a long way to travel."

He turned off the light and slipped under the covers beside her, putting his hand across her swollen stomach. It seemed to him that every little thing that he did now reminded him of something in the past. As he was immersed in darkness he thought of how proud he had been that day several years ago when he finally ran the electric line to the house. All of them had stayed up half the night clicking the lights off and on, like children with new toys on Christmas morning.

Cloma pushed herself closer to Jared and said, "I'm afraid, Jay. Maybe I shouldn't be, but I am."

"Afraid of what, the storm?" he asked.

"No. Not that. I'm afraid of what lies ahead for all of us."

"You got nothin' to fret about," Jared said reassuringly as he moved his hand back and forth across her stomach. "We'll make it fine . . . I promise you. The Lord will look after us. What I'm worried about most is you and that little fellow inside you. You sure you feel up to leavin' now? We could move around and stay with different folks 'til the baby comes."

"I feel fine, and I'd rather go now. That way we could be settled sommers when the baby comes. It'd be easier to go now than wait 'til later."

"All right. We'll go on and go as we planned. But if you get to feelin' poorly along the way, you best let me know. We'll stop sommers and stay put 'til you feel like movin' on again."

Cloma did not answer, and Jared could feel that she had already drifted back to sleep. He held her gently and said softly, "Don't you fret none, Cloma. We'll make out fine. You'll see."

For several minutes Jared listened as the storm moved closer to Teeter Ridge. He knew that soon now it would lash his land with its full fury. He was concerned about the hogs and the chickens and the cow until he realized that they were no longer there. He suddenly sprang upright in the bed as if a bolt of lightning had crashed through the roof and seared into his body. A cold fear of what lay ahead swept through his veins and caused sweat to form on his brow. He tried to calm himself but the flashes of lightning and the booming thunder made the apprehension worse. His hands trembled as he tried to push himself back under the covers.

Cloma came awake and said to him, "What's the matter, Jay? You're jumpin' around like a new colt."

" 'Tain't nothin' but the storm. It sounded like the lightnin' hit awful close by. I'm sorry I woke you again, so just go on back to sleep now."

Again he put his arms around her, this time trying vainly to shut away all consciousness of the storm and to dispel from himself the pent-up spectre of disaster that had finally erupted from every pore of his body.

TWO

THE HOOD of the old Dodge van seemed to be sweating as the vehicle chugged unsteadily along Highway 27, passing a line of Australian pines on the left and an open field on the right. The mid-day Florida sun was sending waves of heat shimmering upward from the cracked concrete. The van suddenly shuddered and belched forth a hissing cloud of angry steam. Valves clanked and rattled as the truck rolled slowly to a stop beside a drainage canal flanking the right side of the highway.

Jared got out of the van and raised the hood. When he removed the radiator cap he released a violent geyser of boiling water. He jumped back, shook his scorched hand and muttered, "Jesus!"

For a moment he stared at the hissing radiator, then he walked to the side of the van and said, "It'll take that thing a while to cool down afore I can put in some water. We might as well eat now."

Cloma pulled herself slowly from the right door of the van. Her stomach seemed more swollen than ever. She was followed by Kristy and Bennie.

Cloma settled herself unsteadily on the ground and spread out a newspaper. From a brown paper bag she removed four cans of Vienna sausage, a box of crackers, and four bottles of hot Coke. They all sat in the white limestone dust and started eating silently.

Jared looked past the drainage canal and across the field that stretched as far as the eye could see toward the horizon. Far in the distance, giant sheets of water were being sprayed into the air, and a group of people followed a truck piled high with crates. Jared took a bite of the sausage and said, 'I ain't never seen a field like that in my lifetime. It looks like the whole world out there, don't it?"

Cloma looked but said nothing.

Bennie said, "Can I let Skip out of the truck, Papa? He probably needs to do his job."

"No. You better not. He might run out in the highway and get himself killed. You better leave him in the van 'til we get there."

"How much farther is it, Papa?" Kristy asked.

" 'Tain't far now. We're almost to Homestead. We'll be there in just a little bit more, and then we can all rest up some."

"I want to see the ocean," Bennie said, excitement in his voice. "You said that when we got to Floridy we would see the ocean, and we ain't seen it yet."

"It's over in the east," Jared said. "You'll get to see it soon enough."

"Will we get to fish in the ocean?" Bennie asked.

"Yes. We'll fish. And someday we might even own our own boat."

"I don't want to catch any smelly ole fish," Kristy said tartly. "I want a bathin' suit. A red one in two pieces, just like you see in the magazines."

"You all better worry about where we'll sleep tonight,

and forget all that foolishness for now," Cloma said wearily as she gathered up the empty cans.

"Are you feelin' all right, Cloma?" Jared asked.

"Yes. I'm fine. I'm just fine."

"Are you sure?"

"Yes, Jay, I'm fine!" she insisted. "I'm just fine."

"Well, if you get to feelin' poorly again, we'll try to find a motel."

"We can't afford a motel," Cloma said firmly. "And I've already said I'm feelin' fine. That spell the other day was just an upset stomach. I'm fine now."

Jared went to the van and came back with a bucket. He filled it in the drainage canal and took the water back to the van. Cloma gathered up the newspapers and bottles and put them back into the brown paper bag.

When Jared cranked the engine, they all got back inside, and the van pulled slowly back onto the highway and headed south.

The Teeter family had been on the road for almost two weeks on a trip they had expected to take no more than four or five days. The morning they left the West Virginia farm before daylight, they had all been drenched by a bone-chilling rainstorm, and the dog Skip had managed to jump from the van and escape into the darkness. Bennie had chased him for a half-hour before hemming him up in the barn and returning him soaking wet to the van.

Misfortune plagued them almost constantly. When Jared traded his pickup truck for the Dodge van, he had taken the word of the salesman that the van was in good condition. Before they reached the West Virginia state line, the water-pump gave out and had to be replaced, causing them the loss of the better part of a day. A universal joint stripped itself in North Carolina, and then the next day two tires blew out and shredded. They spent three days in a small town in north Georgia waiting at a garage for a new generator to be shipped in from Atlanta, a generator that all the while had been on a shelf in the rear of the garage but was now priced higher because of "shipping charges." One night they stayed in a motel, but the rest of the nights they slept in the van. Then it was the spark plug wires and a coil, and finally the radiator became hostile as they moved deeper into warm weather. This slowed them to below the legal speed limit. Just north of Jacksonville, Jared was arrested and fined thirty-five dollars for a faulty brake light. The court appearance and the repairs took another day. Jared's limited supply of cash had diminished quickly in a series of roadside garages and unexpected delays. And then to avoid any more fines on the heavily-policed interstate highways, Jared drove inland and traveled along less used state roads leading south to Lake Okeechobee and then Homestead.

All of this did not dampen the excitement of Kristy and Bennie, but it brought even deeper anxiety to Jared and Cloma. To the youngsters the trip had turned into an adventure; but to Jared and Cloma it was still the end of all things they had ever known.

With each mile they traveled, Jared's emotions ran up and down like a yo-yo. One moment he was optimistic and confident, and the next moment he was cast again into deep doubt. He tried to appear cheerful and confident, but Cloma knew that he was tormented with doubt.

Kristy and Bennie stared out of the window in the rear door of the van as they approached the outskirts of Homestead. They had both been fascinated since they first entered the citrus country to the north of Lake Okeechobee. The miles and miles of trees laden with golden fruit seemed to them to be all the Christmases they had known rolled into one, since the only time they had ever seen or eaten oranges was on Christmas morning when they found them under the sparsely decorated tree.

On both sides of the highway there were now vegetable fields intermingled with groves of avocado and papaya and mangoes and limes and other strange things they had never seen. Farm roads leading off to the left and right were lined with towering Australian pines and stately royal palms and dumpy cabbage palms. Stands displaying an endless variety of fruits and vegetables were located at almost every intersection.

Jared suddenly turned to Cloma and said, as if in an unexpected revelation, "That's what we'll have, Cloma! A roadside stand where we can sell fruits and vegetables. We'll do it as soon as we can save up the money. We can make ourselves a good livin' with a stand. It won't take us no time at all to get one."

Cloma considered the idea for a moment, and then she said enthusiastically, "That would be real good. Maybe we could make some things ourselves and sell them too. You were always good at makin' cane-bottom chairs, and Kristy makes real fine pot-holders. Bennie could make whatnot shelves and those little carved animals he makes, and I could sew aprons and blouses and make those red and yellow sunbonnets some folks like. If we had a little piece of land behind the stand, we could grow our own vegetables too."

Jared was pleased that she agreed. He smiled as he said with his first excitement in weeks, "We'll do it! It won't take us no time at all!"

The two-lane highway was now jammed with huge trucks and cars and pickups, all seemingly frantic to move faster toward a distant destination. Driving became more and more difficult for Jared, and the task took all of his attention. He prayed silently that the radiator would not boil again and force him from the highway.

Highway 27 was also the main street leading through the business section of Homestead, and Jared felt a tremendous sensation of relief when he passed the city limits of this place they had searched for so long and had endured so many difficulties to reach. He sighed when he stopped for the first traffic light. But his feeling of relief that the long trip was finally ended was immediately replaced by the bewilderment of being in a totally strange place and not knowing where to go or what to do. He drove the van even more slowly, backing up traffic behind him and causing other impatient drivers to honk their horns and gesture angrily. They all stared like tourists as they passed block after block of stores and restaurants and cocktail lounges and supermarkets unlike anything they had ever seen in their rural section of West Virginia.

On the southern end of the city they came to an area of huge packing houses where the vegetables were processed before being shipped to distant markets. Before he realized it, Jared had left Homestead and entered Florida City. He finally pulled to the side of the road and stopped.

For a moment they all became silent with exhaustion, and then Bennie said, "I gotta leak, Papa. And I know Skip is about to bust."

The small black and white dog was leaning against one wall of the van, panting.

Cloma said, "We should have never brought that dog with us. We could have given him away. A trip like this is no place for a dog."

"Aw, Cloma, you know the kids couldn't leave Skip behind," Jared said. "And besides, he won't be any trouble."

Bennie put his arm around the dog and said, "I'll take care of him, Mamma. You don't need to worry none about him."

"I'll find a service station and get gas, and you can use the restrooms there," Jared said, cranking the motor again.

He pulled into a station on the next corner. Bennie took

Skip behind the building while his mother and Kristy went to the women's room.

The attendant set the automatic control on the pump nozzle and said to Jared, "You folks tourists?"

"No," Jared said. "We're down here lookin' for work."

"You mean picking?" the man asked.

"Well, anything," Jared replied. "I'm not particular just so long as it's honest work."

"Jobs in the fields are pretty hard to come by right now, and that's about all there is around here," the man said as he stared at Jared's lanky body and faded overalls. "Besides all the regular migrants, the place is swarming with Cubans, and there's been a steady stream of folks like you coming in here from the Carolinas and West Virginia and Georgia and Alabama and all over the place. I ain't never seen nothing like it."

"You mean there ain't no work?" Jared asked, deep concern in his voice.

"Well, there's some, but you sure got to look to find it. And it might be pretty hard for you with no experience. There's a line-up every morning right over yonder on the street corner."

"What's that?" Jared asked.

"All the folks who want jobs in the field gather over there, and the contractors hire who they want. If you want to try that, you better get there early, way before sun-up. There's always a lot more people than jobs."

"I'll be there," Jared said.

The man then turned his attention from Jared and watched Kristy as she came from the restroom and walked back to the van. He noticed every move of her body, the full breasts and hips, and then he said to Jared, "That your girl?"

"That's my daughter Kristy," Jared replied.

"How old is she?"

"She's sixteen, and she's a mighty fine girl," Jared said proudly.

The man studied Kristy closely again, and then he said, "The way she's built, she could easily pass for twenty. She could get a job real easy."

"How's that?" Jared asked curiously.

"Can she dance?"

"Back home we had a barn dance every Saturday night. She's pretty good at it."

"I mean go-go dance," the man said. "She could get a job easy in any of the lounges, and that pays good money. She could get you by 'til you find work."

"What's this go-go dancin'?" Jared asked.

The man looked at Jared curiously and said, "You know, fellow, go-go. Dancing naked from the waist up with the tits showing. The way she's built, she could take her pick of the joints."

An instant rage boiled up within Jared. He said quickly, "How much I owe you, fellow?"

"Eight dollars even. You want the oil checked?"

"I don't want nothin' more from you!" Jared shot back angrily. His hands trembled as he handed the man the money. Then he jumped into the van and screeched the tires as he drove away.

Cloma was startled by the sudden burst of speed. She said, "What's the matter, Jay? Did somethin' happen back there?"

"No. Nothin'," Jared said, trying to calm his voice. "It's gettin' late, and we gotta try and find a place to make camp fer tonight."

Jared turned the van back east, and then he drove slowly along a narrow side street. It took him several minutes to brush from his mind the thought of Kristy dancing naked in a bar. He knew he had come close to striking the man but was glad that he had simply driven away. Trouble was one thing he did not need at this point.

He soon came to a small park with swings, benches and a picnic area with a covered pavilion and barbeque grille. No one was there, so Jared turned the van into the park and stopped by the pavilion. He said, "This looks about as good as we'll find. And there's a roof fer me and Bennie to sleep under while you and Kristy can have the van."

Bennie said, "Can I let Skip out of the truck, Papa?"

"Well, you better put a rope around his neck and tie him to the front bumper. They's bound to be rabbits around here, and I don't feel a mind to be chasin' Skip all over south Floridy."

Jared took two bedrolls out of the van and placed them on the concrete beneath the pavilion. He turned to Cloma and said, "How much vittles we got left?"

Cloma settled herself on a bench and replied, "We got about a half-dozen cans of Vienna sausage, some bread, and a can of peaches."

"That'll do fer tonight," Jared said. "I'll see to some supplies in the mornin'."

Bennie came running around the side of the van and said with excitement, "They's a bunch of funny-lookin' trees right over yonder, Papa! And they got real bananas growin' on them! You want me to go and pick some for supper?"

"No. You better not do that. They probably belong to somebody. But you better scout around and scrape up some branches. We'll need a fire later."

Kristy came from the van and said, "Papa, they's somethin' bitin' all over me. It stings somethin' awful."

Jared suddenly slapped at his face and arms and said, "Skeeters! Jesus, the whole place is swarmin' with skeeters. That's all we need now, to be et alive by skeeters. Maybe we can smoke 'em away."

Bennie slapped his arms and said, "I'll get the wood now, Papa. We'll show them skeeters a thing or two for sure."

The sun was just beginning to set when the patrol car

passed the park. The officer inside noticed the West Virginia
tag and the bedrolls under the pavilion. He turned, came back
and parked beside the van. Then he got out and said, "You
folks having a cookout?"

Jared got up from the bench and said, "No, we're not
doin' any cookin'. We done et. We're just tryin' to run the
skeeters off with the smoke."

The officer was a young man of about thirty. He looked
to the van and then back to Jared. "I see you folks are from
West Virginia. That's a pretty far piece from here. You just
down for a vacation?"

"No, we come to stay," Jared replied. "We just got in this
afternoon, and I'll start lookin' fer work tomorrow."

"Well," the officer said hesitantly, "it's o.k. for you to
eat here and rest for a while, but you can't stay the night.
Overnight camping in a city park is against the law. You'll
have to move on before dark."

Jared didn't understand. He said, "Ain't this public
property?"

"Yes, it's public property," the officer replied.

"Back in West Virginny, anybody who wants to can camp
on public property so long as they don't disturb nothin'. We
ain't doin' no harm."

"I'm sorry," the officer said, noticing that the woman
was heavy with child. "It's the law, and there's nothing I can
do about it. Why don't you go to a motel or a boarding house
for the night?"

"I guess we could," Jared said, "but we just can't rightly
afford it. We had a lot of bad luck comin' down, and we need
to save all the money we can."

"You can go to the Salvation Army place, then," the
officer said.

"The Salvation Army?" Jared questioned. "We're mountain folk, and we don't take charity from nobody."

The officer was trying to be patient because of the

woman and the children. Turning migrants out of the park at night was a regular nightly routine for him. He said, "It wouldn't exactly be charity. The Salvation Army is there just to help folks like you when they need help. They have a big empty lot with trees where you could park the van for tonight and make camp. Just doing that wouldn't be charity."

"I guess we could do that," Jared said. "We do need a place to camp fer tonight, and as soon as I find work tomorrow, I'll look about and find us a boardin' house 'til we can get our own place. We don't want to break any laws. We're peaceable folks. All we want is to make a home here."

The officer was relieved. He said, "Well, you go right up there one block, turn left, go for four more blocks, and the Salvation Army is right on the corner. You can't miss it. It's a big two-story white frame house."

As soon as the patrol car had left, Jared gathered up the bedrolls and put them into the van. Bennie untied Skip and brought him inside, and then they drove slowly up the street. Jared found the house with no trouble, and he parked the van beneath a huge live oak. He then got out and walked to the front of the house.

A man got up from a rocking chair on the porch and came to meet Jared. He looked Jared over carefully and said, "Something we can do for you?"

Jared still did not like the idea of being here, and he was glad that his friends back in West Virginia would never know that he had gone to the Salvation Army. He said reluctantly, "We just need a place to park the van fer tonight and make camp. A policeman sent us here. Is it o.k. there under the tree?"

"That's fine," the man said. "You folks just passing through?"

"No, we're here to stay," Jared answered. "I'll find work tomorrow, and then I'll get us a place. We had some bad luck comin' down."

"If you want, there's empty bunks upstairs. It's free, and you can sleep inside out of the night air. There's also hot showers."

"We'll stay in the van," Jared replied.

"Suit yourself. You can park out there as long as you like. We've got a sitting room inside with a TV. While you're out looking for work tomorrow, your folks can stay here. And supper will be ready in about fifteen minutes. It's nothing fancy — hot franks and beans, cole slaw, and hot coffee. You're welcome to eat with us if you wish."

The thought of hot food and coffee interested Jared. He had not had coffee for more than a week, and he knew that the others were not satisfied with the small cans of Vienna sausage that had been their supper. He said, "How much does it cost?"

"It's free," the man replied.

"We can't take your food fer nothin'," Jared said. "We're mountain folk, and we don't take charity. How much would it cost if we paid?"

The man hesitated for a moment, and then he said, "Well, you can put whatever you wish in the donation box inside the hall. I'd say that fifty cents would be fine for all of you."

"That seems fair enough," Jared said. "We'll all come on inside as soon as we make camp. And we do thank you rightly fer letting us park the van."

"That's what we're here for," the man replied. As he turned and went back up the steps to the porch, he muttered to himself, "Mountain folk!"

THREE

JARED WAS up before dawn the next morning and left the Salvation Army building before breakfast. He drove directly to the street corner where the man at the service station had told him the line-up was held each day. Several pickup trucks and old buses were already parked beneath a street light, and a large group of men and women were milling around silently, waiting for the ritual to begin.

Jared noticed that some of the people were white and some black; some were Cubans and some Mexicans, although he could not tell one from another; and others were long-haired, bearded hippies accompanied by young girls with strings of wooden beads around their necks and sweatbands tied around their foreheads. All of them had expressionless faces and moved about as if in a trance. Each of them — both men and women — somehow resembled the other.

It was but a few minutes when a man stood up in the back of a truck and shouted, "I need twenty-five hands for okra!" People pushed by Jared frantically and formed a line. As soon as the twenty-five were hired and given passes to board a bus, the others in the line moved to another truck.

Jared watched with interest as two more crews were hired. The whole process seemed to him like he had always imagined an ancient slave market to be. He finally realized that unless he fought his way into a line, he would still be standing on the curb when the last bus was filled.

When another man shouted an order for tomato pickers, Jared pushed his way into the crowd and worked his way forward. When he reached the head of the line, the man glanced at him briefly and said, "You got experience picking tomatoes?"

Jared said, "Well, I owned my own farm back in West Virginny, and I growed a few tomatoes. I always picked what I growed."

"Step aside," the man said briskly. "I don't want nothing but experienced pickers. We got a sixty-acre field to clear this morning, and we ain't got time to fool with no friggin' hillbilly."

"But I can do it," Jared insisted. "I owned my own. . ."

"Goddamit, fellow, are you deaf?" the man said impatiently. "Move aside! I ain't got all day to get this bus rolling."

Jared moved out of the line and walked dejectedly back to the curb. He made no other attempt to get into a line as he watched the last bus being loaded. Several dozen other people had also been turned away or had failed to make it to the head of the lines, and they slowly drifted away into the shadows. Jared was alone beneath the street light as dawn streaked through the eastern sky.

For a half-hour Jared sat on the curb, gazing absently at the buses and trucks that ambled by, trying to determine what he must do now. Finally he decided to try the packing houses. He got into the van and drove along the main street into Homestead.

It did not bother him that he had left Cloma and the

children behind while he looked for work, for he knew that watching the TV would be a real treat to them. He had also left the money with Cloma to pay for the meals while he was gone.

When he reached the last packing house on the western outskirts of the city, he stopped and went inside. As soon as he inquired about work, he was told that only experienced graders were needed, and that all other jobs were filled. From one plant he went to another, working his way back toward Florida City; and at each plant the story was the same.

It was mid-morning when he was rejected by the last packing house, and he felt more despondent and hopeless than ever. He then drove the van back into Homestead, parked in a city lot, and started walking the streets. At first the tourists in their shorts and brightly colored shirts and blouses interested him, but then his thoughts went back only to finding a job.

Soon he came to a farm supply store and went inside to inquire about work on the loading platform or driving a truck, but again there was none. He then left the main area of town and walked along a narrow side street lined with dingy pawn shops and bargain stores. Already there were faceless men sitting along the sidewalk, drinking from bottles inside brown paper bags. Jared finally paused when he passed the front of a place called Blue Moon Cafe and noticed a sign in the window that read: "Help Wanted."

Jared went inside reluctantly, almost certain that he would not be suitable for work in a cafe. The small room was dimly lit and smelled strongly of boiled cabbage and stale bacon grease. There was a counter at the back of the room, and tables occupied the center and sides. Except for two men drinking coffee at the counter, the place was empty.

For several moments Jared stood by the counter and shuffled his feet nervously, thinking that perhaps it was a mistake even to come inside. Then a short fat man wearing a dirty apron and a white cap came from the kitchen area and said to him, "What'll it be, fellow?"

"Well," Jared said hesitantly, "I noticed the sign in the window. I'm lookin' fer work, and I just thought I'd come in and ask about it."

The man eyed Jared closely and said, "My dishwasher took sick yesterday and will be out for a couple of days. The pay is a buck an hour, and you can put in seven hours today and thirteen tomorrow. You want it?"

Jared replied quickly, "Yes. I'll do it. When you want me to start?"

"Right now," the man replied. "All them breakfast dishes is piled up back there, and I can't tend to it and cook and wait the tables. Come on back and I'll show you what to do."

Jared followed the man into the kitchen area. On one side there was a stove filled with simmering pots of squash and cabbage and black-eyed peas, and a huge frying pan. Against the opposite wall there were two large sinks, one filled with a combination of greasy water and tired soap suds, and the other plain water.

The man said to Jared, "You wash 'em in here and rinse in there. After you dry 'em, stack 'em on the shelf over yonder. It's also your job to clear the tables and the counter and keep the floor swept. At quitting time, you put out all the slop and garbage. We start serving breakfast at five, so be here a little before that in the morning. And let's get something straight right now, fellow. The pay don't include no meals. What you eat you pay for. And everything you break comes out of your wages. You understand?"

"Yes, I understand," Jared said. He had a sickening feeling as he stared at the huge mound of dirty dishes and utensils stacked on a table beside the sink.

The man turned to leave, and then he looked back at Jared and said, "You better go sommers tonight and take a bath and wash them overalls. The way you look, you'll have the health department down on me."

Jared glanced down briefly at his dirty clothes, and then he grimaced as he picked up a dish and tried to wash the dried egg yolk from it in the greasy water.

It was nearly dark when Jared returned to the Salvation Army building. Cloma, Kristy and Bennie were sitting on a bench beneath the huge oak tree. Jared parked the van, walked over to them and settled himself wearily on the bench.

Cloma said, "We was gettin' real worried about you, Jay. You've been gone so long."

"I tried a little bit of everything," Jared said. "They wouldn't hire me at the line-up because I didn't have no experience, and then I tried all the packin' houses and a few stores. Don't seem to be nothin' around here fer a man to do, so's we might have to move on sommers else. Maybe it would be better up in the cattle country."

Cloma noticed the tiredness in his voice. She said encouragingly, "Maybe it will be better tomorrow. We only been here two days now. Maybe tomorrow you'll find what you want."

"I got work fer tomorrow. And I worked seven hours today. It didn't pay but a dollar an hour, but I guess that's better than nothin'."

Cloma was surprised by this. She asked curiously, "Where'd you work?"

"In a cafe."

"A cafe?" Cloma questioned. "You don't know anything about that kind of work. What'd you do?"

"I worked," Jared said guardedly, wishing that he had not even told them about it.

"Doin' what?" Cloma insisted.

Jared remained silent for a moment, and then he cast his eyes downward and said, "Washin' dishes."

Cloma put her hand on his arm and said, "Jared . . . Jared . . . you didn't have to do that. We're not that hard up yet, are we?"

"It was honest work," he insisted defensively.

Kristy jumped up and said, "Papa, you ought not be washin' dishes in a cafe. I'll wash the dishes tomorrow, and you can look for other work. That's not the kind of thing for you to do."

Jared considered the idea briefly, and then he said, "Would you really do that, Kristy? It would mean thirteen dollars, and I could go on lookin' fer somethin' else. Maybe tomorrow I'll try all the service stations. I sure know how to pump gas and fix flat tires, and somebody is bound to need help."

"I'll do it, Papa!" Kristy said enthusiastically.

For the first time that day, Jared became aware of how hungry he was. He had not eaten since the night before, and now his stomach was rumbling. He said, "Well, it's settled then. I'll look around for another day before we decide what else to do. But right now I sure need to go inside and have some vittles. I'm powerful hongry, and even them franks and beans would go good."

When he got up, Cloma stood by him and took his hand in hers. She said, "Jared, I ain't ashamed of what you did today. I know you did it for all of us. You're a good man, Jared Teeter, and I love you for it. You got no need to be ashamed."

He put his arm around her, and they walked together to the two-story white frame building.

Cloma and Bennie rode with Jared when he took Kristy to the Blue Moon Cafe the next morning. Although it was not yet five, the place was already filled with solemn men dressed as field hands, and the owner was impatient as he told Jared that it was all right for Kristy to substitute for him at the sinks so long as she could keep up with the work. Kristy insisted that she could. Jared paid the man the price of a breakfast and lunch for Kristy, and then he went back to the van and started driving the streets.

Only one service station in Homestead was open at that hour, and the manager had nothing to offer in the way of work. He returned to the Salvation Army, had breakfast with Cloma and Bennie, and then left them behind as he started on his rounds again.

By late morning he had visited every station between Homestead and Florida City, and there were no jobs available. He had given up hope and was ready to quit when he pulled into one last station on the west side of Florida City. He parked behind the building, and walked to the front.

No customers were there, and the manager was standing outside by a pump island. When Jared came to him he said, "Something I can do for you?"

Jared anticipated what the answer would be as he asked, "I'm lookin' fer work, and I thought maybe you needed some help. I can pump gas or fix flats or do 'most anything you want me to do."

The man studied Jared, and then he asked, "Where you from, fellow?"

"West Virginny. We just got down here a couple of days ago."

"How much family you got?"

"I got a girl sixteen and a boy fourteen."

"They good and healthy?"

"Yes," Jared replied, beginning to wonder at the questions that had nothing to do with his request for a job.

"How about your old lady?" the man then asked.

"Well, she's strong, but she's about seven months along with a new baby."

The man looked at Jared closely again and said, "I ain't

got no work here just now, but have you thought about doing any picking?"

"They wouldn't hire me in that line-up yesterday mornin'," Jared said, disappointed at being turned down again. "But I would sure do it or anythin' if I could just find work."

"Well, that line-up don't mean nothing. It's just a one-day shot for drifters and bums. I'm talking about steady work. I can probably help you if you want me to."

"That would be mighty fine of you," Jared said quickly, surprised by the unexpected offer. "I'd sure appreciate anything you can do."

Jared waited outside as the man went into the station office, picked up the phone and dialed. In a moment he said, "This Creedy? . . . yeah . . . this is Hankins at the service station . . . you need some people? . . . no, they're not black, they're white . . . hillbilly types from West Virginia . . . four of them . . . not the kind to give you trouble I don't think . . . man's around forty . . . says he has a strong boy and a girl . . . the woman's knocked up, though . . . a white Dodge van, about a '60 or '61 . . . o.k., I'll send them to the regular place . . . you'll meet them first thing in the morning then . . . three of them can work, so at twenty bucks a head, you owe me sixty dollars, and I want the money tonight . . . bring it to the station around eight."

The man then hung up the phone and came back out to Jared. "Well, I've got you folks fixed up with some jobs," he said.

"You really mean it?" Jared exclaimed, breaking into a broad grin. "I don't know how to thank you. I was about ready to give up."

"Glad to help out. You don't need to thank me. The man who's going to see you is named Creedy. Silas Creedy. You can camp tonight in a hammock about four miles down 27. It's on the left of the road just behind a sign advertising the Everglades National Park. You can't miss it. He'll meet you there first thing in the morning. You do a good job, this'll probably be steady work for a long time to come."

"I'll do a good job," Jared said eagerly, "and I sure don't know how to thank you enough." He extended his hand and said, "My name's Teeter. Jared Teeter. Folks call me Jay."

The man shook his hand briefly. "Glad to meet you, Jay." he said.

Jared then handed the man a ten-dollar bill and said, "This is just a little somethin' to say thanks. I really appreciate it."

The man took the bill and put it into his pocket. He said, "Well, o.k., but I didn't expect any money. I was just helping you out, that's all. Folks has to help each other these days."

"That's what I always believed. Folks has to help each other. And I sure thank you plenty."

Jared then got into the van and drove quickly back to the Salvation Army place. He rushed up the steps and found Cloma and Bennie inside the sitting room. He did a brisk jig on the worn wooden floor and said to them, "I told you! I told you comin' down here, didn't I? We're goin' to be o.k. I've got steady work already!"

"Are you foolin' me, Jared?" Cloma asked anxiously.

"No, it's the God's truth! A man at a filling station made a phone call, and somebody named Creedy is goin' to come in the mornin' and give us work. We're to stay tonight in a hammock down south of here. I've got the directions."

"We'll need food," Cloma said with excitement, trying to control the flood of relief this news was bringing to her.

"And ice," Jared said, "a big bag of ice so's we can have cold drinks. We'll pick up Kristy first, then we'll go to a market and get all the things we need fer tonight and in the mornin'. We'll get some candy bars fer the kids, and some sweet buns and fresh fruit, and some meat scraps fer Skip, and. . . ."

"Oh, Jay, I'm so glad," Cloma interrupted. "I was so

afraid for us."

"We're goin't to be just fine," Jared said, reaching over and pressing her hand. "You needin' worry one bit. We'll have our own place afore time fer the baby to come. And we can send fer the bed, too."

FOUR

A BRISK coolness was in the air as a mid-October dawn broke the clear Florida sky. The sun would soon send waves of dry heat across the land as it inched upward in the sky, making the soil a hostile enemy that scorched plants and strained the endurance of a man; but now the ground was covered with millions of glistening moisture jewels that changed color constantly with the growing light.

Jared awoke slowly and gazed upward into the tops of the cabbage palms. The thickness of the trees, combined with the heavy growths of palmetto, filtered the yet weak sunlight and caused the hammock to glow dimly like the coals of a dying fire. For a moment more he lay still, then he bolted upright and jumped to his feet. He calmed himself only when he looked to the left, saw the van, and realized where he was.

He moved quietly so as not to awaken anyone. After gathering sticks and starting a fire, he turned up the dirt trail leading back to the highway. When he reached the edge of the ribbon of black asphalt, he squatted on his haunches and looked out across the fields that melted into the distant horizon. A thin layer of fog lay motionless just above the ground. It was broken into wisps as egrets swooped upward and downward while searching the fields for food.

Jared gazed intensely for several minutes, thinking not of a time here in this strange Florida hammock, but back once again to those acres in West Virginia where the soil was mixed with the blood of his father and his mother and his wife and children. Times there had been hard, and sometimes almost desperate, but he had been his own man in a world of his own making. He had been beholden to no one as he now must be, but the price for this foolish and stubborn pride had been more than he could pay and was now coming up for collection.

He thought of Cloma, lying pregnant on the hard floor of the van, and of the day so long ago when they met at a church social as he bid fifty cents for her box of fried chicken, which he later shared with her. Their meeting had been nothing more than his contribution to the church build- ing fund, or so it seemed at the exact moment; but as they walked to the picnic table by the church to spread the dinner, he accidentally touched her shoulder, and he knew instantly that he would spend his life with her.

He thought again of all those doubts and anxieties that had tormented him during the trip southward from West Virginia, asking himself if he had really done the right thing or if he should have tried for one more year to hold on to the land. But he knew that his situation there had been hopeless and there was no other way except to leave; but the leaving had been an almost unbearable knife thrust through his heart.

It troubled him deeply to take Kristy and Bennie out of school, for the one thing he was determined to do in life was to give them the education which had been denied to him and to Cloma. He had not gone past the tenth grade, and Cloma had dropped out of the eleventh grade when they married. But there would be schools in Florida, and later there would be college, and roads would open for Kristy and Bennie that had been forever closed to him.

He knew that many things he left behind would haunt his memory forever: the woods where he hunted, the streams where he fished, the hillsides where he cut wood to keep them warm in winter, the fields that produced skimpy crops of corn and pumpkins, the barn with its early morning smells, the hickory grove where his father and mother rested; all these things would linger while the hurt and the pain and the hopelessness and the despair would someday fade away. But he was determined to push all of his former life from his mind, and create something new and good for all of them.

His trance was broken when he heard footsteps coming quickly up the dirt trail. He turned as Kristy ran up and said, "Mamma sent me lookin' for you, Papa. She said the coffee is ready."

Jared motioned and said, "Sit here beside me a minute, Kristy."

When she was settled on the damp grass, he said, "I want to thank you again fer what you did fer me in the cafe."

"It was nothing, Papa," she said. "I was just glad to help out."

"We're all going to be fine," Jared said, reaching over and touching her arm. "You'll see. Everything is going to work out o.k."

For a moment Kristy stared across the misty field in silence, and then she said, "Papa . . . I know everything is going to be fine with us . . . but someday . . . when we're all settled and Mamma and Bennie are taken care of . . . I want to go back to the mountains. Papa . . . do you understand?"

"I reckon as how I do," Jared said, again touching her arm gently. "I'd like to go back someday too. Fact is, I didn't want to leave . . . but there was no choice. I understand, Kristy. Someday you'll get all you want out of life. And that's a promise."

Kristy got up and said, "We better go now, Papa, before Mamma has to come and fetch us. She'll be worried."

He pushed himself up slowly and then followed Kristy back into the hammock.

It was after ten o'clock when the yellow Mark IV turned off the highway and entered the hammock. Jared had been pacing back and forth beside the van for hours, desperately worried that perhaps the man at the service station had played a cruel joke on him, that no one would come looking for him. He almost ran to meet the automobile as it stopped beside a cabbage palm.

A huge man got out and leaned against the front of the car. He was almost six and a half feet tall, and weighed over two hundred and fifty pounds. His hair was red and short-cropped, and his face was almost as red as his hair. He looked to be around fifty years old. He studied Jared carefully and said, "You the folks who're looking for work?"

"Yes," Jared said nervously. "I'm Jared Teeter. Folks call me Jay."

The man snorted and said, "Your last name should have been Bird. Then folks could call you Jay Bird." He looked at Jared closely again and asked, "Where you folks from?"

"West Virginny. We just got down here a few days ago. I met the man at the service station yesterday when I tried to get a job there."

"You got any kin folk around here?"

"No. All our kin is back in West Virginny."

The man seemed to be in deep thought for a moment, and then he said, "I'm Silas Creedy. You ever picked before?"

Jared scratched his head, remembering that this same question had cost him a job once before. He finally said, "Yes, sir, I've done a good bit of it. I owned my own farm, and I've picked plenty of corn and vegetables."

"I mean picking. Worked the fields down here."

"Well, no, I guess not," Jared said uneasily, "but I can do anythin' I'm a mind to do. I'd sure like to try pickin' or anythin' else you want me to do."

Creedy looked toward the van. "Are them younguns healthy?" he asked.

"Yes. They's fine kids."

"But you got your old lady's belly swole up."

"She's 'bout seven months along."

"We don't usually allow nobody in the camp who can't work."

Jared had a sinking feeling that he was not going to get the job. He said quickly, "Her bein' that way won't bother my workin'. She's a good woman, and she can look after herself durin' the day."

Creedy remained silent for a moment, then he said, "Well, I guess you folks will do. Maybe your woman can find something to do around the camp during the day."

"The camp?" Jared asked quizzically.

"Yeah, the camp. You folks will live in my labor camp. It's called Angel City."

"You mean we get housin' too?" Jared asked, surprised.

"Yeah, you get housing," Creedy said impatiently. "How many times do I have to tell you, fellow? You'll live in my labor camp."

"Why, that's fine, Mr. Creedy," Jared said, "just fine. I was awful worried 'bout where we would find a place to stay." He hesitated for a moment, and then he asked, "Mr. Creedy, how much does this work pay?"

"Depends on you," Creedy answered. "Tomatoes pays twenty-five cents a bucket. Other stuff generally pays by the hamper. If we pick fruit, it's by the tub. The more you work the more you make. It's up to you."

"What about the cost of the camp housin'?"

"Ah, there's a little charge for that, but it don't amount

to much of nothing. We take it out of your earnings ev'ry Saturday when you get paid. You get supper cooked at the camp, but you have to look out for yourself for breakfast and whatever you eat in the fields at noon."

"That sounds fair enough," Jared said. "I'd be mighty proud to work fer you, Mr. Creedy."

Creedy then said, "Before we go to the camp I want you to follow me back to Florida City and get signed up for food stamps."

The statement puzzled Jared. He said, "Mr. Creedy, I don't need no food stamps. I've never taken charity in my lifetime. Mountain folk don't take charity."

"It's not charity!" Creedy snapped, annoyed by Jared's unexpected answer. "It's coming to you from your taxes. Ev'rybody at Angel City gets food stamps. All you have to do is sign up, and I take care of it from there. It won't be any bother to you."

"Well, I guess I'll do it if you say so. But we don't take charity from nobody."

"You just follow me back to Florida City, and then we'll go to the camp and get you folks set up."

The Dodge van followed the Mark IV as it left the highway and moved slowly along a dirt road surrounded on both sides by tomato fields. A small island of Australian pines broke the openness of the field about a mile south of the highway. When they reached the camp, Creedy got out, unlocked the gate and opened it. To the right of the gate there was a sign painted in red and blue that read:

ANGEL CITY
LABOR CAMP
POSITIVELY NO TRESPASSING
— *KEEP OUT* —

The camp covered about two acres of ground and was surrounded by an eight-foot chain link fence with three strands of barbed wire on top. The main building was a long concrete block structure with rows of doors on both the north and south sides, but no windows. Dingy whitewash hung in flaked strips from the concrete, and the roof over-hang was sagging badly from rot. Behind this building there was a small block building containing a toilet and shower, and a house trailer was parked beneath the Australian pines in the south corner of the compound. A red pickup truck sat beside the trailer. The place seemed to be deserted except for an old Negro man sitting on the ground beneath one of the trees. He did not look up as the two vehicles entered and parked.

Creedy got out of the car and said, "You folks will have number ten on the north side. You can spend the rest of the afternoon getting settled. The bus will leave for the fields at six o'clock in the morning." With that he drove out, locked the gate and created a cloud of white limestone dust as he raced the Mark IV back toward the highway.

Bennie said, "How come he locked the gate, Papa? We can't get back outside if we want to."

Jared was also puzzled by this. He said, "I don't rightly know. Maybe they don't want folks in here that don't have no business bein' here when ev'rybody is in the fields. That might be a good idea."

They all followed Jared as he walked to the north side of the building and found a door with the number 10 painted above it. He opened the door and entered slowly. A naked light bulb with a string hanging down was in the center of the room. He pulled the string and flooded the eight-foot square cubicle with yellowish light. The heat and the strong smell of stale urine and vomit almost turned his stomach. He jumped back quickly and said, "Phew! We better let some air get in there afore we go in. That place smells like it's real ripe."

They waited for about five minutes and then entered again. The room was totally bare except for two sets of bunk beds against the walls. A pile of empty wine bottles was in one corner and was surrounded by dried vomit.

Jared held his nose and said, "We better get back out of here! I purely can't stand it!"

For several minutes they huddled silently outside the room, and then Jared said dejectedly, "It looks like I done got us in a real mess, don't it?"

"It wouldn't be so bad if it was just cleaned up," Cloma said, trying to ease the guilt in Jared's voice.

"It ain't goin' to be much even when it's cleaned up," he said.

"Why don't you ask that old man under the tree for some soap and a mop? And tomorrow we can get some spray that will take the bad smell out."

"I'll go and see to it now," Jared said.

The old Negro seemed to be asleep as Jared walked up to him. He appeared to be about eighty years old, and his body was nothing more than wrinkled skin and bones. Jared shook his arm and he looked up.

"Where can I get some soap and a mop?" Jared asked. "We want to clean the room."

The old man said, "I's de cook. I don' pick no 'maters no mo, an' I gits two bottles o' wine 'stead o' one. Dey's a mop in de outhouse but ev'rybody buys dey own soap."

Jared said, "You got some soap I can borrow 'til we can buy some? Or I could just buy it from you."

The old man answered, "I's de cook. I don' pick no 'maters no mo, an' I gits two bottles o' wine 'stead o' one. You'll have to go to de sto'."

"But the gate's locked and I can't get out," Jared said, becoming exasperated.

"I's de cook. I don' pick no 'maters no mo, an' . . . ."

Jared turned quickly and walked back to the room. He

said, "That old fool seems to be daffy. We'll just have to wait
'til somebody gets back to the camp. We might as well go sit
under a tree where it's cooler."

They all walked to one of the Australian pines and sat on
the soft needles that covered the ground. Jared said, "I been
doin' some thinkin'. This place is worse than our old hawg
pen, but we don't have to stay here long. If they pay twenty-
five cents fer pickin' a bucket of tomatoes, and I can pick a
hundred in a day, that's twenty-five dollars. If Kristy and
Bennie can pick fifty each, that's another twenty-five bucks,
or fifty dollars fer the day. For six days' work that's three
hundred dollars — more clear money than I ever made in a
month. At that rate it won't take us no time at all to have
our own fruit stand. You think we can stick it out fer a few
weeks?"

"I'll pick more than fifty, Papa," Bennie said with excitement.

"And I'll pick as many as Bennie," Kristy said.

"You won't neither," Bennie shot back. "You're just a
girl. Can't no girl do nothin' like a man."

"We can make do all right, Jay," Cloma said assuredly.
"The room won't be so bad once we get it cleaned up and
the smell out."

Jared felt relief. He was afraid they would all hold it
against him for bringing them to such a place. He said, "Well,
it's settled then. We'll stick it out fer awhile, and we'll fill a
bucket full of money afore you know it. We'll sell fruits and
vegetables and pot-holders and aprons and Bennie can carve
those little wooden animals he's so good at. It won't take us
no time at all."

It was just before six when the two old school buses came
into the camp and parked beside the trailer. One was painted
a faded red and one blue. Both were covered with dust. On

the side of one there was a sign painted in white: ANGEL CITY UNIT 1; on the other, ANGEL CITY UNIT 2.

About sixty people got out of the buses. All were black males except for ten black women, a white man and woman, and a white boy about the same age as Bennie. Some of the people ran and formed a line in front of the shower stall; others disappeared into their rooms; and some just plopped down to the ground and sat.

Jared and his family watched this sudden activity with curiosity, and then they walked back to the building and sat on the ground in front of their room. A black man was sitting in front of the door next to them.

In a few minutes a huge black man carrying a box walked down the side of the building. He handed each person a pint bottle of white wine. When he came to Jared he held the bottle in his outstretched hand and said nothing.

Jared looked up at him and said, "What's this?"

The man jabbed the bottle at Jared and remained silent.

The black man sitting on the ground by the adjacent room watched for a moment, and then he said, "Mistuh, you're payin' a buck-fifty for that bottle of junk whether you take it or not. You better take it."

"But I don't want any wine," Jared said, puzzled by the whole thing.

"You better take it. It'll help you get through the night."

Jared took the bottle, and then the huge black man continued on along the line of rooms. Jared turned the bottle over and over in his hands, staring at it, and then he said to the black man sitting next to him, "You want it?"

"You keep it. You'll need it sooner or later."

Jared took a closer look at this stranger. He was in his early forties, and the coal-black skin of his face was broken by a long white scar running down his left cheek. His clothes and shoes were covered with white dust.

No black people had ever lived anywhere near Teeter

Ridge, and Jared had never really known any. He was curious
to know more about this black man, so he extended his hand
and said, "My name's Jared Teeter. Folks call me Jay."

The black man was surprised by the extended hand. He
reached over reluctantly, touched Jared for only a moment
and then said, "I's called Cy."

For a moment neither of them said anything further,
then the black man said, "Where you come from, Mistuh
Jay?"

"West Virginny," Jared answered.

"What part of West Virginny?"

"Well, my place was out from Dink."

"Dink?" the man questioned. "What's that near?"

"Well, Dink's not far from Wallback or Valley Fork or
Big Otter. Big Otter is close to Nebo, and Nebo is close to
Mudfork, and Mudfork is close to . . . ."

"That be's all right," Cy interrupted. "You don't need to
explain it no further."

Another period of silence prevailed, and then Jared said,
"We can't go in the room, it stinks so bad. I got to have some
soap and a mop. When do we go to the store?"

"We stops at the sto' comin' in ev'ry afternoon."

"Can't I go tonight after supper?"

The black man stared curiously at Jared, and then he said,
"Only in the afternoon comin' in from the fields. But I got
some soap powder you can have, an' they's a mop out by the
shower stalls."

Just then an old black man with a white beard came out
of Cy's room. He was singing an almost incoherent tune, "I
seen Jesus today . . . I seen Jesus in de 'mater patch . . . I seen
Jesus today . . . an' Jesus wuz pickin' 'maters . . . ."

Jared stared curiously at the old man as he walked away,
still singing.

Cy turned to him and said, "Don't pay no never mind to
him. He's tetched, but he don't bother nobody. Ev'rybody

'round here calls him Rude."

"Ain't he kind of old to be workin' in the fields?" Jared asked.

"That old man's past eighty, but he's like a machine. You point him down a tomato row an' he'll pick fo' buckets while anybody else picks one. He's been here three years now, an' if he wadden' so good at pickin', Creedy would-a kilt him a long time ago. I'll get yo soap."

Cy's last statement about the old man and Creedy baffled Jared and was totally beyond any degree of comprehension, but before Jared could question him further, Cy vanished into the room. He returned shortly and handed a box of soap powder to Jared.

"I sure thank you fer this," Jared said. "I'll pay you back tomorrow when I get to the store."

"Don't worry 'bout it. I don't use much soap no more."

"Well, I guess I'll go now and find the mop, and see what we can do with that room," Jared said.

"You best wait 'til after supper. It's 'bout that time, an' if'n you don't et when it's ready, you won't git none."

Cy leaned back against the wall and opened his bottle of wine. Jared watched as he put the bottle to his mouth and drained it in one gulp. He belched loudly, and then he looked at Jared and said, "That cheap junk cost forty-nine cents a pint at the sto', an' we pays Creedy a buck-fifty fo' it here in the camp ev'ry afternoon, whether we wants to buy it or not. Ain't that some crap?"

A loud clanging noise suddenly erupted from somewhere west of the barracks. Cy jumped up and said, "That's it. You gotta hav yo own plates an' foks." Then he hurried around the side of the barracks.

Jared went to the van and brought back a box containing plates and other utensils, and then they all joined a line leading to an open shed in the west corner of the camp. The stove was an iron grate propped up on concrete blocks. A wood fire smoldered beneath it, and three large blackened pots sat on top of the grate.

The frail old man who had called himself the cook was standing behind the grate, dipping from the pots as each person came past. Onto each plate he dumped a glob of boiled pork backbone, a portion of boiled squash and stewed tomatoes, and two slices of white bread. The old man had no teeth, and his mouth popped constantly as he served the food.

Some of the people took their plates back to their rooms, and others squatted on the ground close by the shed. Jared and his family went to a tree by the side of the van. The sun had now sunk deeply into the western horizon, and two floodlights came on at each end of the building.

For a moment they ate in silence, and then Jared said solemnly, "If that old man's a cook, then I'm one of them ballet dancers."

Cloma smiled as Bennie said, "This squash tastes like it's got sand in it."

"He didn't wash it before he cooked it," Cloma said. "Maybe now you'll appreciate more the good food I've been givin' you all this time."

Jared laughed and said, "Well, ev'rybody save a little bit fer Skip. Maybe he can eat it."

Kristy said, "Papa, Skip can have all of mine if he wants it. I'm just not hungry."

When they finished what they could eat of the supper, they joined another line leading to the hydrant close by the side of the outhouse where people were washing their dishes. Jared got a bucket from the van, filled it with water, looked for the mop and found it in the shower stall. Then he went back to the room.

He put the mop and bucket against the wall, and then he said to Cloma, "You want me to help with this?"

"No," she answered. "Bennie and Kristy can do it. I'll watch and see that it's done right."

"You ought not do any work yourself. I'll help if you say so." He moved toward her.

"You'd just be in the way. We can't hardly turn around in this little room as it is. We'll do it."

Jared then left the room and walked to the fence on the north side of the camp. Far in the distance he could see the glow of lights hovering above Florida City and Homestead, creating a huge yellow dome in the darkness of the sky. His thoughts began to drift back again to the farm in West Virginia.

He was startled when he realized that Cy was standing beside him. His body jerked as he spun around.

"I didn't mean to scare you," Cy said.

"That's o.k. I was just thinkin', and I didn't hear you come up."

Cy leaned against the fence, and then he said slowly, "Mistuh, I don't knows how you come to be in here, but you seems like a good man. You ought to take yo woman an' them younguns an' git outen here the fust thing in the mornin' while you still can."

"I don't understand what you're sayin'," Jared said, puzzled.

"I mean, git outen here! You ain't got no business in Angel City!"

"I can't do that," Jared said, even more puzzled by the insistence of this black man he didn't even really know. Then he said emphatically, "I need the work!"

Cy suddenly turned and carefully searched the area next to the barracks. He noticed that the huge black man who had passed out the bottles of wine was standing near the flood-light on the east end of the building. He turned back again and faced Jared as if he had something more to say; but then he wheeled around quickly and walked back toward his room.

FIVE

DAWN HAD not come the next morning when Angel City came to life. Little fires sprang up in front of doors, and people moved about beneath the dim glow of the flood-lights like vague shadows. The smell of coffee drifted through the camp.

Jared stepped from the room and breathed deeply of the cool air, trying to shake the sleep from his head. He had spent a restless night in the concrete cubicle which still reeked with a foul odor. Cy was sitting on the ground beside a fire. He had propped a grille on top of four blackened beer cans, and a small coffee pot bubbled over the flames. The old man called Rude was eating sardines from a can.

Jared looked at Cy and said, "Good mornin'."

"Mornin'," Cy replied.

"Where'd you get the wood fer the fire?" Jared asked.

"Out by the cookshed. They's a pile of branches out there."

Jared went to the shed and returned with a bundle of sticks. By the time the fire came to life, Cloma came outside.

She looked at the fire and said, "How'm I goin' to make coffee over that? We don't have a grille to set the pot on."

"Just set the pot in the fire," Jared said. "I'll take the grille off the camp stove in the van when we get back this afternoon."

Cy looked up and said, "You can use my grille now. I'm through with it. And they's water in the bucket by the wall."

Cloma boiled coffee over the glowing coals, and when Kristy and Bennie came from the room, they all sat on the ground and ate the sweet buns left from the day before. Cy opened a can of Vienna sausage.

Jared looked at Cloma and said, "Do we have any food left to take to the field?"

"Nothin' but a few oranges," she replied.

"I can let you have three cans of sardines," Cy said. "That's all I can spare. But you can eat all the tomatoes you wants in the field."

"I'd appreciate the sardines," Jared said. "I could have brought more food if I had known. We'll leave a can of sardines fer Cloma, and maybe the cook will have something else she can have."

"He won't have nothin' fo' nobody 'til supper," Cy said.

"Don't worry about me," Cloma said. "I'll do fine with sardines and oranges. It's you I'm worried about. You can't work all day without proper food."

"I've always liked tomatoes," Jared said. "I'll probably eat a bushel."

"You'll sho' be stopped up if'n you do," Cy said. He then looked at Jared and said seriously, "You folks better go out back an' relieve yo'selves afore we go to the fields. They ain't no place in the fields to do a job excepin' in front of ev'rybody."

Jared gave the black man a queer look. He said, "Well, thanks fer the information. That's good to know."

Bennie then jumped up and ran toward the outhouse.

Promptly at six a clanging sound came from the area of the cook shed, and people moved immediately toward the two buses. Those who lived in the north side of the barracks were assigned to Unit 1, and those on the south side to Unit 2. A driver stood by each bus, counting the people as they entered. Jared, Kristy and Bennie climbed aboard Unit 1.

Dawn was just breaking when the buses turned onto the highway and headed east. They drove for three miles and then turned north on a narrow paved farm road. Fields seemingly stretched into infinity on both sides of the road, fields that had once been part of the impenetrable Everglades but had been wrenched violently from nature, diked, drained, and stripped bare of flora and fauna, marshland turned into arid soil that now formed one of America's largest vegetable gardens. Each day an army of men and women swarmed across the land, a conglomerate of lifetime migrants and exiles from failure and defeat in rural areas of Appalachia and the Carolinas and Georgia and Tennessee and Alabama. From the green vines they plucked hundreds of thousands of tomatoes that were processed in Florida City and Homestead and then shipped to distant markets to be served in salads and sandwiches in New York and Boston and Chicago and Minneapolis and Detroit and New Orleans and Denver and Toronto.

They also passed fields planted heavily with pole beans and squash and okra and potatoes and cucumbers and peppers. All of the fields were dotted with white splotches as egrets searched for their breakfast.

In some of the tomato fields, the rows were covered with strips of white plastic to hold in moisture and to kill weeds, and the plants grew from holes in the strips. From a distance, these fields looked as if they were covered with snow.

The buses finally turned into the edge of a field and parked beside a row of Australian pines. A flatbed truck loaded with empty crates was parked nearby. As each person was issued a bucket, they selected a row and moved out into the field like lines of advancing soldiers. The flatbed truck followed slowly behind the mass of pickers.

For the first two hours, the picking was like an adventuresome game to Kristy and Bennie. They felt tinges of excitement each time they plucked a tomato from a plant and gradually filled a bucket. They almost ran as they took the buckets back to the truck and dumped them into a crate. But as the sun moved higher into the sky, intensifying the heat reflecting from the rocky soil, they began to move slower and slower and fill the buckets less often.

About mid-morning, Cy came up alongside Kristy and said to her, "Little miss, I been watchin' you. You better take it easy, else you gone be laid out afore noon. It's a long day in the fields when you not use to it. You stay alongside o' me fo' a while an' I'll pick some in yo' bucket."

"That wouldn't be fair," Kristy said, wiping sweat from her forehead with the back of her hand. "That would be taking away from you."

"That don't matter none at all," he said. "You just stay alongside me fo' awhile."

For a half-hour she stayed abreast of the black man as he picked into two buckets at once, and then she began to fall behind. She finally sat down to rest as the other pickers moved farther and farther away from her.

At noon the workers took a half-hour break. Jared, Kristy and Bennie sat on the ground and shared the two cans of sardines. They also ate two tomatoes each. Water was available from a keg on the back of the truck.

By mid-afternoon, even Jared was hurting. The rows became longer and longer, and the buckets bigger and bigger. His shirt was drenched with sweat as he too fell farther and farther behind the experienced pickers.

It was a long walk back to the buses when the day finally ended at five. The smell of sweat-soaked bodies was almost overpowering as the bus lumbered back along the narrow farm road. A mile east of the camp the buses pulled into a parking area adjacent to a concrete block building housing the Gater General Store.

As each person got off the bus, the driver handed them a dollar bill. Cy explained to Jared that this was an advance on earnings to buy food for the next day. The pickers pushed into the store and made purchases quickly. Some returned to the buses drinking cans of cold beer, while others carried brown paper bags containing sardines or Vienna sausage or pickled pigs' feet or slices of hoop cheese or cans of beans or loaves of white bread.

Cloma ran to meet them when Jared, Kristy and Bennie got off the bus inside the camp. They walked back to the room slowly. Kristy and Bennie grabbed towels and went immediately to join the line leading to the shower stall.

Jared sat on one of the bunks and groaned. "I never knowed that pickin' tomatoes could be so rough," he said wearily to Cloma. "My back feels like it's broke. And I know it was tough on them two younguns, but they really tried hard."

"Did you do as well as you hoped you would?" Cloma asked.

"Nope. But we'll do better as we get used to it. I picked eighty-two buckets, Bennie got forty, and Kristy got twenty-seven. That's not too bad, though. One more bucket and we'd have made forty dollars today."

"I hope it won't be long," Cloma said. "Me and that old cook were the only people here today. I tried to talk to him once, but all he would say was some gibberish about him bein' the cook and not havin' to pick anymore. Skip was a real comfort to me. I even got to talkin' to him."

The small dog was lying on a blanket Cloma had placed for him under a bunk.

The giant black man suddenly came into the room and

handed Jared a pint of white wine. Jared took it without comment and sat it against the wall beside the other bottle.

Cloma said, "That's another bad thing here. You just can't have any privacy at all. If you shut the door it's like an oven, and if you leave it open people just walk by and look right in. Did you get the spray?"

"Yes." Jared reached into a brown paper bag and handed her a can of aerosol spray. "But I didn't buy any food except in cans. We can't keep meat or anything like that without a refrigerator or ice. We'll just have to make do fer awhile as best we can."

Cloma started spraying the deodorant around the room. She said, "I scrubbed this place three more times today just to have somethin' to do. It's plenty clean now. But we've got to have some chairs. I can't even sit outside durin' the day 'less I sit on the ground."

"Maybe we can go into town Saturday afternoon and look in the used furniture stores," Jared said. He knew that staying alone all day in the small room was a cruel hardship for her.

"That would be nice. A used chair ought not cost too much."

Jared took a towel from a cardboard box. "I've got to get this white dust off'n me," he said. "It itches worse than pison ivy. I've never seen fields so full of rocks and dust. I don't see how they make things grow at all, but they do. The rocks are nearbouts as thick as a mountain crick bed. We'll have to get better shoes. But I noticed that some of the black people were barefooted. They must have feet like iron."

"They're probably used to it," Cloma said. "And besides that, I've always heard that black folks are as tough as nails."

"They must be. It hurt me clear through the soles of my shoes. But you know, I seen a strange thing today. I looked up two or three times and the black man in the room next to us — the one called Cy — he was pickin' into Kristy's bucket."

"How come him to do that?"

"I don't know, 'less he figured she needed some help and he was willin' to give it. But it looks to me like that would cost him money." Jared got up, stretched, and said, "I'm goin' now and take a bath afore the supper bell rings." He looked back. "That stuff sure makes the room smell better."

The meal that night consisted of fried strips of salt pork, pole beans and stewed tomatoes. All of the Teeters ate on the ground outside their room. When they were finished, Kristy and Bennie walked away to explore the camp, and Cloma went to the hydrant beside the outhouse to wash the day's dirty underclothes. Jared leaned back against the wall as Skip came from the room and sat beside him. He reached over and patted the dog's head.

Cy was also sitting on the ground in front of his room. He looked at Jared and said, "What you call that mutt?"

"His name's Skip," Jared answered. "He's 'bout the best rabbit dog you've ever seen. If they's a rabbit within ten miles, he'll find him."

"They don't 'low no dogs in here," Cy said. "You best get rid of him."

"I couldn't do that. We've had him over eight years."

"You could take him outside when the gate opens in the mornin' an' turn him loose."

"He wouldn't go nowhere," Jared said. "He'd just hang around out there and starve."

"You could take him to the fields an' turn him loose. He'd find a home sommers."

Jared was becoming agitated by the conversation. He snapped, "This little dog won't bother nobody! We'll keep him in the room as much as possible, and he won't hurt a soul!"

"It's yo' dog," Cy said with finality.

Both men remained silent for several minutes, then Jared looked back to Cy and said quizzically, "What does Mr.

Creedy get out of all this?"

Cy gave Jared a piercing look. For a moment he didn't answer, and then he muttered, "Plenty."

"In what way?" Jared asked, wanting to know more about the operation of the camp.

Cy glanced down the side of the building, and then he leaned closer and said, "He's a contractor. He gits two dollars an' fifty cents an hour fo' hisself fo' all the time we're in the fields ev'ry day. And he also gits a dollar each fo' ev'ry picker he puts in the fields ev'ry day. That's a heap o' money, but it ain't enough fo' Creedy. If'n he could figger a way to haul out ev'rybody's do-do from the shithouse an' sell it fo' fertilizer, he'd do it!"

Jared figured briefly in his mind and said, "That is a lot of money fer Creedy, but he's got the expense of this camp and the food at night and the buses."

Cy gave Jared another piercing look. He grunted but did not comment further about Creedy.

Jared then asked, "Who're those two men who drive the buses and hand out the wine?"

Cy said, "The big 'un is called Jabbo, an' the one with the twisted nose is Clug."

"How come they don't pick?" Jared asked.

"Them's Creedy's men. They live in the trailer. They ain't pickers. An' you best stay clear of them two. They's mean niggers." Cy then got up and said, "I'm goin' walk aroun' some. I'll see you later." He was tired of Jared's questions.

Jared got up and put Skip in the room, then he walked around the end of the building. He had wanted to meet the white family living in the south side of the barracks.

He found them sitting on the ground in front of a room. The man was about four years younger than Jared, the woman the same age as Cloma, and the boy was Bennie's age. The man had a sullen look on his face.

Jared squatted in front of them and said, "Howdy. My

name's Jared Teeter. Folks call me Jay." He extended his hand.

The man ignored Jared's offered handshake and said in a flat tone, "What you want?"

Jared was surprised by the reaction. He said, "I don't want nothin'. I just thought I'd visit a spell. We just got here yesterday. We come from West Virginny."

The man became even more sullen. He said, "You come around here 'cause we're white too?"

"No," Jared answered, feeling uncomfortable and wishing he had not even tried to start a conversation with the stranger. "That had nothin' to do with it. I just wanted to visit."

"If you think you're goin' to get special treatment in here 'cause you're white, you can forget it." The man's tone was now hostile. "Creedy don't give a damn if you're white or black or purple. You're just two more hands in the field, that's all. Just two more hands in the field. You won't get nothin' special in here 'cause you're white."

Jared was startled by the outburst, and then it angered him. He said firmly, "I ain't lookin' fer no special favors! I've always pulled my own weight! We's mountain folk!"

"You damned well better pull your own weight!" the man snapped harshly.

Jared had had enough. As he jumped up to leave, the boy looked at him and said, "My pa here is Willard Baxley. My ma is Martha. I'm Lonnie. We come from Alabama." His tone was apologetic.

"I hear that's a good place," Jared said, not knowing what else to say. "It's good to have met you folks." He then turned and walked away quickly.

Cloma had returned to the room when Jared came inside, but Bennie and Kristy were not there. Cloma said, "There's no place for me to hang these wet clothes. The fence is too high, and there's not a single clothes line in the camp."

"Just drape 'em over the side of the bunks," Jared said.

"The heat in here will dry 'em in no time." He was still feeling puzzled and dejected by the man's reaction to his offered friendship.

Cloma said, "We've just got to get an electric fan, Jay. My bunk was soaked with sweat when I got up this morning."

Jared acted as if he did not hear her. Skip came from under the bunk, and he reached down and patted the dog's head. For a moment he pulled at the dog's ears, and then he said, "It's best you look after Skip real good. They's things here I don't understand. You best keep him close to you durin' the day."

"How come he needs special treatment all of a sudden?" Cloma asked. "He can't go anywhere with that fence out there and the gate locked."

"It's just best that you watch after him real good," Jared insisted.

Kristy and Bennie then came running into the room. Bennie's face was flushed with excitement as he said, "We been out to the south side of the camp, Papa, behind the cook shed. Mister Cy was there. He said that the marsh you can see beyond the south field is the Everglades. He said there's alligators out there. Will you take us to see an alligator, Papa? We ain't never seen one."

Jared looked at Bennie's flushed face. He said, "Maybe we can take a hike out there Sunday afternoon. But I don't know if the alligators are there or not."

"Mister Cy said they were," Bennie exclaimed.

Kristy said, "Mister Cy picked in my bucket. He helped me, Papa. I don't think he would tell us about the alligators if it wasn't true."

Jared was pleased that his children were in a happy mood. He said, "Well, if Mister Cy said it, I guess it must be so. We'll go out there Sunday afternoon, and we'll see the alligators then."

"Maybe we can catch a little one and keep him for a pet,"

Bennie said. "Nobody back in Dink ever had a pet alligator."

Jared then got up from the bunk and left the room. He suddenly felt a need to be alone for a few minutes. Night had now come, and he walked out to the north fence and watched the glow of lights in the eastern sky. Occasionally, a car passed along the highway a mile from the camp, its headlights slicing the darkness. Muted sounds drifted outward from the barracks.

When he turned to leave, Jared noticed that Jabbo was standing in the edge of the darkness by the gate, watching him.

SIX

NEITHER JARED, Kristy nor Bennie did much better the remainder of the week than they had done the first day, but they were becoming more accustomed to the work. Jared knew he would improve as time went on, and that he would eventually pick as many tomatoes as anyone in the field. He had doubts only about Kristy, and he wished she did not have to go into the fields at all. He felt pity for the black women who worked each day, although he knew they had probably done this all of their lives.

By the end of Saturday, Jared figured their four-day total at six hundred and two buckets. This was not as high as he had hoped, but he knew it was not bad for their first effort. He believed they could reach a goal of two hundred buckets per day.

The bus went straight back to the camp and did not stop at the store. A half-hour after they had arrived, Creedy drove into the camp in the Mark IV. He had a gray metal cash box with him, and he sat in a chair behind a small table as a line formed.

When Jared finally reached the table, Creedy examined a ledger and then said to him, "Way I got it figured, your total is three hundred, seventy-two dollars and fifty cents."

Jared was surprised. He said, "Mr. Creedy, we didn't earn that much, did we? Not unless the pay was more than the twenty-five cents a bucket as you said it would be."

"I didn't say how much you *earned*," Creedy said. "The amount is what you *owe* me."

Jared was dumbfounded by the words. For a moment he couldn't speak. He finally said, "What did you say, Mr. Creedy?"

"You heard me!" Creedy snapped impatiently. "You owe me three hundred and seventy-two dollars and fifty cents."

Jared said, "There ain't no way I could do that! No way!"

Creedy glanced at the ledger and said, "Well, let's see. There's a fee of one hundred dollars for being put to work, and ev'rybody that stays in the camp pays this whether they works or not. That's four hundred dollars for you and your bunch. That's only a one-time charge. You don't have to pay it no more. Then there's ten dollars each per week for rent. That's forty bucks. And five dollars a week for electricity. The supper is two dollars each, so that's thirty-six bucks for the four days this week. The bus is two dollars a day each to the fields, and I give each one of you a one-dollar advance ev'ry day for food. The wine is a buck-fifty a bottle. That all figures out to five hundred and twenty-three dollars. You earned a hundred and fifty dollars and fifty cents picking, so you're into me for three hundred and seventy-two dollars and fifty cents. You understand now?"

Jared did not understand. His mind was completely addled by Creedy's rapid flow of figures, and to him the whole situation seemed to be unreal. He said, "How come you didn't tell me 'bout all them charges before we came in here? How come you didn't tell me?"

"Well, I'm sure I did. You just don't remember, or else

you wasn't paying attention like you should." Creedy then pushed the ledger aside and looked directly at Jared. "You want to settle this up now with cash, or do you want to work it out?" he asked, knowing that Jared probably did not have the money.

"I don't have that much," Jared replied, still unable to believe that what was happening was real. "We had some bad luck with the van comin' down here."

"Well," Creedy said condescendingly as he reached for the cash box, "it won't take you no time at all to clear the debt and then start making some real money. You'll see. So don't worry about it. I'm going to advance five dollars for you and two-fifty each for your younguns. Here's ten bucks." He handed Jared a ten-dollar bill.

Jared took the money and stepped out of the line. He turned it over and over in his hands, staring at it. Then he watched as each person came up to the table. Everyone was handed only a five-dollar bill for the week's work.

Cloma knew immediately that something was wrong when Jared came into the room. His face was drawn and white. He sat on the bunk and slumped forward, not speaking. She asked anxiously, "Jared? What is it, Jared?"

He tried to explain, but she did not understand the various figures Creedy had quoted any better than Jared did. She said worriedly, "What will we do, Jared?" She always called him Jared when they were discussing something serious or when something frightened her.

He said, "I don't know. I've only got around a hundred and fifty dollars left from the trip. We can't pay off the debt except by workin' it out. We'll just have to pick harder, I guess. I'm sorry I got all of you into such a mess as this."

Jared blinked as Jabbo stepped into the room and handed him the bottle of wine. He put it against the wall with the other bottles. There was no time for him to take a shower before the supper bell rang.

Soon after supper, everyone went to the buses for the usual Saturday trip to the store. Jared walked up to the giant black man and said, "We'll go in the van. I need to run it some to keep the battery up."

"You go in the bus," Jabbo said. "Ev'rybody goes in the bus."

Some of the people seemed almost happy as they reached the store with their five dollars in cash. Others were as grim as Jared. Some made food purchases, while others spent the money for a quart-bottle of whiskey.

Cloma found a small electric fan priced at eight dollars. She said to Jared, "Can we afford to buy this?"

"Yes. But I don't see any chairs at all."

"It doesn't matter," Cloma said. "There's some empty bean hampers behind the cook shed. I'll make myself a chair."

Jared purchased more canned food and a carton of eggs. Kristy and Bennie each spent twenty-five cents for candy, and then they went back to the bus.

Creedy drove up and parked in front of the store, and Jared went over to him. He said, "Mr. Creedy, are we allowed to go outside the camp on Sunday?"

"What for?" Creedy asked.

"Me and my folks are used to services on Sunday. I was a deacon back home."

Creedy chuckled and said, "Well, maybe you can get Jabbo or Clug to say a few words, and get that ding-bat cook to play the fiddle. Some of them niggers can probably sing, too."

"Are you sayin' we can't go?" Jared asked, not amused by Creedy's remarks.

"I got business to take care of," Creedy said impatiently. He turned and walked away briskly.

It was almost dark when the buses pulled back into the camp. Some of the people were already drunk as they headed for their rooms. Shrill laughter broke the usual silence of the compound, and the sound of scuffling came from some of the rooms.

Jared put his packages in the room, came back outside and sat on the ground. Cy was leaning back against the wall, drinking from a bottle of whiskey. He turned to Jared and said, "You want some?"

"No," Jared said. "But thanks anyway." He did not want to let his depression make him speak rudely.

Cy took another drink and said, "I worked a week in them fields fo' this bottle of whuskey, an' they won't be nothin' left of it by tomorrow but dried piss in the dust. A whole week's work shot right through my pecker an' down in the dust."

Jared picked up a stick and scratched absently at the ground. Cy watched for a moment, then he said, "Creedy's a fine man, ain't he? I tried to tell you."

"It won't take long," Jared said. "We'll work it out and be gone from here in no time."

Cy said, "I been here two years an' I ain't worked it out yet. I never seen nobody leave Angel City that didn't leave feet first. Excepin' for two Cubans. That's the only thing Creedy won't bring in here no mo'. Cubans."

"How's that?" Jared asked, mildly interested.

"He brought two of them Cubans in here 'bout six months ago, an' he worked 'em fo' a week an' wouldn't pay 'em. They couldn't hardly speak no English at all, but they was shoutin' all kinds of stuff at Creedy. Then they pulled out them long pig-stickers that Cubans carry. One of 'em held Jabbo an' Clug 'gainst the fence, an' the other one commences to carve his name on ole Creedy's fat belly. Then they took a whole sack o' money from that big Mark IV an' hightailed it out o' here. Creedy couldn't say nothin' 'bout it to the police, an' he knew that if he went over to Miami lookin' fo' them two Cubans, they'd be a hundred more jus' like 'em out lookin' fo' him with them long pig-stickers. So he jus' lets it be, an' then he comes back in here an' beats the hell outen six of us niggers."

"Where do all these people in here come from?" Jared asked.

"Ev'rywhere," Cy said, drinking again. "Creedy even goes up to the Carolinas an' brings folks down here. Promises 'em good jobs. One time I seen him bring a drunk nigger in here who was wearin' one of them red monkey suits like men wear in front of a hotel to open doors an' unload baggage. When he sobered up, he started raisin' hell. They beat that nigger like I ain't never seen befo', but he wouldn't shet up. They finally took him fo' a ride in the pickup."

"How did you get in here?" Jared asked, absorbed by Cy's tales.

The more Cy drank, the freer he seemed willing to talk. He said, "He got me in Belle Glade. He come by this camp where I was livin' an' got me drunk. The next thing I knowed, I was here in Angel City."

Jared said, "Well, if you've been here two years now, you couldn't possibly be still in debt to Creedy."

"You be's in debt if'n you stays here ten," Cy said.

Jared thought that most of the things Cy was saying was just whiskey talk. He said skeptically, "I don't believe that nobody has to stay here if they don't want to, no matter how much Creedy says they owe. If nothin' else, they could just break and run in the field."

"That's been tried befo', an' they always come after you. You ever been pistol-whupped?"

"No."

"It ain't a pretty sight, but it's even worse if'n you on the receivin' end of it."

Jared became silent for a moment, trying to digest all the things Cy was saying. Although he had never really known a black person, Jared had always heard that they always either exaggerate all that they say or outright lie. He could not determine if he should believe this black man or not, but he was interested in the things he was saying. He then said to Cy, "Are all the camps like this one?"

"No, they ain't all like Angel City." He took another drink, then he continued, "They's a few more like this where you can't get out if'n you want to, but it don't make no matter. You can't really get out of none of 'em, an' the livin' is just as bad if they's a gate or not. They all 'bout the same, an' I seen 'em all. I been a picker all my life, movin' from one place to another. I don't even know where I was born. It could 'a been in a tomato patch."

"If you're not bein' paid fer your work here after you've cleared your debt, I still don't see why you don't leave," Jared said stubbornly.

Cy took another deep drink from the bottle. He wiped his mouth and said, "I tried to get away two or three times. They whupped me good, but that just made me madder. But the last time I tried it, Creedy took my boy."

"What?" Jared asked, completely puzzled by this statement. "He did what?"

"He took my boy to stay at his place. He brings him out here ev'ry Sunday afternoon fo' a visit. He's got them white folks' little girl, too, an' five or six more younguns. You ain't goin' to run off with *that* over yo' head."

Jared couldn't bring himself to believe Cy's words. He said, "Nobody can do something like that to someone else. You could tell the police."

"I tell the police, they'll take my boy out in the swamp, in that pickup truck. They'll kill him an' dump him in a sinkhole, an' that'll be the end o' that. Me an' my woman, we made that baby right in the middle of a bean field at noon one day, an' later, when he was born, he was born right in the middle of a bean field. There wasn't no papers or records or nothin', so there ain't no way I could prove that I ever even had a boy."

Jared was again shocked by the words, but he still could not face the reality of what this black man was saying. He then said to Cy, "Where's your wife now? Is she with the boy?"

"She died eight years ago, when the boy was born. We was in the Carolinas, pickin' beans. Migrant folk can't afford one of them sto'-bought funerals, so I buried her out in the woods."

Suddenly Jared did believe. He knew that the black man was incapable of fabricating such a story. For a moment he gazed beyond the fence and across the darkness of the fields; then he turned to Cy and said, "Is this the way it's always been for people like you?"

"You mean nigger field hands?" Cy asked.

"Yes. I guess that's what I mean."

"It's always been the same, an' it goin' always be the same."

Jared said, "I'm sorry, Cy . . . I never knowed. I thought I'd seen all the hard times they was back on that ridge in West Virginny, but I guess I was just a dumb hillbilly. I never knowed what it was really like out here. I'm sorry." Then he got up and walked away quickly into the darkness.

SEVEN

JARED DID not tell Cloma about the conversation with Cy and the things he had said. He did not want her to know the real truth about Angel City or Creedy or for her to be aware of the seriousness of their situation. He was determined that he would pick more tomatoes than anyone in the camp, and work off the debt quickly. Then they would simply leave all this behind them.

Sunday was a long day. The buses did not make a trip to the store, and the gate remained locked. The monotony of the long hours of confinement within the camp became stifling.

Cloma made a Sunday morning breakfast of fried eggs. Jared asked Cy to join them, and he did so eagerly, saying that he had not eaten eggs in more than a year. They offered some to the old man, Rude, but he refused. He ate his usual breakfast of one can of sardines.

It was just after noon when Creedy brought the children to the camp. Jared watched with deep pity as the boy ran to Cy and grabbed him around the neck. Cy took the boy's hand, and they disappeared into their room. Jared now understood why the white man on the other side of the barracks had been so sullen and belligerent when he had visited him. It had not been hostility, but fear. He felt sorrow for all the families whose children had been taken from them, and he wondered what he would do if Creedy or anyone ever tried to take Kristy or Bennie.

Jared entered the field on Monday morning deeply troubled. He picked the tomatoes frantically, filling bucket after bucket, running to the truck and back again. Bennie and Kristy watched him with wonder. He did not even stop at noon when the two of them ate cans of Vienna sausage.

By quitting time he had picked a hundred and thirty-two buckets. Every bone and muscle in his body ached as he walked back to the bus. He also felt a gnawing hunger from not eating since before daylight that morning.

Kristy took a seat beside him. She looked at him distastefully and said, "Papa, you stink. How come you worked so fast today?"

He glanced at himself and noticed for the first time that his clothes were as wet as if he had fallen into a creek. He was also covered with white dust. Her innocent statement made him smile, and he said, "You know, Kristy, you're right. I do stink. I sure better have a bath afore your mother gets a whiff of me."

When they reached the store he purchased food for the next day, and he also bought a can of corned beef, which he wolfed down quickly during the trip from the store to the camp. As soon as he put the package in the room, he headed for the shower stall.

The meal that evening made Jared feel guilty for eating the corned beef and not sharing it. They were served boiled pork neck bones, squash and stewed tomatoes. All of them felt a certain amount of constant hunger, but Jared did not want to spend more than the three dollars a day they were advanced for food unless it became absolutely necessary. He wanted to keep the hundred and fifty dollars intact in case he needed it to help buy their way out of Angel City.

They took the plates back to the barracks and sat on the ground in front of their room. Skip came outside when he smelled the pork. Jared gave him a pile of bones, and he chewed them ravenously. Jared watched for a moment, and then he said to no one in particular, "At least he don't have to eat no stewed tomatoes. I'm gettin' pretty damned sick of 'em, and ripe ones too fer that matter."

Cy was sitting close by, his plate untouched as he finished the bottle of wine. He said to Jared, "This slop they feed us ain't nothin' but the trash they throw out from the packin' plants in Homestead. Creedy gets it in a big garbage can ev'ry day. An' the stuff he does buy, like the salt bacon an' neck bones, he buys it with them food stamps he makes ev'rybody sign up for. It don't cost him nothin'!"

"I used to feed my hawgs better," Jared said, "but I guess folks sommers would be glad to even get this. But it sure do cut down a man's pleasure at meal-time."

Kristy put her plate aside and said, "Papa, if I wrote my name on some of the tomatoes I pick, do you reckon anybody would ever know that I picked them?"

"I guess they might," Jared answered. "But it would be mighty hard to write on a tomato. And they wouldn't have no way of knowing where you are nohow. Folks don't think about where somethin' comes from when they eat it. They jus' eat it, that's all."

"Well, they ought to," Kristy said. "Pickin' is hard work. I might try putting my name on the tomatoes."

Cloma said, "Is Mr. Creedy still here?"

"He was out by the trailer a few minutes ago," Jared said, curious as to why she had asked. "What you want with him?"

"I wrote a letter today to Mamma and Papa. Maybe he'll mail it for me."

Jared got up and said, "I'll go and see."

Kristy said, "I got a letter too, Papa, to Jeff. Will you ask him to mail it too?"

Jared smiled and said, "I thought somethin' pretty serious was goin' on between you and Jeff. So that's why you want to go back to the mountains. Let me have the letter and I'll send it along too."

Kristy blushed as she went into the room and came back with the letter.

When Jared came around the side of the building, the Mark IV was still there. He knocked on the door of the trailer and Creedy came outside. Jared said, "Can you mail a couple of letters fer me, Mr. Creedy?"

"Yeah," Creedy replied.

"I don't have no stamps, but here's two dimes."

"I'll mail 'em when I get back to Homestead," Creedy said. He stepped back into the trailer.

As soon as Jared was gone, Creedy ripped the letters in half and threw them into a waste basket.

It was the next morning when he went out to the cook shed to get firewood that Jared found Skip. The little dog's head had been severed, and was lying about four feet from the body. Jared had not seen Skip in the darkness but had stumbled over the body. He lit a match and discovered that he was standing in a pool of dried blood. For a moment he did not move, then he stooped down and touched the bloody form.

Jared picked up the body and the head and placed them on the ground beside the van. Then he went to the trailer and knocked on the door. Jabbo looked out and said, "Whut you want?"

"Who killed my dog?" Jared demanded angrily.

"Whut dawg?"

"You know damned well what dog!"

"I don't know nothin' 'bout no dawg."

Jabbo started to close the door, but Jared pushed it back violently and demanded, "Who killed him, dammit, you or Clug?"

The giant black man glared at Jared menacingly. He said harshly, "White man, you better move on away from here!"

Jared let his better judgment overcome his anger. He stepped back and said, "I'll need a shovel to bury him."

"You ain't buryin' no dawg inside this camp," Jabbo said. "Mistuh Creedy don't 'low that. You can take him outside the fence an' bury him when we gits back this afternoon."

"I'm not leavin' Skip on the ground all day!" Jared said defiantly. "I'll not leave this camp 'til he's buried!"

Jabbo glared at Jared again and said threateningly, "White man, if'n you ain't on that bus when we leave this mo'nin', I'll bust yo' ass wide open!" Then he slammed the door.

Jared stood there for a moment, and then he went back to the room. Cloma was standing in the doorway, holding the coffee pot. She said anxiously, "Where's the sticks for the fire, Jay? I been waitin' on you. You won't have much time now to eat breakfast."

He ignored her remarks and said, "Skip's dead. Somebody killed him out by the cook shed."

"What?" she said with disbelief. "Why would anybody do that to Skip?"

Bennie and Kristy had heard what Jared had said. "Where is he now, Papa?" Bennie asked. "I want to see."

"He's out by the van, but don't go there. His head's been cut off, and it ain't a pretty sight."

Kristy fell across the bunk and started crying as Bennie ran from the room. Jared shouted, "I said no, Bennie! Don't go out there!"

Bennie stopped and looked back. "I want to see," he repeated.

"No!" Jared said again. "I'll have to wait 'til this afternoon to bury him."

Bennie came back to the room reluctantly. "Who done it, Papa?" he asked, anger in his voice.

"I don't know. It was probably Jabbo or Clug. Cy told me that Creedy don't allow dogs in the camp, but I didn't listen. I guess it's my fault he's dead, but I didn't think nobody would do a thing like this."

"They didn't have to kill him," Bennie said, now trying hard to hold back the tears.

Jared went into the room and put his arm around Kristy. She sat up and leaned against him, and then she said, "I'm sorry, Papa. I didn't mean to cry."

"Ev'rybody cries," Jared said. "Even a man cries sometimes." He brushed his hand against her cheek.

Cloma said, "You all better eat somethin' now. There's no time left for makin' coffee."

Kristy and Bennie both ate a cinnamon bun, but Jared took nothing. He went back to the van and covered Skip's body with brown paper. When he returned to the room Bennie said, "Will we say words over him, Papa?"

"Yes. We'll say words."

Cy had watched it all but said nothing.

When they reached the field, Jared again picked frantically. By mid-morning he had filled forty buckets. But the more he thought about Skip and all the other things that had suddenly engrossed his life, the angrier he became. He stopped once and crushed a tomato in his hand, causing the juice to run down his arm like blood. Then he dumped the bucket on the ground and stomped the tomatoes into a pulp.

Cy came up beside him and said, "Mistuh Jay, you don't

need to be stompin' them 'maters. They don't belong to
Creedy. They just belongs to somebody who's payin' to have
'em picked.''

Jared felt foolish. He said, "I guess you're right." Cy's
words calmed him, and he tried to push the angry thoughts
from his mind. But he did not stop the urgency of his pace.
By noon his bucket had been dumped seventy times.

During the break they sat in the white dust and shared
two cans of mackerel and a package of crackers. Cy came to
them and said, "Mistuh Jay, you better take it easy. You
goin' to kill yo'self. It don't matter none at all how many
buckets you fill."

"I'm fine," Jared insisted. "I feel fine." He wiped sweat
from his eyes and drank the juice from the mackerel can.

When they got back to the camp that afternoon, Jared
went immediately to the van and discovered that Skip was
missing. He searched around the camp but could not find the
body or any trace of a fresh grave. Then he looked across the
south field and saw that buzzards were circling the edge of
the swamp. He cursed to himself as he walked back to the
room.

Bennie met him at the door and said, "Are we goin' to
bury Skip now, Papa?"

"Somebody has already done it. I could see the grave
outside the fence." He did not want Bennie to know that
Skip had been dumped at the edge of the swamp for the
buzzards to eat.

"Did they bury him without words?" Bennie asked.

"I don't know. But we can say words fer him here in the
room. Skip won't know the difference. We'll do it after
supper."

Just after dark, Jared went out to the north fence and
paced back and forth, trying to convince himself that things
were not really as bad as they seemed. He thought that perhaps he was agitating for nothing. In two days he had picked

two hundred and seventy-three buckets of tomatoes, and both Bennie and Kristy were doing better than they had done the previous week. If he could keep up this pace, he should be able to clear the debt in less than two weeks. Then they could either work the fields in another camp or move on somewhere else. Jared stopped the pacing and grabbed the fence with both his hands. He swayed back and forth as he was suddenly overwhelmed with tiredness. Then he walked unsteadily back to the room.

When he came inside, Bennie looked up from his bunk and said, "Papa, we ain't said the words yet for Skip."

Jared had forgotten all about this. He dropped to his knees on the concrete floor and said softly, "Lord . . . bless Skip . . . make a place fer him up there with some woods to roam and a few rabbits to run, and he'll be happy . . . take good care of him, Lord . . . that little dog didn't mean no harm to nobody . . . and Lord, watch over us all . . . ."

When he finished, he got up and fell wearily across his bunk, not even removing his clothes. He was asleep instantly.

EIGHT

ALL OF the words from Cy and the danger signals from his own body did not slow Jared's pace for the rest of the week. Each day he picked more tomatoes than the day before, and each night he was asleep before the orange sunset receded from the western sky. He did not even mind the slop they were fed for the evening meal. He chewed automatically and swallowed, too numb from fatigue to know or care what he was eating.

Cloma noticed this, and it troubled her deeply. She had never seen Jared act this way. He had always enjoyed his food and then sitting around after supper, discussing the events of the day and making trivial talk. Bennie and Kristy also noticed, but they knew the reason for his tiredness. They did not understand why their father was working at such a frantic pace, and they did not question him; but both were concerned as they watched him in the fields each day.

Saturday finally came. When the workday ended, and they reached the camp, Jared went to the room immediately and started figuring. He had picked eight hundred and fifty-two buckets for the week; Bennie had three hundred and six, and Kristy two hundred and forty. He added the figures slowly and carefully. The total of thirteen hundred and ninety-eight buckets was an earning of three hundred, forty-nine dollars and fifty cents. Then he figured the charges: forty dollars for rent, five dollars for electricity, fifty-six for the evening meals, thirty-six for the bus, eighteen dollars advanced for food, and ten dollars and fifty cents for the bottles of wine lining the wall. This came to one hundred and sixty-five dollars and fifty cents. He subtracted this from the earnings and it came to one hundred and eighty-four dollars. Then he remembered the ten dollars Creedy had advanced, and this reduced the amount of clear money to a hundred and seventy-four dollars. This, subtracted from the three hundred and seventy-two dollars and fifty cents that he owed Creedy, brought the debt down to one hundred and ninety-eight dollars and fifty cents.

He felt great relief. With a little more effort they could clear the debt the next week, and if they did not quite make it, he could pay the difference. All of the numbing tiredness suddenly rushed from his body, and his mood became jubilant. He jumped up and kissed Cloma on the forehead, and then he said, "Ev'rything's o.k.! We're goin' to be just fine!"

She gave him a questioning look, then he left the room quickly and joined the pay line.

When Jared reached the table, Creedy examined the ledger; then he looked up and said, "You did pretty good this week, Jay Bird. You've reduced your debt by fifty dollars. That brings the total down to three hundred and twenty-two dollars and fifty cents."

It took several moments for the words to register, and then Jared said angrily, "That ain't so, Mr. Creedy! We made a hundred and seventy-four dollars free and clear! I don't owe but one hundred, ninety-eight dollars and fifty cents! I figgered it myself!"

Creedy's face flushed. He said, "Goddammit, Teeter, I keep the books! You owe what I say you owe!"

Jared stepped back because of the sudden outburst. He looked Creedy directly in the eyes and said, "Mr. Creedy, I'll tell you what I'm goin' to do. I got a hundred and fifty dollars left from the trip down here. I'm goin' to give it to you. Then I'm goin' to get my family in my van and drive out of here. I'm goin' right through that gate and not look back, and you ain't goin' to stop me."

Creedy jumped up and shouted, "Nobody leaves Angel City owin' me money! Nobody! You understand me? You ain't goin' nowhere!"

Jared said calmly, "I'm goin' to drive through that gate and leave. And you ain't goin' to stop me."

Jared had not seen Jabbo standing behind him, and the blow was totally unexpected. He hit the ground on his stomach. He tried to push himself up but was too stunned to move. He lay still for a moment, waiting for his eyes to focus. There was a tremendous ringing in his ears, but he heard Creedy say, "Give him another one, Jabbo!" Then he felt the heavy brogan shoe crash into the side of his head.

Jared did not know how long he had been on the ground. When he finally pushed himself to a sitting position, the line of people was gone. Creedy was standing over him. He threw a ten-dollar bill to the ground and said, "Here's your advance for next week, Jay Bird." Then he turned and left.

The supper line had formed when Jared reached the hydrant beside the shower stall. He turned the water on and let it run over his head, then he walked slowly back to the room.

Cloma, Bennie and Kristy were waiting outside the door. Cloma said, "What took you so long, Jay? We'll miss supper if we don't hurry." She noticed that his head was wet and that his face was beginning to swell. "Jared, what have you been doing out there?" she asked with concern.

"Not anythin'," he answered. "I just stopped by the hydrant to wash up some. We can go to the supper line now."

They went to the cookshed and then returned with plates of food. Jared took only a few bites, then he put the plate down and said, "Cloma, I got a thing to say, and I want all of you to listen real good."

"What is it, Jared?" she asked anxiously, still puzzled and disturbed by his sudden change of mood.

"The gate is open fer the buses to go to the store. I want all of you to stand by the east end of the building. I'm goin' to go out to the van. When I crank it, all of you run and jump in. We're leavin' here."

"How come we're doing this all of a sudden? You told me before supper that ev'rything was goin' to be all right."

"Just do as I say!" he said harshly.

"What about our things here in the room?"

"Leave them! And go now!"

Jared walked to the van slowly. No one was around. He put the key into the ignition and pushed the starter. The engine remained silent. He eased out of the door and opened the hood. When he looked inside he saw immediately that the battery was missing. He closed the hood and walked back to the building.

"We better get on the bus and go to the store now," he said without emotion. "We'll need food fer next week."

Cloma was completely baffled by his actions. She did not understand any of this, and it was causing her great concern. Her thoughts were troubled as they joined the line of people pushing their way into the bus.

When they returned to the camp, Jared sat on the edge of his bunk, his arms draped dejectedly across his lap. His head ached, and the right side of his face had turned purple. Cloma knew that something bad had happened and that he did not wish to talk about it yet, so she remained silent and did not question him further as she mended a rip in his shirt. Kristy was sitting on her bunk making a pot-holder, and Bennie was outside somewhere.

Jared looked closely at Cloma. It seemed to him that her stomach was swelling more and more each day. She also looked very young to him, almost as young as that day in the past when he had purchased her box of fried chicken at the church social and then shared it with her at the picnic table. He remembered the day of their marriage and their first night together, then the long walks in the woods and talk of the life they would share together in the mountains at Teeter Ridge. It had been a hard life but one with many moments of happiness. He also remembered how Cloma had looked when she was carrying Kristy.

He then turned his gaze to Kristy, noticing how much she looked like Cloma at the same age. Her eyes were deep blue and filled with innocence. She could not see the things that he saw, could not comprehend the reality of their present life. It suddenly came to him just how dependent all of them were on him. Their lives were almost totally in his hands, and he could make of them whatever he wished, like a potter molding clay. The thought frightened him. It was a heavy responsibility for any man, but now he had made the weight of it even greater. He looked at them both again, and he knew they did not deserve to be here in this camp or in this dingy concrete room where he had brought them. He had turned into a very bad potter, and it saddened him to think of it. He then got up and went outside.

Cy was leaning against the wall, drinking whiskey from a quart bottle. Jared sat down beside him. Cy said, "I seen what they done to you. But what they done this time ain't nothin' at all when you know what they can do."

"It was enough," Jared said.

"You want a drink?"

"No thanks," Jared said. Then he muttered absently, "They's got to be a way."

Cy put the bottle on the ground and said, "Mistuh Jay, don't you do nothin' foolish. Just bide yo' time an' wait. Ain't nothin' goin' to help you none if you daid."

"They's gotta be a way," Jared repeated. "We could get word to the police or somebody. Somebody would help."

"You'd just be wastin' yo' time," Cy said. He picked up the bottle and drank again, and then he said, "Folks don't care 'bout people like us. We ain't nothin' to nobody. We jus' don't matter none at all. The sooner you learn this, the better off you goin' to be. You gotta take it like it is. If'n you don't, then you goin' to end up doin' somethin' bad you would have never done. This the way it's always goin' to be. You gotta take it like it is, an' fo'get all the rest."

"Is that what all these people have done?" Jared asked.

"That's what they done a long time ago. These folks is daid, Mistuh Jay. A man don't have to stop breathin' to be daid. They done had the life knocked outen them. They was born daid. All they doin' now is hangin' on and waitin' to be planted. If they can get a place to sleep, an' somethin' to et, an' a bottle of whuskey fo' Satteday night, then they don't mind the pain of it."

"They'll not defeat me!" Jared said, a determination in his voice. "Not ever! We's mountain folk!"

"Mountain folk don't mean nothin' at all down here," Cy said. "Don't you do nothin' foolish." He pushed the bottle toward Jared. "Why don't you have yo'self a snort? It would sho' do you good. I know yo' head is bound to be hurtin'."

Jared took the bottle and removed the cap. He took a deep drink and handed the bottle back to Cy. The warmth of the whiskey flowing down his throat felt good, and he could feel it easing the pain in his head. He said, "Thanks. I appreciate it." Then he went back into the room and lay on his bunk.

NINE

JARED DID not slacken his pace when he went into the fields the next Monday. He realized now what Cy had meant when he said it didn't really matter how many tomatoes he picked; but he was determined to try once again to reduce the debt by a large amount. He thought that Creedy just might give him full credit for what he and Kristy and Bennie earned if they all worked as hard as they could and he did not create further trouble. It would at least be worth trying, and there would be nothing for him to lose except energy.

It was just after the noon break on Wednesday when Jared noticed that the old man called Rude was acting even more peculiar than usual. He had been picking all morning in a row next to him, and the old man had been constantly singing the song about seeing Jesus in the tomato patch. This did not puzzle Jared, for Rude sang to himself most of the time; but then he started dumping his buckets of tomatoes on the ground instead of taking them to the truck. As fast as he picked a bucket full, he dumped them where he stood, then he moved on and dumped them again. He was leaving a solid trail of tomatoes between the two rows.

Cy came up to Rude once and said something to him, but the old man continued to sing and dump the tomatoes. A few minutes later he dropped the bucket and wandered off toward a line of Australian pines lining the farm road. Jared watched as Jabbo followed after Rude and then brought him back into the field; but as soon as Jabbo was gone, Rude wandered off again. Jared saw no more of Rude until they got on the bus to return to the camp.

It was after supper when Creedy and Jabbo came around the side of the building. Jared and Cy were sitting on the ground, talking. Cy was the first to see them coming, and he said to Jared, "Mistuh Jay, no matter what happens, don't you take no part in it. They ain't nothin' we can do."

Jared said, "I don't understand what you mean."

"You will in a minute," Cy said. "Just don't you have no part of it."

Creedy walked to the door and looked inside. Rude was sitting on his bunk, still singing. Jared watched curiously as Creedy went inside. The sound of the first blow was like someone smashing a bottle against the concrete floor.

At first the old man screamed, and then he started crying. Jared jumped to his feet as Cloma came running outside. Her voice trembled as she said, "What in God's name is happening in there?"

"Go back in the room!" Jared said to her harshly. "And don't come back out here 'til I say so!"

Cy stepped in front of him as Jared moved toward the door. He said, "I done tole you! They ain't nothin' we can do!"

"We can't just stand here and let them do that to the old man!" Jared said desperately. "They'll kill him if we don't help!"

"They ain't nothin' we can do!" Cy shouted again as he pushed Jared backward. "You want to get the same fo' yo'-

self fo' nothin'?''

Jared could see through a corner of the door as the old man put his hands to his head, trying vainly to ward off the blows. The pistol smashed into his face again and again. The more times he was struck, the harder he cried; and then with each blow he started shouting, "Jesus! Jesus!"

Creedy finally came from the room and started to walk away. Then suddenly he seemed to become angrier. He said to Jabbo, "That ain't enough! Go back in and give the old fool a few more licks!" He turned and walked away as Jabbo went back into the room and started pounding Rude again with the pistol.

As soon as Jabbo was gone, Jared rushed into the room. Rude was swaying back and forth, his head in his hands. He was moaning, "Oh Jesus . . . Oh Jesus . . . Oh Jesus . . ." He was covered with blood, and blood was splattered over the walls and floor.

Jared went to his room and said urgently to Cloma, "Get some rags. We need your help. And hurry!" Then he took a bucket and ran to the hydrant for water. When he returned, Cy helped him place the old man on a bunk.

Cloma tried to wash the blood from the old man's head, but it came back as fast as she wiped it away. She finally said, "He needs help badly. There's nothin' I can do for these wounds. We don't have medicine or bandages."

"We'll have to do the best we can," Jared said.

Cy looked again at the smashed head and said, "The pore ole fool was tetched, but he sho' knowed how to pick. They should 'a let him go out o' here a long time ago. Now he'll leave fo' sho'. He might 'a made it outen here if he hadden been so good at pickin'. That's why Creedy kept him in here and wouldn't let him go."

Rude finally stopped moaning and then lay still. Cloma put another wet rag on his forehead, and then she said, "All we can do for him is keep his head cool and watch him during the night. The blood is beginning to slow. Do either one of you know what he did to make them so mad at him?"

"He didn't do nothin'," Cy said. "He was jus' old an' wore out. He stayed in the fields too long."

Jared and Cy went outside and sat on the ground while Cloma remained in the room with Rude. Jared leaned back against the wall and said, "I've seen mean folk in my lifetime, but I ain't never seen nobody like Creedy. He ain't real."

"He's real," Cy said. "They's men like Creedy ev'rywhere. The woods is full of 'em. But you just now findin' it out."

"Back in West Virginny, they'd take a man like Creedy and hang him to the nearest tree," Jared said.

"They wouldn't nowhere I ever been," Cy replied.

Jared thought for a moment, and then he said, "I'm glad I ain't been where you been. I couldn't have stood it fer this long." He got up and moved toward his room. "I'm dead tired, and I'm goin' to bed now. If you need help with Rude later in the night, jus' let me know."

"He ain't likely to need no help," Cy said. "And at least he won't have to pick tomorrow."

Cloma was waiting anxiously the next afternoon when the buses returned from the fields. She ran to Jared and said, "I've been takin' care of that old man all day, but since noon I can't tell if he's breathin'."

Jared and Cy went straight to the room. Jared felt Rude's wrist, and then listened to his chest. He turned to Cy and said, "He's dead. I better go and tell somebody."

Ten minutes after Jared had spoken to Jabbo, the giant black man backed the red pickup to the door. He and Clug loaded Rude into the back of the truck, then they covered the body with a piece of canvas.

Jared watched as the truck went through the gate and raced along the dirt road leading to the highway. It was creating a dense cloud of white dust. He turned to Cy and said, "I wonder how they'll explain those wounds on Rude's head?"

"Explain to who?" Cy asked.

"To the people at the funeral home, and maybe the police."

"He ain't goin' to no funeral home," Cy said. "He's headed fo' the swamp."

"You mean they'll just take him out and bury him?" Jared asked doubtfully.

"Either that or dump him in a sinkhole. Rude ain't the first one to leave in that pickup. They's been others. An' it don't make no difference if'n you daid or alive when you leave, you ain't comin' back."

"You sure you ain't just stretchin' it a bit?" Jared asked, still doubtful.

Cy said, "Mistuh Jay, if'n they ever tries to put you in that pickup, you best fight like a wildcat. That ain't no truck; it's a hearse. If you ever get in that pickup, you ain't never comin' back."

He said it so simply that again Jared believed.

As the week passed, Jared's pace began to slacken. It was not intentional, and for a time he did not realize he was picking fewer tomatoes. It became difficult for him to concentrate on the work with so many thoughts clouding his mind. He wondered how he could have stood idly by and only watched what was in reality a murder. But then it was as Cy said; there was nothing he could do. It also saddened him that the old man had died so alone with apparently no one anywhere who cared. It was as if a mule had died instead of a man. He thought that everyone should have someone somewhere who cared. Even Skip had been mourned. It also frightened him that Creedy or Jabbo or Clug apparently thought no more of beating a man to death than they would think of going into a barnyard and killing a chicken for supper. Such men were totally alien to his upbringing and previous way of life, and he could not bring himself to now accept them and their actions as a natural way of this new life he had ventured into. He also did not want his children to be witnesses to such things.

Each time he realized he was filling fewer buckets, he doubled his efforts during the next hour, but then he would again fall into a mood of depression and lag behind the others. He did not notice the rocks or the dust or the heat or the hunger; and he was not aware that Jabbo was watching him constantly.

When Saturday ended, he figured their week's total of thirteen hundred and twenty buckets. This gave them three hundred and thirty dollars, and deducting the expenses, there was one hundred and sixty-five dollars and fifty cents left. He subtracted this from the three hundred and twenty-two dollars and fifty cents, and the debt was reduced to a hundred and fifty-seven dollars. But he felt no jubilation as he had the previous Saturday.

He joined the silent pay line, and when he reached the table, Creedy glanced briefly at the ledger and said, "You've reduced the debt by thirty-five dollars this week. You're down to two hundred and eighty-seven dollars and fifty cents now."

Jared felt no surge of anger, and he was surprised at himself for this. He did not even argue. He accepted the ten-dollar bill and walked back to the east end of the building. Then he watched as each man and woman took the five-dollar bill handed them and then went back to their rooms. When the ritual was ended, he walked back to Creedy and said, "Mr. Creedy, I want to talk to you fer a minute."

"What is it now?" Creedy asked impatiently.

"I'll give you my van fer the debt."

Creedy glanced briefly at the truck, and then he said, "That old thing ain't worth nothing."

Jared said, "I gave my pickup truck and five hundred dollars fer it before we left West Virginny, and I spent a lot of money on it comin' down here. It ought to be worth a heap more than the debt. You can have it and we'll call ev'rything square. Me and my folks can walk back to Homestead."

"You must think I'm crazy," Creedy said. "That ain't no good deal at all. It ain't my fault if you let some used-car salesman ram a shaft up your rear. I'll take the thing and sell it and put what I get on the debt. You want me to do that?"

"If that's all you'll do, yes." Jared handed him the keys; then he walked back to the building. He looked back around the corner and watched as Jabbo brought the battery from the trailer and put it into the van.

TEN

THERE WAS more chill at dawn as October passed into November, but the Florida days were just as humid. Soon now there would be snow in West Virginia, with logs to chop and deer to hunt. The trees would be bare and somber, and the fields would lie fallow and brown. The earth would be crusty beneath the step as white layers of frost blanketed the yards and the houses and the woods. The days would be shorter and the nights longer; the glowing logs in the fireplaces would send thin spirals of black smoke upward into the gray sky. The beds at night would be piled with thick layers of quilts. Jared sensed that Cloma and Kristy and Bennie were thinking of these things, although they never spoke of them.

There was no visual change of season in the tomato fields or in the surrounding areas. The Australian pines and the cabbage palms and the royal palms all stayed the same as they had been. The fruit trees did not drop their leaves and become bare, and the tomato plants did not turn brown and wither. Instead, the buses continued to dump their human cargoes into the fields each day; the trucks continued to rumble along narrow farm roads, transporting thousands of crates of tomatoes and beans and squash and okra to packing houses in Homestead and Florida City; the rocky fields continued producing the fruits and vegetables which filled the shelves of supermarkets in distant towns and cities, and were eaten by snowbound people who had no thoughts about the where and the how of fresh fruits and vegetables during the winter. These things just magically appeared in supermarkets and were taken for granted by snowbound people.

The days also did not change for the residents of Angel City. There were cans of sardines and Vienna sausage to be eaten before dawn; there was a bus ride to the fields, where ten hours of picking awaited them; there were cans of sardines and slabs of cheese to be eaten at noon; there were late afternoon stops at the Gater General Store to purchase more cans of sardines and Vienna sausage and cheese to be eaten the next day; there was wine to drink and then a hot supper; and there were the stifling, airless rooms at night, and whiskey on Saturday. There were also the occasional sounds of pistol butts cracking skulls. It was all a part of providing the tomatoes for salads and sandwiches to be eaten in New York and Boston and Chicago and Detroit and New Orleans and Minneapolis and Denver and Toronto.

Each day was the same to Jared Teeter as he waited anxiously to learn if Creedy had sold his 1960 Dodge van. It was now the end of another week, and he had not seen Creedy since he had given him the keys the previous Saturday. He felt sure the van would clear the debt, so he had discontinued the frantic pace he had endured the previous two weeks. He worked at a steady pace and averaged ninety buckets per day.

As Jared waited in the pay line, he wondered if Creedy

might possibly give him some cash for the van as well as clearing the debt. If he received even a small amount of money he could purchase an old clunker in Homestead that would do for transportation until he could afford something better.

When he reached the table, Creedy looked up at him and said, "You didn't hardly even break even with the picking this week. How come you to slow down so much?"

At first Jared didn't answer. He was more interested in the van than the picking, and he did not want to say anything that might make Creedy angry. He finally said apologetically, "I was tired, Mr. Creedy. But I didn't think I did too bad."

Creedy said, "Well, you better step up the pace again if you're ever going to work off this debt. I got fifty dollars for your van at a junkyard, so you're down to two hundred and thirty-seven dollars and fifty cents now."

For a moment Jared remained motionless. He felt the blood drain from his face and his hands tremble. He suddenly bellowed, "Shit fire, Creedy! What the hell you take me fer, a goddam idiot?"

The boom of his voice startled the people standing behind him, and they began to back away. Jabbo and Clug moved closer to Jared. Creedy pushed the chair from the table and started to get up.

Jared looked first to Creedy and then to Jabbo and Clug. He had an overpowering urge to smash something with his fists, to strike Creedy regardless of the price he would have to pay. For several moments he hesitated, his body frozen rigid with anger; and then he picked up the ten-dollar bill from the table and walked quickly toward the barracks.

During supper he did not speak to Cloma or Kristy or Bennie. Just before he boarded the bus for the store, he took three twenty-dollar bills from their savings. After making his purchases, he changed the twenties into ones and stuffed the thick roll of bills into his pocket.

When they returned to the camp, Jared asked Cy to step aside with him. The two men walked out to the north fence. Jared stepped close to Cy and said, "I want you to help me with somethin'."

"What's that, Mistuh Jay?" Cy asked apprehensively.

"I got a plan," Jared said. "I know how we can make Creedy pay ev'rybody what they got comin'."

"How's that?" Cy asked, eyeing Jared closely.

"We just won't work. If we refuse to work, then Creedy won't make anything. And he can't beat up ev'rybody in the camp."

"I don't get what you mean," Cy said.

"When we go to the field Monday morning, we refuse to leave the bus 'til Creedy pays ev'rybody fer this week's work."

Cy scratched his head. "These folks in here won't do that. They be's afraid."

"He can't beat up ev'rybody on the bus," Jared insisted.

"I guess he can't at that," Cy admitted. "But I just don't believe nobody will do it."

"Maybe I got somethin' here that might help persuade them," Jared said. He pulled the roll of bills from his pocket. "How many folks ride our bus ev'ry mornin', 'bout twenty-five or thirty?" he asked.

"Somethin' like that," Cy answered.

"We'll give each of 'em two dollars. We'll try it first with just our bus. If it works, then the other crew can do it too."

"I don't know, Mistuh Jay," Cy said doubtfully. "I just don't know 'bout this. Creedy'll get maddern hell fo' sho'. Ain't no tellin' what he'll do."

"He can't beat up ev'rybody on the bus," Jared said again. "And it's worth a try. We don't have nothin' to lose but my money. Will you give out the bills and tell ev'rybody what to do?"

"How come you wants me to give out the money?" Cy

asked, again becoming apprehensive.

"They'll probably listen to you quicker than me."

" 'Cause I's a nigger?"

"Yes," Jared answered simply. "You don't have to argue with anyone. Just hand out the money and tell them what to do. That's all. If they get off the bus Monday mornin', there's nothin' we can do 'bout it. But maybe they won't."

Cy took the rolls of bills reluctantly. He said nervously, "O.k., Mistuh Jay. I'll do it. But soon's I'm done, I'm goin' to drink that whole bottle o' whuskey as fast as I can. Ole Creedy'll get maddern hell."

Jared watched as Cy entered the first room on the west end of the building.

ELEVEN

NO ONE spoke to anyone else as the workers boarded the bus Monday morning, and the trip to the fields was made in silence. Jared wondered if his plan would work, but there was no clue on anyone's face as to what they intended to do. An air of gloom permeated the bus, and each person glanced suspiciously at the others.

When the bus reached the field, Jabbo parked it beside an Australian pine and got out. No one moved. For a moment Jabbo seemed puzzled, then he got back in and said, "Git offen the bus!"

Still nobody moved. Jared stood up and said, "Nobody works this mornin' 'til we get paid. And you can tell that to Creedy."

Jabbo seemed to be totally bewildered. He glared angrily at the workers for several minutes, and then he backed the bus from beneath the tree and into the edge of the field. Then he closed the windows, got out and shut the door.

Minutes turned into hours as the workers remained in their seats. By mid-morning, the sun had turned the bus into an oven. Jared wiped sweat from his face as he wondered how long these people would hold out. For the first time, he felt a closeness to others in the camp besides Cy. Perhaps they weren't all dead yet after all, he thought.

Noon came, and the heat became even more intense. There was no water to drink and no place to perform the necessary bodily functions. Some people were beginning to squirm; but still no one moved toward the door.

At mid-afternoon Creedy came to the field. He spoke briefly with Jabbo and then left. Jared watched the Mark IV as it disappeared down the farm road. He smiled briefly. He too was beginning to hurt badly, but he felt a strong comradeship with the others on the bus who were also suffering. Even Kristy and Bennie didn't complain, although they did not understand what was happening.

The workers got off the bus silently when it returned to the camp. Not one word had been spoken during the entire day except for the brief statement made by Jared. Everyone seemed to be more tired than they would have been if they had picked.

Jared and Cy were sitting on the ground outside the room when Creedy, Jabbo and Clug came around the side of the building. Creedy was in a trot. He stopped in front of Cy and said harshly, "What the hell you mean, nigger?"

Cy didn't move, and there was deep fear in his eyes. Before he could speak, Jared got up and said to Creedy, "He didn't have nothin' to do with it. It was me who made up the plan."

Creedy turned to Jared and said, "If it was you, how come it was this nigger who gave out the money?"

"I gave it to him and told him what to do," Jared said calmly.

Creedy snorted. "You mean to tell me that a white man gave a nigger a fistful of money and told him to give it to other niggers? I don't believe it!"

"Where else you think he could have gotten it?" Jared asked. "You sure don't pay him anythin'."

Creedy gave Jared a menacing look. He said, "Do you mean to tell me you want to take this nigger's whuppin' for him?"

"I'm tellin' you it wasn't his plan," Jared insisted. "It was mine. He didn't have nothin' to do with it."

Cy stepped up and said, "That ain't true, Mistuh Creedy. I been savin' that money fo' a long time. This white man didn't have nothin' to do with it. He didn't even know. It was us niggers who planned it."

"That's what I thought!" Creedy snapped, again turning his attention to Cy. "You better go with us out to the cookshed."

Cy walked ahead of them as they turned the west corner of the building. Jared followed close behind, but Creedy wouldn't listen to anything he tried to say. When the little group reached the cookshed, Creedy rang the bell.

People came slowly from their rooms as Creedy continued ringing the bell. Many had stark terror in their eyes. When they were all assembled in front of him, Creedy said loudly, "They ain't going to be any supper tonight for nobody! And the buses ain't going to stop at the store again 'til Saturday! You can eat tomatoes in the field if you get hongry! And I want all of you to see what happens to any son of a bitch who causes trouble and won't work!"

Creedy turned suddenly and smashed his fist into Cy's mouth. Cy went to his knees, and Creedy kicked him in the stomach. He kicked him twice more, then he turned to Jabbo and said, "You and Clug can have him now. Give him one he'll remember."

Cy tried to get away as the two men pounded him with fists and feet. Jared's face turned ashen as he watched, and then he leaned forward and vomited into the dust.

The beating lasted until Cy lay still on the ground. When

it was over, all of the workers went silently to their rooms. Jabbo and Clug stood over the body for a moment, then they turned and walked back to the trailer.

Jared lifted Cy from the ground and placed him in a sitting position. He squatted in front of him and said, "Can you get up if I help you?"

"I can try," Cy answered feebly. Blood was flowing from his nose and mouth.

Cy got up slowly and put his arm around Jared's shoulder. They moved one step at a time around the corner of the building and to Cy's room. Cloma was waiting with water and rags. She bathed the blood from his face as Cy slumped on the edge of the bunk.

Jared said in a pleading tone, "Why'd you do this, Cy? Why? That should a' been me out there, not you."

Cy looked at Jared and said unsteadily, "It don't . . . matter none 'bout me . . . Mistuh Jay . . . you got a . . . family to look after. . . ."

Jared suddenly felt a bond with this black man he knew would be with him for the rest of his life. He put his hand on Cy's shoulder and said, "You didn't have to do this. I can take my own beatin's."

Cy managed a feeble smile. He said softly, "Don't you know . . . you can't kill a nigger . . . by beatin' him on the head . . . white man hit me once . . . wid a crowbar . . . an' it busted the bar . . . I'll be all right . . . Mistuh Jay. . . ."

Jared didn't know whether to laugh or cry. He said, "Do you want wine? We have some in the room."

"That would sho' be fine," Cy said, seeming to catch a second breath like a runner. "But I sho' would like to have me some whuskey 'bout now."

"I'll buy you two bottles Saturday night," Jared said quickly. "And we'll have eggs Sunday mornin'."

"That sounds mighty fine," Cy said. Then he lay back on the bunk and closed his eyes.

It was three days before Cy was strong enough to go into the fields again. Cloma looked after him during the day, and Jared brought tomatoes from the field for him to eat. They also shared with him their meager supply of sardines and Vienna sausage, which would have to last the rest of the week. It hurt Jared deeply that Cloma and Kristy and Bennie and all the other people in the camp were constantly hungry. He wished he had never tried the useless plan that had brought all this trouble to everyone; and he vowed he would never again do anything that created a risk to anyone other than himself.

Jared continued to pick at a slower pace and ignored Creedy's previous warning to produce more if he wanted to reduce the debt. He did not count the number of buckets he picked. He thought only of finding a way out of Angel City, and this one goal became an obsession which pushed all else from his mind. Rather than frightening him into submission, the witnessing of Cy's cruel beating had made him more determined than ever to take his family and leave.

That Saturday afternoon when he joined the pay line, he did not care if Creedy did or did not reduce the debt and he stared blankly as Creedy told him that he had only broken even again that week. He accepted the ten-dollar bill without protest, and went back to join Cloma and Kristy and Bennie at the supper line.

After the trip to the store, he and Cy sat on the ground outside the room. Both remained silent as the sun disappeared from the sky and darkness crept into the camp. Neither of them had said anything more about the trouble earlier that week, but each day Jared thought he detected a hatred toward him in the eyes of the other workers. He knew that it was he alone who had caused all of them to be denied food and the one daily pleasure of visiting the store each afternoon. This hostility toward him — real or imagined — saddened him greatly, for he had not meant to bring harm to any of them.

Jared finally broke the silence and said, "I've got another plan."

Cy looked at him with disbelief. He said, "Mistuh Jay, ain't you learned nuthin' yet? You best take 'nother look at my face."

"This won't involve anyone but me," Jared said quickly, still feeling deep guilt and sorrow for what had happened to Cy because of him. "But all this has got to come to an end. I'll put a stop to it next week."

Cy still couldn't believe what he was hearing. "What you goin' to do now?" he asked apprehensively. He did not really even want to hear the answer.

"I'll buy my way out of the gate, then I'll go to Homestead and bring back the police. This thing has got to stop. It can't go on forever."

Cy shook his head. He said, "You goin' to fool around an' get yo'self hurt real bad. Creedy ain't playin'. You ought to know that by now."

Jared ignored the remark. He said, "It won't involve anyone but me. I'll go to Homestead and bring back the police."

Cy took a deep drink from his bottle. He wiped his mouth and said, "Are you sho' you know what you doin'? They's other folks in here 'sides you."

"I know that," Jared said. "And this time I won't bring trouble to them. But they're all in the same trap I'm in."

Cy pushed himself back against the wall. His eyes were troubled. He fumbled with the bottle for a moment, and then he said, "If these folks gets outen here, where they goin' to go? To another camp?"

"At least they'll have a choice," Jared replied.

"They ain't got no choice noways. The camps is all the

same. Only diff'rence 'tween Angel City an' any other is that the gate's locked here an' they ain't as much money to buy whuskey.''

"I'm not sure what you're sayin' to me," Jared said. He looked again at Cy's battered, expressionless face. "Are you tryin' to tell me that all these people in here want to live this way?"

Cy said, "I ain't sure myself what I'm tryin' to say. I'm just a dumb nigger, an' I knows it. But these folks is diff'rent from you, just like you an' me is diff'rent. You come in here 'cause you wanted to. Nobody made you. Us folks was born in the camps. It's all we knows, an' we ain't got no place else to go even if we wanted to. An' one camp's the same as another. But I just ain't sho' 'bout nothin' no more.''

Jared gave Cy a penetrating look. "Do you want to stay here the rest of your life?" he asked. "Or do you want out, like me?"

For a moment Cy didn't seem sure of his answer. He seemed to be weighing the question. He finally said, "I wants out. But it's 'cause o' the boy. I wants somethin' better fo' the boy.''

Jared also became silent for a moment, then he said to Cy, "How come you think I want out of here so bad? You think it's just fer me?"

A sudden understanding came into Cy's eyes. He said, "No. I knows now, an' I shoulda knowed all along. It ain't fo' you.''

Both of them gazed into the darkness for several minutes, and then Jared spoke as if saying the words to himself, "It won't involve nobody but me.''

Cy took another deep drink from the bottle and muttered, "I sho' hope you knows what you doin'.''

TWELVE

IT WAS Wednesday afternoon just after supper when Jared approached Jabbo out by the trailer. Jabbo was eating a Moon Pie and sucking the chocolate from his fingers. He eyed Jared with distrust.

At first Jared just stared at Jabbo, and then he said hesitantly, "Can I talk to you fer a minute?"

"Whut you want?" Jabbo asked harshly.

Jabbo's tone made Jared reluctant, and he asked cautiously, "How'd you like to make some money?"

Jared watched the giant black man's reaction closely.

"Doin' whut?"

"Nothin' much. It would be worth fifty dollars to you."

Jabbo appeared interested. He said in a guarded tone, "Whut you want me to do?"

"Just open the gate tonight and let me out. My woman's feelin' poorly, and I need to go to the store real bad and get some stuff fer her. You let me out, nobody will ever know you did it, and I'll come back real soon."

"You got the money?" Jabbo asked.

Jared reached into his pocket and pulled out a wad of crumpled bills. He handed them to Jabbo and said, "Fifty dollars."

Jabbo took the money and put it into his pocket. He said, "Whut time you want to go?"

"As soon as it gets dark."

Jabbo wheeled suddenly and went into the trailer.

For a moment Jared stared after him, wondering if Jabbo would really open the gate or if he had given his money away for nothing. He knew that if Jabbo kept the money and left the gate locked, there was nothing he could do about it. But he was willing to take the risk.

He went back to the barracks and sat on the ground outside the room. He had said nothing of this to Cloma, for he knew she would be frightened by the danger involved and would try to persuade him not to do it, and he had not told Cy when he intended to put this plan into action.

Cy came back outside and sat beside him. For a few minutes they made trivial talk, but Jared was completely detached from everything except the approaching darkness. Cy noticed this, and wondered about it. Always before, Jared had seemed to enjoy their conversation as the camp settled into the night; but now, for all the attention he was paying to Cy's remarks, Cy might as well have not been there at all.

Jared did not speak to Cloma or even look into the room when he got up and walked slowly toward the east end of the building. The moon had not yet arisen, and the fields outside the fence were seas of darkness. He could not see the fence or the gate as he skirted the edge of the yellow cone being cast outward by the floodlight. His heart pounded as he moved past the clump of Australian pines.

When he reached the fence, he stopped and let his eyes adjust to the darkness. Then he pushed his body against the gate. It opened. He stepped outside and closed the gate behind him.

For a moment he looked back and searched the area around the gate. When he detected no sign of movement, he turned and started along the dirt road. He had an overpowering urge to break and run, but he knew he must not allow his footsteps to shatter the quietness of the fields and echo back into the camp. He moved slowly and carefully, one step at a time, feeling his way along the powdery trail as would a blind man. He looked back only once, and it seemed to him that the floodlit buildings were a thousand miles away.

Just as he reached a point forty yards from the highway, the truck's headlights came on and centered on him. The unexpected shafts of brilliant light blinded him, and he tried to shield his eyes. He heard the roar of the engine as it came to life, and then he heard the screech of tires. He realized vaguely that the pickup was moving directly toward him. For a moment he was unable to control his body; then at the last possible second he jumped aside as the truck rushed past him and skidded around wildly, once again bathing him in the blinding headlights.

Jared felt terror invade every part of his body as the pickup rushed at him again. He turned and ran into the field to his right. The truck also turned and came at him again. He stumbled as the limbs of the tomato plants grabbed at his legs; and when he tried to break free of them, the pickup started circling him. It did not come directly at him again until he ran blindly toward the south end of the field.

Each time the headlights seemed certain to smash into him, he managed to jump to the side; and then the game began again. He ran and circled and dodged and fell and then ran again; but no matter what he did, he could not escape the menacing beams of light.

He had reached almost total exhaustion when he felt the sharp sawgrass cut into his legs. He fell forward and landed in soft muck that splattered across his face. For a moment he lay still, panting and unable to breathe, then he looked back

just as the headlights were turned off. He did not realize until
then that the truck had been herding him into the marsh.

For several minutes more he did not move. There was no
sound coming from anywhere except a bellowing off to his
right. He had never before heard such a sound, and then he
remembered what Cy had said about the alligators. The total
darkness addled him, and he could not tell from which direction he had stumbled into the swamp.

He finally pushed himself up and staggered forward, but
with each step he took, he sank deeper and deeper into muck
and water. He could hear swishing sounds as snakes scurried
out of his path. When the water level reached his chest, he
turned and moved in the direction he thought he had come.
The water gradually became shallow again, and then he was
suddenly back in the edge of the field.

He sank down to the rocky soil and breathed deeply.
About a mile to the west he could see the dim lights of the
camp. After he rested for a few minutes, he got up and
headed east across the field. He had moved only a few yards
when the headlights came on and once again centered on him.
He felt he did not have the strength left to even try, but he
started staggering through the tomato plants.

The truck came at him again and again as he ran and
stumbled and fell and ran again, and then he realized that the
game was ended. If he continued to run they would kill him,
so he dropped to the ground and lay still.

He heard the door swing open as the truck stopped ten
yards from him, then he heard the rush of feet. The first
blow stunned him as the pistol smashed against his face. He
was surprised that it caused so little pain, and he did not put
up his hands to ward off the blows. He was too exhausted to
care what they did to him, and it was a relief when he felt
consciousness slip away.

The jolt of his body hitting the floor of the truck bed
aroused him, and he heard Clug say, "We goin' to take him to

the sinkhole?''

"Naw," Jabbo's voice came to him. "Mistuh Creedy say bring him back to the camp. We goin' to take the girl."

Blackness closed in on him again, and he knew nothing more until he hit the ground outside his room. He felt himself being pulled inside and thrown on the bunk, and he had a twilight realization that Cloma and Kristy and Bennie were crying hysterically; but he could not force words from his mouth.

Jared looked up and discovered that he could see and hear, but he could not move or speak. He listened as Jabbo grabbed Kristy by the arm and said, "Mistuh Creedy say fo' you to come to his place."

He heard Kristy scream, "No! No, Papa! I'm afraid! I don't want to go, Papa! I'm afraid!"

Jared tried with all that was left in his body to push himself up, but he could not do so. He watched helplessly as Jabbo dragged Kristy to the door.

Cy suddenly stepped out of the darkness and said, "Why don't you two niggers leave that girl alone? Is Creedy payin' you that much? You done enough to her pa already."

"You want some too," Jabbo asked, his eyes glazed with hostility.

"I'd as soon as not!" Cy shot back angrily. "You goin' to give it to me by yo'self, without no help from Clug? You try it by yo'self, I'm goin' to beat tha' livin' shit outen you."

Jabbo stepped toward Cy, dragging Kristy with him, then he stopped and said, "I'll settle wid you later. We gotta take the girl now."

Cy watched Kristy struggle as Jabbo pulled her to the pickup; then he stepped into the room and said to Cloma, "Is Mistuh Jay hurt bad?"

"I don't know," Cloma sobbed. "Oh my God, I just don't know!"

Cy went to the bunk and examined Jared's face and head.

Then he turned to Cloma and said, "I don't think he's got nothin' broke, but they sho' whupped up on him real good. Ain't no need fo' you to fret so. He'll git all right in a few days, an' I'll help look after him."

Cloma sat on the edge of the bunk and bathed Jared's head. She said to Cy, "What did he do?"

"He snuck out fo' Homestead," Cy answered. "I tried to tell him, but he wouldn't listen. He thought it were a game. I tried to tell him these folks ain't playin'."

THIRTEEN

THE NEXT morning when he awoke, Jared could hardly push himself from the bunk. Both of his eyes were almost swollen shut, and he had a purple welt down the right side of his face. The muscles in his arms and legs ached each time he moved, and sharp pains shot through his ribs where he had been kicked.

He took the coffee Cloma handed him and sipped it slowly. At first he did not remember the events of the previous night, then they started coming back to him like fragments of a dream. He could see Kristy being dragged from the room, and the thought of her being held as a prisoner by Creedy made him sick. He put the coffee mug on the floor and pushed it away.

For several minutes he sat on the edge of the bunk, trying to put all of the pieces together in his mind. He knew now that what Cy had said was true: this was no game. Each day since he had learned the harsh reality about Angel City, he had hoped that it was all a bad dream that would fade away, that he would awake one morning and find it did not exist at all; but he knew from the empty bunk where Kristy had been, and the pains in his own body, that this was not to be. His situation was totally beyond his understanding, but it was a deadly serious reality.

Jared got up and forced himself outside when the bell rang for the loading of the buses. Cloma pleaded with him to remain in bed, and Cy cautioned him not to go to the fields, but he paid no heed to either of them. He was determined at any cost to show Creedy that he had not been beaten into something less than a man. Walking slowly and painfully one step at a time, he reached the bus and climbed aboard.

There were times that day when Jared could not remember filling the bucket or taking it to the truck. His eyes were narrow slits, and he picked by feel rather than sight. As the heat became more intense, his head pounded beyond endurance; and several times he dropped to his knees and vomited into the green plants. It was mid-afternoon when he finally sank to the ground between the rows and did not move again until Bennie and Cy helped him to the bus at the end of the day.

Each day for the rest of the week, Jared went back into the fields, and gradually his strength began to return. On Saturday afternoon, when he reached the pay table, he glared defiantly at Creedy as he was handed the ten-dollar bill.

Before going to the store, Jared took ten dollars from the sixty dollars left of his savings, and after making his food purchases, he bought two quarts of whiskey. Cloma watched the precious money change hands but said nothing. She knew what he felt he must do.

Late that afternoon, Jared sat on the ground outside the room, a bottle on each side of him. He had already taken several drinks when Cy came out and sat beside him. Cy opened his own bottle, then he said to Jared, "It looks like you plannin' a party tonight."

"I thought I'd do some drinkin'," Jared replied, not fully

aware of what Cy had said.

"Don't blame you none," Cy said. "Man take a whuppin' like you did, an' then go back to the fields, he oughta drink some. You the most stubborn white man I ever seen."

Jared turned the bottle up and drained it three inches, then he said, "Folks is killin' hawgs now in West Virginny." He was trying to flush the present from his mind and submerge himself into the past, but the mountains and streams seemed to be too far away, if they ever existed at all.

Cy said, "I sho' would like to have me a big ole fresh ham an' some baked sweet taters. I could et a ham as big as a watermelon."

"We made our own hams and bacon and sausage and lard," Jared said, drinking deeply again. "Smoked the meat with hickory. I always liked to put a piece of fried sausage between a hot biscuit. We had real butter too, and in the winter there was deer meat."

Cy said, "Mistuh Jay, you oughta hush up. You makin' that salt poke an' stewed squash we et fo' supper swish aroun' in my belly. I's gittin' hongry just listenin' to you. How come you to up an' leave all them good vittles an' come down here?"

Jared drank again, and then he said, "Well, I didn't rightly want to, and when we finally pulled up stakes and shucked out for Floridy, I was scared spitless. Times just got too hard in the mountains, and I couldn't make it no more. Taxes was too high, and they wasn't much way a man could make cash money. I cut logs on one of my ridges 'til they ran out, and I hauled some firewood. Two winters I left home and worked in the coal mines, but I couldn't stand it down there under the ground. The Lord didn't mean fer a man to burrow around like a mole and then die with that black stuff in his lungs."

"I wouldn't like that neither," Cy said. "I just got to have me some fresh air all the time."

Jared turned up the half-full bottle and drained it in one gulp. Then he threw the empty bottle toward the fence and opened another. Cy watched him curiously and said, "You oughta take it kind of easy, Mistuh Jay. They's plenty of the night left ahead o' us."

Jared turned to him and said sharply, "Goddamit, you think I don't know how to drink?"

"I didn't mean nothin' at all," Cy said quickly, startled by Jared's angry response.

"Folks aroun' Dink make they own whuskey," Jared said, his voice now as calm as if he had not made the previous remark to Cy. "It's a heap better'n this store-bought stuff. When it comes outen the still it's white, but you put it in a charcoal keg and it turns brown."

For a moment Jared fell silent, then he turned back to Cy and said, "You ever do any coon huntin'?"

"I done some once up in Georgie," Cy answered.

"We used to go ev'ry chance we'd get," Jared said. "Went mostly just to hear the dogs run. Go out in the woods and build a fire. Never did mess with the coons, though. But I had a uncle who did. His name sounded almost like my wife's. It was Clomer. He always got drunk before the hunt started, and when ev'rybody else was just sittin' round the fire, listenin' and talkin', Uncle Clomer would run after the dogs and go up in a tree after the coon. He'd catch one and then bring him back to the fire and turn him loose so's the dogs would run after him again. One night Uncle Clomer went up in a tree, and he was really shirt-tailed drunk. He grabbed that coon by the rear legs and started jerkin'. Only it wadden no coon. It was a wildcat. But Uncle Clomer was too drunk to tell the diff'rence. At first the wildcat thought Uncle Clomer wanted to play, so he gives Uncle Clomer three or four quick jabs with them big back feet. Kicked just like a mule. But Uncle Clomer didn't turn loose. Then that ole cat commences to get mad. He started makin' a nest in Uncle

Clomer's hair, only he was takin' it all off Uncle Clomer's head. It sounded like they was tearin' the whole top out of that tree. Leaves and branches was flyin' ev'rywhere. Then the wildcat decided he'd take off Uncle Clomer's ears, but Uncle Clomer had other plans. He just couldn't understand why a coon would carry on so. About then Uncle Clomer gets mad too. In a few minutes we heard the damndest whump you ever heard, so we all run over to the tree, and there on the ground . . ."

Jared suddenly stopped talking, leaned back against the wall and took another deep drink. When he said nothing more, Cy asked anxiously, "Well, Mistuh Jay, what happened to yo' Uncle Clomer?"

Jared remained silent for several more moments, his eyes transfixed on something past the fence and the fields; then he finally turned to Cy and said, "I ain't a nobody! I was a deacon in the church! I had a cousin who was a town alderman in Mudfork. I ain't a dried cow turd you can stomp on and kick!"

Cy couldn't understand Jared's sudden shift of conversation, and was confused as to how to respond to it. He said hesitantly, "I knows you ain't no cow turd, Mistuh Jay. I can tell you's fine folks."

Jared drank again, and then he said softly, "Oughta be snow soon in West Virginny. Kristy was born durin' a snow. I got the pickup stuck and had to fetch the doctor on a mule. I was a heap more scared than Cloma. She just laughed at me after it was over. And that baby was so little. She looked just like a doll. Never did cry much. I'd pick her up and bounce her up and down on my knees. She really liked that. She would coo just like a pigeon. Never did really cry much. She was a good baby and . . ."

Cy watched as tears welled in Jared's eyes. He put his hand on Jared's shoulder and said, "Mistuh Jay, you needen' fret so. Yo' girl goin' be all right. They ain't done nothin' to my boy since he been over there. She goin' be all right, Mistuh Jay."

"They's a diff'rence," Jared said, "a heap o' diff'rence. That girl never been away from home even one night before we came here. She ain't been aroun' like your boy, and she won't know how to handle it. And besides that, they's a big diff'rence 'tween a boy and a girl. You oughta know that."

Cy wanted to say something that might help ease Jared's fear, but he could not do so. He merely repeated, "She goin' be all right, Mistuh Jay."

Jared turned up the bottle, drained it half-way and started singing, "Wes - Vir - Ginny . . . mountain mamma . . . take me home . . . where I belong . . . Wes - Vir - Ginny . . . mountain mamma . . . country roads . . . take me home . . ."

Suddenly he pushed himself up and staggered unsteadily to the north fence. He laced his fingers through the heavy wire and shook the fence violently, then he dropped to his knees and said, "I ain't never done nothin' really bad in my lifetime, Lord . . . not a really bad thing . . . but You better help me now, Lord . . . You better help . . ."

Jared fell forward and lay still against the fence. He was not aware when Cy picked him up and carried him back to the room.

FOURTEEN

ON SUNDAY, Jared's moods changed constantly from anger to depression, and he moped around the compound like someone in a trance. Cloma tried to talk to him and cheer him, but she couldn't get through to him no matter what she said. When the Mark IV pulled into the camp and parked by the trailer, Jared ran to it anxiously. Kristy was not with the other children, and this caused him great fear. For the rest of the afternoon, he sat by the north fence alone, staring across the field and at the highway leading to Homestead.

The next day Jared picked the tomatoes automatically, filling the bucket and emptying it and filling it again. At noon he ate a can of sardines and a tomato, but the chewed pulp stuck in his throat. He spat the tomato to the ground and washed his mouth with water.

When he walked into the store at the end of the day, he appeared to be calm. After purchasing food he handed the sack to Bennie, then he walked to the store manager and said loudly, "You got to help us! We're prisoners! You got to help us!"

Jabbo moved toward him immediately. The store manager backed away and said, "You must 'a got too much sun, fellow. You better sit down and rest for awhile." Then he turned aside and waited on another customer.

Jared backed toward the door, repeating loudly, "You got to help! . . . somebody has to help!. . . ."

When he reached the front of the store, he turned right and ran up the highway. A car approached from the west, and Jared jumped in front of it, waving his arms wildly. The car swerved to avoid hitting him, then it increased speed. He ran again until he reached a house a quarter-mile up the highway, then he crossed the yard and knocked on the front door. When a woman opened it, he said urgently, "You got to help us . . . we need help . . . somebody has to help . . ." The woman slammed the door quickly and locked it.

Jared then looked down the highway and saw that Jabbo was coming after him. For a moment his senses were overcome with panic, then he jumped from the porch and ran into an orange grove to the south of the house. It was dark when he finally stopped running and paused for a few minutes beneath a papaya tree. After pulling one of the gourd-like fruits and sucking the juice, he wandered again for another hour until he dropped to the ground exhausted and fell asleep.

The sun was already mid-way in the morning sky when Jared awoke. He sprang to his feet startled and bewildered, not knowing where he was or how he got there. As reality gradually drifted back to him, he looked around and saw that he had spent the night at the edge of a bean field. Far in the distance he could see men and women picking into hampers. He knew that if he turned north again, he would eventually come back to the highway.

When he reached the road leading to Florida City, he dared not walk along its edge for fear that Jabbo or Clug would be looking for him; so he stayed behind houses and in the fields and groves until the outskirts of town came into view. At the first service station he came to, he asked directions to the police station.

It was another two miles to the Homestead branch of the sheriff's department, and as Jared walked along the roadway and sidewalks, people stared at his torn, filthy clothes and his battered face. He glanced around constantly to see if he was being followed. When he reached the small brown stucco building he went inside quickly.

The first room was a small lobby area, and as Jared entered, a man behind a desk eyed him suspiciously. "Something I can do for you?" he asked quizzically.

"We need help," Jared answered quickly. "We're bein' held against our will, and they've taken my daughter. Somebody has to help us."

The man gave Jared another penetrating look as he said, "Just have a seat over there and Deputy Drummond will talk to you in a few minutes. I'm just a clerk."

Jared waited nervously for ten minutes until finally he was asked to step inside an office. As he took a seat in front of the desk, an officer said, "I'm Deputy Drummond. What's your problem?"

Jared spoke rapidly, "We're bein' held like slaves! . . . . They've taken my daughter! . . . . You got to help us! . . . ."

"Just take it easy, fellow," the deputy interrupted. "Calm down a bit. Are you a migrant?"

"I work in the fields," Jared replied, trying to calm himself. "We came here from West Virginny."

"What's your name?"

"Jared Teeter. Folks call me Jay."

For a moment the deputy toyed with a pencil on the desk, then he looked back to Jared and said, "Just tell me the truth, Mr. Teeter. Have you been shooting junk or drinking too much wine? You could save us both a lot of time if you tell me the truth."

Jared was surprised by the question, and he answered firmly, "I ain't been doin' nothin' like that! We need help real bad."

The deputy looked closely at Jared's condition and said, "O.k. Now who is it that's doing all this to you?"

"His name's Creedy. Silas Creedy. We live at Angel City."

"I've never heard of either one of them. But we don't keep track too much of the migrant camps. There's just too many of them."

Again the deputy studied Jared closely. "Just exactly what is this man Creedy doing to you?" he asked.

"He keeps us in the camp and won't pay nobody," Jared said, trying to think of all the things he should say. "Claims we all owe him money and we got to stay there and work it out. Can't nobody get outside the camp. I tried to get out and go fer help, but they caught me and then they took my girl off to Creedy's place as a prisoner. He's got the other folks' children there too."

"Where does Creedy live?" the deputy asked.

"I don't know," Jared replied, troubled by not knowing, for he wanted to go there immediately. "I guess it's sommers around here or Floridy City, or maybe in Miami. And it could be out in the country sommers."

"That's not much help," the deputy muttered. He then said, "How'd your face get so beat up?"

"They pistol-whupped me," Jared said, wincing as the memories came back. "They beat one old man to death that way, then they took him into a swamp to get rid of him. I seen it. My friend's been in Angel City two years. He says they've killed a whole bunch of folks and put them into a sinkhole."

The deputy thought for a moment, trying to digest all of the things Jared was saying. "That's a pretty bad story, Mr. Teeter," he said. "How far is it to this Angel City camp?"

"I can't rightly say fer sure," Jared answered, "but I can show you the way. It's not too fer out of Floridy City."

From Jared's straightforward answers, his simple sincerity and the urgency in his voice, the deputy surmised there must be some truth in the things Jared had said. He got up from the desk and said, "Maybe we might better go out to this Angel City and take a look."

Jared followed the officer outside, then they got into a green patrol car with a red flasher on its top. As they drove into Florida City, the officer turned to Jared and said, "How long's it been since you've eaten anything?"

Until then Jared had not even thought of food. He said, "I don't rightly remember. It must be nigh on two days now."

The deputy stopped at a hamburger stand and bought Jared two hamburgers and a milk shake, and he wolfed them down eagerly as they passed through the town and turned west on the highway leading to the camp.

It was after six when the patrol car turned from the highway and crossed the field to the camp. To Jared's surprise, the gate was open. The deputy parked beside the trailer and got out.

Creedy came from the trailer immediately, approached the deputy and said calmly, "I see you got ole Teeter. He's kinda daffy, if you ain't found it out already."

The deputy ignored Creedy's remark about Jared and said, "Are you Creedy?"

"That's right," Creedy answered. "I'm the contractor who runs this camp."

"Mr. Teeter here has told me some pretty bad things about you," the deputy said, watching Creedy closely.

"I done already told you he's tetched. I do everything I can to look out for him, but sometimes he goes plumb loco and runs off. You can ask his family about him."

"Mr. Teeter says you're holding his daughter and some other children at your house. Is this true?"

Creedy began shuffling his feet. "I ain't never heard such a wild tale," he said indignantly. "I live right here in the trailer. You can look for yourself."

Jared had been standing to the side, listening. He turned to the deputy and said, "That's a lie! Jabbo and Clug live in the trailer! Creedy don't live here at all!"

The deputy looked at the flash of anger in Jared's eyes, then he turned back to Creedy. "You mind if I have a look around?" he asked.

"Suit yourself," Creedy said, his voice unconcerned. "Look all you want to."

As the deputy went into the trailer, Creedy turned to Jared and said in hushed tones, "If anything comes of this, you're in bad trouble. You must 'a forgot where your girl's at."

Jared was worried, for he had not expected things to go as they were. He had surmised that the deputy would simply arrest Creedy and then return Kristy to him. But he still thought that the officer would surely learn the truth before leaving the camp. Thus far he had only heard Creedy's side of the story, and he knew that Cloma and Cy would tell the truth.

When the deputy came back outside, he said to Creedy, "I'll look around the camp for a while. You wait here until I return."

Jared followed the deputy as he went to the first room on the north side of the building. He looked inside and said, "You folks got anything to say to me?"

Four somber black faces stared back. One said, "Naw suh."

"Can you leave this camp if you want to?" he then asked.

"Yas suh. We can leave anytime we wants."

Jared's face was ashen as he listened to the unexpected answers.

The deputy moved on down the line and received the

same reply in each room, then he came to Jared's room. Cloma was sitting on one bunk and Bennie on another. She looked at Jared and said, "Where've you been, Jared? We've been worried sick about you."

Before Jared could speak, the deputy asked, "Is this your husband?"

"Yes," Cloma answered calmly. "That's Jared."

"Where's your daughter?" he then asked.

"We don't have a daughter." Cloma stared downward, avoiding Jared's eyes. "We only got Bennie here."

Jared's heart sank, and he knew now why the gate had been open instead of locked. Creedy had had ample time to prepare the camp. Jared was not surprised when Cy told the deputy he had no son.

After questioning several more people, the deputy walked back to the trailer with Jared following. He leaned against the side of the patrol car, staring intensely at Creedy, then he said casually, "That's a mighty fancy car for a labor contractor."

Creedy looked toward the Mark IV and said defensively, "I earned ev'ry penny of it. I works hard. I go into the fields ev'ry day and picks right alongside my people."

The deputy was unimpressed by Creedy's remarks. "How come this man's face is so beat up?" he asked, studying Creedy's reaction.

"How would I know?" Creedy snorted. "He ran around in the woods all last night. Maybe he fell over something. I try to take good care of him, but sometimes he goes plumb loco."

The deputy sensed that Creedy and all the others were lying, but he couldn't take the word of one man against all the others in the camp. He turned to Jared and said, "I guess I'll be going now, Mr. Teeter."

"Ain't you goin' to arrest him?" Jared asked feebly.

"For what?" the deputy said. "Nobody here will back up

your story, not even your wife."

"I told you he's tetched," Creedy said, now feeling confident.

"Maybe he is and maybe he isn't," the deputy snapped, looking directly into Creedy's eyes. "I can't prove anything now, but this whole place don't look right. How come you've got it fenced like a prison compound?"

"Too much thievin' goin' on," Creedy said warily. "You know how it is with these migrants wandering around all over the countryside. They'll take anything that ain't nailed down. And besides that, it ain't against no law to put a fence around your own property."

When he reached the patrol car, the deputy turned and said, "You take it easy, Mr. Teeter. And Creedy, I might be seeing you again."

Jared watched the patrol car as it turned through the gate and moved toward the highway, taking with it his one hope of getting Kristy back and escaping from Angel City. As he walked dejectedly toward the barracks, Creedy shouted, "Hold up there, Teeter!"

Creedy came to him and said, "We ain't goin' to whup you this time, 'cause it don't seem to do no good. But you owe me a fair and honest debt, and you're goin' to pay it one way or another. You pull another stunt like this, or cause trouble of any kind, and that gal of yourn might have a real bad accident. You understand what I'm saying, Jay Bird?"

"I understand," Jared said, his face and voice strained with defeat. "I ain't goin' to cause no more trouble. I swear it."

Creedy was pleased by Jared's answer. He said, "It's about time you figured it out. I ain't never had nobody come in here before who acted like you over an honest debt. From now on, you get only four dollars on Saturday instead of what I been givin' you. If your belly starts to hurt, it ought to make your brains work better."

"My wife needs plenty of food," Jared said, concerned by Creedy's remark about the money. "Her time's not too far off, and she needs to keep up her strength. Do what you want to me, but don't punish her fer what I done. She had nothin' to do with it, and she needs her strength."

"You ought to have thought about all that before," Creedy said. "If your woman gets hungry, you can give her part of your vittles from now on."

"I'll do that," Jared said as he turned quickly and walked away.

When he entered the room, Cloma grabbed his arm and cried, "I'm sorry, Jared! I'm sorry! I ain't never lied before, and you know it. But Mr. Creedy said he'd hurt Kristy real bad if I didn't do as he said. And he threatened Cy and all them other folks, too. I'm real truly honest sorry, Jared, but I didn't know what else to do! I was afraid for Kristy!"

"I understand," Jared said, looking deeply into her eyes as he took her into his arms and tried to calm her. "It's all right. I know you couldn't do nothin' else but what you did. It's all right, Cloma, don't fret about it. You done the right thing."

Two days later, late in the afternoon, Creedy entered the camp with a drunken black man sitting beside him in the Mark IV. The man got out and staggered around the side of the building. When he came to where Jared and Cy were sitting on the ground, he said, "Is this room 'leben? Mistuh Creedy say I'm in room 'leben. I's goin' work fo' Mistuh Creedy."

"You found it," Cy said.

The man had a brown paper sack in his hand. He said, "I's called Hoot, an' I comes from Orlanda. Mistuh Creedy, he let me have ten dollars in advance. He a good man. He goin' pay me twenty-five cents a bucket fo' pickin' 'maters."

Cy pointed into the room and said, "You got the bunk on the right. The man what had it befo' you had to leave here a short while ago. Just go on in an' make yo'self at home."

Hoot went inside for a moment, then he came back out and said, "You folks wants a drink? Mistuh Creedy, he give me this here whole quart bottle o' whuskey."

"Don't mind if I do," Cy said, eyeing the bottle. "You can sit down here on the ground an' join us fo' a spell, a good long spell. We sits out here ev'ry afternoon after supper."

FIFTEEN

DAYS MERGED into each other as the buses left the camp each morning before dawn and returned in late afternoon. The routine was broken twice when the workers were shifted from tomato fields into bean fields; and for three other days they planted tomatoes instead of picking them. They did not know what they were being paid as planters, and the money Creedy gave them each week remained the same.

When the month changed to December, the daylight hours were shorter, and sometimes the light did not come until a half-hour after they entered the fields. Dusk settled before supper was finished, and the wind at night was strong and piercing. Flights of ducks and geese passed overhead as they headed out into the vast marshlands of the Everglades. Rain came more often, and sometimes the ground inside the camp turned into a quagmire that sucked at shoes and covered the concrete floors of the rooms.

Since Kristy was no longer in the fields, Jared received only two dollars each day for food, and this, combined with the four dollars he received on Saturdays, gave him sixteen dollars each week for food and all the other necessities. He ate less and gave Cloma and Bennie more, and at night he bathed without soap in order to divert every possible penny into additional cans of sardines and Vienna sausage. He brought tomatoes from the fields, and sometimes he would slip from the fields into adjoining orange groves and steal fruit, which he brought back to the camp in a brown paper sack he kept inside his shirt. He also asked the store manager for waste beef and pork bones, which he boiled into broth each night and left for Cloma to drink during the day.

Kristy came for visits on Sunday afternoons, and each visit they saw a change in her personality. The constant smile she once wore was now gone, and she showed little interest in anything. Jared tried to question her about how she was being treated, but she would not answer. Instead, she would turn and walk away alone, ignoring his pleading calls for her to come back and be with the family. Sometimes she would stand for hours clinging to the fence, gazing out across the empty fields; and when it came time to leave the camp, she would walk away without saying goodbye to any of them. This caused both Jared and Cloma great anguish and concern, but there was nothing they could do but hope that the change was only temporary.

Jared made no further plans for escape. Instead, he decided to do as Cy suggested and bide his time, waiting for something unexpected to come from some unknown somewhere and set him free. He wanted to get out of Angel City as badly as ever, but his spirit was shattered, and he was determined to do nothing more so long as Kristy remained outside the camp, and so long as his actions might endanger her life. Each day was lived as it came, and his life slipped into a routine just as regimented and drab and as accepted as that known by any of the workers who had spent lifetimes in the camps.

He began to think and feel and act more as Cy did. Sometimes he hated himself for letting his life become so totally controlled and guided by Creedy. When he became angry enough because of this, he would share Cy's bottle of whiskey on Saturday nights. He would look forward to those few hours on Sunday afternoons when all of his family could be together, although most of the time Kristy was not with them at all; then on Monday mornings he would go into the fields and lose all conception of hours and days until another weekend came again.

It was on a Saturday night that Jabbo came down the line of rooms on the north side of the barracks. Jared and Cy were sitting on the ground outside Cy's room, and they were immersed in darkness except for a narrow shaft of light drifting through the partially closed door. Hoot was inside, passed out on his bunk. Jabbo suddenly appeared out of the shadows and said, "Mistuh Creedy say fo' you to be on the bus at six in the mornin'."

"What fer?" Jared asked harshly, startled and annoyed by Jabbo's unexpected presence on a Saturday night. "We ain't never picked on Sunday."

"Mistuh Creedy say we takin' one bus full o' men to work in Belle Glade fo' awhile. He say all men on the north side be on the bus at six."

It took a moment for the meaning of Jabbo's words to register on Jared, and when they did, Jared said, "I ain't goin' to do it! I'm not leavin' this camp with my wife the way she is!"

Jabbo repeated, "Mistuh Creedy say fo' you to be on the bus at six. An' you leave the boy. We ain't takin' nothin' but men on the bus." Then he walked on down the line of rooms.

Jared turned to Cy and said, "What's this all about? How come they'd take us to Belle Glade?"

"To pick," Cy said, without surprise or concern because

of the sudden order. "Up there they grows sweet corn an' celery an' lettuce. He might even put us in the sugar cane fields. If he puts us in them cane fields, then you sho' goin' need you a bottle ev'ry night."

"I thought we stayed here all the time. Creedy didn't tell me nothin' about goin' some place else."

"We goes where they's work," Cy said. "Beans an' cukes in Carolina, peaches in Georgie, 'taters in Alabam, oranges anywhere he wants us to go. If them buses wadden so old an' rattly, we'd go up to Noo Yawk an' pick grapes an' apples, but Creedy ain't goin' spend the money to fix 'em up to go that far."

Jared became silent for a moment, "I ain't goin' to go! They'll have to drag me on that bus feet first an' kickin'!"

Cy shook his head with exasperation and said, "I thought you'd done learnt better. You don't go, all you goin' do is make things worse fo' yo'self an' bring on a heap o' trouble fo' yo' girl."

Jared realized that again Cy was right. He asked, "How long will we be gone?"

"It's hard to say. Depends on the crops an' how many folks is already workin' up there. Most times it's two-three weeks or a month, but the crops lasts all winter up there. Could be a long time, but sometimes the pickin' gets better down here, an' he brings us back. We follow the crops anywhere they points that old bus."

"I can't leave Cloma that long, the baby is due soon."

"They ain't nothin' you can do 'cepin' get yo' head bashed in or yo' girl in trouble. That wouldn't help yo' woman none, would it?"

"Maybe Creedy would let Kristy come back to the camp and stay with her."

"They's a woman called Bertha in the other side of the buildin'. She's a midwife, an' she's a good woman, too. I'll speak to her 'bout lookin' out fo' yo' wife."

"What if she needs a doctor?" Jared asked.

"She won't get no doctor even if you's here. An' you knows that. I'll go speak to Bertha."

Cy got up and went around the side of the building.

Before he went in to tell Cloma, Jared decided that he would see if Creedy was still in the camp. He walked to the trailer, and the Mark IV was there. When he knocked on the door, Creedy came out.

Jared said, "Mr. Creedy, will you bring my girl back to the camp when we leave for Belle Glade tomorrow?"

"What for?" Creedy asked.

"My wife's expectin' soon. Kristy could look out fer her while I'm gone."

"You must think I'm crazy!" Creedy snapped. "I wouldn't let you go four feet outside the gate with that girl back here. You'd probably shuck out for West Virginia."

"Let her come back to the camp," Jared pleaded. "If you do, I swear 'fore God I won't do nothin'. I ain't caused no trouble lately. Let her come back, Mr. Creedy."

For a moment Creedy seemed hesitant, then he said, "I ain't going to do it! You got a boy to look after your woman. You ought not to have gotten her belly swelled up like that noway. She ain't been to the fields a day since she's been here."

"Who'll be here if she needs help?" Jared asked, realizing that Creedy would never grant his request.

"Clug is stayin' here with the south crew. While ev'rybody's in the fields, the cook will be here during the day. Ain't that enough? And besides that, they's some nigger women who can help out. Hell, them nigger women knows how to handle it. They has babies out in the fields, then goes on picking the rest of the day."

Jared knew it was useless even talking to Creedy. Without speaking further, he turned and walked back to the room. He dreaded telling Cloma.

SIXTEEN

CLOMA AND Bennie walked with him as Jared answered the bell to board the bus. To Jared the shrill clanging seemed to be an ominous forewarning of impending doom. It was as if some pagan temple bell were tolling him away so that his wife and unborn child could be sacrificed to a god of the fields he could not accept or comprehend. He wanted desperately not to go, to stay and share with Cloma the agony and joy of this thing they had created together, this intimate moment of love they had shared in the past which would soon produce life. He knew this desire was hopeless, so he consoled himself with the thought that perhaps he would return to Angel City before the time of the birth.

When they reached the bus, he kissed Cloma and cautioned Bennie to look after her as best he could; then he turned away from them quickly and stepped into the dark interior of the old vehicle. As they passed through the gate and moved slowly along the dirt road, he looked back and could see Cloma and Bennie standing alone beneath the floodlight on the east end of the building.

The sky was overcast that morning, and dawn did not come until they reached the northern outskirts of Homestead. Jared looked through the grimy window and watched the houses and the vegetable stands and the fields flow by. The fields were now empty and forlorn, resting until the next day when hordes of pickers would swarm over them like locusts.

A few miles north of Homestead, Jared thought he recognized the spot beside the highway where they had stopped to let the van's radiator cool on the day they arrived in Homestead. He remembered the lunch of sausage and crackers and hot Coke, and the conversations about the fruit stand and the ocean and fishing and bathing suits and things to come. He knew now that all those dreams they had talked about were only dreams, and they had been washed away like a sandcastle in a mountain stream.

They soon passed the junction of Highway 27 and the Tamiami Trail, and continued north on Highway 27. Jared passed the time by looking out of the window constantly, watching the people and the cars and the houses and the groves and the vast stretches of sawgrass at places where the Everglades swooped in and touched the edge of the highway. He also saw migrant camps which were in even worse condition than Angel City, rotten wooden shacks on stilts and unpainted concrete block barracks with bare yards and naked children and junked cars and trash and beer cans and people with hopeless faces looking out of broken windows, watching the flow of traffic along the highway.

When they reached Andytown, a light rain was falling, and the sky far in the north was a solid wall of black. "Cold front movin' in," Cy said to Jared. "It rain hard 'nough we won't be able to pick, then ole Creedy'll blow out his flue fo' sho'."

For several miles north of Andytown the highway cut through another section of the Everglades; then they reached the beginning of the vast areas of the sugar cane farms, fields of solid cane that stretched to and beyond the horizon and dwarfed even the largest tomato fields Jared had seen around Angel City. He looked in wonder at the soil, which was as black as thick layers of soot, and was puzzled by smoke boiling upwards from walls of fire stretching across the land.

Cy watched Jared with amusement, then he said, "They burnin' the cane fields befo' the cane's cut. Burns off the leaves an' trash. Most o' the cane's cut by voodoo niggers."

"What's voodoo niggers?" Jared questioned.

"Niggers from the islands. Pickers won't cut no cane lessen they ain't nothin' nowhere to pick an' they has to. It's too hard work. But them men they brings here from down at Jamaica swings them heavy machetes like they was made o' paper. You ain't never seen nothin' like how them niggers can go down a row o' cane."

Jared continued to stare at the endless fields. He asked, "You ever cut any?"

"I done it some, but I sho' don't like to. I'd ruther pick a thousand buckets of 'maters than spend a day in the cane."

"I don't see how they ever get it all chopped," Jared said.

"You would if you knowed how many men they puts out there in them fields at one time. All you can see is voodoo niggers swingin' them big blades."

It was just before noon when the old bus ambled into South Bay. Here the highway skirted the south shore of Lake Okeechobee. To the left were Bean City and Lake Harbor and Clewiston and Moore Haven; to the right, Belle Glade and Pahokee. The bus turned to the right.

Two miles out of South Bay the bus left the highway and followed a dirt road flanking a drainage canal on the right and a cane field on the left. A mile down the road they came to a clump of Australian pines. Just as Jabbo parked the bus beneath the trees, a solid sheet of rain poured down on them.

The pounding rain lasted for more than two hours, and

the men sat in the bus in silence. No mention was made of food, and Jared's stomach rumbled as he wondered when they would be given something to eat. When the rain finally stopped, they got off the bus and wandered around the small area beneath the trees.

It was late in the afternoon when the Mark IV pulled up beside the bus. Creedy got out and had a lengthy conversation with Jabbo. He opened the trunk of the car, took out a cardboard box and sat it on the ground; then he got back into the car and drove off.

The box contained cans of sardines and beans and loaves of white bread. Jabbo gave each man a can of each and two slices of bread. Jared and Cy sat on a bed of wet pine needles and ate from the cans with their fingers. Jared said, "Where'll we stay tonight? Does Creedy have a camp up here too?"

"We in his camp now," Cy said, drinking the oil from the sardine can. "You can sleep on the ground or in the bus."

There was no water except that in the nearby drainage canal, and it was covered with green slime and had a foul odor. Jared drank just enough to wash the food down his throat.

Some of the men gathered wet firewood which they coaxed into burning, but the wet wood produced more smoke than warmth. The temperature dropped rapidly as the wind became stronger and made a mournful wailing sound as it rushed through the thick limbs of the pines. Jared went into the bus and got a blanket he had brought with him. He draped it around his shoulders and sat as close to the weak fire as possible, but even this didn't help. His body shivered with cold as he got up and went back into the bus, and finally he fell asleep on the seat with Cy huddled close against him.

SEVENTEEN

DAWN WAS far off when Jabbo awoke the men the next morning. He again gave them cans of sardines and beans and slices of bread, but there was no coffee to ease the biting chill. During the night, the temperature had dropped into the mid-thirties. Jared had not brought even a light jacket with him, for he had no prior knowledge of the cold fronts that rush through Florida in the winter, dropping the temperature forty degrees overnight.

The meal was finished quickly, and then the workers were ordered into the bus. Just as they turned right on the highway toward Belle Glade, a feeble dawn revealed a steel-gray sky. Two miles down the highway they again turned onto a dirt road flanking a cane field. Cy looked out of the window and moaned, "Ah, crap! We ain't headin' to the corn fields. They must be too wet. He's takin' us to a cane field."

Jared didn't know the difference between a vegetable field and a cane field except for the remarks Cy had made about cane cutting, so he made no reply to Cy's seemingly disturbed remark.

When the bus stopped, Jared noticed that the Mark IV was parked beside a pickup truck. Creedy was talking to a man in the truck. All of the men were then ordered off the bus, and Jared shivered with cold as the piercing wind bit into his body.

Another truck was parked nearby, and a man at that truck issued each of the workers a machete and assigned him a row of cane. For those like Jared, who had never cut before, he demonstrated that the cane must be cut at ground level and then cut again into four-foot lengths. Jared gripped the handle of the huge blade and swished it through the air. The weight of it caused his arm to drop, and he almost sliced the blade into his leg.

The first hour of cutting was a novelty to Jared, and he swung the blade back and forth vigorously, striking down the hard stalks, cutting them again and throwing the lengths to the ground for the automatic loaders to scoop up. Soot from the burned stalks covered his face and arms and got into his eyes, and the black muck sucked at his shoes; but still the uniqueness of the work made the first of the morning bearable.

By noon his arms and back and legs ached almost beyond endurance, and the machete became heavier and heavier. It took all his strength just to lift the blade after he had swung it downward into the base of a stalk. He stopped almost continuously to rest, and each time he looked up, the row seemed to grow longer and longer. When the work was finished that afternoon, Cy had to push him back into the bus.

That night they again ate the cold food from cans and drank in the drainage canal. Jared managed to wash some of the grime from his face and arms, but his clothes were caked with thick layers of mud and soot. He made a bed of pine needles and then rolled himself into his blanket. He was so tired he didn't notice the cold or the dampness of the ground or the wailing sound of the wind in the pines, and it was just after dusk when he fell into a deep sleep.

The temperature dropped again to twenty-nine degrees, and even the constant swinging of the heavy machete did not warm Jared's body. His hands shook as he chopped again and again at the thick stalks, and at noon he huddled against Cy in the bus to gain some warmth. He wished that Jabbo would pass out the bottles of wine at night as he had at Angel City, for this might help bring some relief from the cold and the ache in his bones.

It was late in the afternoon on the fourth day in the cane fields when the pickup followed the bus back to the camp in the Australian pines. The emblem of a sugar company was painted on the doors of the pickup, and a tall radio antenna was mounted on the truck's cab.

A man got out of the pickup and looked at the ANGEL CITY sign on the side of the old bus, then he walked to Jabbo and said, "Is this the crew run by a man named Creedy?"

"Yassah, this it," Jabbo replied.

"You people been camping here all week?" the man asked.

"That's right," Jabbo said. "This our camp."

"Creedy stay here too?"

"Nawsuh. He stay at the motel in Belle Glade. He be out here soon with the food."

The man went back and sat in the truck until the Mark IV drove in and parked by the bus. He watched as Creedy put the box on the ground and Jabbo issued each man the cans of food and slices of bread; then he walked over to Creedy and said, "You Creedy, the contractor with this crew?"

"That's right," Creedy answered. "What you want?"

"I'm one of the field supervisors with the sugar company, and you're camping in my section. How long you had these men here?"

"Since Sunday," Creedy said warily.

"Are they sleeping on the ground?"

"They can sleep in the bus if they want to."

"It's a damned wonder they all don't have pneumonia." The man watched the workers as they sat on the pine needles and ate with their fingers from the cans. He said, "I've never seen a crew that looked worse than this. When's the last time these men had a bath?"

"I don't know nothin' about their personal habits," Creedy said, becoming agitated by the questions. "They can take a bath in the canal anytime they want to. Hell, I ain't no nursemaid. I'm a contractor."

"They can't stay out here any longer," the man said. "You can move them into a barracks at Camp 9."

"What's that going to cost?" Creedy asked.

"We'll give them the same deal as the offshore workers. The rooms are free, and the meals are seventy-five cents each."

Creedy thought for a moment, and then he said, "I ain't going to pay no two and a quarter a day per man just for meals. I can feed 'em myself for less than a buck."

"What do you mean, you're not going to pay?" the man questioned. "The meals are deducted from the men's wages. It has nothing to do with you."

"I get all the money and I pay the men," Creedy said firmly.

"What?" The man gave Creedy a penetrating look, then he said, "There's no way you're going to do that! We'll pay you the same as any contractor for putting these men in the field, but every man receives his own wages."

"I ain't going to do that!" Creedy said defiantly. "I get the money and I pay the men. Some of these people owe me money, and I have to take it out of their wages."

"You got a court order to do that?"

"A court order? Hell, I don't need no court order to collect a honest debt."

"You do up here." The man stepped closer to Creedy and said, "Fellow, I don't know what kind of an outfit you're running wherever you come from, but these men look worse than a bunch of pigs. Are you going to move them into the barracks or not?"

"Before I do, I'll take 'em out of the field!"

"You just do that!" the man snapped angrily. "And you get the hell off this property! You're on company property without permission! You're trespassing!"

"We got some money coming," Creedy said quickly.

"I know that. I'm going over to the field office and see exactly how much each of these men have earned. Then I'll come back and pay them. I'll be gone about a half-hour." He walked to the pickup, got in and drove off quickly, spraying mud from beneath the truck's rear wheels onto the side of the bus.

As soon as the truck was gone, Creedy kicked the cardboard box violently, scattering cans across the small clearing. He shouted loudly, "Bastards! Sons o' bitches! A man can't even make a honest livin' no more on account of them supervisors!"

The men sitting beneath the trees watched curiously as Creedy kicked the box again and again until finally it landed in the drainage canal.

When the supervisor returned, each man was given an envelope with his wages inside. The workers were paid according to the amount of cane each had cut, and Jared's envelope contained fifty-two dollars. He stuffed the bills into his pocket. Creedy stood to the side and glared angrily as the supervisor finished his task and got back into the pickup. He leaned out the window and said to Creedy, "I want you off this property within thirty minutes! And I don't want to ever see you back!"

Creedy watched the truck until it disappeared into the growing darkness, then he turned to the men and said, "I'm going to be fair with all of you. I got expenses bringing you up here, and the food. I'll let you keep half what the man gave you, and I'll take half. That's more'n you got comin'. And I'll let the bus stop at a store when we leave here."

Each man got up silently and walked to Creedy, handing him half the money he had received. Creedy stuffed the bills into a brown paper sack and then took Jabbo aside. They talked for several minutes, then Creedy got into the Mark IV and drove off. At Jabbo's signal, the men gathered up their blankets and boarded the bus.

When they reached the highway they turned right and drove to Belle Glade, then they turned north toward Paho-kee. A mile out of town the bus stopped at a country store. The men scrambled out and rushed into the building, hurriedly purchasing cartons of beer and bottles of wine and Moon pies and jars of pickled pigs' feet and boxes of sugar cookies. Jared bought a denim jacket for eight dollars, several cans of corned beef and sardines, a quart of red wine, and two candy bars. He thought immediately of Cloma and Bennie back at Angel City without enough food, but he was too cold and too hungry to resist spending this much of the unexpected money. He still had over fifteen dollars left.

They drove north again for two miles, then the bus turned from the highway and followed a dirt path to an abandoned labor camp. The wooden cabins contained about nine square feet of space each and were propped on stilts four feet off the ground. The windows and doors were missing from all of them, and some of the cabins had gaping holes in their sides and roofs.

Jabbo cut the engine and said, "Mistuh Creedy say we stay here fo' a while."

Jared and Cy entered one of the cabins cautiously. They

were immediately covered with cobwebs, and the rotten floor sagged with their weight. There was a strong smell of decay. Cy said, "It ain't much, but it's better'n the ground. Makes me kinda homesick, too. Let's look aroun' an' see if we can find somethin' to build a fire in."

They went outside and searched the area surrounding the cabin. Jared found a rusted bucket half buried in the dirt, and Cy gathered a bundle of twigs. A few minutes later, a small fire inside the bucket illuminated the interior of the cabin. Both men held their hands over the flames to warm them.

Jared and Cy both opened cans of corned beef, then they drank deeply from bottles of wine. Cy said, "It sho' did me good to see that sugar man give it to Creedy. I thought ole Creedy was goin' choke to death on his own spit."

"Where'll he take us now?" Jared asked between bites.

Cy swallowed a huge chunk of corned beef, washed it down with wine, and then said, "Mos' anywhere. Probably the corn fields, but he sho' ain't goin' to take us back to the cane fields. Them folks don't want no more truck with Creedy."

"Suits me fine," Jared said. "I don't never want to cut another stalk noways." He spread out his blanket and lay down. The wine warmed him, and the new jacket felt good to his arms and shoulders. "How long these cold spells last?" he asked. "I always thought it was hot all the time in Floridy."

Cy drank again, then he put the bottle down and said, "Sometimes it gets cold enough to freeze the oranges on the trees, an' they has to fire the groves. But these spells don't last long. This one last much longer, the vegetables be in real trouble."

"I wouldn't care if ev'rything froze solid tonight. Maybe then we would go back to Angel City."

"You's worried 'bout yo' woman, ain't you?"

"Yes." Jared had not realized it showed so much on his

face and in his voice.

Cy said, "You don't need to worry so. Bertha a good woman. She'll see to yo' wife. Bertha will take good care o' her."

"Maybe," Jared said doubtfully. "But I sure wish I was back there now."

EIGHTEEN

IT WAS after ten the next morning when Creedy arrived at the camp. He passed out the cans of food, then he said impatiently, "You men can eat on the bus. We're runnin' late."

The workers boarded the bus hurriedly, and Jabbo followed the Mark IV back to Belle Glade and then east on Highway 441. Five miles out of town they pulled to the edge of a sweet corn field and stopped. A driver was waiting in a flat-bed truck piled high with empty crates. As soon as the bus was emptied, the workers followed the truck into the field, pulling the ears from the stalks and packing them into crates, then loading the crates on the truck and starting again with empty crates. When the truck was loaded, another took its place, and the loaded truck headed back to the packing house in Belle Glade, where the corn would be pre-chilled and then packed into other trucks to be shipped to markets in the East and the Mid-West and Canada and the Far West.

After work that day they returned to the abandoned camp for the night, and the next day they picked in the same field. It was Saturday, but when Creedy came to the camp late that afternoon, he did not hand out any money. Jared didn't really expect to receive any, since he had been allowed to keep half the money he earned in the cane fields, which was more than several weeks' pay at Angel City. The other men in the crew didn't seem to be concerned one way or another. They took the cans of sardines and beans and went back into the dilapidated shacks.

Jared and Cy sat on the floor of the cabin, eating in silence. Jared was glad there would be no trip to a store that afternoon. He still had some degree of pride left within him, and he was ashamed of the way he looked. Grime and soot were ground into his face and hands, and his clothes were stiff with caked dirt. He longed for a bath even if in a slimy drainage canal, but it was still too cold to risk such exposure.

They had not finished eating when Jabbo came to the cabin and ordered them outside. As they got up, Jared said, "We must be goin' to move again. Maybe it's back to Angel City this time."

Creedy was standing at the front of the bus, his red face flushed even redder with anger. When all the men were outside, he said, "We got a nigger missing. The one called Hoot. Who knows about it?"

The men glanced around at each other, but no one spoke. Creedy walked to the Mark IV and returned with a bottle. He said, "I'll give this quart of whiskey to the first man who tells me where the bastard went."

The group remained silent for several moments, then an old man of about sixty-five spoke up and said, "I seen him, Mistuh Creedy. Right after we got to the camp I seen him runnin' t'ward the highway. I seen him, Mistuh Creedy."

"Which way did he go when he got to the highway?"

"I don't know, suh. I couldn't tell fo' the trees. But I seen him runnin' t'ward the highway."

Creedy turned to Jabbo. "He couldn't have gotten far by now." Then he handed the bottle to Jabbo and said, "Put this back in the car. I ain't givin' away a quart of whiskey for no more information than that."

The old man stepped back into the group and cast his face downward.

Creedy then said, "I want you two men over there to go with Jabbo to Pahokee, and you two there to go with me to Belle Glade. The rest of you stay here at the camp, and you damned well better be here when we get back, or we'll be out lookin' for you next. You understand me?"

The men nodded their heads silently.

The first two men Creedy pointed to were Jared and Cy. All of those he selected to leave the camp and help search for Hoot were ones whose children were at his house.

Jared and Cy followed Jabbo to the bus as Creedy and the two men left in the Mark IV. When the bus reached the highway it turned right and followed the narrow highway which wound past cane and vegetable fields and was bordered on both sides by thick lines of Australian pines.

Darkness was flooding the highway as they arrived at the southern outskirts of Pahokee. This was the Negro section of the town, and on each side of the road, two-story concrete-block apartment buildings were jammed one against another. Some had once been painted in garish colors of pink and red and yellow which were now faded badly. All of them looked as if a stiff wind would send them tumbling down one against another like a line of dominoes. Clothes hung from sagging wooden balconies, and the yards were bare of grass and littered with trash and with rusted junk cars without wheels, propped up on wooden blocks.

Jabbo pulled onto a side street, parked the bus and motioned for Jared and Cy to get out. He said, "You two work the west side an' I'll take the east. If'n you find him, bring him back to the bus."

Jared and Cy walked together for a block. Silent men were huddled against walls and squatting along the sidewalk, some drinking beer and wine and whiskey, and others just looking and spitting into the street.

As they stopped beneath a dim street light, Cy said, "I'll work this side an' you work over in the next block. We'll meet down at the south end."

Jared touched Cy's arm and said, "What you goin' to do with Hoot if you find him?"

"I'm goin' tell him to run like hell an' never look back."

Jared smiled. "That's what I thought."

As Jared turned to cross the street, Cy said, "You best be real careful around here. This a bad part o' town." Then they walked in different directions.

Jared paused on the next corner and watched the people move about and the flow of traffic along the street. He was not aware of the police car's presence until it pulled to the curb beside him and stopped. An officer got out and came over to him.

Jared became apprehensive as the officer stared closely at his physical appearance. Finally the officer said, "What are you doing here, fellow?"

For a moment the situation addled Jared, and then he said, "I'm just walkin' around some."

"You a migrant?" the officer asked.

"I work in the corn fields. We live in a camp just south of here."

"What company's camp?"

Jared hesitated again, then he said, "I don't know the name of the company. We work for a contractor. He brought us into town in the bus."

"Is it the red bus parked on the side street over yonder?" the officer asked, pointing across the street.

"Yes, that's the one. We're just spendin' a while in town. We'll go back to the camp pretty soon."

The officer looked closely at Jared again and said, "You ain't got no business in nigger town on Saturday night. Don't you know that?"

"No, sir, I didn't know," Jared said nervously. "I was just walkin' around some."

"Well, you better walk in another area. We have enough trouble as it is without you just plain asking for more."

Jared felt relieved as the officer got back into the patrol car and drove away. He thought of the night he had so desperately wanted to talk to a police officer, and now he had lied to get rid of one. But he knew that if the police in Homestead wouldn't believe him, an officer in Pahokee would probably think him even crazier. And he was also thinking of Kristy.

As he walked along the street he could feel eyes following him, and finally he turned into a place called the Pastime Cafe. There was a counter along one end of the room, tables jammed along the sides and center, and a constantly flashing Budweiser sign on one wall. The air smelled heavily of smoke and fried fish and onions and hamburgers.

Several black men and women were sitting at the tables, and a fat black woman of about forty was behind the counter. When Jared walked to the counter and leaned against it, the woman gave him a hostile look and said, "What you want, mister? This is nigger town. You ain't got no business in here."

Jared was startled by the anger in the woman's voice. He said, "I'm lookin' fer a man called Hoot. He's a black man, 'bout my age, six feet tall and about a hundred and fifty pounds. Have you seen him tonight?"

"I seen a hundred like him," the woman said, becoming even more sullen. "What you want with him?"

"I need to talk to him. Has he been in here?"

"You want to buy somethin'? If you don't want to buy somethin', why don't you just get the hell on out o' here?"

"I'm just lookin' fer Hoot," Jared tried to explain again.

A man at a table by the counter had been watching and listening. He got up and came over to Jared. Suddenly he pulled a knife from his pocket, touched a button and a six-inch blade swished out. He pointed the knife at Jared and said, "Why don't you quit pesterin' her? You tryin' to start trouble? You lookin' fo' trouble, then you come to the right place."

Jared eyed the knife and the hostility in the man's face. He said as calmly as possible, "I'm not lookin' fer trouble. I just need to find a man called Hoot. I got to talk to him and help him out."

"I ought to drop yo' guts on the flo'!" the man said, moving closer as Jared backed away. Others in the room stopped drinking and watched.

Jared backed against the wall and kept his eyes on the glint of the knife blade. He was totally bewildered, not understanding what he had said to cause such trouble. He wanted to run, but now the man had moved between him and the door.

Jared glanced to the side just as Cy entered, and relief flashed through him at the sight of Cy's muscled body. For a moment Cy froze, and then he said loudly, "Hold up there, fellow! That white man's a friend o' mine!"

The man turned and stared at Cy. For a moment he hesitated, then he folded the knife and put it back into his pocket. He said to Cy, "If he's a friend of yourn, then you tell him to keep his damned mouth shut an' stop askin' questions in here!" Then he turned and walked back to his table.

Cy said to Jared, "We better get on outen here now. You just lucky I came in when I did. That fellow looked like he was 'bout ready to make bacon outen you."

They went outside and stood by the curb. Jared's hands were trembling as he said, "I sure don't know what that was all about. All I did was ask if they'd seen Hoot."

"It's best you fo'get it," Cy said. "But we better stay

together from now on."

They continued down the street and came to a building with a sign on the outside: BEER AND POOL. When they entered, Hoot was standing at a counter alone, drinking a bottle of beer. Cy went to him immediately and said, "What the hell you doin' in here? Don't you know Creedy's out lookin' fo' you? He's got folks here an' in Belle Glade."

Hoot wheeled around in surprise. He said, "I wadden runnin' away. I swear fo' God I wadden. I just wanted to come into town an' get me a beer. I was comin' back."

"You crazy nigger fool!" Cy snapped harshly. "Don't you know Creedy's just as liable to kill you as not?"

"I swear fo' God I wadden runnin' away," Hoot said again, his eyes bulging with fear. "You goin' take me back now?"

"We ain't takin' you nowhere," Cy said, his voice calmer. "But you better hide sommers the rest of the night an' then shuck out o' here as fast as you can in the mornin'. You can go up to Avon Park or Frostproof. They's plenty of work there in the groves, an' Creedy won't find you. An' you better not ever come aroun' Homestead or here again."

"I can't get away lessen I gets back on the road an' catches a ride," Hoot said desperately. "I ain't got a cent left. Mistuh Creedy he goin' find me fo' sho'."

Jared reached into his pocket, took out a ten-dollar bill, handed it to Hoot and said, "This'll get you on the bus with a little left over."

Hoot looked surprised. He grabbed the money eagerly and said, "You jus' givin' it to me fo' nothin'?"

"Yes. To help you get away from Creedy. But you better get outa here. Jabbo's with us."

Hoot's eyes flashed with fear again at the mention of Jabbo. As he glanced nervously toward the door, he said to Jared, "I sho' 'preciate you doin' this, I sho' do. I won't fo'get you fo' it."

Cy said, "I better look outside an' see if it's clear." He walked to the door and glanced down the street, then he came back inside quickly and said, "Jabbo's comin' down the sidewalk right now! You better get under the counter quick an' hide there 'til we're gone."

Hoot ran behind the counter as Cy hurriedly purchased two beers. He motioned for Jared to take a seat at an empty table. Just as they sat down, Jabbo entered. He walked over to them and said, "Mistuh Creedy didn't say fo' you to come into town to drink. You supposed to be lookin' fo' Hoot, not drinkin' beer."

"We done looked ev'rywhere," Cy said calmly, "an' we ain't seen hide or hair o' him. We thought we'd have a beer befo' goin' back to the bus. You want one?"

Jabbo stared at Cy. "You mean you goin' pay fo' it?" he questioned.

"That's what I said, ain't it?" Cy snapped. "You want one or not?"

Jabbo hesitated for a moment, and then he said, "I guess I'll have one. Then we got to go." He took a seat at the table while Cy went back to the counter.

Cy came back and handed Jabbo a bottle of beer. Jabbo took a drink and then said, "Mistuh Creedy goin' be maddern hell 'cause we didn't find that nigger."

"We looked ev'rywhere, but we didn't see nothin' at all of him," Cy said.

Jabbo's face became worried. "Maybe Mistuh Creedy find him in Belle Glade," he said.

"Maybe he will an' maybe he won't," Cy said. "If Hoot caught a ride on a truck, he could 'a shirt-tailed it halfway to Orlanda by now."

Cy took another drink, then he looked across the table and said, "Jabbo, how much Creedy payin' you to do what you doin' to yo' own folks? You a nigger too if you don't know it, just like me an' just like old Rude an' just like Hoot.

How much he payin' you?''

Jabbo ignored Cy's question. He turned up the bottle of beer, drained it, belched twice and said, "We better go now. We got to get back to the camp. Mistuh Creedy goin' be maddern hell.''

The three of them walked back to the bus in silence. When they reached the camp, Jared and Cy went into the cabin and built a fire in the bucket; then they sat on the floor, eating a can of corned beef and drinking the rest of the wine.

Jared became thoughtful for several minutes, eating in silence. Then he turned to Cy and said, "How come them people back there in the cafe got so mad at me? I didn't do nothin' at all to make them mad.''

"How come you so mad at Creedy?''

Cy's remark puzzled Jared. He said, "What you mean by that? I don't see that Creedy has anything to do with it.''

Cy stopped eating and looked directly at Jared. "Did you see much diff'rence 'tween them nigger' quarters an' Angel City? Them folks back there works in the fields ev'ry day an' has to come back to them quarters ev'ry night. They can't get away no more than you can.''

"You mean they think I'm to blame for it?'' Jared asked, still puzzled.

"They don't think nothin'. They's just mad, just like you, mad 'cause they's trapped an' can't get out.''

Jared became silent again for several moments, and then he muttered, "Well damn!''

They finished the can of corned beef as the small fire died down in the bucket. When the wine was gone, Jared lay down and wrapped himself in the blanket. For a long time he thought of what had happened in the cafe and why Cy said it happened. Although he was very tired, he felt restless. He turned to Cy and said, "You asleep?''

Cy grunted, "I was, but I ain't now.''

"How come Creedy calls the camp Angel City?" Jared asked.

"I don't know," Cy answered, his voice reflecting a disinterest in further conversation. "Maybe he thinks it's the end o' the line fo' ev'rybody."

"Well, one angel flew the coop tonight, didn't he?"

Cy chuckled. "He sho' did. That's the God's truth."

Again Jared became silent for a moment, and then he said, "When my Papa died, they brung him into the house in a coffin, and then they opened it . . . I was sittin' there alone in that cold room, lookin' at him and feelin' sorrow fer Papa . . . and then all of a sudden I wasn't seein' Papa in that box at all . . . I was seein' me . . . me myself, right there in that pine box . . . not Papa in the coffin but me . . . and then I was alone in a city of angels, just like the Bible says . . . with nothin' around me but white forms . . . white forms driftin' all about me, speakin' in tongues I couldn't understand. . . . It was so real it like to have scared the life outen me, and it was a year or two afore I stopped seein' myself in that coffin . . . and that's the same way I've felt ever since I come to Angel City . . . like as if I'm just sittin' there lookin' at myself in a coffin, and there ain't no way out of it. I got a real bad feelin' in my gut, a mountain-bad feelin', and that's the worst kind."

Jared got up, gathered a few twigs from a pile in the corner and put them onto the coals in the bucket. After rolling himself back into the blanket, he said, "When we first come down here, all Kristy wanted was a red bathin' suit to wear to the beach, and all Bennie wanted was to see the ocean and fish in it. We been in Floridy all this time now and we ain't seen the ocean yet. I don't even know if it's really out there sommer or not."

"It's out there," Cy said. "But why don't you shut up now an' let me get some sleep? I'm bone tired, an' we got tomorrow to face. You ain't in no coffin yet."

Jared lay still for a long while, thinking again of the trip into Pahokee and the incident in the cafe and of Hoot escaping and of the things Cy had said to him. It was late in the night when he heard Creedy somewhere out in the darkness. Creedy was screaming wildly and shouting obscenities at Jabbo. Jared listened for several minutes, then he pulled the blanket over his head and went to sleep.

NINETEEN

ON MONDAY morning, the workers went back into the corn fields. The cold front had now passed, and Jared had spent most of Sunday afternoon bathing and washing his clothes in a drainage canal close by the camp. Later, he huddled in a blanket while the clothes dried slowly beside the small fire in the bucket.

Creedy was still in a rage over not finding Hoot, and each time Jared and Cy looked at his red face, they laughed inwardly because of the part they had played in Hoot's escape. By now he would be safely in Frostproof or Avon Park, and they knew that Hoot would never again come close to Homestead or to Belle Glade.

At mid-week they were shifted into a celery field, where they ripped the white stalks from the soot-black soil and threw them into dump trucks. The stalks were then hauled to the packing house in Belle Glade where they were dumped into vats of water, washed and cooled, packed into crates and shipped to distant supermarkets where they would be purchased, chopped into soups or salads or stuffed with pimiento cheese and served with hors d'oeuvres at cocktail parties.

Jared was thinking more and more of Cloma. Sometimes he worked an entire row without realizing it, and at times he threw the stalks of celery over the top of the truck and had to run back and pick them up. But Creedy made no mention, or showed any inclination of returning the crew to Angel City.

On Saturday afternoon, Creedy gave each of the men five dollars. They were waiting to board the bus for a trip to the country store when the pickup came down the dirt trail and stopped beside the Mark IV. A man got out of the truck and came over to Creedy.

Creedy glanced at the sign on the door of the pickup: *Okeechobee Produce Corporation.* The man looked around for a moment, studying the workers and the cabins. He then said to Creedy, "I was told somebody had moved into this camp. Are these your men?"

"I'm the contractor," Creedy replied cautiously.

"How long you been here?" the man asked.

"About a week and a half. How come you want to know?"

The man glanced around again and said, "This camp was condemned over five years ago. Who told you you could move in here?"

"Nobody," Creedy said, shuffling his feet. "I didn't think nobody would mind."

"This is company property, and you could get us in trouble with the health department. You'll have to move these people out of here."

"We ain't hurtin' nobody," Creedy said sullenly.

"We've got room for these men in a new camp east of Belle Glade. You can move them there right now. I'll radio ahead that you're coming."

"How much is it going to cost?" Creedy asked.

"The rent is ten dollars a man per week, but it's a new

building with baths, kitchens, heat and air conditioning. How many men you got here?"

Creedy didn't respond to the question. His face flushed as he said angrily, "I ain't payin' no ten dollars a week just for rent! You must think I'm crazy. That would run me around five hundred dollars just for a place for them to sleep."

"It won't cost you anything. It's taken out of each man's earnings, and they don't have to pay anything in advance."

"I ain't goin' to do it!" Creedy exploded. "I get the money and I pay the workers! They all owe me money, and I have to take it from their wages!"

The man stepped back and watched Creedy's face turn redder and redder. He said, "Listen, fellow! I'm not trying to tell you what to do with these men. That's between you and them. I'm just trying to help. But I'll tell you one thing for certain. You're going to move out of this camp. If you don't, I'll have the law out here."

Creedy calmed himself when he heard the law mentioned. He said in a more cooperative tone, "I don't mean to cause trouble. I just didn't think nobody would mind if we stayed here. We didn't mean no harm."

"You ought to know better than to come into an abandoned camp without permission!" the man snapped.

Creedy shuffled his feet again. "Can we stay here just for tonight and move in the morning?"

"I'm not saying that you can or can't. But at eight tomorrow morning I'm sending a deputy sheriff out here to check this property, and you better be to hell and gone out of here by then. You understand what I mean?"

"I understand," Creedy said, subdued.

The pickup was not out of sight down the dirt trail when Creedy kicked the rear tire of the bus violently and bellowed, "Goddamit to hell! A man can't even make a honest livin' no more!"

He had a lengthy conversation with Jabbo, then he got

into the Mark IV and screeched the tires down the dirt path.

The trip to the store was cancelled.

At daylight the next morning the men were loaded into the bus. Creedy did not come back to the camp, and there was no box of canned food for breakfast. Jared shared the last of his corned beef with Cy, but most of the men had nothing.

The bus traveled back to Belle Glade and then to South Bay, but it didn't turn down Highway 27 toward Homestead. Instead, it continued west to Clewiston and out Highway 80 to LaBelle, where it turned south on Highway 29. Just after mid-morning, the old vehicle rolled into Immokalee.

Jabbo parked beside a service station on the highway leading through the main part of the town. Except for an occasional car or cattle truck ambling along, the streets were deserted. In the distance a church bell was tolling.

Jared gave Cy a questioning look, but Cy just shook his head in bewilderment. Jared had been in high spirits that morning, thinking that they were at last heading back to Angel City; but as they passed the junction of the highway to Homestead, and continued mile after mile into strange country, he became more and more puzzled and concerned.

It was two hours later when the Mark IV pulled in and parked beside the bus. Jabbo got out and went over to the car, and in a few minutes he came back, cranked the bus and followed Creedy through the town and south on Highway 29.

Seven miles past Immokalee the Mark IV turned left off the highway and followed a dirt path leading across a cow pasture. After a half mile they entered an area of dense loblolly pines, and then they came to an open field. Jabbo parked the bus and all of the men got out.

Creedy came over to the workers and said impatiently, "We got three hundred acres of cucumbers here to pick. I've contracted for the whole field 'stead of by the hamper. You men can sit on your butts the rest of the afternoon if you want to, but the sooner you get this field picked, the quicker we'll get out of here and head back to Homestead." He opened the car trunk and removed a box of canned food and a keg of water, then he got into the car and drove swiftly back across the pasture.

Some of the men took their blankets from the bus and started making a camp beneath a thick clump of pines. Others sat on the ground beside the bus.

Along a barbed wire fence separating the pasture from the field there were several stacks of empty hampers. Jared walked to the fence and picked up one of the hampers, then he went into the field alone and started picking.

TWENTY

IT WAS at two o'clock on Monday afternoon when Cloma felt the first sharp pain sear her stomach. She was sitting on an empty bean hamper outside the room, watching pickers in a field across the highway. She went into the room and sat on the edge of the bunk.

Another pain came in about fifteen minutes, this one more severe than the first. She lay down on the bunk, hoping that nothing more would happen. Then another came.

Cloma got up slowly and walked around the side of the building. The cook, sitting beneath a tree to the right of the trailer, did not look up as she approached. She watched the old man as he scratched idly in the dirt, and then she said, "I might need help before the others come back. I'm havin' pains."

The old man looked up blankly and said, "I's de cook. I don' pick no 'maters no mo', an' I gets two bottles o' wine 'stead o' one."

Cloma stared at him for a moment, then she said, "Don't you understand? I'm havin' pains! I might need help!"

He looked downward and started scratching in the dirt again. "I's de cook. I don' pick no 'maters no. . . ."

Cloma turned and walked away before he could finish. She went back to the room and sat on the bunk.

For an hour she sat still, flinching each time the pains came. She knew that she must not panic, and that there would be no one to help her until the workers came in from the fields.

Sweat beads formed on her forehead as time passed slowly, and her hands began to tremble. She concentrated as hard as she could and tried to close her mind to the pain. She thought of Jared, and wondered where he was and if he was all right. Then she drifted back to a time when she was a little girl, helping her mother make jelly from wild fox grapes her father picked in the woods behind their house. The smell of hot biscuits and fried chicken and baked ham drifted through the dim concrete room. She remembered a Christmas when a small porcelain doll had been left for her under a tree beside the fireplace; then her thoughts drifted to the day when she graduated from the sixth grade, and of the white dress her mother made for her, and the yellow ribbon her father bought for her to wear in her hair; and of how she was chosen to recite a poem by Lord Byron, and the piano music and the people in their Sunday suits and the two American flags in stands on each side of the stage; and in the summers there were fruits and vegetables to preserve for the winter, and games to play, and long Sunday afternoons spent exploring the woods and swimming in the creek. She then remembered the day she first noticed Jared, and how lanky and awkward he looked as he bid for her box of fried chicken at the church social, and how tenderly he brushed her shoulder as they walked to a picnic table to share the food, and how shy he was until they became one and shared their lives together; and how afraid he was when Kristy and Bennie were born; and the anger and fear and then sorrow when he lost the farm. Memories flashed through her mind like patterns in a kaleidoscope as she tossed and turned on the bunk. Several times she cried out, "Jared! Jared! My bed!"

Bennie came into the room just as his mother screamed. His face turned ashen, and for a moment he couldn't move. Then he raced around the west end of the barracks, shouting as he ran, "Miz Bertha! Miz Bertha!"

The Negro woman was about sixty years old. She was just over five feet tall and weighed nearly two hundred pounds, and she waddled like a goose as she walked. Her head was wrapped in a red bandana. As she came around the end of the building she was shouting, "Move outen de way! Move outen de way!" There was no one in front of her.

Bennie put a bucket of water on the cookshed grille and then stood outside the closed door of the room. Each time he heard his mother scream, he felt his stomach turn over and come into his throat. He ran back constantly to see if the water was hot, and when finally it was bubbling, he took it to the room. The woman met him at the door and said, "Now you stay outen here!"

Word spread rapidly through the camp what was happening. After supper, people began drifting to the room, attracted to birth just as people are attracted to death. It was not long before every person in the camp was sitting on the ground outside the door.

Bertha came outside once and was met by the unexpected audience. She said loudly, "You folks git on away from here! Dis ain't no circus! Ain't you never seen a baby borned befo'?" Still the people did not leave.

It was just past eight when the sound of a baby crying came from the room. Bennie wiped sweat from his face as Bertha came outside and announced triumphantly, "It's a boy! A fine baby boy!" She grinned broadly, then she went back into the room.

All of the people got up and left, and in a few minutes

they returned. Some were carrying cans of sardines and some beans and some Vienna sausage and some pickled pigs' feet and some slices of stale bread and some brought half-eaten pieces of hoop cheese. One by one they came to the door and placed the food on the floor just inside the room, then they disappeared again into the darkness.

Cloma looked through hazy eyes at the gifts. She said to Bertha, "They shouldn't have brought those things. They don't have food enough for themselves."

Bertha said, "They wants to, Miz Cloma. They's good folk."

Bertha continued sitting by the bunk, bathing Cloma's face with wet rags. Bennie darted in and out of the room, asking constantly, "Is my Mamma all right?"

Each time Bertha would answer in a commanding voice, "Yo' Mamma's fine! Now you git outen here! Dis ain't no place fo' a boy!"

About ten o'clock, Cloma sat up for a few minutes and held the baby. Bertha fed Cloma a few bites of Vienna sausage and said, "Yo' man sho' goin' be proud o' you. Dis a fine baby. What you goin' call him?"

"I don't know," Cloma answered. "It'll be up to Jared when he returns."

At midnight, Bennie came into the room and lay on his bunk. Although Bertha had to be in the fields at dawn, she continued sitting by the bunk, watching Cloma and the baby. She was still there when the bell rang for the bus to be loaded.

TWENTY-ONE

THE LAST of the cucumbers were picked at mid-morning Wednesday. The men gathered up their blankets from beneath the pine trees and boarded the bus, then the old vehicle crossed the dirt trail through the cow pasture and turned south on Highway 29.

At Carnestown they intersected with the Tamiami Trail and turned eastward into the Everglades. This change of scenery, so different from the rocky soil of Homestead or the black muck of Belle Glade, occupied Jared's attention for a time. He gazed out of the window and watched in fascination as they passed the clusters of Seminole and Miccosukee chickees scattered along the canals that flanked the highway; and the women in long colorful dresses, the souvenir stands and the air-boat riders; and then the vast open spaces of saw-grass broken in the distance by hammocks of somber cabbage palms.

When they came back to Highway 27 and turned south, Jared began to see things familiar to him: the drab brown rocky soil, the lines of Australian pines bordering drainage canals, the fruit and vegetable stands at each intersection, the farm roads that looked like strips of black ribbons as they met the horizon, and the swarms of pickers following trucks and tractors across fields. As his memory of all these things came back to reality, it seemed to him that he had been gone from Angel City for decades.

With each turn of the wheels, Jared thought more and more of Cloma. He knew her time must have either come or was very near. When they approached the outskirts of Homestead, he wanted to get out and push the old bus faster. Cy noticed his extreme anxiety and said to him jokingly, "I never thought I'd see you wantin' so bad to get back to Angel City."

"I never thought I would," Jared replied, as he pictured the camp in his mind.

He again stared out of the window as they passed the small stucco building that housed the Homestead branch of the sheriff's department; then they ambled through Florida City and turned onto the highway leading to the camp.

Jared stood up in the bus when it reached the dirt road leading through the tomato field. He moved to the front as Jabbo got out and unlocked the gate, then he jumped from the bus and ran quickly toward the barracks.

The camp was deserted, but Jared didn't notice this or anything else. He found Cloma alone in the room, lying on the bunk, the baby at her side. She sat up quickly when he entered. For a moment they just looked at each other in silence, then Jared dropped to his knees beside the bunk. He touched her tenderly, and then his hand brushed against the baby. He said, "Cloma, Cloma, I didn't want it to be this way! I didn't want the baby born here. I thought we would have our own place by now. I'm sorry, Cloma, I'm truly sorry!"

As he leaned against her, she put her arm around his shoulders and said softly, "It's all right, Jared. The baby's fine, and that's all that matters. It's a boy."

He looked up when she said this. "A boy?"

"Yes. A boy."

He touched the baby again. "A boy," he repeated. "What'll we name him?"

First he looked at her again, then he gazed at the baby. For a moment he drifted into deep thought, and then he said, "We'll call him Cy."

She smiled. "That's a fine name. Cy Teeter. That's a fine name for a boy."

He leaned over and kissed her, then he got up to leave the room. Cloma suddenly became serious and said, "Jared, you best see to Kristy as soon as you can. All she ever does now when she comes here is sit in a corner and sulk. Sometimes she holds her stomach and cries for a long time, and she hasn't said a dozen words to me since you been gone. I'm afraid they've done somethin' real bad to her, Jared. You best see to her soon as you can."

Jared was so elated by the birth of the baby that Cloma's concern for Kristy did not come through to him. He said hurriedly, "I'll see to it, Cloma. Don't you worry none. You just look after the boy." Then he turned quickly and passed through the door.

Cy was coming around the end of the building as Jared came from the room. Jared ran to him. "The baby's born!" he said, grabbing Cy's shoulders. "It's a boy! They're both fine, Cy! They're fine!"

Cy grinned. "A boy? Sho' nuff? A baby boy. That's good. I'm real proud fo' you."

Jared said, "We've named him Cy, after you."

Surprise flashed into Cy's eyes. He said, "Mistuh Jay, you sho' you want to name yo' boy after a nigger?"

"No," Jared said quickly, shaking his head. "I don't want to name him after a nigger. I want to name him after a friend. I want you to be his godfather."

Cy looked puzzled. He scratched his head and said, "Well, I ain't never been no godfather. What I have to do?"

"You don't have to do nothin'. You already done it."

Cy smiled. "Mistuh Jay, I'd be right pleased fo' that boy to be called Cy." He scratched his head again. "Cy Teeter. But I ain't never been no godfather."

Jared laughed. "You'll do fine. Now, don't you want to see your godson?"

"I sho' do!"

They both went into the room. Cy looked down and said, "That sho' be's a fine baby, Miz Cloma."

She looked up and smiled.

"A godfather," Cy said again. "Now ain't that somethin'. Me a godfather!"

Jared was smiling too.

TWENTY-TWO

JARED WENT back into the tomato fields the next day, but it would have made no difference to him if he were picking tomatoes or beans or corn or celery or cucumbers or cutting sugar cane. His thoughts were only on Cloma and the baby. He knew he must now get them out of Angel City, that it was beyond reason for the boy to either survive or grow up in such a place and under such conditions, but he also knew he must not do anything to endanger Kristy. He would not even think of risking one life for another. Although he constantly searched his mind for every possible avenue of escape, his answers came up blank.

Late that afternoon, Jared sat on the ground outside the room, still totally preoccupied with his thoughts of leaving Angel City. Cy was drinking the wine Jabbo had given him before supper. Jared turned to him and said, "You think Creedy might let us go now that the baby has come?"

Cy put down the bottle. "You know better'n that."

"We've got to get out of here. There must be a way."

"Don't you fool aroun' an' get yo'self in bad trouble

again," Cy said. "You got that baby to look out for now."

"That's why we've got to leave here now," Jared insisted. Then he got up suddenly. "I'll go and ask Creedy." Cy shook his head in dismay as he watched Jared go around the side of the building.

Creedy was standing by the trailer, talking to Jabbo. Jared walked up, stopped directly in front of Creedy and said abruptly, "Why don't you let us go now?"

The question caught Creedy by surprise. He said, "How come?"

"This ain't no fit place for a baby, and you know that as well as I do."

"What's wrong with it? I've seen nigger women pickin' in the fields with babies strapped to their backs. What's so diff'rent about your woman?"

Jared wanted to lash out and strike Creedy with his fists, but he controlled the anger and said, "I've been pickin' fer you fer a long time, and I know I've more than paid off the debt several times over. Why don't you let us go now?"

"Ain't nobody leaving Angel City owing me money!" Creedy exploded. "Nobody! You ought to know that by now! I ain't got time to listen no more! I'm busy!"

Jared glared harshly at Creedy, then he turned and went back to the barracks. He dropped down beside Cy and said, "What kind of a man is Creedy? Where'd he come from?"

"Most likely he was hatched in a buzzard's nest." Cy looked at the anger in Jared's eyes, knowing how the foolish quest with Creedy had ended. He said, "I done tole you befo'. The woods is full o' men like Creedy. He's scratchin' fo' ev'rything he can get, an' he don't care how he gets it. He done gone so far he couldn't turn back if he wanted to. He used to do this just to us niggers, but now he don't care who it is. You best stay clear o' him. He ain't human no more. He's daid too, just like all these folks in here he's done knocked the life out of."

"They's some good in ev'ry man," Jared said. "The Lord tells us so."

"The Lord ain't never lived in no migrant camp," Cy said. "Creedy ain't human no more. You best stay clear o' him."

For the rest of the week, Jared tried to brush the anger from his mind. He thought of many things other than Creedy and Angel City and the apparent hopelessness of his situation. He also spent more time after work with Cloma and the baby, and he didn't mention escape to Cy again.

On Sunday afternoon, Creedy brought all the children to the camp for the regular weekly visit. The next Tuesday would be Christmas Day, and Creedy had decided to leave them in the camp until Tuesday afternoon and avoid the expense of his housekeeper cooking them a Christmas dinner. Jared was thankful that Kristy would be with them for a few days, giving him a chance to try and find out what was bothering her so badly and perhaps bring her out of her deep depression. When Cloma first told him about Kristy's change, he did not listen, but what she had said gradually came through to him. He hoped that the change was simply because she was separated from the family.

The buses left for the fields as usual Monday morning, and a clear dawn was breaking as Jared started down the tomato row. He had decided to use Christmas as a tool to bring joy back to Kristy and make her her old self again, and he was sure this would work. He wanted to do something good for her and for everyone, and he was consumed with the same excitement he had always known on Christmas Eve. Cy watched him suspiciously when he started humming as he worked.

When the bus stopped at the store that afternoon, Jared made purchases other than the necessary food. He wanted to buy a red bathing suit for Kristy, but the store did not stock such items. Instead, he bought large bottles of cologne for Kristy and Cloma, a straw cowboy hat for Bennie, and knitted blue shoes for the baby. For Cy he selected a shaving mug, for Cy's son a toy bugle, and for Bertha a yellow cloth bonnet. He also bought a roll of pink ribbon, a package of red crepe paper, three boxes of paper cups, a basket of apples, a carton of eggs, and two pounds of bacon.

When he came into the room and Cloma saw all of these things, she knew that he must have spent the last of their savings, but she said nothing. This was the first time since they arrived in Angel City that she had seen happiness in his face, and she wanted to share this with him. She cut the sacks into pieces and wrapped each gift in brown paper, then she tied them with pieces of pink ribbon. Jared took the gift for Cloma out to the cookshed and wrapped it himself.

After supper, Jared did things that puzzled all of them. He brought three empty bean hampers from behind the cookshed and placed them together like a flat-topped Christmas tree; then he wrapped them with red crepe paper. Next, he brought the washtub from beside the hydrant and placed it on top of the hampers. On another hamper he sat the basket of apples.

Inside the room, lined against the walls, there were sixty-eight bottles of wine. With Bennie helping, all of the bottles were taken outside and emptied into the tub.

When all of this was finished, Jared asked Bennie and Kristy to go with him to the hampers. Bennie was puzzled but excited and eager, but Kristy turned back toward the room. Jared stepped in front of her and said, "It's Christmas Eve, Kristy. We're goin' to have a party just like we've always had."

For a moment Kristy remained silent, and then she said slowly, "It would be Christmas . . . in West Virginny . . . but there's no Christmas here."

"That's not so, Kristy," Jared said gently. "It's Christmas

ev'rywhere. God isn't just in West Virginny. We'll have a fine party . . . it's Christmas ev'rywhere." He reached out and gripped her hand tightly.

Cloma held the baby on a hamper outside the room and watched as Jared led Kristy out to the decorated hampers with Bennie following. Jared started to sing, "Silent Night . . . Holy Night . . . All is calm . . . All is bright. . . ." Bennie joined in immediately, but Kristy remained silent.

People came out of the rooms and peered curiously at the strange gathering. One by one, and then in groups, they gradually drifted forward, forming a circle around the hampers and blending their voices into the singing of the carols. Soon all the camp was there. Jared marveled at the perfect blending of the rich Negro voices. He had never heard Christmas music sung so beautifully.

Kristy did not join in the singing, but she suddenly looked up and said, "Don't you worry none about me, Papa. I'm not fittin' to cause you worry. I'm sorry, Papa, I don't mean to be a bother to you." Jared tightened his grip on her hand.

After several more carols, paper cups were dipped into the tub of wine. The apples would be given out and eaten later. Soon again the camp and the surrounding fields were ringing with the sounds of Christmas.

Once Jared looked over and noticed Jabbo and Clug standing beneath the floodlight on the east end of the building, watching. He walked over to them and said, "Why don't you join us? It's Christmas Eve."

They both looked perplexed. Jabbo said, "Mistuh Creedy didn't say nothin' 'bout no singin'."

"Creedy's not here tonight," Jared said. "You can join us if you want to. It's up to you."

For a moment they seemed hesitant, but as Jared walked back to the circle, Jabbo and Clug turned and disappeared in the direction of the trailer.

No one wanted the music to stop. It was after midnight when the camp again became silent, and the people drifted slowly back to their rooms.

TWENTY-THREE

ON CHRISTMAS morning, Jared asked Cy and his son and Bertha to join them. While the gifts were being opened, Jared fixed everyone a breakfast of the eggs and bacon. All of them felt a tinge of guilt as the odor of frying bacon drifted throughout the camp. Others were having sardines and Vienna sausage.

It was shortly after noon when Creedy came to the camp. Jared and Cy were sitting on the ground outside the room when Jabbo and Clug approached. Jabbo stopped in front of Jared and said, "Mistuh Creedy say the girl stay here now an' work in the fields. He want the baby."

"What?" Jared said, springing to his feet. "What'd you say?"

Jabbo repeated, "Mistuh Creedy say he want the baby. He's done with the girl, an' you can have her back now. He say she's tetched, an' she ain't much of a woman noways. She don't know how to take a man. I tried 'er myself when Mistuh Creedy was gone."

Jared lunged furiously at the giant black man as Cy

jumped up and ran into his room. Jabbo whipped a pistol from his belt and smashed it into Jared's face. The blow spun him backward against the wall. For a moment he stared at Jabbo, then he slumped to the ground.

Cy came out of the room holding a butcher knife. He stepped in front of Jabbo and said, "You tetch that baby it goin' be the last thing you ever tetch! You understand me, black nigger?" He pointed the knife at Jabbo's throat.

Jabbo looked at the long blade as he stepped back and said, "We goin' take the baby. You want to get yo'self killed fo' it?"

Cy went into a crouching position. He said, "You'll have to kill me right here in the camp! It won't be out in the swamp where nobody can see! You'll have to do it right here in front of ev'rybody!"

Jabbo pointed the pistol at Cy and said, "You go with us to see Mistuh Creedy. You don't go, I'll blow yo' guts all over the ground."

Cy straightened up to a standing position. He gripped the knife handle harder and said, "I'll go see Creedy, but you ain't tetchin' that baby. You'll have to kill me first."

Jared pushed himself up and saw Cy walking with Jabbo and Clug around the side of the building. Cloma, Kristy and Bennie rushed from the room, and all of them had stark terror in their faces. Jared motioned frantically for them to go back inside, then he staggered along the wall and out to the cookshed.

Hanging on a rafter in the shed there was a large steel hook the cook used to remove pots from the grille. Jared took it down and made his way slowly along the south fence. When he passed the end of the building he could see Cy standing in front of Creedy, with Jabbo and Clug behind him. They were arguing violently. Creedy also had a pistol in his hand. Jabbo and Clug suddenly grabbed Cy and started dragging him toward the pickup. He broke free and came at

Creedy with the knife. Jared watched as Creedy fired point blank; then Cy slumped to the ground. Jabbo and Clug picked him up and threw him into the back of the pickup.

Sweat was pouring from Jared's face as he crept closer, coming in behind the trailer so they couldn't see him. He eased around the side of the trailer and was just to the side of Creedy when Creedy turned. Disbelief flashed into Creedy's eyes as the steel hook smashed into the center of his head. He stared blankly for a moment, then he toppled backward. The pistol fell at Jared's feet.

The bullet stung like a wasp when it hit Jared's left shoulder. He grabbed Creedy's pistol and looked up. Jabbo was about to fire at him again. He pointed quickly and pulled the trigger, and the bullet caught Jabbo in the right arm. Jabbo dropped the pistol and stepped back.

For a moment Jared couldn't move, and he felt hot blood running down the inside of his shirt. He finally pushed himself up and walked to Jabbo and Clug.

Clug looked at the pistol in the trembling hand and at the anger in Jared's eyes. He took a step backward and said wildly, "I didn't mean no harm! I swear fo' God I didn't! Mistuh Creedy made me do it!"

Jabbo remained silent, also watching Jared's trembling hand.

Jared turned to Jabbo and said, "Jabbo, I ought to kill you right now! You ain't fitten to live, the things you've did." He pointed the pistol directly at the giant black man's head, and then he hesitated, as if trying to make a decision. He finally lowered the gun and said, "I'll tell you what I want. I want both of you to walk down to the gate and step outside. Then I want you to run. And I don't want you to stop or look back 'til you reach Homestead. You understand me?"

Clug nodded his head in agreement, but Jabbo stood still and said, "You must be crazy, white man!"

Jared aimed the pistol and fired. The bullet knocked a

piece of leather from Jabbo's right shoe. He jumped back quickly and then he followed Clug to the gate. Jared watched as the two men ran down the dirt road toward the highway.

Bennie came around the corner of the building and ran to his father. He said wildly, "Are you hurt, Papa? Are you hurt?"

Jared shook Bennie's shoulder to calm him, then he said, "I want you to run to the store and get them to call Deputy Drummond at the sheriff's department. Tell him to come out here real quick and send an ambulance, that they's people hurt out here. You'll have to run faster than you've ever run before. Can you do this, Bennie?"

"I can do it, Papa," Bennie said. "It won't take me no time at all to get to the store." He bounded across the clearing and out the gate, then he cut at an angle across the tomato field toward the highway.

Jared's head was beginning to pound, but he paid no heed to this or to the severe pain in his shoulder. For a moment he watched after Bennie, then he walked back to where Creedy was lying on the ground. Creedy didn't move as Jared dropped down and straddled the huge hulk. He sat on Creedy's chest and pointed the pistol directly into Creedy's face. Jared's hand trembled harder as he pressed his finger against the trigger.

From behind him he heard a voice calling, "Mistuh Jay! Mistuh Jay!"

Cy was dragging himself across the ground. Jared was startled, for he thought they had killed Cy. The pistol barrel was still pressed against Creedy's face when Cy yelled, "Don't do it, Mistuh Jay! Don't do it! He ain't worth it! Let it be!"

For a moment Jared did not remove the pistol, then he suddenly remembered something Cy had once said to him, ". . . *you goin' end up doin' somethin' bad you would have never done.*" He threw the pistol to the ground and went over to Cy.

The front of Cy's shirt was soaked with blood. Jared bent over him and said, "How bad is it?"

Cy tried to manage a smile. "If I had a choice, I'd ruther not have it at all. But they ain't done me in yet. It's a hard job to kill a nigger."

Jared looked into his eyes and said, "When this's all over, Cy, let's do somethin' together. We'll be pardners in somethin'."

"That would sho' be fine," Cy said weakly. "But let's see if we can do somethin' 'sides pick 'maters."

Jared put his arms under Cy and picked him up. The weight of Cy's body sent sharp pains searing through his shoulder, yet he didn't waver as he walked slowly to the room and placed Cy on one of the bunks.

Kristy was sitting on a bunk against the opposite wall, clutching the rag doll that Jeff Billings had given her the night before they left West Virginia. Jared turned to her and said, "See to Cy as best you can, Kristy. Bennie has gone fer an ambulance."

Kristy didn't answer, and she seemed not to hear or see Jared. She pushed herself back against the wall and tightened her grip on the doll.

Jared said harshly, "Kristy! Don't you hear me? I want you to look after Cy!"

A wildness came into her eyes, and suddenly she jumped up and ran screaming from the room.

Jared stumbled outside and found Cloma sitting cross-legged on the ground, holding the baby. She was swaying back and forth, singing, "Jesus . . . loves me . . . this I know . . . for the . . . Bible . . . tells me so . . . little ones . . . to Him belong . . . they are weak . . . and He . . . is strong. . . ."

For a moment Jared stared at her blankly, as if seeing someone other than Cloma, and then he said, "Cloma . . . are you all right, Cloma?"

She looked up, but her eyes showed no recognition. She

said, "There's snow now in West Virginny. The school will be a long walk for the children." Then she started swaying again, swaying and singing, "Yes . . . Jesus loves me . . . yes . . . Jesus loves me . . . yes . . . Jesus loves me . . . the Bible tells . . . me so. . . ."

Jared dropped down beside her and said in anguish, "Oh my God! My God have mercy! What have I done to them? What have I done . . . ?"

For a moment more he watched her, trying to disbelieve what he was seeing, wanting to reach out and touch her and the baby, but not doing so; and then he was suddenly overwhelmed with rage. He jumped up and rushed around the east side of the building, totally unaware of the people huddled in groups along the wall, people watching with fear and bewilderment in their eyes. He climbed into the red bus and cranked it, then he backed it into the clearing. When he gave it full throttle, the old vehicle shuddered forward and crashed into the side of the trailer, sending it tumbling over on its side.

Jared then backed the bus again, turned it and aimed it full speed at the north fence. It rammed into the thick mesh wire and seemed to bounce back. The fence swayed for a moment, then it toppled to the ground.

Jared got out of the bus and walked trance-like to the pickup. His eyes were glazed, and the pounding in his head had become almost unbearable. He noticed that Creedy had dragged himself to a sitting position beside the Mark IV, but his eyes were still closed.

When Jared reached the pickup, he removed the gas cap and dropped a lighted match into the tank. The force of the explosion knocked him backward, and he crawled away as a mushroom of fire enveloped the truck.

Jared lay on the ground and watched without emotion as the flames consumed the pickup, then he pushed himself up and went out of the gate and into the tomato field. He pulled one of the plants from the ground and threw it into the air. Then he pulled another and another, throwing them wildly. He was still moving down the row, sailing plants into the air, when he heard the scream of a siren. The wailing sound brought him back to consciousness, and he turned and went back to the gate.

The patrol car was leading an ambulance, and Bennie was on the front seat with the deputy. Jared stepped aside as the two vehicles rushed past him and parked just inside the gate. White dust boiled into his face as he forced himself to the ambulance. He held on to the front fender and said, "My friend's down there in room ten. See to him first. He's been shot pretty bad." Then he felt darkness rush in as he toppled to the ground.

Jared was not aware again until he looked up into the face of one of the ambulance attendants. The deputy and Bennie were standing to one side. He asked, "How's my friend?"

"He took a good one," the attendant said, "but we think he'll make it."

"What about Creedy?"

"You mean the big one?"

"Yes. The big one. Is he dead?"

"Naw, he's o.k. His skull's probably cracked, but that's nothing new. We get plenty of those every day out of these camps. But you can bet he'll have some kind of a headache tomorrow. You folks sure had some donnybrook of a Christmas party out here."

The deputy leaned over Jared and said, "He'll have more than a headache for a long time to come. Your son has told me all the things you told me before, and now maybe some of these other people will talk. He's got a lot to answer for, including that bullet in your friend."

The words meant nothing to Jared. He was glad that he hadn't killed Creedy, but he no longer cared about him or

Angel City, and he received no satisfaction from the thought of what might happen to Creedy. He said absently, ". . . it don't matter none noway . . . the woods is full of 'em . . . ."

The deputy leaned over him again. "Don't worry about your family or any of these other people," he said. "I'm sending welfare workers out here to help them. They'll be o.k."

Bennie came to his father and said, "What we goin' to do when we leave here, Papa? I need to know what we'll do."

"I don't know, Bennie," Jared said weakly. "I just don't rightly know. Maybe that fruit stand is still out there sommers, and maybe we'll have to go back to the mountains so's I can work in the mines. We'll make it somehow, I promise you. But you got to take care of your Mamma and the baby and Kristy while I'm gone. You just got to do it, son. You hear?"

"I can do it, Papa," Bennie said. "Don't you worry none at all. I'll see to them."

Jared reached out and squeezed Bennie's hand as he felt himself being lifted into the ambulance. He said urgently, "Do your best by them, Bennie! They're goin' need all the help you can give."

As soon as the two flashing vehicles crossed the dirt road and turned onto the highway, some of the people trudged slowly back to their rooms. Others did not.

Several men went to the open gate and stepped out. For several minutes they stood still, looking back at the barracks and the flattened fence and the smoldering hulk of the pickup. Then they moved forward hesitantly. Suddenly they started running, and soon there was a pounding of feet as they rushed across the tomato field toward the open highway.

Here are some other books from Pineapple Press on related topics. For a complete catalog, write to Pineapple Press, P.O. Box 3889, Sarasota, Florida 34230-3889, or call (800) 746-3275. Or visit our website at www.pineapplepress.com.

Other Books by Patrick Smith

Forever Island and *Allapattah*. A Patrick Smith Reader with two novels in one volume. *Forever Island* has been called the classic novel of the Everglades. It tells the story of Charlie Jumper, a Seminole Indian who clings to the old ways and teaches them to his grandson. *Allapattah* is the story of a young Seminole in despair in the white man's world. (hb)

A Land Remembered. In this best-selling novel, Patrick Smith tells the story of three generations of the MacIveys, a Florida family who battle the hardships of the frontier to rise from a dirt-poor Cracker life to the wealth and standing of real estate tycoons. The story opens in 1858, when Tobias MacIvey arrives in the Florida wilderness to start a new life with his wife and infant son, and ends two generations later in 1968 with Solomon MacIvey, who realizes that the land has been exploited far beyond human need.

The sweeping story that emerges is a rich, rugged Florida history featuring a memorable cast of crusty, indomitable Crackers battling wild animals, rustlers, Confederate deserters, mosquitoes, starvation, hurricanes, and freezes to carve a kingdom out of the swamp. But their most formidable adversary turns out to be greed, including finally their own.

Love and tenderness are here too: the hopes and passions of each new generation, friendships with the persecuted blacks and Indians, and respect for the land and its wildlife.

A Land Remembered was winner of the Florida Historical Society's Tebeau Prize as Most Outstanding Florida Historical Novel. (hb, pb)

A Land Remembered: Student Edition. Patrick Smith's novel is now available in two volumes for young readers. Teacher's manuals for elementary and middle schools are available for using *A Land Remembered* to teach language arts, social studies, and science coordinated with the Sunshine State Standards of the Florida Department of Education. (hb, pb)